GRASPING SMOKE:
A CADE TAYLOR NOVEL

MICHAEL HEARNS

BEATI BELLICOSI
BEATI BELLICOSI PUBLISHING · A DIVISION OF BEATI BELLICOSI MEDIA

Copyright © 2021 by Michael Hearns

Beati Bellicosi is in full agreement and support of copyright. The passion of written works and the appreciation of written works are a symbiotic benefit to both author and reader. Thank you for purchasing an authorized edition of this book and for your support of copyright laws by not reproducing, scanning, or distributing any portion or form of this literary work without permission.

ISBN: 978-1-7344075-4-9 Paperback

ISBN: 978-1-7344075-5-6 Electronic Book Text

ISBN: 978-1-7344075-3-2 Hardback

Library of Congress Cataloging-in-Publication Data Names: Hearns, Michael, author

Title: Grasping Smoke: A Cade Taylor Novel /Michael Hearns

Description: First edition. Miami: Beati Bellicosi (2021) Identifiers: LCCN ISBN

First Edition: May 2021

Editor Julie Hutchings

Cover Design and Conceptualization by Dillon Hearns

Author Photo by Dillon Hearns

For Additional information and speaking engagements visit Michael Hearns on the worldwide web:

http://www.MichaelHearns.com

Beati Bellicosi Publishing a division of Beati Bellicosi multimedia Copyright 2021 by Beati Bellicosi

Printed in the U.S.A

Also by Author Michael Hearns:

"*Trust No One*" 2020 Beati Bellicosi

Acknowledgements

We often hear that "this film, this book, this piece of art this anything could not have been made possible if not for the …."

There is a large amount of truth in those comments of gratitude and recognition. This book could not of been written without the continual, unwavering, dedicated, loyal love and affection from my wife Ricki Witt Braswell. Her consistent praise and positive affirmations have filled my empty cup beyond the brim each and every day. Her presence in my life is beyond a treasure. It is an absolute heavenly blessing. There are not enough words to effectively convey all that she means to me. She has my eternal love and gratitude. I love her with every ounce of my being and I thank her every day for choosing me to be in her life.

I would also like to say thank you to my son Dillon Hearns for the man that he is and for the man that he inspires in me. We have moved to that place in our relationship where the teacher and master is now learning from the student. I thank you Dillon for all that I have learned from you and I love you endlessly.

My gratitude also extends mightily to my editor Julie Hutchings who was onboard for my debut novel *Trust No One*. She fell hopelessly in love with main character Cade Taylor. My apologies to her husband Tim. Working with Julie Hutchings again on the sequel to *Trust No One* and having her fall in love with Cade Taylor all over again in *Grasping Smoke: A Cade Taylor Novel* was for me the author; both exciting and fun. Her editing was incredibly rich to the telling of the story.

I'd like to quietly thank Dr. Lewis Earnest, Stephanie Witt, and Dr. Padrick O'Malley for all they have done for Ricki and I in the past year.

I would like to thank everyone who has ever been kind to me. Whether it is family, coworkers, friends I have known for fifty plus years, or strangers who have extended kindness in large and small ways. I thank you all. From the immensely large dilemmas in my life to everything as minor as opening doors, helping to change a tire on a dark highway, holding elevators, and smiling on crowded subways; it is all so very much appreciated. Kindness is what sets all of us apart as people and as a society. Everyone carries their pain and challenges deep within themselves. We all struggle from time to time. Let's all recognize that and extend kindness to each other. I ask that you spread limitless intentional kindness.

In closing I thank you the reader for having the confidence in me to bring you an enjoyable reading experience. Now, let's get on with the story...

To Ricki and Dillon I love you both

Chapter One

"**F**OUR DOORS FOR more whores."

I could *not* believe he actually said that. I just looked at him, dumbstruck.

I was with U.S. Customs Special Agent Ritchie Tavino. He was talking about his choice of undercover vehicle, which was currently a 1998 Ford F150 XLT Extra Cab 4X4. He'd picked the truck up from the rental agency about two weeks ago.

"Ritchie, you're married, how can you be saying that?"

With a deadpan expression, he said, "Yeah I'm married. So is my wife."

I gave him an equally blank look.

"I'm just playing with you. Actually, it comes in handy on weekends when I'm picking stuff up at Home Depot," he said.

One of the unspoken tenets of working undercover is having the full use of the undercover car. Undercover agents in Miami frequently swapped out cars based on their personal needs, which varied from week to week, even day to day sometimes. It could be tailgating for Miami Dolphin games, hunting season in the Everglades, even an upcoming baby's christening. Whatever the event may be dictates the vehicle an agent chooses off the rental lot. It's not uncommon after a long weekend to see red Georgia clay caked up under an undercover SUV, or Sanibel Island parking passes in the door wells.

I'd always chosen fairly practical cars. Functional. Better for moving surveillance. Cars that also blend in with the general population. Although most recently, I allowed Ramon, the rental car agency manager to convince me that now that I was divorced, I needed a car more suitable to my new single status. That's how I ended up having a midnight blue 1998 IROC Z28 Camaro. It was parked here, in the same parking lot as Ritchie's pick-up truck.

Six months earlier as my marriage was disintegrating to my now ex-wife Gina, I was doing everything to keep a tight cover on the simmering cesspool of my life. The domestic turmoil eventually reared up and bit me right in the ass in the most incalculable ways. Sooner than later, nearly everyone knew I was getting divorced. Now, less than a half year later, it seemed that my every acquaintance had knowledge of what I considered to be the biggest failure in my life.

Divorce.

It's like a hockey goalie who allows a cheap, greasy goal into his net. A spotlight lights him up, a red bulb flashes, and a foghorn sounds to tell everyone that he made a mistake. If the goalie's lucky he won't have to see it on the 11pm sportscast or in the next day's sports page. That's how divorce makes you feel. You begin to think everyone knows that someone on this earth was willing to give up possessions and money just to be away from you.

Compound those feelings with the pressures of my job and you have a perfect formula for a psychoactive clinical drug trial for depression, isolation, paranoia, insomnia, and far entrenched continual retrospection.

I am not a dull-cornered person. I am not a tree-shaded road or a hue-dappled sunset. I can be a 2am doorbell. I can be gunshots muffled by the distance of a few city blocks. Certainly, living with me may not have been ideal for Gina. My life is occupationally chaotic. I've been an undercover detective in Miami for nearly nine years, working large cocaine and high-volume money laundering cases. I have been assigned to the Vice Intelligence Narcotics (VIN) unit of the Coral Gables Police Department for the past nine years.

I think I fell from Gina's heart with an alarming crash. The divorce was eviscerating. They say time heals all. I don't think so. Time taunts me with the memories of squandered remnants of a previous life. A normal life. A life devoid of drug dealers, money launderers and murder.

My career started out "on loan" to the City of Miami Police Department doing "jump out" with their street narcotics unit. It's called "jump out" because we detectives would wait for a more experienced undercover detective to make a drug buy or sale, and then we'd come screaming around the corner in cars and vans and *jump out* to make an arrest, which invariably led to many a foot chase and just as many rough and tumble encounters in some of Miami's most deplorable alleys and streets. Eventually I *became* that more experienced undercover detective and was doing the drug buys. With that experience as a launching point, I quickly found myself detached to U.S. Customs and then here, with a multi-jurisdictional DEA task force.

I hadn't seen Ritchie Tavino in about three years. Back then we'd both been assigned to the U.S. Customs Anti-Money Laundering Task Force "Operation Greenback." I was actually detached to the task force before he transferred down from the New York field office. He always teased me about my love for the Hartford Whalers, all the while relishing the fact that his New York Rangers won the Stanley Cup. That happened the same year he came down to South Florida.

Coming to Miami for the first time was a culture shock for Tavino. He was a neophyte to South Florida. Miami isn't as adaptable as many would have you believe. Either you get Miami or Miami gets you.

Multiple police agencies have hired police chiefs from outside South Florida to head a teetering or troublesome police department. It never works. Without an understanding of how Miami operates— or in some cases fails to operate—can be treacherous for a novice. It was also an occupational adjustment for Tavino to work with locals on a task force whose sole objective was to disrupt the narcotic money pipeline from South Florida to the Medellín and Cali drug cartels in Colombia. He was used to being King Shit on Turd Island in Manhattan. In the undercover world, you need to have locals who can turn the wheels necessary; if not well you're going to get crushed under those wheels. He soon learned that some of us locals were plugged into the narco trade pretty tightly.

Now it was early October and getting late in the afternoon. The traffic on Southwest 8th Street was bumper to bumper. No one was moving anywhere anytime soon. The street is more commonly called "*Calle Ocho*," which is the street leading into Miami's Little Havana section. The Miami rain coming down wasn't especially hard, but it was steady. Tavino and I were dry at the moment. We were at the coffee window at the La Caretta restaurant. We were outside under a large green canvas awning protecting us from the rain, though a few steps in either direction would've changed our dry status quickly. The awning's aged metal support rods clearly showed signs of rust, cobwebs, and the usual urban grunge in the form of calcified chewing gum and grimy fingerprints. These coffee windows are called "*Ventanitas*," which translates literally to "little windows." These walkup *ventanitas* are most often attached to larger indoor cafeterias and restaurants. They're such a unique cultural phenomenon in South Florida that they've become regionally very common. Follow that logic.

La Caretta was a restaurant institution. Its coffee window was a rectangular portal to all that is Miami. A rectangular view into the inner workings of an industrious Cuban restaurant. Conversely, looking out, it's a rectangular view of the constantly changing faces and conversations of Miami. A twenty-four hour conduit of information and conversation flowed and spewed like one of those earthly signals sent by NASA into deep outer space. It mattered not if anyone heard it; but just knowing that it could be sent it out was the main purpose. Many times it seemed people at the *ventanitas* just wanted to have their voice heard even if it only mattered to themselves. Those conversations often centered around Cuban politics, the weather, a funeral's attendees, or anything that its continually revolving patrons would be discussing. Conversations weren't afforded nor expected to have any privacy. The matronly, overly made-up Cuban women who created cup after cup of aromatic steaming Cuban coffee concoctions heard all of it, just as well as the intended conversationalists. The background noise of humanity; a *vox humana* that never ceased. Dialects, curse words, anguish, and joy were intermixed with every topic worth discussing. It never ceased, nor was it ever desired to cease. It was the language of commerce and prosperity to the women inside the restaurant serving coffee with ease and skill.

Cafecito

Café con leche

Colada

Cortadito

It made no difference what you desired. These women were speedily adept at fulfilling your caffeine choice. With unimaginable precision often punctuated by the loud rapt of a coffee grinder emptying its crushed grounds into a plastic garbage can, they smiled gamely, often collecting a few quarters but most often a single dollar bill as a tip each time they came to the window and asked a patron:

"Que te Gustaría?"

What would you like?

Ritchie had called me earlier in the day and asked me to meet him "at the wheel." The wheel was a slang term for *La Caretta* because of its enormous decorative mill wheel, which was just a few feet from where we stood. In the darkness the wheel was lit by faded hazy yellow light bulbs, lighting the way into Little Havana and lending itself as a beacon to night stragglers seeking coffee, Cuban cuisine, or companionship, even if it comes in the form of an overly tired waitress. The watery basin of the wheel always held silver coins and pennies in the bottom.

In the throes of despair nearly anything can be seen as a wishing well.

"Cade Taylor. Wow, man I can't believe you're still in the business," Ritchie said.

Calling me by my actual name in public can be a serious problem—but not amongst the undercovers in Miami. We're an exclusive fraternity, and we all either know each other, know of each other, or have heard of each other.

"Ritchie, I was wondering if you were still here in Miami. When you called I figured it must be important, if you want to meet here in the open at *La Caretta*."

"What? Can't a guy from Bedford Sty have a hankering for a *papa rellena y cortadito*?"

I was impressed with his improved Spanish and assimilation into the Miami lifestyle. The coffee window was usually a bustling place of commerce but its current clientele was relegated to just me and Ritchie. Rain will do that in Miami. It's the only city where the drivers drive with their hazard lights on when it rains. I ordered a café con leche. While waiting for the industrious woman in the window to concoct the hot, steamy, and much anticipated drink, I leaned against the wall adorned with a Florida Lottery advertisement and looked at Ritchie.

He was as I remembered him. Stocky, with creeping gray spreading across his thin beard and hairline. He was tanned and he seemed much more acclimated to his assignment here in South Florida. The coffee and his *papa rellena*—a rounded fried mashed-type potato surrounding a center core of aromatic, spicy ground beef—arrived on clattering little plates. The requisite Lance cellophaned wrapped saltines adorned his plate as well. As we indulged ourselves, Ritchie began talking in a low, hush tone, defying the coffee waitresses to hear.

"Cade, as you know we've had a major problem with D.C. since Forty-one lost the election."

President George Bush, or Forty-one, had lost his reelection campaign to Arkansas Governor Bill Clinton. With that defeat a lot of funding for The War on Drugs was lost as well. Calling it a *war* on drugs put a dramatic connotation to it. It made for a great t-shirt and for powerful photo opportunities at elementary schools with school yards of children chanting, "Say no to drugs." In reality, it was a boondoggled failed campaign that many profited from, both in Colombia and in Washington. Then again, if you're in the throes of drug addiction, or have a loved one who's addicted, then I guess it is a war—a personal war. Under President Reagan, George Bush was the Vice President of the United States. He instituted the "Vice President's Drug Task Force." It poured millions of dollars and resources into South Florida to combat the waves of Colombian cocaine washing upon our shores.

"Once Clinton put Janet Reno in as U.S. Attorney, she all but shut us down. She thinks money deals are unethical. Imagine that? A career Miami Dade politician, now Washington elitist talking about ethnics?"

I couldn't argue that point. When I'd come out of the police academy, Janet Reno had been the State Attorney for Miami Dade County. Now she was the U.S. Attorney. As for Miami Dade having a lack of ethics in their political base? Well, coming from a guy who in his career witnessed the mayor of the city of Hialeah be led out of his office in handcuffs and still win reelection two weeks later, and a crack cocaine-smoking county commissioner who fled to Australia from the very same justice building that was named after his father... let's just say that I couldn't argue with the transplanted New Yorker here wiping *papa relleno* from his mouth and standing under the awning with me.

"So Reno shut us down. She slammed us and IRS. No more money laundering cases. Shit, we had a ton of informants and wires up when she just unilaterally said, 'That's it boys, go check shipping containers for feral monkeys and invasive potato species.' Hell, Cade you were there. You were able to keep going with the DEA but us Customs guys at the Koger Center in Doral, we're sitting around with our thumbs up our asses."

My only response was, "Well, the next election isn't for two more years."

"Yeah, well me and a few of the guys have been keeping our ears to the ground. We think that if we can do a couple deals with you and your group, we can get back in the game."

I took a long sip of my café con leche and watched him as the rain came down heavier. The clattering of the dishes from just inside the window and the continuous mentioning of *"mi amour"* to every customer inside the restaurant from the waitresses was constant.

"I don't know if we can do that. I mean, I'm sure we still have a mutual aid agreement and all."

"Of course you have an MUA with us. Look, we're Treasury, you're now with Justice and DEA. Of course there's an MUA. We don't want any of the seizure. You can have our portion. We'll put in a DAG 71. You just give us a wish list of what you want and we'll endow it back to you. We just have to get back in the game so in two years we can hit the ground running. It takes a good fourteen months for the seizure to clear the legal pipe line anyway. The timing is right."

What Tavino was basically saying is that if we allowed his team to play in our sandbox and we ended up seizing drug money, U.S. Customs would put in for their share of the drug money seizure via an Equitable Sharing Request Form, also known as a DAG-71. But rather than take their portion of the seizure, they'd circle back to ask us what we needed in terms of equipment or resources, and we'd make them a wish list. U.S. Customs would then use their portion of the seizure to fill our wish list, endowing them back to us as a cooperative law enforcement partner. It was a serious win—a win for my task force. A legal loophole that we could exploit a few times until the next election.

U.S. Customs just wanted to get operational again. The DEA wasn't being hampered by Reno's vision of a no-money-laundering world because drug money was considered ancillary to a drug seizure. The focus wasn't on drug money as much as it was on drugs. At least that was our mission statement, and what we told ourselves. By being granted a special dispensation from the Justice Department via the DEA, Customs could skirt around Reno's directive and still get back in the money laundering world as cooperative law enforcement partners, rather than a lead agency.

And to think that Janet Reno thought money deals were unethical.

"It sounds like you got a lock on something. What is it?" I asked him.

"Do you remember when you were with us in Greenback and we had that confidential informant, Chuco?"

"Yeah, I remember Chuco. He sucked as a C.I. Five foot nothing, but with the cowlicks in his hair he was about five foot four and all mouth. Talked a big game but never delivered. You can't be serious going back to that guy. He's a mess," I said.

"*Was* a mess. *Was* a mess, Cade. He went back to Colombia and his cousin married high up into the cartel. His cousin brought him in as family. Chuco has been in Bucaramanga. You know where that is?"

"No."

"Bucaramanga is the capital of the Santander region in Colombia. Dead center-framed by the Cordillera Oriental Range in the Colombian Andes. I'm talking primo coca comes right through there. He's coordinating all the kilos coming up from the Caparo Valley in Peru. Bucaramanga is the third point in the right triangle between Medellín and Bogota. That little fucker has parlayed himself into a sweet position, but he's greedy as fuck. He reached out to us via an intermediary last week about a large contract here in Miami. According to him, there's seven million they want to move quickly. And get this—he wants a minimum of eleven-and-half percent to turn us onto it."

"There is no way we're giving anybody an eleven percent tax-free commission for *any* deal. I don't care how big the seizure is. We top our best guys out at maybe nine percent, and that's even rare. This guy's been off the screen for a few years, and besides, when he *was* in play he was a dick. I think he might even be black-balled," I said.

"It's a hard eleven-and-a-half percent. And it's okay! We'll pay him from our DAG. Out of the seven million, we're going to ask for two. We'll pay him the $800,000 plus on his percent, then endow up to another $800,000 back to you guys. When it clears the pipeline we will take our $400,000 to use as start-up, get us running again after Reno is gone. So you get $5.8 million just for letting us play in your yard."

The opportunity was enticing, and the numbers were definitely in our favor. It would fall on me to try and convince the task force that our former big brother, U.S. Customs, wanted to get back in the game. As lucrative as it may seem, the DEA may not want to go back to the old days of competing with Customs. The clamoring for cases and informants was hard fought many times when the DEA was running Operation Pisces and Customs was running Operation Greenback. The territorial fighting, arguments, continual filing of DAGs, the poaching of agents, informants, and legal teams was harsh.

"You know Ritchie, there's only so much I can do with this. I have to check with my people and we need to debrief on how reputable Chuco is, and who'll be the intermediary... I mean, there are a lot of angles that have to be covered."

"I know, I know. We're trying to get that all covered and get it out of the way. As a competency test, Chuco's client wants to try and move $150,000 as soon as possible to gauge our reputation as well," he said.

"What assurances do you have that there actually *is* a full seven million and this $150,000 isn't just a remainder circling the drain that Chuco wants to grind your wheels on as he screws with you?" I asked him.

"Cade, its money. Not only is it money but it's *illegal* money. Hell, even the government has to put 'In God We Trust' on it just to get us schmuckos to believe in it. When he was with us in the Greenback days he delivered adequately. I mean, as best as can be expected from a slimeball like him. Remember, he worked for us. He's a documented C.I., and if he tries to fuck us on this his snitch file is going to land smack dab in the middle of Bucaramanga. It isn't the eight hundred

G's I give a shit about. I want operational integrity moving forward. And bigger cases," he said.

I couldn't argue with his logic, and as far as I was concerned, if Chuco ended up in a rusty barrel in a Colombian river I couldn't of cared less. I was beginning to sense that Ritchie had learned the money laundering game hard and fast. He was playing it the same way I would have played it, had the roles been reversed.

"How soon is soon?" I asked.

"As soon as we can. If we can do it as early as tomorrow, we'd be happy to get it going. Kind of like the first hit in football, you know? Once we get it out of the way, we're back in."

"That's not something I think I can push up the channels in twenty-four hours. I mean, I'll start the conversation, but it is really quick you know?" I said.

"Cade. We want in and we want in on your slipstream—but in the end, we are still the feds. With or without that shrieking banshee Reno, we are getting back into the money business. So jump on this runaway train and make some cash, or get run over by it. But we *are* coming back in. You got me?"

"No I don't have you. What I do have is established position and play. I'm in position and I'm in play. You and your JC Penney suit wearing buddies may have been around since 1789 but this is 1998 and right now you are out and you are asking me to help you get back in. Don't pull that we are the feds shit with me Ritchie. Not here. Not now. Storage containers and invasive potato species might be your absolute future because I can sell this or kill this. You talk to me like I'm sort of feral monkey you can go back to sticking your thumb up your ass. *You got me?*"

The rain poured down as heavy as the threat to squeeze U.S. Customs back into the money laundering world. If I wasn't careful, I'd be crushed like the Jùpina Soda can clattering in the storm drain alongside the cigarette butts outside.

Our DEA task force was opportunistic. When U.S Customs got tossed out of the game we doubled up our resources and scooped up many of their informants and cases. The DEA had stepped in where Customs left off and the DEA had created their own inroads and trying to explain…

Explain?

Who was kidding who? There was no explaining this to the DEA. It would be forewarning. It would not be an easy sell, telling my people that the other big kid on the block was back from detention and wanted to rule the schoolyard. I turned my thoughts back to Ritchie and studied him for a second. I diverted my gaze and looked up at the falling rain.

"October rain, huh? I remember many a Halloween trick or treating as a kid in a rain-soaked costume. No amount of rain would stop me from getting my candy, right? This is still hurricane season, but this? This isn't the big, nasty, demolishing storm the hurricane trackers always say is coming to erase South Florida off the map, though. Is it? We both know if that storm didn't come in September, there's a good chance it won't come at all." I leaned in close to Ritchie, eyes locked on his. "No, this is just another late afternoon, near-dusk, steady rain, falling without storm front or direction," I said, waving my hand at the downpour. "It's not that bad. South Florida is staying right here," I said with a smile. Ritchie gulped. I turned to look Ritchie right in the eye, and lowered my voice.

"So. What kind of setup do you have?" I asked him.

"We set up some accounts with Sunbank, we got a counting room set aside out in Doral and a team of guys that we brought in slowly but steadily. One used to be a Mendocino California cop who came to us from Glynco about three years ago. So he's got cop sense and U.S Customs blessings now as a GS-12."

Glynco was a training facility for U.S. Customs in Georgia and as a GS-12 he was designated a General Service pay grade as an upper middle level agent.

"We've got a good squad, about eight guys. Some are from Miami, Atlanta, one from Tampa, and a really good analyst on loan from EPIC," he said.

EPIC was an acronym for the El Paso Intelligence Center. The El Paso Intelligence Center was a clearing house of all narcotic-related intelligence gathering for the DEA.

"Wait a minute. You have an analyst for EPIC? Why don't you use that cross designation as a bridge to link us? Let me see if I can sell it that way. I'll say we can have a local EPIC designee, that will be like using a DEA asset. It will grease the DAG through quicker and open more acceptability to having us cooperate on this case."

Ritchie looked at me as he polished off his *cortadito* with a knowing smile. It was obvious that he had already figured that angle out. He was assessing me to see how receptive I'd be to joining up with him and the U.S. Customs agents. Testing me to see if I was still a collaborating guy or if was I jaded from my time with the DEA. He was measuring me to see if I was available and agreeable to broaden my case log and lend a hand on helping his 239 year old agency get reestablished in the money laundering business.

"So do you need my DEA group or do you need me?" I asked him bluntly.

Ritchie was brushing the crumbs of the *papa rellena* off his shirt and he looked up and locked eyes with me.

"Both. But right now we want you."

Chapter Two

THERE REALLY IS no separation between me and the task force. We are melded as one. The agreements between the Coral Gables Police Department and the DEA stipulates that all my cases go through the task force for operational viability before they are investigated.

"Our SAC is going to be in touch with your Major Brunson. Is this Brunson a stand-up guy?"

Major Theodore "Ted " Brunson was a veritable old school traditional cop who was currently the acting police chief while our chief of police, Robert McIntyre was convalescing from a near-fatal stroke he suffered just over a year ago. Brunson was acerbic, caustic, sometimes ill-mannered and used profanity with such an ardency that to the uninitiated it seemed that all he ever did was swear and then swear some more. He was prone to vent his anger on inanimate objects, often kicking waste baskets, slamming doors, and throwing wads of paper in disgust. I think the coursing animosity in his veins was actually the propulsion his blood needed to circulate. He collected and sampled hot sauces from all over the world and was apparently always thinking about what he could eat next. I learned a few months ago not to underestimate his ability to harness and decipher information. He often pointed out to the non-believers that he sat in the biggest office in the building for a reason. Now Tavino was saying that he didn't care whether I was onboard willingly or not; his special agent in charge (SAC) would be reaching out to my direct supervisor anyway.

"Brunson is an acquired taste," was all I said in response.

Ritchie looked off in to the teeming stalled traffic on Southwest 8th Street and simply replied,

"Well I think this job has made us all an acquired taste."

"Who's your SAC?" I asked him.

"SAC's Dale Sorenson. He got here from Charleston, South Carolina about two months ago. He seems like a lifer. Not a bad guy, just he's all about keeping it from coming back on him. Very Teflon. Remember, you don't get ahead in the federal government by doing the right thing. You get ahead by not doing the wrong thing."

I was beginning to wonder how this problem with U.S. Customs and money laundering cases had somehow, in the past thirty minutes, become *my* problem.

The rain continued, not in waves, not in sheets, but in a steady curtain of small droplets that looked almost like snowflakes as they cascaded from the sky. The lit *La Caretta* sign backdropped their descent to the ground, casting the droplets with a yellow hue. There weren't many spaces in the parking lot near the *ventanita*. Some of the spaces were occupied by cars with their wipers still wavering across their windshields, the occupants thinking they'd wait out the rain, not having the vaguest idea that from my vantage, it just wasn't going to happen. The rain was steady. As a born and raised Miamian I knew that it would be a while until it would even begin let up.

A marked uniform City of Miami police car pulled up. Rather than seek an open parking space the officer chose to beach his cruiser behind the cars in the parking lot. Such an act of arrogance would eventually necessitate the officer to have to go back in the rain and move his car if he should choose to get out of it, or the cars pinned in by him would have to wait until he was finished with his business. If I was to wager any sum, it would be on making people wait on him. His windshield was partially fogged from the condensation, but I was able to identify the officer, Alvaro Dominguez. I had previous dealings with him.

Dominguez was one of those officers that had been hired eighteen years earlier when the City of Miami was desperate to fill their depleted ranks. The Mariel boatlift from Cuba had swept over Miami with tens of thousands of hardened criminals and mentally challenged individuals. Fidel Castro saw the benevolence of a weak Jimmy Carter administration and emptied his jails and insane asylums, comingling fleeing refugees with some of the most hardened criminals to ever walk the earth. Castro preyed on the tenet of American liberty:

"Give me your tired, your poor, your huddled masses yearning to breathe free, the wretched refuse of your teeming shore. Send these, the homeless, tempest-tossed to me, I lift my lamp beside the golden door!"

Well, they came to the golden door alright. Actually, it seemed as though they came to every door in Miami. The crime statistics and homicide rate in Miami spiked like a fruit punch at a high school dance. Combine that with the Arthur McDuffie riots of 1980, and Miami was desperate to bolster its law enforcement ranks. The Miami Police Department recruited for applicants at the Miami Dade Youth Fair, shopping malls, movie theater lobbies, even in adjudicated courtrooms. They lowered their standards to such a seepage point that criminal background checks were forged, altered, or skipped entirely on a few applicants. Fluent English was not deemed necessary, and conversational English passed as a qualifier.

Dominguez more than likely would never have been hired as a police officer in normal circumstances, but he slithered through the process. He was now one of those officers that the department worked around rather than with. Dominguez was problematic and he was entrenched via seniority—a terrible combination for any police administration. His appearances before civilian oversight boards and internal affairs were common and often comical. Fully protected by the police union and the bond of the blue, he feared nothing in the form of a police administration. Union dues garnered via payroll deduction were never better spent by any police officer prior than him, and I imagine ever since. Like most everyone in life, he found a groove that worked for him, but his brusque and obnoxious personality, paired with a continued penchant for irritating citizens and fellow cops alike, made him *persona non grata* nearly everywhere. So although high in seniority, his career path never amounted to anything other than the uniform patrol division. A career he spent largely in the Little Havana section of Miami where he could glad hand and ass grab his way through his shift. He oozed distrust and uncooperativeness. I watched him start to get out of the car, the cars he blocked none of his concern at all.

I turned my back to Dominguez, hoping he wouldn't recognize me. *Just go inside the restaurant. Do not come to the ventanita.*

"Well, look here! If it ain't the big secret squirrel himself, Cade Taylor!" he bellowed as he drew near.

Ritchie was surprised to hear the unspoken rule of never acknowledging undercovers in public so flagrantly broken. Ritchie looked at me for my reaction. Before Dominguez could get within ear shot I softly said, "Ritchie let's talk tomorrow. I'll see you later."

"That one of your nut buddies there?" asked Dominguez as he came under the awning, nodding towards the departing Tavino.

"Dominguez. We got nothing to talk about and you need to quit using my real name in public."

"Well, since no one can hear us now, can I just say pretty please, 'Fuck you Cade Taylor?'"

"Dominguez I'm not going to say it again."

"Say what? I called you by your name in public? You think they're going to write me up for that? You don't even work for us. You're a pussy, and you're Coral Gables. You run all over Miami thinking you're hot shit and you haven't done any police work in years. You're an asshole and I'll call you whatever I want whenever I want."

Dominguez has a brother Yordani Dominguez who was doing a life sentence for trafficking four kilograms of high-grade Colombian cocaine within a thousand feet of a school. The undercover set the deal up in one of those shopping plazas where a storefront was being used as a language center. An accredited language center. The designation made the school a legitimate qualifier for the Florida state statue for drug trafficking within a thousand feet of a school stick. It not only stuck, but it sealed Yordani Dominguez's fate. Yordani would be eating with a plastic spork for the rest of his life. Alvaro Dominguez from that moment on, viewed any undercovers as an enemy and often tried to single me out. He felt I should have told him his brother was going to be arrested by the DEA. With that insight, he could have tipped his brother off. His skewed view of police blue allegiance was wacked and sorely misguided. There wasn't anything I could have done to avert Yordani from going down, but Alvaro would hear nothing of it.

"Dominguez I've told you a hundred times, I had nothing to do with your brother getting popped by the DEA. It's not my fault he's in jail. I wasn't even part of that case. So you and your shithead brother can both kiss my surprisingly firm ass."

Before he could retort something stupid again, the Miami police radio attached to his gun belt issued the universally known "three tone" for an emergency. The three tone is a high octave wailing sound that supersedes all verbal traffic on the radio. It's intended to alert anyone who's listening that a serious emergency is about to be dispatched. The long-entrenched police training that both Dominguez and myself possessed caused us to both stop talking and listen.

"*Units standby for an emergency. Any unit in the area of Douglas Metrorail. A 3-30 just occurred in the vicinity of the 3000 block of Mundy Street in Coconut Grove. Subject is a white male armed with a handgun last seen running towards the Douglas Metrorail station.*"

3-30. A shooting with injuries and/or death.

Dominguez was a louse and an unscrupulous cop but he did adhere to the basic premises of law enforcement which was to respond to bona fide emergencies. He didn't say a word to me, just turned around and quickly walked through the rain to his patrol car. A 3-30 can be a serious police call. There could be not just one shooter, but possibly multiple armed individuals. Bullets had already been fired. Someone may be shot.

The shooter was heading towards the Douglas Metrorail Station. The Douglas Metrorail station was just a few hundred yards from the eastern boarder of Coral Gables. My city.

Miami Dade's elevated train system connects the majority of the county with twenty-three Metrorail stations north to south. The Douglas Metrorail station is one of the busiest. The shooter could quickly get lost in the crowd and get off at any one of those twenty-three stations.

Dominguez hadn't parked in a proper parking space, so he was able to quickly enter his car and take off fast south onto Southwest 36th Court, causing puddles to splash away from his rolling tires and make large arcing waves that crashed over the parked cars he passed. He flicked on his red and blue lights and then activated his police siren as he tore away from *La Caretta*.

Southwest 36th isn't a through street, so at Southwest 12th Dominguez needed to turn west to get to Southwest 37th Avenue, also known as Douglas Road. Once on Southwest 37th it would be a straight-out run south to the Douglas Metrorail station.

I decided to go as well.

I didn't have all the requisite police equipment that Dominguez did and my journey to the Douglas Metrorail station would need to be more cautious, but still expedited. I jumped in the Z28 and turned the ignition. The performance engine purred as if to say, "Finally, now we can get some real speed." I backed out and cut the steering wheel sharply, causing the nose-heavy vehicle to swing like an open barroom door in the breeze. The front end swung with engineered precision. I quickly threw the transmission into drive causing the inertia of the swinging front end to settle lower. The tires fought to find a piece of the wet asphalt to lock down upon. The back tires spun causing the Z28 to fishtail until the front tires gripped. Once the car found its way, the low-slung design was like an insulated arrow. The very same puddles that Dominguez had parted were just coming together as I too sprayed a crescendo of water on either side of the car. I was splashing anything and anyone on the side of the road. I could barely see Dominguez's tire tracks in the reforming flooded street, although I could still see him a block or two in front of me, his red and blue emergency lights vividly clear as cars parted for him. I wanted to catch up closer so that I could piggyback his ability to get through the thick traffic.

I think I was hoping for too much. Way too much. His emergency lights and siren parted seams in the congested traffic I could only wish to have at my disposal. My trip to the Douglas Metrorail station was more of a stop and go, expletive-filled, herky jerky series of acts of frustration. I utilized all three southbound lanes of Douglas Road. I dodged, cut and weaved my way but Dominguez was just a speck, his flashing lights my only indication he was even in front of me. Every car on the road was either an impediment or an adversary as I tried to continue my controlled, yet erratic driving. My two biggest obstacles would be the crossing streets of Coral Way and Bird Road. Both streets are sixteen blocks apart. I treacherously snaked my way south. I was secretly happy that the nearness of Coral Gables Hospital was actually on my route, God forbid anything should happen to me in this self-created maniacal run I was on.

The rain continued to come down on the Z28. Aside from me concentrating on my driving, I think the windshield wipers were the next hardest working part of the car. Coral Way was a mess. To my left the Sears Department Store parking lot looked like a lake. Cross traffic was partially grid-blocking the intersection. I pushed the Z28 up to the front of the line via the turn lane and cut back across the lanes, angering everyone behind me. I pushed and nosed my way into the gridlock, causing some cars to inch up and others to creep back, allowing me just enough room to squeeze between them with inches to spare on either side.

Dominguez was nowhere to be seen.

I rocketed past the Bank of America and shortly thereafter, the hospital. I continued accelerating right on past Douglas Park until I approached the stalled and going nowhere lines of cars waiting for the light to change at Bird Road. There was a Florida Power and Light mini substation directly west of the intersection and that caused heavier than normal traffic backlogs because the right-hand lane can't turn right on a red light. The cars were in a complete stand-still as I drew rapidly closer.

I needed to make a decision.

As I drew near Southwest 29th Street I turned hard right from the center lane and across the inside lane. I cut off a Mercury Sable, causing the driver to simultaneously slam on the brakes and in Spanish call me, "*Comer meirda.*"

Being called a shit eater was not foreign to me nor was it my concern at the moment.

I knew that there was a Tire Kingdom and a Sherwin Williams on the corner of SW 38th Avenue and Bird Road. They'd be closed at this late hour, so traffic on this feeder street would be minimal. I was only on 29th Street a scant few seconds when I could feel my hands palming the steering wheel left and the car cycling into a rapid spinning turn onto Southwest 38th Avenue. The car responded well but to my relief, it recovered even better. It now tracked straight south on the road.

The intersection was a clogged mess as three cars on Bird Road were involved in a fender bender. The accident more than likely was caused by cars trying to avoid Dominguez as he went through that very same intersection minutes earlier. People stood in the rain, surveying the damage, yelling, arguing, and gesturing. I saw cross traffic had a gap, and shot out to Bird Road, then turned hard right. I stomped on the gas and the car responded with an eagerness to accelerate ,which it did mightily. I'd effectively bypassed all the waiting cars with that one deviation. At Ponce de Leon Boulevard I slid through the intersection, fighting the spinning steering wheel hard to maintain control. I passed the opulent show room of the Collection Car Dealership, its windows loaded with Ferraris and Porsches. I sensed automotive envy as my American muscle car was free to slide and speed in the rain while those automobiles were stuck behind velvet ropes relegated to only being touched by salesmen in white gloves.

Douglas Metrorail would be in front of me soon.

I had no police radio or any other information. For all I knew, it could have been a false alarm and I'd come peeling into the parking lot to an assembly of cops just looking at each other and wondering what kind of crazed maniac I was. San Lorenzo Avenue was wide open and I floored it straight onto Ruiz Avenue which brought me into the west parking lot of the Douglas Metrorail.

Cars were parked in patches throughout the flooded large lot, with wide puddles dotting it like muddy lily pads. Concrete-based light poles jutted up from the water. The yellow striping of the empty parking spaces had an inch or two of standing water obscuring them partially. The first thing I saw was Dominguez's car.

The police car was crashed up against one of the light poles. The red and blue lights were still on and spinning languidly, reflecting the hues in the adjacent puddles around the car. The backend of the patrol car was damaged where it had hit the pole. The driver's side airbag had been deployed. I drove rapidly up to the car, approaching the crash from behind, and spun the Z28 tightly in front of it.

I could see seven bullet holes in his front windshield.

Dominguez was still inside. The bullet holes were in an arching semi-circle, the pattern reflective of a shooter that had opened fire on Dominguez from left to right.

I slammed on the brakes and put my car between Dominguez and where I thought the shooter might be. I bailed out of the Z28 in low crouch, simultaneously pulling my Glock. Weaving between the passenger side of the Miami patrol car and my car, I kept as low as I could. I used that narrow automotive canyon as my pathway to Dominguez in case the shooter was on the upper rail platform. It would make it harder for him to shoot at me if I was in this ad hoc metallic trench. Still in a low crouch, I came around the back of the police car. I transitioned my gun to my left hand. With my left arm fully extended, I hugged the patrol car with my right hand, pressing my right cheek against the wet blue-and-white striping of the rear quarter panel. I scanned in front of both cars and as much of the upper platform as I could see. Switching gun hands, I slowly reached for the driver's side door and flung it open as far as it would go. I then held back against the rear door in case Dominguez was still alive or in shock and might start shooting me, thinking me to be the shooter.

"Alvaro! Alvaro! Dominguez! Dominguez! You okay? You QRU? Talk to me, buddy. Alvaro!" I yelled in the open space in front of me.

I then did an "Israeli Peek," or what's commonly now known as a "Quick Peek Technique." I momentarily leaned inside. I visually assessed the situation, then just as quickly pulled my head back from the open door. Dominguez was still strapped into his seat. His dash-mounted MCT computer looked as though it had taken one of the rounds directly from the back, as its computer screen was shattered. The passenger headrest also had a cotton-like material pushing out of a bullet hole.

He appeared to be dead or unconscious.

From my crouched position I duck-walked into the open door frame until I was directly abreast Dominguez. He had his head back and his eyes closed. The car was still in reverse. His foot was off the gas and the car was held in place from rolling further backward by the light pole he'd hit. I reached in with my left hand and shoved the transmission into park. I did a very quick, sloppy check to see if he was shot.

He's breathing.

And I didn't see any immediate bullet wounds.

Sticking my Glock momentarily into my pants at the small of my back, I reached across his body and grabbed his police microphone. I switched the microphone to my left hand and used my right to hold Dominguez's Glock locked into his holster. I couldn't risk him being knocked out then waking up and instinctively drawing his weapon and shooting me. I took a knee on the wet ground just inside the open door. I keyed the microphone.

"Coral Gables 923, Coral Gables 923 priority emergency!"

The Miami Police dispatcher responded with expected confusion.

"QSK Coral Gables unit on Miami frequency?"

"Coral Gables 923, I need a 3-15 at Douglas Metrorail west parking lot. Miami officer down. Miami officer down! Shots fired. Shots fired. Shooter unknown. Scene unsecured. Douglas Metrorail parking lot!"

With that came an ear-piercing electronic tone across the Miami radio. Immediately a barrage of voices and units announced their locations, where they were coming from, asking who is Coral Gables 923, what Miami unit and so on. I didn't answer any of them. My focus was on Dominguez and now our collective safety with a shooter amongst us somewhere. I knew help was on the way. I turned my attention to Dominguez with one eye looking out of the spider webbed windshield for the possible shooter ambushing us both. Little glass shards were all over the interior of the police car. The glass fragments on him were nearly miniscule and looked like glitter interspersed against Dominguez's dark police uniform. I did a more thorough assessment of Dominguez and checked him from his neck on down for any bullet holes or wounds. His knee looked like it was swelling from being rammed into the steering column. He had no obstructions in his airway and he was breathing on his own without any labored or hard breathing. His pulse seemed normal. I shook him hard while calling him by name repeatedly. He started to show some signs of regaining consciousness and his eyes started to flutter a little. The police radio was still a continuous stream of voices and commands. In the far distance I heard approaching sirens. Dominguez started to awaken even more. I kept yelling his name and grabbing him by his face, trying to stir him even further awake. Dominguez was now waking up. He was visibly confused and momentarily perplexed to see me leaning over him in his bullet-riddled car.

"Taylor? Taylor, that you? What the fuck?" he stammered, nearly incoherent.

"Dominguez. Talk to me. What happened. Talk to me, Alvaro. Are you hit?"

"Taylor where the fuck, where the fuck are we, oh shit what the fuck is this?"

"Dominguez, what happened? How many are there? Who did this? Talk to me man, talk to me man."

He was becoming more lucid by the second and the sirens were drawing closer. He focused his eyes on me and seemed to be respooling his immediate memory.

"Shooter. Male. Gray hoodie. Gray hoodie, Cade" he said softly.

Two Miami police cars came screaming into the parking lot right towards us. Under my shirt I carried my badge on a chain around my neck attached to a soft piece leather. I pulled my badge out. I stood up with both hands raised as the cars approached holding my badge in my hand. As the cars drew closer I was already yelling.

"QRU. QRU I'm a cop! I'm a cop!"

Even though it potentially put me in harm's way if the shooter was still in range, I continued to stand alongside the open door against the patrol car, my arms raised, yelling, "I'm a cop." I felt a tug on my pants leg as I stood there and the Miami cops were now running towards me. They weren't running at me in a threatening manner and their gazes were intently on Dominguez. I continued to feel Dominguez pulling on my pants leg. I put one arm across the top of the patrol car and the other across the door frame so the cops would still be able to see my hands. I leaned down and looked into the car at Dominguez.

He looked at me.

"Cade, he's on the train. He's on the train. Go get him. Get him Cade!"

Chapter Three

I TOLD THE APPROACHING Miami officers that Dominguez appeared to have not been hit by any of the bullets. I stepped away from the open doorframe of the patrol car to let them have better access to Dominguez. Up on the Metrorail platform, I saw the train just starting to depart the station. It was heading north towards downtown Miami.

There are two stops between the Douglas Station and the Brickell Metrorail station. Brickell is considered the first stop into downtown Miami. The two stops in the middle were Coconut Grove and Viscaya. I'd never get the train stopped in time for either of those stations. I was banking on getting the train stopped at Brickell.

I made a frantic run to the Z28. I swung the door open and jumped into the driver's seat as more Miami police units arrived. I suspect a rescue truck might be staging outside of the parking lot by the Shell gas station at least until the scene was declared secured. To me, it was just a slew of officers and cars streaming in from all sides with lights and sirens. I slammed the door shut. I jammed the center transmission shifter into drive and stepped on the gas as hard as I could. The Z28 responded with a ferocity that was nothing short of push-you-back-in-the-seat, full-out torque. The Douglas Metrorail parking lot is very large. It afforded me the opportunity to gain some quick speed and not worry about curbs, or an abundance of parked cars.

I knew that I had two crucial things to do if I had any hope of catching the shooter. The first thing I needed to do was alert my dispatch to contact Metro Transit and have my people tell them to stop the train. The second thing that was equally crucial was avoiding as much traffic as possible as I chased the elevated train.

Still maneuvering through the parking lot, I grabbed my Nokia 3210 cell phone and dialed the police dispatch for the Coral Gables Police Department. If I dialed 911, I'd have been continuously passed from one department to another as I crossed jurisdictions. The direct line was the best route. I put the phone on speaker and wedged it tightly into the visor above my head. The dispatcher picked up on the second ring.

"Coral Gables Police and Fire, Operator J.R. Richards, how can I direct your call?"

"Jeanie Rae, this is Cade Taylor 923!"

"Cade is that you? I haven't seen—"

"Jeanie Rae! I need you to listen. There was a 3-30 in the Grove and the shooter opened up on a marked Miami unit. The shooter is on the Metrorail heading north from Douglas. I need you to notify Metro Transit and have the train stopped at the Brickell station!" I screamed into the phone poised over my head as I continued accelerating through the flooded parking lot.

"You need what? What train? Are you on the train?" she asked.

I didn't want to get infuriated but I was feeling the tension and the time sensitivity of what I was saying.

"Listen! Call Metro Transit. Have them stop the northbound Metrorail at Brickell. There is a potential shooter on board who just shot at Miami P.D. Stop the fucking train at Brickell!"

I kept the line open as I could hear her trying to tell a nearby call-taker who handles communiques to notify Metro Transit of my request. The train was gaining speed northward on the tracks above me. It had nothing to slow it down until it approached its next stop, which would be Coconut Grove.

I, on the other hand, had slippery, oily, wet streets, thousands of commuters, traffic lights, and pedestrians in my way.

I'd have to take one of the biggest vehicle arteries in South Florida if I had any chance of getting the shooter. I was going to try and chase the elevated train parallel from U.S 1. I needed to make a decision quickly. If I were to turn onto Douglas Road I'd just get slowed by the meandering curve to the next intersection where Bird Road crossed U.S.1 into Coconut Grove. Both the Bird Road and Douglas intersections in this weather, and with this amount of traffic would be a quagmire to try and traverse. I opted for the proverbial road less traveled and jumped the parking lot curb, and put the Z28 right onto the pedestrian crosswalk that went across Douglas Road. Years ago, the Royal Palm Ice Plant had once stood at this same very location; now it was gravel and shrub and across the crosswalk was a new Walgreens. I pressed on the horn of the car and floored it as I was now using a stretch of asphalt that meandered under the pilings of the Metrorail. The shrill blare of the horn brought Jeanie Rae back on the phone.

"Cade, are you QRU? We are contacting Metro Transit. Are you driving?"

"QSL. I'm trying to catch the train," I yelled into the phone.

Now I was under the actual Metrorail tracks on what can best be described as a narrow bicycle path. The Walgreens and its back-loading area overpopulated with bins and dumpsters went by in a flash. I could survey the traffic momentarily on U.S.1, as I was now essentially paralleling the busy thoroughfare. My time on the bike path bought me valuable seconds, as I was able to bypass the Douglas intersection, but the Bird Road intersection would be dicey at best.

As I approached Bird Road, the traffic engineering gods smiled upon me by making the stop bar for the traffic lights set back a few feet from the intersection. I squeezed the car past a lone palm tree and the backside of a car wash. Using the curving sidewalk as my new driving surface, I cut in front of all the cars waiting at the light. Frustrated, I watched for a gap in the southbound traffic for a few seconds. When the light began to cycle, I didn't wait for it to end. The car pitched sideways as I over-accelerated onto the wet road. I let out a stream of curse words as I fought to regain control of the Z28. The typical Miami drivers who consider a yellow light as a different shade of green screeched their tires and nearly hit me as I shot through. I wasn't concerned with the open phone line but could hear voices once again asking me if I was in pursuit of the train. Since the police department had a no chase policy, I yelled in my best cover-your-ass legal way, "Negative! It's a moving surveillance."

The car fell under my wavering control. I was now speeding north on U.S.1; speeding being the operative word as I was definitely accelerating and pushing the car to react in what any logical person would consider to be an unsafe manner. Looking up through the rain-washed glass T-Tops, I could see the tree line and elevated Metrorail track. The speed of the car caused the rain drops to instantly wash back off the T-Tops. The train was about forty yards in front of me, which was actually momentarily ideal. If the shooter was indeed on the train, with me being just behind, he might not be able to look down and see me rapidly weaving through the sloppy traffic. I'd be able to make up lost ground as the train made its next stop at Coconut Grove on Southwest 27th Avenue. I had ten blocks of traffic to navigate before I had any shot at getting close to the train. The car was fighting the road and felt as though it was fighting me as well. The driver's seat was like a cockpit as it wrapped around me and I felt myself becoming one with the car. I glanced briefly down at the speedometer and saw the driver's side airbag icon lit and felt the tiniest of a small relief knowing that the airbag was active.

The rear window was fogging up. I just didn't have the luxury of searching for the rear defroster button so I cracked both windows open which immediately filled the car with cool, wet air and the sound of accumulated puddle water spewing off the tires. More and more taillights and a few drivers with flashers on were in front of me. I kept weaving in between them until I was even with the train. Each of my deft maneuvers elicited a honking horn or a crude hand gesture from the offended motorist I'd either cut off, cut in front of, or intimidated to move out of my way.

As I approached Southwest 27th Avenue, I knew my best bet was to stay to the right as that lane would bleed off quicker with people turning right. There was a Shell station there, too. I might be able to use the gas station as a cut-through, to avoid the busy intersection.

Luck was not in my favor. The light was horrifically backed up. I'd just not be able to accomplish this. The shooter was more than likely going to get away.

It was at that moment that I saw an entrance to a private parking lot on my right side. There was a strip shopping center that had a cell phone store, a dry cleaner, and a Dunkin' Donuts that abutted a Weight Watchers Clinic. The logic of that arrangement I had no time to even try and understand. I cut the wheel hard right and clipped a hedge as I bounded into the parking lot. Blasting north through the parking lot, past the storefronts, I prayed nobody would absent-mindedly back out of a space into me.

The Shell station owner was very entrepreneurial, as he'd cut the curbing from his back property and adjoined the strip mall lot with a crudely-laid patch of asphalt, allowing egress to his gas station from nearly all sides. I took full advantage of that as I went right into the gas station and under the overhang, and skidded past the pumps. A soaking wet man holding a damaged umbrella and a bottle in a tattered paper bag sat on a bench at the intersection of Southwest 27th and U.S.1. I put the car into a hedge line, fearing I'd hit him. The hedges gave way, bristling and breaking under the weight of the car. I overcorrected the steering and I spun almost 360 degrees into the intersection. Once the spin stopped, I was straddling the crosswalk. Cars on either side of me were stopped in combinations of caution, fear, anger, and surprise. Fortunately, the Z28 was still facing north. Voices on the phone above me yelled, "QSM. Repeat."

Jeanie Rae said that they were still on the telephone with Metro Transit and Metro Transit was not understanding the exact reason to hold a train at the Brickell Metrorail station.

"Tell them they're transporting a gunman who just shot at Miami P.D.!" I yelled into the roofline of the car.

"Copy that, Cade. They're asking for details," she replied.

Details? What more did they need to know? I chose to not even answer.

Zooming back northbound, the train was slightly behind me as it was delayed with its stop at the Coconut Grove Station. But within ninety seconds the train was abreast of me and pulling ahead. Once it got to the Viscaya Station the tracks veer away and are not visible from U.S.1 and the approaching ramp to I-95. I'd lose sight of the train when it angled more northwesterly.

I kept the speed as fast as I could, knowing I might get a small reprieve as the train would still have to stop at the Viscaya Station. With all the streets to Coconut Grove blocked, U.S.1 started to have a traffic rhythm. The stream of vehicles was moving more steadily. Most of the traffic heading north on U.S.1 was intending to merge onto the North I-95 ramp or would be going to the island community of Key Biscayne. There was an under-used surface street route to downtown—that's what I'd be taking. I stayed to the right, intimidating cars to move over and avoiding the often confusing entrance ramp North to I-95. The train was now at the Viscaya Station and my only hope was that Jeanie Rae and the Coral Gables dispatchers had convinced Metro Transit to hold the train.

The I-95 North exit was a quick-rising concrete ramp that had decorative sandstone-colored bricks along its side. I stayed way right of the ramp and continued on U.S.1 for another two hundred yards, and then took advantage of a stalled truck in the intersection of U.S.1 and South Miami Avenue. The truck had its hood up, the driver was standing in the rain directing traffic around his stalled vehicle. I barreled towards him, sounding the horn the whole way. He stepped aside but was astute enough to stop traffic for me as he did. I used the blocking aspect of the truck to skitter through the intersection and turn north onto South Miami Avenue.

A grassy median runs the entire length of the avenue as does a canopy of majestic Poinciana trees. Opulent homes with well-manicured lawns and late model cars in their driveways whizzed by my water-streaked windows.

This was where I'd have to make up any lost time.

The straight roadway and open visual sightlines of South Miami were going to hopefully allow me that gain-time I desperately needed. I felt the car hyper-jump into another accelerated gear as it leveled on the straight avenue and sprint north. The skyscrapers and high-rise condominiums of Brickell came into view, the tops of them nearly obscured in the rain and low cloud cover. Their lights and neon decorative adornments were just colorful smudges in a dusky sky. The heavily wooded Simpson Park was on my left-hand side as I roared by, its tree line descending the street into early darkness.

The rain fell harder as I tore right into the traffic circle at Southwest 15th Street, which was thankfully empty. I pierced the circle like an errant spear with the slightest adjustment of the steering wheel and the Z28 caught some air under it as the road dipped. All four wheels left the ground and then came down hard on South Miami Avenue as I rocketed towards Southwest 13th street. The car fought to gather its tractional equilibrium. I pushed myself down to be as bounded in the seat as far as I could as it came back onto the street.

At 13th Street I power-slid westbound, then immediately spun the wheel a full revolution on Southwest 1st Avenue.

I could hear the train's wheels screeching to a halt as it entered the Brickell Station just ahead of me. The car shook as the train rumbled right above me. The Metrorail was directly over my head.

I searched for the quickest staircase to the top of the station; wherever it was would determine where I parked. *An escalator.* That's where the quickest route would be. Because of the weather the escalator was locked down. It looked slippery and treacherous. Water was falling down the metal stairs like a modern art waterfall. I slammed on the brakes and yanked the car into park. I jumped out into a puddle with slick, oily residue on top of it.

The train wasn't moving.

The noise of the idling train reverberated as I started up the inoperable escalator. The slick glass sidewalls were of no use as a safety rail, and I struggled to stay on my feet. The ascent was unsafe and difficult as water trickled down over each rising step. Rivulets of rainwater washed over my shoes with each step upward. Midway up the precarious escalator I could finally see the silver roofline of the train idling with its doors closed. As I continued up the escalator more of the train came into my view. What I saw first were the train's recognizable blue and green striping and white train numbers. Three steps more and now the wide windows were revealed. I could see the first car more clearly than any of the rest, and was surprised by how packed the train was with riders.

Riders and an attempted cop killer.

Wind gusts on the upper platform brought the rain down in swirling waves. I was soaked to the bone. My hair, when not matted against my face, was blowing wildly with the elevated winds.

I was nearing the top of the escalator.

Quickly, I drew my Glock from my waistband and held it tightly behind my right thigh, careful not to expose it and alarm—or more precisely, alert—any passengers looking out at me. North of me further down the train line, numerous searchlights tried to pierce the opaque gray sky. Something was going on at the Miami Arena.

The train was a spectral image. The line of cars were stacked. The idling engine and falling rain were the only sounds on the platform. The train was like a seething combatant, I had chased it so ardently and risked so much to catch it. Now that it was before me. It had the appearance of an electronic metal beast defying me to come closer. It seemed to be waiting for me, taunting me, daring me to approach it.

All I could think of was that a potential homicide suspect and attempted cop killer was somewhere in those linked cars.

I stepped onto the platform the density of the passengers on the train was still oddly surprising, a look of confusion on their faces. Some even displayed frustration at the fact the train wasn't moving. What was more startling to me was the commonality of many of the passengers. They were almost themed in the way they were dressed. Some wore top hats, others had sequin jackets and oversized eyeglasses. I even saw a few feather boas. I quickly recalled a news article about Elton John playing a concert at the Miami Arena. Now it made sense to me. Still too many people packed in with a shooter, but I felt a bit of relief that I might be able to ferret him out in this crowd. Absurdly, trying to blend in with his gray hoodie, it would only make him stand out now.

He'll be wet, alone, and not interacting with any of the other passengers.

I stood off to the side, trying to get the conductor's attention. The conductor was in the last train and I needed to do a car-by-car search. Thank God for Jeanie Rae. She had gotten the message across to Metro Transit. Now it was all on me.

The wind and the driving rain made seeing down the full line of cars nearly impossible which meant the conductor most likely couldn't see me either. I'd have to walk along the train line until he spotted me—which would potentially expose me to the shooter.

I kept my badge under my dark t-shirt and concealed my weapon as best I could as I walked with my gun behind my thigh. I kept my eyes on the train windows, scanning as many people as I could. A few of the passengers had taken notice of my attempt to conceal my gun. I could sense their murmured comments. I felt as if the wave of information was trailing my drenched walk as I passed the first car and moved onto the second. It was as though all eyes were locked on me. I just kept intently scanning, looking for a gray hoodie in the mass of faces and people.

Without warning or announcement, the train began to move.

I was aghast. My astonishment rapidly turned to red hot anger.

I started walking faster towards the back of the train, which was now moving towards me. I was trying to look into the lit windows as the train gained speed. The windows began to whizz by me with too much speed, I couldn't get a good bearing on any faces now. I started yelling some pretty harsh curse words, just standing on the platform as the train pulled out of the station in full force. The last car went by and the swirling water from the train washed over me. No conductor to talk to, no shooter to apprehend.

Chapter Four

Like one of those times
That's never the same
Like when something dies
Like runaway trains

~ Runaway Trains by Tom Petty

THE TRAIN WAS streaking northward out of the Brickell Metrorail Station. Glowering, with my gun in my hand, I could only watch as it pulled further away. I was wet, angry, and feeling defeated.

The sound of the departing train faded off and the platform became eerily quiet with just the rainwater splashing off the edges of the roofline. Normally, I would have had an impressive vantage point to see the Miami skyline from where I was standing, but it was cloaked in low-ceilinged clouds and tumbling rain. About thirty yards ahead of me the center bank of elevators hummed with activity, bodies moving behind the decorative block glass.

Two wet uniformed Miami police officers and an equally soaked female detective stepped off the elevator. I was fed up with constantly identifying myself. I just chose to holster my gun which I knew they all clearly saw me do. One of the officers split off from the detective and the other cop and he strategically walked the outer edge of the platform. He was tactically splitting my target area, eliminating my ability to shoot all three of them out in a cluster if I made a move. As they drew closer, without any fanfare, I simply pulled my badge out from under my shirt and let it hang on its chain around my neck.

The burly uniformed officer leading the pack of three towards me called out, "You Gables 923?"

"I'm Cade Taylor. Vice Intelligence Narcotics with the Gables, unit 923," I called back.

"Detective Taylor. I'm Cynthia Clay, Miami Homicide," said the detective as a way of introduction.

She was somewhat diminutive in size and had tightly curled jet-black hair that she'd most likely tied back hastily in a ponytail before heading out in this torrential rain. Her features were soft and her skin was smooth. As she drew closer I could see her wide expressive brown eyes.

"Where's the train?" the burly officer asked as he walked up to me.

I was tempted to tell him that the craziest thing happened, and that Magician David Copperfield had made the train disappear. I held my tongue and simply said the train was northbound.

Detective Clay immediately turned to the other Miami officer on the platform fringe.

"Raise Bravo 517 at the command post for the Elton John concert. Tell him to advise all assigned off-duty officers at the concert to bolo a white male in a gray hoodie, possibly exiting the Metrorail, possibly armed, wanted in connection to a 3-31 in Coconut Grove."

During my hell ride to the Brickell Metrorail Station, the police code had upgraded from a possible shooting to a homicide.

The officer turned away and began transmitting verbatim what Detective Clay had said to him into his portable radio. The burly officer idled himself before turning to Clay and said, "C.C. I'll be downstairs if you need me." He walked away, leaving me and Clay alone on the platform.

"You know my people got the train stopped," I said to her.

"I know. We got word that someone at Metro Transit got pressured by the concert promotors and the Miami Dade Entertainment Authority to have the train leave here. They had it bypass Government Center and go straight to the Overtown Station where the Miami Arena is. They figured we have more cops there than just one Coral Gables cop here."

"So I nearly killed myself getting here, trying to protect one of your own, and you pulled the train on me?"

"I'm willing to bet you probably nearly killed more people than just yourself getting here," she said dismissively.

"What's that supposed to mean? I didn't see any of your guys going with me?"

"What you didn't see is because of your own actions. Did you tell anyone that Dominguez said the killer was on the train? Did you tell anyone where you were going? From my perspective—and you might be surprised, but my perspective *does* matter since this is my case—it seems maybe a little communication from you and we could've done a better job here," she shot back.

"Well since this is your case, you obviously don't need me here."

I started toward the same slippery escalator that I used to climb up to the platform.

"Taylor... Wait."

I stopped at the top of the inoperable escalator. I turned back and looked at her and said, "Your officer was in need of medical attention. I left him with his backups. There wasn't anyone to say anything to—the few officers that were there were needed for Officer Dominguez. It wasn't like I just chose to slip and slide my way into downtown Miami by myself. You may notice that radios and blue lights aren't part of my Batman utility belt here."

"We have a team in Coconut Grove and this case has been assigned to me. Why don't you ride with me back to the Grove? I can get your statement in the car. Either myself, or one of our guys will bring you back here to your car afterwards."

I looked down at the Z28 parked below. I thought about it for a second. I looked up at the small droplets still falling. I then relented.

"I'm in the Z28. I need to get some things out of it. I'll meet you by my car." I turned and started the wet treacherous descent to my car.

I learned a few months earlier the importance of having a "go bag" with me at all times. It's called a go bag so that when a crisis occurs you can just grab the bag and go. I opened the trunk of the car.

In my go bag I carry a change of clothing and other necessities when I find myself in need of being rapidly mobile. I stripped off my soaked t-shirt and tossed it into the trunk, then used a towel from the go bag to, as adequately as I could, dry myself all over. I donned a dark dry Henley and felt better almost immediately not being completely sopping wet. My jeans were soaked especially from the knees down, but I figured my pants would continue to get wet so why change them? My goatee and mustache were moist from the rain. I dug my face into the towel one last time before grabbing a Hartford Whalers ballcap from the go bag. I pushed my shoulder-length hair back and underneath it. The baseball style cap would keep whatever rain was in my immediate future off my face.

Detective Clay pulled up to me in her car.

"My car's okay here, right? I won't get a ticket or anything?" I said, leaning into her open window.

"It'll be fine. There's no one out here doing traffic enforcement. If you're worried, I'll let my people know," she said.

I climbed into her car—the all-too-common Dodge Intrepid which nearly every detective in Miami had been assigned. I'd just closed the door when she pulled briskly away from the curve only to pull over about fifty yards down the street from the Metrorail station. Two uniformed City of Miami patrol cars with their overhead lights on shot up behind us and whizzed on by. Once in front of us, they enacted their sirens. Clay immediately pulled out right behind them. *They've got to be the two officers from the Metrorail platform.* Between the urgency of her needing to be on the scene and the weather conditions, it was a wise choice to have a uniform escort back to Coconut Grove.

On the seat between us was her city identification attached to a lanyard. Her identification picture was more flattering than the way she'd first appeared on the platform. Her skin was a slight mocha complexion, it reminded me of a phrase I once saw on a Lancôme counter display at Macy's.

Pecan tan

The identification also noted her date of hire: February 1991. She had eight years on at the City of Miami. After Hurricane Andrew raged through the southern suburbs of Miami Dade County in 1992, many of the residents in those quiet neighborhoods opted to move north of the Miami Dade County line to Southern Broward County. Many of those very same suburbs they moved from and then reestablished were jokingly called "Copland" and "Copland II" due to the inordinate amount of law enforcement people who'd clustered in those idyllic Miami Dade neighborhoods, only to repeat the same patterns in Broward County. There was a mass exodus from South Florida entirely. I was willing to venture her quick ascent into homicide was due to post-Hurricane Andrew flight.

"So how long have you been in homicide?" I asked her.

"Three months."

Well, there went that theory about post hurricane attrition and movement.

"What were you before homicide?" I asked her.

"I started out in uniform in Flagami, out by Westchester, after reasonable potion of time I spent a few boring years in data management. Now I'm homicide," she said.

She intently tried to keep her car tires aligned within the recent tire tracks of the patrol car she was closely following. My confidence in her ability as a homicide detective was faltering due to her lack of experience. I kept that feeling to myself.

We were moving south nearly retracing the exact route I'd taken on the way north to downtown. She asked me how it was that I ended up at the Douglas Metrorail Station. Without going into the exact conversation, I took her back to the *ventanita* at *La Caretta* and Dominguez had come up to me to say "hello." I mentioned the 3-30 and three tone call on Dominguez's radio and after seeing him head off by himself I decided to also go to the Douglas Metrorail Station. I didn't want Dominguez to go alone, and the station is very close to the eastern Coral Gables border. I told her Dominguez arrived before me and when I arrived in the parking lot I detailed what I saw. I told her what I did leading up to me leaving the parking lot and heading north on U.S.1. She took it all in and didn't ask too many questions.

"Anything else, Detective Clay?"

"Call me C.C., everyone does."

"Cynthia Clay, C.C. Got it."

With the uniformed escort we made great time to Coconut Grove. By the time I'd finished talking we were nearly pulling up to the homicide scene. The 3000 block of Mundy street intersects with U.S.1. The most discernable thing in the block is an Advance Auto Parts Store on the corner. Now the Advance Auto Parts Store west parking lot was a cordoned-off crime scene. It was a short walk across U.S.1 from the homicide scene to the Douglas Metrorail parking lot. The *safest* route is west along U.S.1 and crossing Douglas Road on the elevated pedestrian walk. But the quickest route is walking diagonally west through the Walgreens lot, then across Douglas Road.

Pulling up to the macabre scene was gut-wrenching. Under a yellow tarp laid a body, and judging by the victim's sport shoes peeking out of the tarp, I surmised the victim was a relatively young male. A young life snuffed out entirely too quickly. Yellow crime scene tape fluttered in the occasional post-storm breeze. Every inch of the crime scene tape was wet from the rain. Droplets of water fell off in a steady *tap-tap-tap* rhythm.

The Miami police had the scene contained very well, although there were still many onlookers. Some straddled bicycles, others stood off to the side, and some were eating burgers fresh from the

Wendy's next door. The Advance Auto Parts store was closed for the remainder of the day, its front door held open by a garbage can. Miami Police technicians had portable lights and cables being fed from outlets inside the business and a uniformed officer standing by the open door. His position was designed primarily to prevent any theft of air fresheners, Armor All, and steering wheel covers. C.C. hugged the curb and parked on Mundy street. We both stepped out of her car.

Two detectives ambled over and spoke in a quiet hushed circle with her. They were likely the on-call detectives tasked with holding the scene until she arrived. They'd turn it over to her and head out only to be summoned to the next homicide call that came in before their shift ended. I stood by the side of her car not venturing to go any further unless summoned. After a few minutes one of the detectives lifted the crime scene tape and C.C. and the two detectives entered the homicide scene. More quiet reflective walking and talking by the three, with one of the detectives motioning to the yellow evidence markers on the ground; three yellow triangles that I assumed were covering spent cartridges. I just became another onlooker, albeit one without a Wendy's burger. After about twenty minutes C.C. lifted the tarp over the body as slightly as she could, trying to shield the view of the deceased form the curious people outside the cordoned-off area. I heard a young woman in a vibrant pink top near me say, "That look like Reggie."

I turned to her and asked her what she meant by that.

"He always wearing them green Pumas. He stay on Franklin. I think he works for the county because I seen him in a county truck at his house. He was nice enough, but he ain't from here. He was just staying on Franklin."

"Do you know his last name?" I asked her.

"No. He just Reggie."

"Do you know where on Franklin?"

"I seen him near Plaza."

I motioned to C.C. We stood with the tape between us.

"Did you get an I.D. yet? If not, that young woman in the flamingo pink top over there thinks it's a young man named Reggie. She thinks its him because of the green Pumas. Said he might live on Franklin Avenue near Plaza Street."

C.C. looked past me at the young woman and then called to a uniform officer to gather what information he could from her. "I'll get you a ride back to your car," C.C. said. I let her continue with her investigation. Ten minutes later a Public Service Aide—also known as a PSA—pulled up adjacent to me in a Ford Taurus. The car had similar striping as Miami Police car with just a few deviations, and instead of a full red and blue lightbar affixed on the roof there was an amber yellow lensed light bar. The driver lowered the window.

"Are you the Gables guy?" said the PSA officer.

"I guess I am," I said.

I plopped into the passenger seat and the PSA wordlessly eased out towards U.S.1. I looked over at C.C. and the processing of the homicide scene.

I was very relived to be leaving.

The ride back to the Brickell Metrorail Station was quiet and uneventful if you didn't count all the times the PSA told me about his great law enforcement career working traffic accidents and citing barking dog owners. Had the ride continued any further, I would have rather of shaved my neck with a rusty cheese grater than listen to him drone on about his exploits. Finally at the Z28, I thanked him and exited the car. As he drove off, I just smirked looking at the wet parking ticket wedged under the front windshield wiper of my car. I removed the damp, crumbling ticket and threw it into the glove compartment.

I realized that I hadn't eaten anything since my meeting with Special Agent Tavino. I turned on the ignition and the car purred to life, almost begging me to put it through its paces again. Much to its disappointment, I was more than happy to leisurely drive away from the Brickell Metrorail station. I drove north on Southwest 1st Avenue towards the Miami River. I decided to head to Miami's oldest bar, "Tobacco Road." I drove past the iconic watering hole, and its sizeable line of patrons waiting to get in. Up on my right, just before the bridge starts to cross the Miami River, was a Florida Department of Transportation satellite office, with its requisite state-issued "No Parking" signs. I parked in one of the spaces anyway. I reached into the glove compartment, pulled out the tattered parking ticket I received earlier in the day and put it back on the windshield.

Tobacco Road had survived Prohibition and multiple owners over the years. During Prohibition the upstairs lounge was a known hangout for many imbibers, including gangster and part time Miami Beach resident, Al Capone. The bar proudly held liquor license number 0001. For decades it was without a doubt one of Miami's oldest, grittiest, jovial, and most importantly rollicking bars. "The Road," as its devotees called it, had a moniker: "The Road is Always Open." Closing time was 5am each and every night of the week; it was always tested and never failed.

Here I was standing a few paces from the Miami River and it was easy to see why.

The building was boxed between a row of storefronts. The storefronts always changed but Tobacco Road stayed consistent. Aside from its copious drinks and decent bar food, The Road was a serious live music venue with stages both up and downstairs for performances. Top acts willingly stopped in to play for small crowds just so they could add themselves to the great list of performers who'd previously darkened its doorway. Internationally known acts such as Miles Davis, Koko Taylor, Eva Cassidy, and John Lee Hooker had performed there in its storied history. The bar had an allure that called to its denizens each and every night. It was an everyman saloon with a big heart and decades of stories that were as numerous and varied as the shells on a beach. Everyone in Miami went to The Road at least once in their life. Federal prosecutors bellied up to the bar beside drug smugglers. A-list actors rubbed elbows with plumbers and delivery drivers. World-renowned musicians often heard great renditions of their top hits being played by a guy who, when not a baritone player at night, was a day construction laborer on Key Biscayne.

I stood by my car for the briefest of moments and looked up at the night sky. Over my shoulder the Metrorail was lit underneath its arching track with long neon strips, illuminating the river underneath. The colors dazzled on the choppy Miami River a good sixty feet below the elevated train line. The city's skyline was in full growth mode with multiple new gleaming high rise office buildings and condominiums. The low cloud cover cast these behemoths in a hazy whitish blend of streaming color and illuminated shadows, fighting to shine and simultaneously stay dark. In available pockets of space between the buildings were numerous steel girders, frames, and scaffolding. I do believe the state bird of Florida should be a "construction crane."

The rain had dwindled into the finest of mists and was nearly nonexistent by the time it hit terra-firma. The Hartford Whalers hat would be enough to keep me dry. As I neared the door, I saw a flyer posted on a telephone pole. Graham Wood Drout, would be appearing with his band, Iko Iko. The popular Iko Iko band had become a staple over the years and their appearances at Tobacco Road had made them nearly the de facto house band. I'm sure many waiting to get in were secretly hoping Elton John might stop in after his concert. I found that notion unlikely but then again after the afternoon and evening I'd just experienced, what could I possibly know about unforeseen events?

I started toward the long line of people waiting to get in the bar. Many cops upon seeing such a crowd would often pull out their police badge and try to "badge" their way in and bypass the line. It's a common practice in South Florida. Management and bouncers often view a cop patron as one who won't wreck the place, will pay their tab, and be available as extra security if something were to happen inside. "Masterbadge." As in, "There are some things money can't buy. For everything else, there's Mastercard."

I had a better plan.

I strode past the deepening line of people. They were from all aspects of Miami, young, old, professionally attired, and casually dressed. The outside of the bar is painted in the oddest shade of green ever devised by man. A concocted combination of gumball green, seafoam green, and asparagus tip green all blended together. The façade of the building is a mashup of unfinished rough stucco laid over brick. Near the roof line is an archaic but still functioning neon sign that has three illuminated stanzas. The top line says in fiery red neon, "Tobacco Road." The middle line says in a leprechaun green argon-filled tube of gas, "Liquor Bar." The bottom line, and I'm sure the primary reason that has caused many a taxi patron to yell, "Stop here" to their cab drivers were the neon lines, "Til 5 A M." If the sign wasn't enough to grab your attention, emblazoned across the front tier of the building was a black-painted banner with "Tobacco Road" written in red and white lettering in a huge bold antique font. A very imposing bouncer was standing under the front door's green curved awning. He was wearing a stretched way too tight black t-shirt that barely covered his impressively muscled chest and arms. I walked right to the front of the line. I looked at him. He looked at me. I stood as close as I could to him without alarming him and said very softly:

"I slept with Jack."

He looked at me quizzically and then instinctively leaned down even closer where I repeated nearly in his ear, "I slept with Jack."

He pulled back to study me. Then he stepped aside and opened the overworn, often-kicked, scuffed and faded yellow French door to the bar. I strolled in and he quietly closed the door behind me.

One of the advantages of having a police badge is getting into certain venues and places unchallenged. An even better advantage is knowing the very secret password that only a few people knew. Jack is a bearded, paunchy bartender who is very passionate about snow skiing in Colorado. He travels out west every chance he gets. On one of my many forays into The Road, we'd become familiar with each other. He told me of the foolproof password to bypass any line at the front door.

"Just tell 'em you slept with me," he said one night as he cleaned glasses behind the bar. We were both nearing the 5am closing time. It stuck with me and it always worked.

The interior of Tobacco Road is like a time capsule of Miami history. More importantly, it is a living breathing shrine to blues music and the pantheons of rock and roll. Just inside the weathered front door is a framed black and white photograph of "Doctor Feelgood." The photograph is mounted on a plaque and it shows a big facial close up of a weathered black man with tufts of gray hair peeking out from under his denim baseball cap. His eyes are squinting with his natural smile, although it was tightly held. When he was alive, Dr. Feelgood was actually a skinny ex-con named William Bell. His favorite drink was vodka and Coca Cola. He slept next door on an outdoor porch for years and was an honorary bouncer. It was rumored his ghost still haunted the bar. An engraved plate under his photograph was what I surmised to be his most famous quote.

"That's what she said, Goddamn it!"

I moved through the extremely linear bar towards the back. There are a few tables on the left side, a large wooden scratched and human-scarred bar runs nearly the length of the ground floor on the right. In the midst of the tables is a small stage—or actually more of a cleared area. It is forged into the overhang space where the staircase leading upstairs has a landing. The staircase is positioned between the lower tables and the narrow, hot, noisy kitchen. Going upstairs is always a treat and reminiscent of a visit to a New Orleans bordello. The wallpaper is a red velvet with the bulbs in the fringe shaded lamps all painted red. The bar upstairs is functional but most patrons "got their drunk on' downstairs then amble up to let the music and the vibe float them into their night. Downstairs, the aisle between the tables and the bar are narrow. If you had any compunction about anyone ever rubbing against you—and by rubbing against you, consider all body parts in play—this is not the place for you. The bar is dark and nearly every inch of the walls has a framed photograph of a famous blues singer, a signed copy of sheet music, or a concert announcement, all of which are intrinsically part of the essence of Tobacco Road. I found a seat midway at the downstairs bar.

Through the open back door to my left I could see the courtyard. The Iko Iko roadies—or more specifically, band friends—were carrying in equipment and then turning upstairs. The bartender was a large guy who had one of those beards that either he intended to let grow wooly or he was just too lazy to shave his neck. He swirled a Newcastle Ale coaster down in front of me. After sixty years of all the alcohol, blood, snot, and water that had been splashed across this bar I don't think a coaster would have mattered.

"Jameson neat. How's the barbecue shrimp?" I asked him.

"Well, Captain Gonzo just brought it in an hour ago on one of our fleet shrimp boats," he answered sarcastically.

"I'll have the cheeseburger, medium, with fries, no ketchup, no mayonnaise. If you put mayonnaise on the burger we're both going to end up on the eleven o'clock news."

He smiled and as he walked down the length of the bar but said loud enough for me to hear, "Got it. One cheeseburger extra mayonnaise."

The first Jameson came rather quickly and I think the second Jameson came even faster. I sat there listening to the track music playing downstairs that had been curated by their in-house music guru named Dave. Dave was responsible for finding live music acts and booking them. He also was adept at creating looping tracks of house music when there wasn't anybody playing live. I wasn't certain, but I think at the moment I was listening to The Groove Hogs, or it might have been the Thunder Row Hellions. I started thinking about the day's events which soon led me to think about where I was and how I ended up here. Not just here in the bar.

Here.

Eight months ago, I was married and living in a quiet suburban house in southwest Miami Dade County. My marriage to my then-burgeoning artist wife Gina imploded with the revelation of her affair with the guy she rented an artist studio from. His loyalty to his own long-term marriage was obviously nonexistent as he moved out on his wife and was now living with Gina in Palm Beach

Gardens. The divorce was a long, drawn-out barrage of legal filings and motions for discovery. Her attorney, Phillip Gilot, was not very skilled, but he knew enough to constantly ask for documentation on nearly every aspect of my life. It had no bearing on the divorce. It was intended to keep me off balance. As a "public servant," I had to answer frivolous inquiries and allow for my personal files, my performance files, financial files, even an accounting of the yard guy's visits had to be produced. The state of Florida is a no-fault marriage state. Florida divorce judges aren't concerned with who wronged who, they just look for equitable distribution of marital assets. Anybody who thinks they'll get divorced in Florida and plead a case for understanding is going to be sorely disappointed. As for the attorneys… well, keep in mind they have to deal with each other all the time. You, on the other hand, are a one-time client. If you're *smart* you'll be a one-time client. Do the math on the loyalty scale on that one.

Days before our court hearing I'd taken a four-day trip to Toronto. When I came home nearly everything in the house of value was gone. What wasn't taken was toppled over, strewn on the floor, or damaged. Gina had used a hide a key and crew of people to come into the house and arrogantly took "equitable distribution of marital assets" into her own hands. Phillip Gilot had requested a list of days I would be unavailable for deposition, and knowing I was out of town, forwarded that information to Gina. It was as though human locusts had descended on my home and privacy. She even took the kitchen paper towel holder. What kind of demented person needs a paper towel holder that bad?

It was a legal mess. It wasn't entirely *burglary*, although she had moved out and was no longer paying the mortgage. Her things had still been there and the mortgage deed still had her name on it as well as mine. A divorce judge would order her to return all the possessions which would end up in a big pile in my driveway. We'd then have to sift through the possessions in an embarrassing game of adults acting like children playing eeny meeny miny mo. I chose to go with the expediated version. I tabulated everything that was removed and its true value and my attorney sought financial restitution, which much to her and her dipshit attorney's chagrined surprise, the judge agreed to. The house sold rather quickly and with the proceeds from the sale, and the little bump in the renumeration of all that was taken, I was actively still looking for a place to live. I'd briefly stayed a few miles north of here in a two-story house in El Portal. From there I couch surfed and vagabonded my way for a week or two. A doctor friend I met through a contact at the Miami Dade Medical Examiner's Office had purchased a condominium in Paradise Point for his mother. She was in the Dominican Republic. The day before his mother was to move to Miami, she broke her hip and now will remain in the Dominican Republic for a few months convalescing. He kindly offered me the unused, furnished condominium in Paradise Point until she was healthy enough to move. I saw it as a good way to regroup. I gladly accepted his offer. The condominium is far away from where I was currently sitting, way down south in the county off of Coral Reef Drive and Ludlum Road.

Since the divorce, my penchant for Jameson Scotch Whiskey was becoming a little too much. To me, the wonderful Irish whiskey elixirs were edge-of-life-cutters, cope-with-the-miseries, heal-the-unhealable shots. I was aware they were becoming a little more prevalent than I liked to admit. It faded Gina from memory and it dulled the synapsis in my brain that tended to revisit some of the traumatic and upsetting aspects of being a VIN detective. A VIN detective, I might add, in a city that seems to invent crime. I was contemplating my drinking history which was ironically running in my mind congruently with my drinking habits. I was ashamed to think that this was not the first time I'd sat at a bar in damp underwear. It probably wouldn't be the last, but then again in this particular situation I reasoned it was acceptable.

This time.

The cheeseburger arrived with fries, and the bartender as a way of demonstrating his comedic touch, included a side of mayonnaise on the plate. He chuckled as he walked away. The burger was thick and seared well and I chomped into it greedily. The bottom of the bun had that slightly moist red meat residue indicating the cook plopped it onto the bun seconds earlier.

The bar was still filling up. I didn't look up to gauge the growing crowd but could tell it was growing by how many times my high back barstool got jostled by people. The noise level was amplifying and the music volume rose as well. The seat next to me opened up and a young woman eased into it post haste. I didn't even look up. My burger was nearly finished, and I was contemplating a third Jameson shot. *A third would go quite nicely*, I told myself. The bartender who I inwardly named Mr. Mayonnaise was quick to respond. He set a generous pour before me. I showed my approval with a tight smile and an ever-so-slight bow of my head to him. I was just reaching for the golden mind soother when the young woman next to me spoke.

"Are those truffle fries?" she asked me.

"I'm sorry, what?"

"Are those truffle fries? They look like truffle fries."

I spun the plate in her direction. She picked up on the nonverbal invitation and removed two fries from my plate and ate them both.

"No, not truffle fries. Too bad. There's a place in Malibu called the Duck and Dive that has great truffle fries. Have you ever been to Malibu?

Before I could answer she was onto another round of questions.

"What brings you here? Me and my girlfriends have a game that never fails. Tell me what you do and I can guess your name."

I had no idea that offering a French fry to someone in an attempt to get them to leave you alone could morph so fast to playing guessing games with a chattering bar seatmate. I wanted to get up and leave but the Jameson was still settling at the rim of the shot. I turned more towards her. I looked at her. Even in the dim lights I could see she had a high wattage smile. She was probably in her early thirties. Long brown hair that with each flowing inch seemed to take on the russet colors of a New England fall. Her hair wasn't a brassy red at the ends. It just went from a gradual brown to a resplendent red. Her skin was an even-toned, fresh-scrubbed whiteness. She appeared to be someone who either takes care of her skin or sees someone in a spa who does it for her. I was willing to bet her makeup counter at home had thirteen different lotions and creams. She was wearing a long sleeve purple sweater with blue jeans. She was attractive and two Jamesons into the night I couldn't see the harm in playing along.

"You can guess my name by my occupation?" I said back.

"Absolutely. It never fails," she said with a devilish smile.

"Okay. I own a pool liner company."

"Oh, you're in the building trade. Guys like you have those curt, right-to-the-point names. Pool liner... cement, vinyl, piping...okay I got it. Your name is Dave."

"No, but it's a good try," I said, turning my stool back towards my drink.

"Was I even close?" she asked.

I turned back towards her and said, "Well you got the vowels in the right place."

"So it's not Dave. How about Sage?"

"Nope," I said, still wanting to start in on my waiting shot of Jameson.

"Abe."

"No."

"Nate."

"Seriously. Is this really going to go on like this? You and your girlfriends might need to find a new game to play," I said with a hint of exasperation.

"Okay, I give up. What is it? What's your name?"

"Cade. My name is Cade," I said, hoping the party game was over.

"Cade? I don't think I've ever heard that name before. Cade. Well, you got me."

"Do I? Did I get you?" I asked flirtatiously.

She picked up on the entendre and smiled.

"Okay. Your turn. I'm a flight attendant for American Airlines," she volunteered.

"Unexpected Turbulence," I said.

She laughed heartily.

"Well, Mr. Cade, I'll let you know that I can most certainly be unexpected turbulence."

"I really don't think that coming from you, turbulence would be unexpected," I said.

"What's that supposed to mean? I don't know if I like you, or your fries anymore."

"Yes, you do. Besides you're only using me for my fries. We both know that. When the fries are gone you'll use me and throw me on the scrap pile with all the other men in your life you've ruined."

"You know, you got some crazy ideas there. Seriously, see if you can guess my name."

"Lorraine," I said without any conviction it could even possibly be right.

"What? Do I look like a Lorraine to you?"

"Do I like an Abe?"

"Good point. Okay, for real, one more honest try. What do you think my name is?"

"Tammy."

She furrowed her brow and let me know that Tammy, Stacey, Tricia, Lacey, or Vanessa were all cliché flight attendant names instilled in the male psyche since the days of overtly sexist airline advertising from the 1970s. I don't think I ever wanted to savor a shot of Jameson and simultaneously down it at the same time as much as I did right then. I was sufficiently informed and equally bored with the lesson on the pitfalls of Madison Avenue advertising. This time I was able to actually put my hand around the Jameson and draw a smooth pull of it to my lips.

"Since I'm not very good at this what is your name?"

"Kaitlyn. Actually, its Kaitlyn Sara. Everyone calls me Katie. I spell it K-e-i-g-h-t-y. Keighty."

"Since I'm not everyone, what should I call you?"

"You can call me Katie, although I like the rolling aspect of being a high number, like eighty."

That entire comment made absolutely no sense to me but she was very attractive. The sharp edges of the day were starting to melt away. Hours ago, I'd been in Coconut Grove watching a dead young man's ankles get wet as the rest of him laid dry under a tarp. Here I was, now satiated by a colossal burger, and having a repertoire with a pretty woman whose attractiveness was growing on me.

"So tell me Katie-Eighty, what's the best thing about being a stewardess?" I asked her.

"It's *flight attendant*. Not stewardess. I like it. I like the travel. That's the best thing."

"I thought it might be at the end of a flight as you walk down the aisle with a hefty bag and look everyone in the face and say, 'Trash?'"

"That's part of it, but it's not as glamourous as staring at everyone's crotch before we take off to see if their seatbelt's fastened."

"Tell me something about being a flight attendant that would surprise me."

"Hmmm. Well, you know those beverage carts that all the drinks are on?"

"You mean the carts where you and your crewmates steal those little bottles of Johnnie Walker and Dewar's from?" I joked.

"Hey, those bottles are strictly accounted for, but if you're ever in need for small bags of peanuts, I'm your girl."

"No thanks on the peanuts but I like you being my girl."

Even in the dark I saw the pink light up her cheeks. She motioned to Mr. Mayonnaise for a refill of her Cosmo. I did the universal hand-circle-wave thing that conveyed one more shot of Jameson for me and put her tab on mine.

"Well," she continued, "those beverage carts are actually made in Europe and the latches and compartments on them are a bitch to try and figure out. Nothing more embarrassing than opening drawer after drawer to get some fat ass a Cheez-it bag and you can't find it. Plus, they seem to be really heavy sometimes and really light other times. You'll wreck your back if you try and push one, thinking it's light.

"Are you from Miami?" I asked her

I'm based here in Miami, but I'm originally from North Carolina. American is thinking of expanding their presence in Boston so if I get based there, I might actually commute in from New Hampshire, it's cheaper."

"So you're Miami based? Where do you live?"

"Wouldn't you like to know!"

"Actually, yes I'd like to know," I said suggestively

"I live in North Bay Village." She studied me with a grin. "I don't know. I always thought if I got Miami-based I'd meet some exotic guy. Drug smuggler, gun runner or some other bad boy. Not a pool liner guy," she said.

"Drug smuggler, or gun runner? Well, some of us guys just don't have the guts to be in that world. No, I'm just a pool liner guy. I can find and fix leaks. Seal cracks, if you know what I mean. Besides you're too good a girl to get mixed up with bad boys."

"The only difference between a good girl and a bad girl is that good girls are very selective with who they're bad with," she said as she drew a big sip from her chilly Cosmo.

"Yeah, I heard that ladies like bad boys. Lucky for them I'm bad at everything," I replied.

We talked for another hour or so and the crowd was still growing. *Breakfast in America* by Supertramp was playing on the music loop. An intentional deviation I'm sure by Dave the music guru to signal the working bar crew of something. "I saw these guys in concert a long time ago at Miami Jai Alai," I said.

"Who are they?" she asked.

"Supertramp. Breakfast in America."

"Well, how do you feel about mediocre tramp and breakfast at my place?" she said as she looked me deep in my eyes.

I'd already cleared our tab with Mr. Mayonnaise and there was nothing to stop us from leaving the bar. I agreed to follow her to North Bay Village. She hastily wrote her number on a paper napkin in case we got separated. As we started for the door she remarked that she knew she made the right choice in wearing her lucky bra.

"Of all the things in life, you chose undergarments as a lucky charm?" I asked as we stepped outside.

"I'm a woman. Everything under my clothes had better be lucky."

I let her lead me toward her car. She climbed into a dark green Chevrolet Prizm, waited for me to get in my car, and we headed north on South Miami Avenue. I pictured her adjusting her rearview mirror ever-so-slightly to see me behind her, maybe adjusting her lip gloss, and doing a mental checklist of how clean her place was. Did she take out the garbage? Are there dishes in the sink? Things like that. As for me, I knew that if Ritchie Tavino's SAC did call Major Brunson I'd have to be in the office Monday and try and mitigate that. I had thoughts about C.C.'s homicide victim, and the adrenaline rush of my entire night. I also thought about my still-smoldering divorce. I thought that maybe I had one too many Jamesons, and that maybe I needed to honor myself, and things more in my life rather than just "hop a flight with Katie Eighty."

We crossed the bridge spanning the deep dark Miami River. Looking off to the right, the Metrorail track neon lights reflected back up from the choppy, dark water below in the most amazing kaleidoscope of colors. At the curve by the James L Knight Center, I was right behind her at the traffic light. The light changed and she made the turn toward the north ramp onto I-95. I did too, except I veered at the last second and took the south ramp instead.

Chapter Five

I VEERED. I SWERVED. I bailed. I made an Irish exit. Unlike Katie Eighty, I may have never been to Malibu, but I just did my own duck and dive. Call it what you may, but with the events of my life especially in the past six months, I just didn't need the potential entanglements. I'd assume that Katie Eighty would think I was just an idiot, and made a wrong choice at the entrance ramp, but it was intentional. I just wasn't ready for another romp with anybody, least of which someone who knew where the exits were in the front, middle, and aft of the cabin. I said a silent internal toast to myself.

"Here's to always staying positive and testing negative."

I gunned the Z28 up the south ramp and continued south where I-95 merges into U.S.1. As I neared Mundy Street I looked over at the Advance Auto Parts.

No sign of any police crime scene. They must of all cleared it hours ago.

I continued south right through Coral Gables, passing Fire Station Two and the gas pumps. I went all the way to the western border of the city. To my right, past the elevated Metrorail tracks the University of Miami looked quiet and tucked in for the night. At Southwest 67th Avenue, I turned south. Many would say I was turning for home, but no place had felt like home in months. The nomadic disconnected aspects of my life post-divorce were like a lingering odor in an old house. Sometimes if the conditions were right, it was overpowering. Other times it was subtle, barely noticeable. The worst part of it was wondering if everyone else noticed the omnipresent smell.

Do they see the carnage? Do they see me struggling with the divorce? The constant doubt was a millstone.

The residential neighborhood of The Village of Pinecrest was quiet. The fact they called themselves a village spoke to the nature of their populace.

Pinecrest was granted city status only two years earlier from unincorporated Miami Dade County. Many of the officers in their newly formed police department were recent retirees from other agencies. I was hoping that like all experienced officers working the midnight shift in a quite city, they were ensconced in the deeply wooded empty lots and "reserving their energy," rather than being on the look-out for speeders like me.

The run south on Southwest 67th was quick and easy and once I crossed Old Cutler Road I could see the Florida Power and Light shuttered and mothballed overflow station up ahead. In the 1960s FPL bult this monstrosity of pipes, catwalks, smokestacks, and steam valves that rose easily ten stories above the abundant banyan and palm trees. Back then there wasn't much in the area. Now it was an industrial eyesore and rumored too expensive to demolish, so it sat unused like an Erector Set from a bygone era. It was always rumored that FPL would dismantle the plant and ship it to a seller in Venezuela, but that rumor never materialized. Sadly, it sat on about sixty-five acres of prime Biscayne Bay real estate. I cruised right past the eastern border of The Westminster Christian School, known for being the alma mater of baseball icon Alex Rodriguez. It is also known for being built on the former location of the long gone but notorious Black Cesar Forage restaurant where many a 1950s era Miami Dade politician conducted backwater deals, corrupt land options, and received payoffs. They were rumored to have clandestine meetings and most probably consummated some of those lunches with young women they always introduced as their "nieces." In its time the restaurant and the open fields and trails leading to tucked away barns were the appeal of its remote location. Now suburban sprawl had caught up to the area—including my current place of residence at Paradise Point.

Turning east onto Coral Reef Drive is a South Florida horticulturist's dream. The narrow lane is framed on both sides with soft pink, luscious fuchsia, fiery orange, scarlet bougainvillea, fragrant frangipani, as well as billowing sea grape and mangrove trees. The official title of the gated community is Royal Harbour Yacht Club, but everyone knows it as Paradise Point. The guard at the gate was familiar with my odd comings and goings. He barely looked up as I used the remote attached on the passenger visor to open the gate.

Midway down the stretch of road I pulled into my temporary dwelling: 6211 Paradise Point Drive. The community is essentially high-end row houses, each adjacent to the next one by a shared external wall. Each residence has surprising depth and each unit is, at minimum, two stories high. Most, including my unit, have a third level used as an outdoor deck. From the outdoor decks of these houses manatees and dolphins can be often seen swimming in the narrow channel that leads directly out to Biscayne Bay. My unit is on the southside of the lane. The view is an unobstructed spectacular vista of trees, mangroves, and Biscayne Bay looking south towards Boca Chita Key, Elliott Key, Chicken Key and the rest of Biscayne National Park.

I parked in the courtyard driveway. I never park in the garage—it slows me down. The garage was under the entrance staircase, and had a large oval kelly green wooden door. My headlights illuminated the thick, climbing fig that covered nearly the entire arched exterior staircase. The terra cotta tiled stairs were still wet from the earlier rains.

My unit is furnished very tastefully. Large, comfortable couches and polished wood built-in shelves. There are some pre-Colombian art pieces. A few tastefully-sized, imitation Botero pieces. Paintings from Sebastian Spreng, Alberto Pancorbo, and Connie Lloveras hung on the walls. Even an imitation Wilfredo Lamb lithograph was in the condo. I only know this because the doctor left a binder describing the artwork and the artists. The interior was very spacious with large white ceramic tiles and white walls. In the daytime the large windows and terraces let in natural light very nicely.

I trudged into the condominium, plodded upstairs to the master bedroom and fell right onto the plush mattress and comfortable cushions. I was asleep within minutes of hitting the bed.

The next morning was one of those mornings of accelerating slow motion. I was slow to get started but as the minutes wore on, I got more in step with the day. I put ESPN College Game Day on the fifty-five-inch TV. The heavily favored Miami Hurricanes were playing Rutgers at noon in New Jersey. I didn't think any networks would be carrying the football game unless the local CBS affiliate picked the game up. I gathered some mail and was getting ready to go up to the top deck and see if I needed to push any of last night's rain deluge off the deck when my cell phone rang.

"Taylor."

"Cade, it's C.C. I have a couple of questions."

"Okay."

"Hey, I was wondering if you could tell me, who is Llyod Trentlocke?" she asked me.

I briefly closed my eyes and knew that whatever she was asking about was not something I needed right now.

"He's Miami Dade Homicide. Why?"

"Well, the young lady you singled out in the crowd, it seems her information was good. Our victim last night is Reginald LaMarr, AKA Reggie."

"Okay, but what does that have to do with Trentlocke?"

"Reggie LaMarr was staying on Franklin, right off of Plaza, but he doesn't work for the county. His uncle does. LaMarr is actually from Baltimore. He's been staying with his uncle and aunt the past six months," she said.

"Okay, but again, what does this have to do with Trentlocke?" I repeated.

"We want to search his house—or more specifically, his room—but the uncle won't let us in without a warrant. We can get a warrant but it's a pain in the ass and will take hours, especially on a Saturday. The uncle says he'll only let us in if either you or this Trentlocke guy is with us. He says he only trusts you two. "

"Me? Who's his uncle?"

"A guy named Godfrey Pinder."

"Pinder? Slim older black guy who smokes?" I asked her.

"Obviously, you know him. If I pick you up will you come with us so we can bypass the warrant and get going on this case?"

"You do realize it is Saturday, right? I mean, seriously?"

"Yes. I know it's Saturday. It's Saturday for me, too. I hate imposing on you but seeing as it *is* the weekend it makes my securing a warrant even more difficult. I mean, I'm getting really pressed here. Can you please say yes? Please."

I looked around the condominium and the peacefulness of it all. It was indeed Saturday. A rare day off, not just for me, but for few in law enforcement. Getting weekends off was a perk in the detective world. I mulled it over briefly and finally relented.

"Okay, but last time I rode with you some PSA who smelled of way too much Paco Rabbane cologne regaled me with his great stories of being a PSA. Thanks but no thanks, I'll meet you there. What's the address and how soon will you be there?"

"I'm here now. I'm sitting outside in my car. The address is 3589 Franklin Avenue."

"You may have to wait a few. I will be there in about a half hour. I'm pretty far south." I said as I hung up the cell phone.

Godfrey Pinder. I'd met Godfrey Pinder last winter when he was interviewed by Llyod Trentlocke, and later by me about his job as a facilities manager with Miami Dade County. A former informant of mine was found dead at Matheson Hammock Park and Trentlocke was assigned the investigation. Part of Pinder's job responsibilities were checking the Matheson Hammock Marina at night. Pinder was interviewed about what he might've seen or heard the night the informant was killed. I was actually surprised he even remembered me as we only spoke briefly. Pinder told me he lived on Franklin Avenue. I was a little miffed with myself because I should've put two and two together when the young girl said she saw a county truck on Franklin Avenue. I should've made that connection last night on the scene.

The drive from Paradise Point to Franklin Avenue was quicker than normal because it was the weekend. My biggest impediment was passing the thirty or so road cyclists on Old Cutler Road who, although they all come in various body shapes and sizes, seem to wear the same type of tight lycra biking gear, thus making them look like a poor man's Tour de France. I cut over from Lejeune Road and turned east onto Loquat Drive and cruised the leafy tree-shaded street until it forked at Kumquat Street. From Kumquat it was a quick jot to Franklin Avenue. C.C. was indeed sitting in her white Dodge Intrepid in front of the house. When she saw me pulling up she gathered her binder and met me in the street. By way of greeting I handed her the now crinkly, dry, weathered parking ticket from last night.

"I'm sure you let your people know, but obviously someone didn't get the message," I said as I thrust the ticket in her hand.

She looked down at the ticket and slipped it into the back of her binder.

"Being cheap is not a very endearing quality," she muttered.

"So, this is the house, huh? Is Pinder here?" I asked her.

"If he isn't then a different skinny black man keeps coming out to the porch looking at me and smoking cigarettes," she said.

The house is different than some of the other houses on the street. It is what is termed as a classic Coconut Grove Bahamian shotgun shack. It is very narrow. The term "shotgun shack" is because when they were built in the 1920s the builder had said, "You could shoot a shotgun through the front door and have the pellets go right out the back door." The house has a gabled end over the roof and a raised, but narrow front porch with four support pillars emerging from the rail. There is an air vent just under the gabled end that is intended to vent out the excruciating hot summer air that could accumulate in these wooden structures. The front ship lap siding is painted in a soft baby blue, serene against the singular front window framed in ivory white. The front door is painted the same ivory white. The house is neatly maintained and protected by a four-foot-high chain link fence running the length of the front of the property. The fence continued uninterrupted west to the house next door and all the way around the second house. Upon closer inspection I saw that both houses are connected in the back by a common wall behind a small wooden gate. The house next door is identical in the Bahamian style but in a muted peach. The front door of the peach house has no numerical address.

It seemed that the Pinder household was actually two houses conjoined in either an illegal addition, or in an addition that had squeaked past the Miami building inspectors.

"Which door has he been using to come out of when he smokes?" I asked her.

"He comes out the other door at the peach house, he barely opens it. Probably thinks I don't see him looking at me," she said.

"Go knock on the white door of the blue house," I said.

C.C. opened the partially rusty gate to the chain link fence. I followed closely behind her. She ascended the few stairs to the white door at the blue house and I cut over to the door by the peach-colored house. She rapped on the door repeatedly and once again made her verbal police announcement.

"This is Detective Clay from the Miami Police Department."

I stood just off to the side of the door at the peach house. After a few knocks and announcements from C.C., the door which was inches from me opened ever so slightly. Then opened a little more. I could see the back of the head of a black male peering at C.C. from the door through the miniscule opening. He never saw me behind him when I turned my hand inward and locked three fingers into the opening, and then pulled back on the door to reveal Godfrey Pinder.

"Mr. Pinder, it's me Cade Taylor from the Coral Gables Police Department. I understand you wanted to see me."

Startled, Pinder wheeled around, wide-eyed. A Salem Light cigarette hung precariously on his bottom lip, tethered only by a saliva droplet. He squinted at me. I could see that he recognized my name but was trying to place my face.

"The county still got you zimming and zamming all over the place?" I asked him.

When I'd interviewed him months ago he said that the county had him "zimming and zamming all over the place." By using his exact phrasing, I was hoping to jar his memory. He was still processing my surprise appearance on his porch, but recognition ignited in his eyes. A very tight smile formed across his face. He still had that face that was weathered and wrinkled. I remember thinking he was a man who'd seen a lot in his days when I first spoke to him last winter.

"You're him, aren't you ? It's you. You're Cade," he said.

C.C. saw me talking through the door and crept towards the porch we were on as Pinder reacquainted himself with me. I spoke very softly to him, refreshing his memory of the night we met.

"You know, it wasn't like I didn't want to cooperate with the police. It's just they were here in the late evening, asking all these questions about Reggie. We were just so stunned that he was *dead*. I mean, how's that happen? We just didn't want all these people in our house. It wasn't like Reggie died here in the house. Me and P.G., we just needed some time to process it all."

"P.G.?" I asked, one eye on C.C. approaching the porch.

"Patricia Gayle. My wife. We call her P.G.," he said, now with his eyes fully on C.C. as she ascended the first step. Pinder watched her every slow step, with each rise and fall of her legs.

"Well, Mr. Pinder, the woman you see here with me is also called by her initials. This is C.C. She's Cynthia Clay, and she's a detective with the Miami Police Department. C.C. is handling Reggie's case.

She said you'd feel better if I was here, too. So, here I am, to make you feel better. I also want to assure you that C.C. has your best interest, and most importantly, Reggie's best interest in mind."

Godfrey Pinder's eyes slid back and forth with dubious suspicion between C.C. and me. Then he hung his head. He let out an exhale that still had the lingering odor of his menthol cigarette habit. He glanced back into the house, then slowly retreated inside, extending his arm to keep the door open.

I took that as an invitation and stepped past him, followed by C.C. Pinder closed the door behind us.

The Bahamian shutters shielded the morning South Florida sun, leaving the house a bit dark, but cool inside. The interior was neatly appointed, decorated with a variety of artwork. Some of it I recognized. There was a piece from one of his Coconut Grove neighbors, Neith Nevelson.

"I see you have a few paintings from Neith," I said by way of creating even more familiarity.

Pinder looked at a framed rendition of a horse, drawn with wide swipes of brown paint on a finger-smudged canvas.

"She lives on Brooker near Frow. She keeps hanging them on our fence at night. Once in a while we wake up and there's a new canvas, draped over the fence. P.G. and her used to talk years ago, so she keeps dropping her art by. A lot of it we donated to the Frost Museum at FIU, but we kept a few."

"Yes, I'm familiar with her, too. When I first started in the Gables, the Grove was my patrol zone," I said.

C.C. probably wasn't familiar with Neith Nevelson, but she also wasn't immune to this warm, fuzzy familiarity talk. She knew that it would be beneficial to further her investigation if we had a rapport with the Pinders. It was C.C. who spoke next.

"Mr. Pinder, you mentioned your wife? P.G.? Is she here now?"

"No, P.G. owns a salon, she's there now. She's trying to get her assistant manager to run it for a few days until we can get through this."

"Mr. Pinder, first of all both Detective Clay and I want to convey our condolences about Reggie. I paused. "Can you please tell us about him and your relationship to him?"

"Reggie was our nephew, from P.G.'s side of the family. He'd been living in Baltimore, running with a bad crowd. His mother, P.G.'s sister, was having *fits* with him. He'd been a good athlete, was doing good in school but the enticement of that street money and those street hustles got the better of him. So her sister asked if we'd host him here. She hoped we could try and help him get away from those thugs. Pretty ironic when you have to leave Baltimore and come to Miami to avoid a life of crime, ain't it?"

"So how long was he living here with you?" asked C.C.

"He came down around May of this year, so it had been about five months. Shortly after he arrived P.G.'s sister passed away unexpectedly from an aneurism and we just figured Reggie would have been ours. Now we just don't know anything. It all just doesn't make any sense."

"Mr. Pinder, I can understand the confusion and the shock of all of this. We're as confused as you are. That's why, with Cade's help, I wanted to talk to you today," said C.C.

Pinder had settled into a comfortable La-Z-Boy, and both C.C. and I took a seat on an adjacent sofa. I sat with my hands folded across my knees. I decided to let C.C. do most of the talking.

"Mr. Pinder, what can you tell us about Reggie that might help us find the person responsible for this?" she asked him.

Pinder rubbed his left hand across his stubbled chin and looked past the both of us. He set his eyes on a spot somewhere on the wall. He started speaking slowly, but intentionally all the while, not really looking at either of us.

"He wasn't the big criminal he thought he was. He wasn't the bad seed his mother portrayed him to be. He was kind. Thoughtful. He helped out a lot here in the house. His being here was actually a good thing. I saw at the county job board that the airport was moving away from airline baggage handlers. They were looking to go with contracted baggage handlers. After all the labor issues of Eastern and Pan Am, I guess the airlines thought that by contracting them folks they could save on costs and benefits. They could avoid the labor issues, too. So I suggested he try and get on with one of those outfits. I would've preferred to see him try and go to Miami Dade or FIU but ..."

C.C. was taking notes and asked for clarification. "I'm sorry, Mr. Pinder—did you say FAU?"

"No. FIU. Florida International University. But it could have been anywhere as far as I was concerned. So he applied and this outfit at the airport hired him. He'd been working with them about three months."

"As a baggage handler?" she asked.

"Yup. He was a baggage handler, loading and unloading airplanes. It didn't really matter which ones although mostly American and United. He called it the 'ramp.' It was always 'the ramp was hot today,' or ' they shut down the ramp for lightning today,' that sort of talk. He seemed to like the work. It helped him get in better shape, too. We were happy to see him working. Sometimes he took the train to work, sometimes he took the bus up Lejeune Road, other times he got a ride to work, but he *did* it. He sure as hell did it. He went and he never missed a shift."

"Did he ever mention any of his coworkers or bosses? Did he have any problems with any of them?" she asked.

"No, he never mentioned any problems or anybody."

"What was the name of the company he worked for?" she asked.

"Reliable Flight Services. They just called it RFS," he said.

"They?"

"Some of the guys he worked with were here a few times. They all just called it RFS."

"Mr. Pinder, I know this is a difficult time but I just asked if Reggie ever mentioned any of his coworkers or bosses—and you said no. But some of his coworkers were, in fact, here. Reggie *had* made contacts. Do you recall any of their names?"

A crease of agitation momentarily flashed across Pinder's forehead, but he remained calm and said that he didn't recall the names of any of his coworkers.

"Mr. Pinder, would you mind if Cade and I looked at his room here?" C.C. asked hopefully.

"First door past the table in the hallway," was all he said which we both took as verbal consent to search Reggie's room. C.C. and I both got up from the sofa. Mr. Pinder wasn't inclined to move from his chair. C.C. reached into her front pocket and retrieved light blue latex gloves. She donned a pair for herself and offered me a pair as well.

Gloves on, we quietly walked down the hall to the door just past the wobbly table in the hallway. Before going in, I inspected the door for any kick marks, or forced pry marks. Just because Pinder said they had a peaceful existence with Reggie doesn't mean it was exactly like that. The buffed wood of the door was smooth and the seal around the trimming led me to believe it was authentic and original from when the house was built.

I turned the knob and the door eased open.

The first thing I noticed was an unmade full-size bed. The sheets and coverings were in a tangled mess. There was a locker box at the foot of the bed. Across the room was an upright four drawer dresser. C.C. opened the bottom drawer first. It was full of blue jeans, but there was a green sweatshirt from Baltimore's Forest Gray High School in there, too. In gray script it said "Foresters." The third drawer from the bottom had a wide collection of boxer briefs in dark colors like navy, black, and gray and socks balled up like woolen softballs. The second drawer had a menagerie of t-shirts and basketball shorts. The top drawer was a dump drawer with some loose change, a bottle of Pierre Cardin cologne, chewing gum packets, two cheap gas station condoms, and a mix of odds and ends. C.C. took interest in a pocketknife, but upon opening and closing it a few times, she lost interest and placed it back into the drawer.

"Who's that?" I said, spotting a small, framed picture of an African American woman. I joined her at the junk drawer.

"Probably his mother," C.C. said.

I mentally catalogued the rest of the drawer's contents; a Ziploc baggie with about fifty screws in it. The heads of the screws were a very odd slot. His RFS identification and Miami International ramp access laminated cards were in there too, all attached to a Baltimore Ravens lanyard. I studied it intently. I had not seen nor knew what Reggie looked like until then. He'd signed his identification "Reginald LaMarr," with a big flourish of a signature. It was the signature of a young man with ambition in front of him and demons behind him. He was a handsome young man with a wide smile and big brown eyes. A young man with a forged future and an abandoned past. C.C. looked at the I.D.s as well and made a comment about the lanyard.

"Ravens fan huh? Harbaugh at quarterback, I don't think so. I'm sure he got ribbed wearing that out at the airport," C.C. said, looking at the lanyard.

"You know football?" I asked her.

"I had to. My uncle Billy was drafted by the Broncos but ended up playing for Washington. He was the first from my father's side of the family to go to college. He went to Mississippi but only lasted one year in the NFL. He was a cornerback, but rarely ever got in."

"Well, it's still an accomplishment," I said.

I dropped the lanyard and started in on his closet, where some jackets and RFS rain gear hung. Every inch of the bottom of the closet was littered with all types of shoes just thrown in. It probably took Reggie a minute or two each day to find matching shoes. I made a mental note that he might have worn certain pairs almost exclusively, because with as many shoes as he owned the young girl at the murder scene recognized him by his green Pumas. I checked all the pockets of the hanging jackets; nothing in any of them.

We turned our attention to the footlocker at the end of the bed.

I got on my knees and tried to get the locking mechanism to open, while C.C. looked under the bed.

"Anything?" I asked her.

"Nothing."

"I can't get the lock to open," I said when I felt a presence in the room. We both turned to see Godfrey Pinder standing in the doorway, looking down at us.

"That used to be mine. I had it in country. It's been all over. Hanoi, Kon Tum, Quang Ngai, on down to the Quàng Tri Province. P.G. thought it would be a good idea to let Reggie have it to keep his stuff in. I set the lock sideways right after boot camp to keep people from surprise inspecting my locker. You know, rat fucking my stuff. As I went up in rank I just kept it that way."

Pinder stepped into the room and both C.C. and I got up off the floor so he could bend down, and with a quick twist of his wrist, he had the top of the locker lifted open. It was then that I saw the stencil on the top.

"Captain Godfrey Pinder."

C.C. and I looked inside. There were some quilts and rolled towels inside. Other than that, there wasn't much inside that appeared to be helpful in C.C.'s investigation. To me, the towels didn't seem to have any heirloom or vintage value. In fact, one had a Bed, Bath and Beyond tag still on it.

I thought it seemed odd to keep your bath towels in a closed locker, especially if you needed them for daily showers.

I got back down on my knees and felt the towels and could feel heavy objects in them.

I started pulling the towels out and handed them up to C.C., who laid them on the bed and started unrolling them.

The first two towels had two 35mm cameras in them. A Pentax and an Olympus. The next towel was tightly wrapped around a canvas U.S. Mail pouch.

Inside the mail pouch was cash.

From a cursory look I'd have guessed it to be about $35,000. The money was wrapped in rubber bands and was in various denominations. We both looked at Pinder and he just stared at the cash then slowly moved his hand over his mouth. He was as perplexed as we were.

Chapter Six

THE SIGHT OF the cash made Pinder's eyes water a little. It was as though he'd believed that Reggie had redirected his life in the palm trees of South Florida—but his brickyard Baltimore ways were still here.

"Did you know anything about this?" C.C. asked Pinder, as a qualifier. He shook his head no, but we both already knew that. To her credit, C.C. was very gentle as she explained the upcoming process. Because the cash was found in a U.S. Mail pouch she was unable to determine if a federal crime had occurred or if the pouch was just a receptacle to hold the cash. She explained that she'd be calling crime scene technicians. The technicians would arrive and they would photograph the cameras, the mail pouch, the cash, quilts, towels, and locker itself. She explained a property receipt would be left with Godfrey Pinder, listing all of the items that the crime scene would be taking with them. The cash would be noted as uncounted, but once the cash was counted a PSA would come by later with an accurate property receipt. C.C. said the Miami Police Department would not be seizing anything at this time, just impounding the contents of the footlocker, including the locker itself. As the investigation of Reggie's death continued, at some point Mr. Pinder could come to Miami Police headquarters and retrieve some of the items, most likely the locker, towels, and quilts. But not the cameras and cash. Maybe they'd be released at a later date, she said.

Godfrey Pinder. Captain Godfrey Pinder, the man who had told me six months ago he'd "seen a lot," was at a loss for words. He was at a crossroads with himself. He truly felt that he and P.G. had made a difference in Reggie's life. Now with Reggie dead and the discovery of this cash, he didn't have to say anything. The self-doubt was evident. I could see the torment in his eyes.

"Mr. Pinder, there's a lot of conjecture that can come from this. C.C. is good at what she does. Before we make any assumptions, let's all get behind her investigation and see what unanswered questions she can find the answers to," I said.

C.C. asked us all to step out of the room, and she closed the door behind us. She used her cell phone and requested crime scene technicians to come to the Pinder home as we walked down the narrow hallway.

Pinder sat down again in the same chair in the living room. I heard a car pull up outside and looked at C.C., knowing that the Miami Crime Scene technicians could not have gotten here that fast. It was Pinder who clarified it for us with a few softly spoken words.

"P.G. is here."

We hrard a car door close and heel strikes on the front steps. The front door opened and in stepped an attractive, thin African American woman. She looked at both C.C. and I then quickly over to Godfrey. I stood up and introduced myself and C.C. She didn't say anything, only watched us with a combined look of surprise, dismay, regret, and futility.

"Mrs. Pinder," C.C. said, "I am so sorry for your loss and for everything that you must be feeling."

"Feeling? How do you know what I'm feeling? What do you know about knocks on your door late at night except when you're the one doing the knocking? What do you know about a young life wasted senselessly? Tell me. Why don't you stand here in my house and tell me what you know about all of that?"

C.C took a sharp inhale and held it, eyes on mine. What could either of us say that would assuage her feelings? P.G. Pinder was hurt. She was angry. She was grieving.

I decided that rather than keep on the same vein of thought, it would be best to just inform her of what we'd discovered in the footlocker. I didn't want to make her feel we were leading her through a series of questions blindly.

"Mrs. Pinder. Miami Crime Scene technicians will be arriving here soon. We found some items in Reggie's bedroom that merit further investigation and I don't want you to be surprised when they get here," I said.

"'*Found some items*?' What kind of *items*? Drugs? What?" she retorted, firing one question after another, not allowing me a moment to answer any of them.

"They found cash and cameras in my footlocker," Godfrey said as he rose from his chair.

"That's right. It's my footlocker. We wanted Reggie to have something for his stuff but in the end it's my locker, so I'm prepared to take whatever consequences come of this."

Godfrey Pinder was laying groundwork to take the hit for Reggie if C.C.'s investigation should unearth something unforeseen. Like a true soldier, he was trying to not dishonor the dead. Both C.C. and I could see what he was doing and I think she took the same mental note of it being an admirable try—but we both felt that those items in the locker were Reggie's.

We explained further to P.G. what was discovered in the locker and how it was discovered. P.G. asked a few questions about the cash. Most of them we didn't have any answers for. Eventually Mrs. Pinder calmed down a little and wasn't as acerbic as she was when she first walked into the house, but her resolve was still hard.

"I think I want you both out of my house and I want an attorney," she said.

"We have already been provided consent to be here. Our leaving won't change anything other than that we'll have to ask everyone to leave until I secure a warrant and then come back. Or, if we continue on the path we're on, we should all be done here in less than an hour. As for an attorney, that's up to you, Mrs. Pinder. I'm not going to ask you any questions about what was discovered here . I would like to ask you about Reggie and maybe some of his friends or coworkers, but aside from that I have nothing else to ask about, and there isn't anything else for me to look at. So, if you want an attorney, that is your prerogative. I think it would be money unwisely spent. By the time an attorney gets here we'll have secured a warrant anyway. Once again—I am truly sorry for your loss. But I can't help you if you don't help me to help you. Do you still want an attorney?" said C.C.

With a great sigh, "I think I'd rather have a steaming cup of hot tea," P.G. said.

"I don't think the Miami Police Department can provide that for you, but I would gladly follow you into the kitchen and have some with you," said C.C.

A measurable détente was established and both women went into the kitchen. I followed a few minutes later and stood in the doorway as they talked.

"Is there something you can tell me about Reggie that would help me to understand him better?" asked C.C.

"Reggie was a stalled rocket. An aborted take-off. He just needed to *launch*, and to have him launch the conditions just had to be right. We were *making* those conditions right. We were all systems go here."

Her aerospace analogies were odd coming from a salon owner, but it was clearly understood that the Pinders had been doing all they could for Reggie. I stayed in the doorway listening to them talk when C.C. asked a question that made me zero in even more.

"Mrs. Pinder, what can you tell me about any of Reggie's visitors he may have had here?"

"Reggie didn't have many visitors here. He didn't know a lot of people. There was one young buck that he worked with that came by a few times. His name was Cooper something. Reggie just called him Jabo. I guess Jabo was some sort of nickname. He was only here once or twice. He was polite and mannerly when he was around me and the Captain."

I smiled at her endearing term for her husband. "Well, this Jabo fellow," P.G. continued, "he must not have known these two houses are connected because he only came over on this side. One night I overheard him on his cell phone as he sat on the other porch. He was really worried about some guy named Zeus. It was all about some guy named Zeus being pissed. He was trying to explain to whoever he was talking to that they had, as he said, 'fucked up,' and Zeus was pissed, and they needed to correct whatever it was or Zeus was going to 'fuck them up.'"

"Mrs. Pinder, how long ago was that?"

"I don't know. Maybe about two weeks ago."

"You're sure he said *they* fucked up not *he* fucked up?" I asked her.

"Oh yeah, it was plural," she affirmed.

I stayed until the Miami Crime Scene technicians and a uniformed officer arrived. Two technicians went into the bedroom to process and photograph the room. When they finished, C.C. intended to put the cash in the uniformed officer's car trunk for transport back to the Miami Police Department.

I caught the officer on his own and asked the officer if he knew how Alvaro Dominguez was doing. He said that Dominguez was at Jackson Memorial Hospital with a concussion, bruised knee, and a bruised sternum. We talked at length about how fortunate Dominguez was and how he was lucky to be alive.

The technicians were done in about thirty minutes. The U.S Mail pouch and the cash were put into a big clear plastic bag and sealed tightly with red evidence tape. C.C. signed the tape, followed by the Miami officer. We both said our goodbyes to the Pinders and C.C. vowed she would be in touch.

I hung back just a little.

The locker and its contents were put in the backseat of the Miami police car. The sealed bag of cash was put into the trunk. The crime scene technicians left. C.C. stayed with the Miami police car to insure chain of custody integrity. I spoke with Mr. Pinder at the front door before leaving.

"Remember what I said earlier: There can be lots of explanations. Let's not jump to some crazy conclusion about Reggie until we can get more answers," I said.

"You said she was really good at what she does," he said, nodding towards C.C.

"Yes, she is," I said.

"You know I spent a lot of time in country, Cade. I have seen a lot. I told you that once before. I've also seen newness. I've seen shiny new. I have seen sparkle-new, so new it doesn't know what to do unless someone tells it what to do." His eyes bore into me deeper. "You aren't Miami, but as a favor to me, P.G., and especially Reggie... stay with this. Will you?" he implored of me.

"Mr. Pinder. I am not homicide. It's not my case..."

He grabbed me by the arm and leaned up near my ear. "For us. Do it for us. Jump the curb on this one for us. Please."

I looked in his eyes which were welling with tears and just nodded my head affirmatively. I moved slowly away from him and down the steps to C.C. and the Miami officer. I heard the Pinders' front door close. I didn't look back.

"What was that all about?" C.C. asked.

"He wanted to see if I could stop Neith from leaving paintings on his fence," I said.

The street was quiet. C.C. motioned to the Miami officer that she wanted a little privacy. She and I walked to the back of the patrol car as the officer sat behind the wheel and closed the car door. He would no doubt be enjoying the air-conditioned comfort of the car.

"So. What do you think?" she asked me.

"I don't know. What do you know so far about this Reggie kid that you didn't find out from his uncle and aunt?"

"There isn't too much. He didn't grow up here so not many know him or care about him. The young girl who recognized him by his shoes said he was a nice guy. She must've seen him in his uncle's truck; that's how we made the county connection."

"Where was he shot?" I asked her.

"He was shot three times. Twice in the chest and once in the head," she said.

"Two in the chest and one in the head?" I repeated.

"Yeah, the shell casings look as though the first two were the chest shots, the third was the head shot. The third shell casing was found thirty-two inches north of the first two. The first two shell casings were pretty close to each other."

"North? So the shooter was moving toward U.S.1 when he shot Reggie."

"That's what we're thinking too. We're thinking the shooter encounters Reggie on the perimeter area of the Advance Auto Parts Store. He pumps the first two into him, Reggie staggers back, which in this case, was north. The shooter advances and puts the third one in in his forehead."

"Do you think Reggie was down and he was finished off or was he still upright when the third round went in?" I asked.

"The third shell casing has a slight scratch on the rim like it had hit the asphalt from a height then bounced briefly and landed again. Plus, the entry wound and blood splatter on Reggie's forehead are strong indicators he was still standing. There's blood splatter on the back of his right hand. Reggie was more than likely clutching his chest when the third round went right through his cerebral cortex," she said.

"Cerebral cortex. Why not just say it went through his head or his brain?" I asked.

"Because 'the head' can mean lots of things. There's nothing worse than being on the stand in a murder trial and have a medical doctor lecture you about the functionality and divergent aspects of the head. Ask me how I know. Likewise, the brain can also mean lots of things. Cerebral cortex is where the third round lodged itself."

I started sensing that C.C., although new to homicide, was more skilled than many gave her credit for—including Godfrey Pinder. She glanced over her binder at the notes she was able to take inside the Pinder home.

"I'll be checking with this RFS company and see if they have this Cooper guy on their payroll. I'll also be checking our databases for anybody in our system named Zeus," she said.

"I don't know how much money was there in that bag, but based on Reggie only having five months of employment, I'd suggest checking with your street narcotics and S.I.S. units for dopers who go by the name Zeus. I'll check our side of the drug world and send word out to Miami Dade's TNT units. If that's okay with you," I said.

She readily agreed to that idea of checking with the Special Investigation Section (S.I.S) inside Miami Police Department and the Miami Dade's Tactical Narcotic Team (TNT). She turned the conversation back to informing me about the crime scene of Reggie LaMarr's death.

"Cade, we're dealing with a really contaminated scene. The rain washed a lot of evidence away. We have no thread ware. We have no shoe impressions. There are no fingerprints on the shell casings. The cameras at Advance Auto Parts were turned toward the front door instead of the parking lot. The Advance manager took it upon himself to do that because he thought his day stock room worker was stealing Purolator filters. You hear what I'm saying? Valuable surveillance footage lost because of a six-dollar oil filter! This frustrates me to no end."

"What kind of rounds was he shot with?"

"Oh yeah, that's another kicker. You ready for this? It was a Walther P-88. They call it the P-88 because Walther produced the first one in 1988. We have two of our light duty guys assisting making calls. There isn't a gun shop in Miami that sells the Walther P-88. We checked them all. Tamiami, Garcia, not even Miami Police Supply sell this gun. We even checked with Kiffney's in Key Largo. A wire request has gone out to ATF for registered owners in Miami Dade

County; so far, nothing. Walther stopped production of the P-88 two years ago and went to a compact version because it was cheaper. The P-88's got a fifteen-round capacity, nine by nineteen millimeter Parabellum round known affectionately as 'the world's most popular and widely used military handgun and submachine gun cartridge.' So I got a common kid, killed on a common street, with common ammunition, fired from an *un*common gun."

There was a pause while I just looked at her.

"I'm sorry if I seem a little sharp about this. I grew up in Carol City. My neighborhood was very similar to what we're standing in right now. You know, where the people put their license plates in the back windows of their cars to keep the plates from being stolen right off their bumpers. Then they get pulled over and cited for having their plate improperly displayed. You know, the same neighborhood the ice cream man doesn't drive through because he got robbed at gunpoint for $13.58 one summer. One of those *UPS, do not leave a package on the porch* neighborhoods. I remember being a little girl and thinking the streets were 'diamondized' because of all the pulverized broken glass smashed into the asphalt. Kids like Reggie were as common to us as fireflies are on a North Carolina summer night. They lived short lives and died just as quickly. That's why I needed to make a change. I needed to get out of those streets myself, and find a way to get those streets out of me. That's why I became a cop. My mother is white and my dad is black. By the time I was four she was gone, and I was just like Reggie. I was raised by aunts and uncles because my dad just couldn't stop drinking to take the time to take care of his little Cynthia. So when I see a case like this, I feel this jagged ripping pain in my side because I know his death won't even make it in the *Miami Herald*. Yeah, the newspaper of record won't even record the death of this young man. What will be his claim to fame? Green fucking Pumas."

The frustration rose in her voice, and she'd become animated, waving her arms as she spoke. I saw the Miami officer watching us though his driver's side mirror. On his face he wore a concerned expression about C.C.'s gestures.

Standing out in the morning light I could see her features even more clearly now. She was an attractive mulatto woman who had faced strife and turmoil growing up. Now she was working hard in a system that very rarely rewards the effort. Not to mention that she was also trying to make it in a male-dominated workplace. She was fighting for credibility and for her cases. She was pushing boulders uphill.

"What about other cameras? Where there any other cameras?" I asked her.

The ire in her voice continued on an upward steady rise.

"Cameras? Oh, like the one at the gas station on the corner of Douglas and U.S.1 that was positioned under the vinyl awning? Giving us a rain-splattered shot of the shooter from the knees down? Or what about the cameras at the Douglas Metrorail that were partially obscured by condensation because some nitwit decided to clean them once with Fabulouso, leaving a purplish-tinted smear. I swear I'm going to pull my hair out over all these missed opportunities. This young man was shot three times. One. Two. Three times!" She mimicked the pulling of a trigger three times with her hand as she finished her comment.

"Was Dominguez able to provide any other information? All he told me was the shooter was wearing a gray hoodie."

"Dominguez. I cannot fault him. He's a terrible cop and a scourge to all of us, but in this case he did what he was supposed to do. He responded on a three and the siren probably alerted the shooter. The shooter waited for him—at least from what we can tell in the purple haze of the Metrorail surveillance camera closest to the sidewalk on the west side. As Dominguez came in and started getting closer, the shooter had been ducking behind a *Miami New Times* box and leaned out. Hear what I'm saying? He leaned *out*! He was still using the box as concealment and partial cover and cranked a rapid succession seven rounds, all center windshield, on Dominguez's *moving* car. The fact that Dominguez even saw a gray hoodie is remarkable because to see it through that lavender lens, it's pretty crazy."

"You realize C.C., from what you're telling me, there's a bigger problem here?"

"Bigger problem here, how?" she said.

"Let's look at what you know and have told me. Reggie got killed just a few feet off of U.S.1. That's a half mile from here. Easily a ten minute or more walk. Reggie was summoned there. He doesn't own a car. You heard what Pinder said about him taking buses, trains and rides to work. Why would Reggie be at Advance Auto Parts in the rain? He *walked* there in the rain. No, this was a prearranged meeting. Now let's look at your shooter. He was prepared for the weather—he had a hoodie on. Or at least he was prepared for the shooting, knowing the hoodie tight around his head would obscure him from witnesses," I said.

C.C. locked her eyes on mine, drinking in what I had to say.

"So, Reggie meets up with the shooter. The shooter comes up behind him. Reggie had to walk south to north to get to the Advance Auto Parts parking lot, but he died facing *south*. The shooter came up behind him. The shooter was waiting for him. He encounters, or calls out to Reggie, and Reggie turned to face south again. The shooter either didn't think about cameras or wasn't concerned with the cameras. The hoodie and the rain were working in his favor. How many people plan an execution and don't have a means of escape? Where's the getaway car? Where's the shooter's car?"

"The Douglas Metrorail station!" C.C. said in a breathless gasp.

"Maybe. Actually, probably. The shooter, after shooting Reggie, doesn't want to chance being seen by the congested stop-and-go traffic on U.S.1. So he decides to not weave through the stalled cars in the rain and take a direct path to the Metrorail. No, he takes the long route to the Douglas Metrorail. This guy's got confidence. Rather than press the chance that someone might remember him, he decides to just casually walk southbound on U.S.1 past the gas station. He took the pedestrian flyover to the Metrorail station. I say he walked casually because it took Dominguez, even with lights and a siren, a while to get to the parking lot. The shooter was in no hurry.

He didn't want to call any attention to himself. Cool as a cucumber. So, he's heading to the parking lot and he hears the siren. He weighs his chances of getting to his car unseen, decides it's too risky, and he takes a defensive position to ambush Dominguez. You said he leaned out from behind the newspaper box? He's got confidence in aiming and shooting one-handed."

C.C. looked off to the side and nodded her head in agreement.

"So, let's look at Dominguez. He comes screaming into the parking lot and ends up taking seven rounds in a perfect half-moon across his windshield. He slams the brakes, throws the car in reverse to get away from the incoming bullets, and ends up crashing into the light pole. So *why didn't the shooter finish him off?*"

"I see everything you're saying, Cade, but aside from the obvious this is an even bigger problem…because of how?"

"The shooter is a pro. Reggie was a *hit*. He was shot Mozambique: two in the chest and one in the forehead. To professionals it's called the 'Mozambique Drill.' Two quick shots in the chest and a very quick shot to the head. You said Reggie had blood splatter on the back of his right hand. He was probably just like you said, clutching his chest. It was very fast. You said the third round was found north of the other two rounds. The shooter walked him. Walked him right up. The first two shots were done on the move, and so was the third. The shooter never even stopped to look back, just walked him right there in the rain."

"Well, if he's such a pro why didn't he hit Dominguez with any of those seven shots?" she asked.

"Because he *is* a pro. He didn't *want* to kill Dominguez. He just wanted to back him off. Those shots were intended to penetrate the car, but not hit the driver. Alvaro Dominguez just got in his way. You said the P-88 has fifteen rounds. Three for Reggie and seven for Dominguez. He had five rounds left, at least in that magazine. He knew that. He was still ready to go. He just didn't want to kill Dominguez. The bigger problem is this: This shooter is well-trained and knows what he's doing. He's either ex-military or he's a cop."

Chapter Seven

She says, "I understand
I'm used to being alone
And holding my own hand
I'm stronger than you know."

~ Runaway Trains by Tom Petty

THE REALIZATION THAT a highly trained professional killer was walking the streets of Miami washed over both of us at about the same time. This was not something either of us wanted to contemplate.

My involvement with aiding Dominguez could have put me as the direct recipient of those final five bullets in that P-88 magazine.

At least it isn't my case, I thought.

But it surely fell heavily upon C.C.'s shoulders. She momentarily seemed a little overwhelmed. She looked down at the hot asphalt of the street and tried to pull her hair back behind her ear. This was not going to be easy for her. It wouldn't be easy for any seasoned homicide investigator, for that matter. Her workload concerning this case just exponentially grew.

She had to follow the Miami officer back to the Miami Police

Department where she'd have to count the money and then secure it in their property evidence room. There were countless crimes scene photographs, charts, and reports to go through. She'd need to make contact with someone at the RFS and find out what she could about Reggie, that Cooper guy, and Zeus. A trained assassin using an obscure gun that fires every day, usable ammunition would not be easy to trace. Ballistic tests on the shell casings would be needed to send to the Alcohol, Tobacco, and Firearms national data clearing house in Washington D.C. She would probably have to interview Dominguez again. The necessary steps and retracing of steps was just beginning for her.

"You know, if the shooter's car was in the Douglas Metrorail parking lot you may want to look over all the crime scene photographs taken of Dominguez's car, see what vehicles are in the background," I said.

"Already thought of that. On our way to the station I'm going to have him go over there with me first," she said, tilting her head at the uniformed Miami police car. "I'll also check the tow logs and see if any cars were towed from there in the last twenty-four hours."

I was impressed with her thinking and told her so. I also reiterated that if she needed anything she could call me. She thanked me. With a sigh and quick shake of her head, she got in her Dodge Intrepid through the car window she twirled her finger in a *follow me* gesture to the Miami officer. They both went into the roundabout at the corner of Franklin Avenue and Plaza Street and then were northbound on Plaza out of my sight.

I looked at my watch. It was 11:23 am on a Saturday. I still hadn't heard a word from Ritchie Tavino. He was probably at Home Depot, loading up that Ford F150 XLT Extra Cab 4X4 with mulch and planting soil.

Up the street east, the assembly of cars, trash cans, and houses seemed to carry on for blocks and blocks. Even though it was October, I spied a slight shimmering of a wavering, watery mirage as the heat rose up off the asphalt.

I needed to get somewhere to collect my thoughts and await a call if it ever came in from Tavino. If the call didn't come in from Tavino, well, that was just fine by me too. I got into my sweltering car and drove east on Franklin Avenue. Midway through the roundabout, I cut south on Royal to avoid all the constant construction at the end of Franklin. I was quickly at the intersection of Royal and Main Highway, and fortunately traffic was light. The Banyan trees that make Main Highway such a pleasurable canopied road also have such massive trunks that it's hard to see oncoming traffic. Soon I was cruising into the business district of the Grove in the light Saturday traffic. I drove past the Barnacle Estate—now a historic national park—although you'd never know it was even there; the tree line and walls shielding it from the road all but hide it completely. At the three-point intersection where Grand Avenue, Main Highway and McFarland converge, I turned south on McFarland. I thought of stopping at Cozzoli's for a slice of pizza. Although the outdoor tables had umbrellas, it just seemed too hot to eat outside under partial shade. Aside from that, the pedestrian traffic weaving around the haphazard tables out on the sidewalk didn't appeal to me either.

I did want to eat outside, but I wanted total shade. I wanted to be out of the spotlight and take the heat off myself for one blessed minute. Just a composure moment would be nice for once in the last 24 hours.

McFarland bends east and in doing so turns into South Bayshore Drive. That bend in the road is like a magic arching curve into tropical beauty. The left side of the road has high rise condominiums and hotels, each one an architectural masterpiece. They're festooned with royal majestic palm trees, fountains, landscaped facades, and flowering bougainvillea. Some of the buildings are round, square, some are clustered in identical towers with each offering vibrantly magnificent views of Biscayne Bay. The scenic drive is very calming, and I needed it. The beauty of Peacock Park on my right and the occasional glimpses of the shimmering Biscayne Bay blue water are absolute tonics for whatever may ail you. Leaving the open green space of Peacock Park behind me, I turned even further south on

Pan American Drive right past the Regatta Park and Miami City Hall signs. At the end of the road is Miami City Hall. City Hall is directly adjacent to Biscayne Bay. How appropriate.

Miami City Hall is located in the former Pan American Airlines Terminal Building on Dinner Key, which was designed by the then-renown architectural firm Delano & Aldrich. Pan American President and CEO Juan Tripp was said to have overseen the construction himself. It was constructed for Pan American Airlines in 1934 and repurposed as Miami City Hall in 1954. The building itself is still stunning. It fronts Biscayne Bay and has a large, landscaped circle in the front that visitors and city officials park around like spokes coming off a wheel. When it was the Pan American Airlines Terminal Building, flying passengers were met curbside by stewards in full uniform and white gloves. The fleet of aircraft were called clipper ships or flying boats because they took off and landed on water. A total of twenty-eight clipper ships flew out of this terminal from 1931 to 1946. During that time, Pan American operated clipper services to Latin America right from this International Airport. Now known simply as Dinner Key, the City of Miami retained much of the splendor of the bygone aviation era. The beautiful features of the Pan American terminal were preserved inside City Hall in its imported Spanish tile, Brazilian hardwood, and Italian terrazzo, all of it still intact. City commissioners and the mayor argue over political issues now in what had been the ticketing lobby of the terminal. The building still has the large paned glass windows that were there in 1934. Inside, in the smooth terrazzo on the floor remains the route structure for Pan American, denoting the Latin America cities they served from Dinner Key and Havana onto Buenos Aires. It really is a sight to behold.

I parked in one of the center circle spots and walked across the parking lot toward the boat yards that are just east of the circle. A chain link fence runs by a stand of sea grape trees, and an opening with a well-worn white gravel path surrounds a concrete pavilion. Three marina workers were sitting underneath it in the cool shade taking a cigarette break. If you're going to smoke this has to be one of the more picturesque places to do it in greater Miami. In the distance I could hear the diesel engine of a forklift.

There are four very large concrete and aluminum structures that, in the Pan American era, were the actual hangars that the clipper ships were housed in. Now they were used to dry dock boats in multiple racks that towered up to the rafters of the buildings. The forklifts are massive diesel belching machines that retrieved these recreational boats down for the casual boaters who owned them. Past the pavilion, was the former launching ramps for the clipper ships. They looked like two boat slips but you could still see the ramps that led into the bay from the topside sea walls. The marina workers barely noticed me as I passed them. I continued a few more feet across the greasy, oil-stained parking lot to Scotty's Landing.

As soon as I entered the open-air restaurant, I immediately felt some of the tensions of the morning slough off of me. Scotty's Landing, a green and white tented seafood restaurant, sits directly on Biscayne Bay. It's extremely casual with lots of oval white plastic tables and matching four plastic chairs that quite honestly, are right out of an outdoor patio aisle in Costco. The owners made the most of the bar. Wooden barstools line the shiplap bar in a ninety-degree angle. It's the only bar I've ever seen that has green padded barstools, twenty-five of them or more. The length and angle of the bar, coupled with the corner pillars, must drive the bartenders crazy trying to tend to all the customers who, by happy hour, cram this oasis. At this time of the day the lunch crowd was growing but wasn't in full swing yet. I nodded at the waitress, more so to let her know I was there but I'd find my own seat. I chose a table furthest from the kitchen and the bar but still shaded by the expansive green and white canvas. There were plenty of salt-affected, rusty but still functionally operable fans in the eaves of the tent and the place was comfortably cool. The waitress came over after a few minutes. She was relatively young and Hispanic. She was also an experienced waitress because she brought a glass of ice water in a tall red plastic Coca Cola cup and a menu with her. She must've learned early the perils of walking back and forth continuously from the kitchen to the far tables unnecessarily.

The laminated, double-sided menu had the standard seafood, salad, and burger fare. I put the menu aside and didn't even look at it.

"What's your name?" I asked her.

"Alicia."

"Hi, Alicia. What kind of beer do you have?"

"On tap we have Bud, Bud Light, Coors, and Miller Lite. In the bottle we have Stella, Corona, Heineken and Amstel Light."

"Alicia, is Santiago back there in the kitchen today?"

She looked at me, a little perplexed, but told me Santiago was indeed in the kitchen. Santiago Fonseca was the assistant manager. He oversaw the seafood and products that came in from the Bahamas, like conch for their Bahamian conch chowder, or for making conch fritters.

"Super. I'll have the grouper sandwich with fries and a beer. Can you please tell Santiago that Cade is here? He knows the beer I like."

Alicia's face momentarily showed the angst of talking to Santiago and asking him what beer I liked, but she was actually good about it and took it in stride. She took the menu back with her and said my name once out loud as a reminder to herself as she went towards the bar and the kitchen. She returned a few minutes later with two ice cold bottles of Kalik Bahamian beer in a plastic bucket.

"Santiago says you owe him," she said as she put the imported and very hard to get beer on the table.

"Tell Santiago I always owe him," I said.

Kalik was one of my favorite beers, but even though the closest Bahamian island of Bimini is only fifty-seven miles from Miami, finding Kalik here was nearly impossible. Santiago always had his suppliers throw in a few cases of Kalik beer with the seafood he was purchasing from the fishing cooperatives in Nassau and Freeport. He kept a few of them aside on ice for his closest friends and longtime customers.

I'd met Santiago about six years ago and it became a relationship of favors and information passed between us. Santiago knew the restaurant and seafood business. He knew all about fish. It could be snapper, cobia, grouper, or even square grouper; he knew it all. Square grouper was a nickname for seafaring discarded bales of marijuana. When the U.S. Coast Guard was highly funded, the marine interdiction units in the Reagan and Bush years were in optimum form. Many maritime dopers cast their marijuana cargo overboard to lighten their load and avoid the law enforcement boats descending upon them. Those large bales of marijuana became known as "square grouper," as they washed ashore days later anywhere from the beaches of Hallandale, on down to Barnes Sound in Key Largo. He also was connected in the cocaine trade. Santiago was intimate with the traders and sellers in the business. It made no difference what you called it; blow, *La Reina, perico, farlopa*, snow, *basuco, blanquita*, nose candy, or coke. He had a pipeline of information that I had tapped into on a few occasions. Santiago was a black bag. Black bag people walk amongst us every day with seemingly normal lives and jobs, but in a time of need they either do the things many won't do, or they know the people who will do those things for a price. Santiago had always been in the restaurant business, and he had his ear to the ground about many things in Miami. Some would consider him an informant. I liked to think of him as a "fixer."

The view from the table was splendid. The blue-green water of the bay had a very slight chop, and the lapping of the waves was just discernable enough to be heard. Little skiffs plied the waterway, shuttling groceries and people to live aboard sailboats anchored offshore in what's called "the anchorage." Small mangrove spoiler islands dotted the immediate horizon with nothing but blue water looking south past them. I could see the east side of City Hall, and the imagery of those majestic flying boats idling and then slowly churning out toward the terminal filled my imagination and pushed everything else out, if just for a moment.

Before the grouper sandwich arrived, Santiago came wading through the maze of plastic tables and pulled up a chair across from me.

"Cade, you got Alicia all freaked, she thinks you're from the Health Department or something."

We both had a laugh about that.

"Santiago. How are you doing, my friend? What's the good word?"

"The good word? The *good* word is 'competent cable guy.' We're trying to get the Hurricanes game on now and have the TVs set for the Dolphins/Jets game tomorrow. There's some guy here now working on what he calls a 'multi feed split.' I could give a shit about the split, I told him, just make it work."

"Do you get a crowd on Sundays for the games?"

"It's Dolphins/Jets and I heard there's forty New Yorkers from some dental conference staying across the street at the Grand Bay, so I got word to the concierge that we could be Jets central tomorrow."

"Smooth. What about your local Dolphins fan?"

"They won't care. It'll spike the energy, and as long as the taps flow it'll be football by the bay. In the end it's all about palm trees and eighty degrees."

Alicia approached the table, and with a slight smile placed my delicious-looking grouper sandwich and fries in front of me. After she was sufficiently out of earshot I said to Santiago, "You ever hear of a guy named Zeus in the business?"

Santiago leaned back and looked up at the whirling fans above us. After some contemplation, he looked across the table at me and said, "No. If I do hear, what do you want me to do?"

"If it comes up or you hear something, without being too obvious see what you can learn. Don't go to deep. This guy Zeus might be a hard-edger," I said as I took a bite of the great-tasting sandwich.

Santiago gave it some thought. "You got anything else or is that it?"

"Were you around when we used to deal with a Colombian named Chuco?"

"Chuco. Chuco? Didn't that guy go back to Colombia and work with his cousin or something?" he said in the vaguest of ways.

It was obvious that Santiago was still very connected to the comings and goings in the narco trade. I pretended to know as little as he did and answered back also in the vaguest of terms.

"Yeah, that's what I heard too, but I was just thinking about him and wondering what happened to him?"

"What I remember is that he was a short little asshole who couldn't be trusted. He left some guys holding on a restaurant investment deal in Miami Lakes. You remember Fermin Rivacoba? He was one of the guys Chuco left holding about 65k on the deal. Fermin's in Palmetto General Hospital in total renal failure. Doctors think he has about three to four days, tops."

Unbeknownst to Santiago, Fermin Rivacoba had actually worked as a C.I. for me and Ritchie a few years ago. He produced enough information to warrant being documented by us as a confidential informant (C.I.). Fermin Rivacoba was somewhere deep in the C.I. files, fingerprinted, photographed, and documented by me personally. Santiago was not documented. No one in the task force was aware of who he was. I kept my relationship with Santiago to myself. Guys like Santiago, you don't document. You rarely pay them for their tips or information. It's usually a tit for tat type of thing.

"Well, rumor is Chuco may be looking to come back and start up again. Keep me in the loop if you hear anything," I said.

"If I hear something I'll let you know, but it might be after I tell the guys in Miami Lakes. Especially Fermin if he makes it. I can negotiate a finder's fee on that one. A big one."

The staff was beckoning him back to the kitchen. Santiago stood up and just nodded his head and smiled before heading towards the kitchen/bar area.

"I appreciate you hooking me up with the Kalik," I said as he walked away.

I continued to take in the view and relish the frosty cold Kalik. Alicia came back and checked to see if I needed anything. She also told me Santiago comped my lunch. Like I said, it was a relationship of favors and information passed between us.

I hung around a little longer; just in time to see the TVs at the bar come to life with the Miami Hurricanes versus Rutgers football game. I guess the word of the day was indeed "competent cable guy." I over-tipped Alicia and headed for my car.

The marina workers were done with their smoking break. I cut past the pavilion and got in the Z28. It was still very hot outside, but us native Miamians could feel a hint, a slice, a glimmer of fall in the air and the minor dip in humidity was enough of an enticement to take the T-tops off of the Camaro and put them in the backseat for convenient retrieval later. I drove back home to Paradise Point. The tree canopy of Main Highway and Old Cutler Road cast fleeting shadows and interspersed blasts of light upon the interior of the car. It was a good day to be alive.

Unfortunately, Reggie Lamar was not around to see it.

Chapter Eight

Monday, 8:05 am

THE MELODIC PITCH of my cell phone woke me up. I was still on top of the bed, I hadn't even attempted to get under the covers. Too much Sunday fun day at a local marina, drinking. The sun streamed in from the louvered blinds. As I sat up I realized my mouth felt like a band of gypsies had held a horse auction in it. I had to search for my cell phone at first and found it under a pillow in the bed on the third ring. The caller I.D. said it was the VIN office. I tried to make myself sound as alert and awake as I could as I answered my phone.

"Hello?"

"Cade, *ju* are being *jasked* to be in *Broonsoon's* office at nine," said the voice on the line.

It was the VIN secretary, Ileana Portillo. She was a Cuban American twice divorced, single mother of two, whose pronunciation of certain words were horrific mash ups of English with a heavy Spanish accent. She could never pronounce Brunson's last name. It always sounded like *Broon-soon.*

"Okay, Ileana I'll see you in a few," I said.

"Don't *ju* come to see me. *Ju* need to be at *Broonsoon's.*" she said.

"Yes, Ileana I just thought I'd see you on the way in."

"Uh huh, *juts* don't be late, *ju* know what a *pinga* he can be," she said as a way of signing off.

Ileana had been with us six years. She worked in the center of the three-office suite that was the VIN office. It was Ileana that visitors always saw first. The office to the left of Ileana's was where Gary Fowler worked. Gary was our in-house financial administrator. I always called him "Big G." It had nothing to do with his size or girth, but simply a nickname I heard a guy once call his buddy in an elevator in Chicago. Although nearly the same age as me, he liked to call everyone 'dude,' a holdover from his days growing up in Hobe Sound, Florida's surfing Mecca. He had a buzz cut and the straightest, whitest teeth of anyone in the department. He also had a bar code tattoo at the base of the back of his neck and a small "F" tattooed on his right middle finger. He once told me that when he waves his hand in greeting or when accepting a volley of directions from someone he doesn't care for, the tattoo signified inwardly to him that he could "give a flying fuck."

The third office was the lieutenant's office. The VIN unit had been without a lieutenant for six months and there were rumors that Major Brunson would be appointing someone to lead the unit; but with the fiscally maniacal city manager watching every penny, each day that Brunson wasn't appointed chief, or the VIN unit operated without a lieutenant, was money saved. The unit was functioning well without the middle management of a lieutenant but it meant that I and the other VIN detectives would have to see Major Brunson more than we cared to. Major Brunson was probably the last of a dying breed. His father was an American G.I. who'd been stationed during World War II at the Richmond Airfield Blimp base in the scrub pine and palmetto section of southwestern Miami Dade County. His mother was a local girl whose parents had owned a five and dime store in downtown Miami. He was born and raised in Miami where his parents settled in the northeast corridor neighborhood known as Lemon City. By his early teens, as Lemon City became more integrated, his family moved blocks north on Biscayne Boulevard to the village of Miami Shores. He still lived there to this day. Brunson was a fair man but a man of uncompromising ideals. His accent was neither pure southern nor one that can fully be defined. More like a subdued, slower cadence of the cartoon character Foghorn Leghorn. He pronounced Miami "Mia-A-Muh," and was prone to profanity in such a haphazard way that it caused many a quizzical look when he went into one of his tirades. He was a quick-tempered man, prone to kicking the standard department-issued army green metal waste-basket in his office. He was fastidious about his perceived image, and usually feeling guilty about an outburst, he'd try to swap out his dented waste basket with someone else's on the odd chance the mayor or city manager should visit his office. He wore black western-style boots always under his suit and uniform pants and he had a strong inclination to sample hot sauces, of which there was usually one or two on his desk. They always had eye-catching names like "Scalding Tonsillectomy," "Assplosion," or "Belligerent Blaze."

Getting from Paradise Point to The Coral Gables Police Department by 9tam was going to be a stretch. I rolled off the bed and hopped on my shoeless foot as I threw the shoe off my other foot. I walked briskly to the opulent master bath and turned on the dual-headed shower. I waited for the hot water to work its way up to the second floor from the hot water heater in the garage. I quickly brushed my teeth and then jumped into the shower. The water was tepid at first but soon was comfortably warm and I showered very quickly. I was out the door in less than ten minutes after exiting the shower. Dressed in jeans and a long sleeve maroon t-shirt, I backed the Z28 out of the courtyard and set my sights and the car west on Coral Reef Drive. At the intersection of Mitchell Drive and Ludlum Road I turned east into the Kings Bay subdivision and used a secondary remote I kept tucked into the glove compartment to open the gate to the Kings Bay Marina and barely waited for the gate to open. I cut through the marina parking lot and wound my way to Old Cutler Road through the Deering Bay high rise condo devel-opment. This little jaunt would save me easily fifteen minutes in Old Cutler Road traffic. It was a cut-through many didn't know about nor could they attempt without the marina gate remote. Thankfully,

I made friends with the dockmaster and he'd given me the remote a few weeks ago for this exact purpose.

Coming out of Deering Bay I cut over Chapman Field Drive. I just fell into the flow of the traffic on Old Cutler Road. I took the meandering and tree-shaded road all the way to Sunset Drive, then to Lejeune Road, with traffic moving well enough that I was confident I could make it to the police station by 9 o'clock.

As I neared the police station I was as always struck by the absurd ugliness and nonfunctional architectural design of the building. It was a hideous Gulden's mustard-colored brick façade. The building was designed sometime in the early seventies. It has a glass atrium on the westside that broil-roasted all of its inhabitants in the brutal South Florida afternoon sun. The result of this short-sighted design gaffe was the necessity of installing an enhanced air conditioning system that blew such frigid air you could make ice in the building. Every civilian employee wore a pilfered winter jacket from a road patrol officer. Conversely, as they moved about the building they were constantly being mistaken as officers by the visiting public. The dispatch division had already fried two computer networks in the past two years because employees had plugged space heaters into orange designated hi-tech electrical outlets. The four-story building had been designed for a heliport until the poured concrete roof was deemed too weak to hold a helicopter. Two ladder fire trucks were parked out on the street because the adjoining fire department couldn't park them in their own parking bay—the threat of the trucks' weight caving through to the often-flooded basement below was too great. I drove up the parking ramps to the third-floor apron area where the detectives parked. The neighboring high rise office buildings that looked down upon the parking apron were counter-productive to any type of covert use of undercover cars. I parked as far as I could from the open-air apron closer to the east overhang, backing into a spot to avoid my license plate being seen by the surrounding larger office buildings. In the undercover world you can never be too sure who sees what and where.

I went into the building through the east stairwell door, up a short flight of stairs, and breezed past the open door to the VIN office. I saw Ileana at her desk but she didn't see me, as she had her head buried in a document she was reading. I continued down the hall to Major Brunson's office. It was 8:57am and I was feeling good about my timing.

I went down to Major Brunson's office and stepped into the outer office where his secretary, Charlene Muscanera, was already at her desk, sorting through a pile of papers. She looked up at me and said, "You're early."

"Yep, by three minutes," I said with an air of cockiness.

"No. It's more like thirty-three minutes early," she replied.

From the inner office I heard Major Brunson's distinct voice call out, "Charlene is that Williamson?"

"No. It's Taylor. He's early," was her reply.

"Send him in anyway," Brunson barked back.

As I started walking into the office, I asked Charlene exactly what time I was supposed to be there. She mouthed the words "Nine. Thirty."

"I apologize for being ea—" I started but Major Brunson waved a dismissive hand at me from behind his massive desk.

"That damn Ileana, she can't pronounce nine-thirty so she rounds my appointments either up or down. She drives me goddamn crazy. I mean how hard can it be to say *thirty*? It always sounds like 'dirty.' As in 'nine-dirty.' So she rounds the appointments off and expects people to sit in the office chatting with Charlene 'til I can't stand hearing their voices through these paper-ass thin walls, and I end up having people in my fucking office much earlier than I wanted, like now, with you, Cade."

"I can leave if you want me to," I answered.

"I always enjoy seeing you leave my office, don't get me wrong. It really is an absolute fucking joy for me, but sit tight. I don't feel like greeting you all over again. I got a little something I have to do then we can get started."

At that moment Charlene buzzed the Major's intercom and informed him that Detective Johan Williamson was outside the office door. Brunson just sort of leaned off to the side in his chair and stared incredulously at Charlene through the open adjoining door. He simply said, "Do you think the goddamn intercom is necessary when we're basically looking at each other? I'd tell you to send him in but why don't I just say it myself and save us the possibility of it getting lost in translation. Williamson, get your ass in here."

Johan Williamson was a newly-appointed detective in the General Investigations Unit (GIU). Being detached to the DEA task force, I was rarely ever in our police station. I didn't really know Williamson too well, I'd only seen him once or twice in passing. I ventured to guess he may have been with the police department less than five years. His promotion to detective must have been very recent.

Johan stepped into the office with a twinge of nervousness.

"You wanted to see me, Major?" he asked.

Brunson got up from his desk and stepped around it. "Ah, Detective Williamson. Good morning, Detective. I don't know if you know Cade Taylor, here. He's also a detective. No officers here, just detectives."

Whatever Brunson was angling towards, I could tell it wasn't going to be pretty. Johan nodded to me politely, but also looked at me for some sort of answer as to why he was in the Major's office at 9 o'clock in the morning. I had nothing to offer. I mean nothing. All I could provide was quiet sympathy and a head nod back at him.

"So. Detective Williamson. This is your first time in my office. You may notice that it is the largest office in the building. There's a reason why I sit in the biggest office in this place."

I'd heard this speech before and knew that whatever was coming at Johan Williamson would not be pleasant. Major Brunson walked over to Williamson, put a paternal hand on Johan's shoulder and said, "Come over here by the window. I want to show you something."

I stayed in my chair. No way, no how I wanted any part of this at all. Whatever was outside the window had nothing to do with me, and I wasn't interested in knowing either.

"So, Detective Williamson, if my memory serves me correctly you have been a detective now five months. I hope you like your promotion to detective. I hope the adjustment to being a detective has been a smooth one. We like our detectives here, Williamson, and what we like most about our detectives is when they act like detectives."

With those words, Brunson opened the window shade. The morning light of a typical October Miami morning came streaming in. He asked Williamson to look down at the street and tell him what he saw.

"There are two marked units parked on the street," said Williamson.

"Two marked units? Two actual uniform police cars parked right below us. Imagine that? Is there anybody in them?

"No sir," said Williamson.

"Well, we can always change that. We can get someone to be in one of those cars real quickly. It's real easy to find someone to drive one of those cars. Whoever we get, they can work eight hours a day in a postage stamp-sized patrol zone, driving the same streets over and over, day after day. What color's the striping on those cars, Williamson?"

"Blue and white, sir," answered Williamson.

"Well, you're partially correct. Yes, they are marked units, and yes, they are two of ours. Every car dealer will give a descriptive name to a color to enhance the appeal of their car—the striping on those cars isn't just simply called 'blue and white.' They aren't sapphire blue, or igloo white or some other fancy dancy color name either. No, those colors are actually called 'career-ending white, and 'stuck-in-patrol blue.' Can you say those colors back to me, Detective?"

"Career-ending white and stuck-in-patrol blue," said Williamson with a hint of confusion.

"So I hope you'll remember that color scheme the next time you fucking decide to use your goddamned unmarked detective car to make a traffic stop on the way into work. You see, we pay you to be a *detective*, not a traffic cop in a clip-on tie and Hagar slacks. But if you want to drive one of those 'career-ending white, stuck-in-patrol blue' cars, we have plenty of them for you to drive. Plenty. Take your pick. I can have one ready for you in ten fucking minutes. Because Williamson, we made you a goddamn detective for a reason and we want to reasonably believe we made the correct choice in making you a detective. If I wanted another ticket-happy writing fool I'd have grabbed some other fucking moron from patrol, but you're the moron I chose to be a detective; at least for the next five fucking minutes. So quit acting like a motor cop, or as Cade here is my unwilling witness, I will ship your scrawny ass back to patrol. You can write all the tickets you want until your fucking fingers fall off. Do I make myself crystal clear, Officer Williamson? Officer Williamson. I kind of like the sound of that more than Detective Williamson. So, what's it going to be: officer or detective?"

"Detective, sir," stammered Williamson.

"Then I guess I made my point. Goodbye Williamson."

The chastised Williamson exited the office and now it was just me and Major Brunson. I looked at him and he looked at me, still fuming.

"What's this about U.S. Customs wanting to engage us on our money laundering deals?" he asked.

The ability that Major Brunson had for switching gears from threatening to transfer a newly appointed detective to obtaining information was eerie. He transitioned his mood and train of thought with incredible ease. The speed that information funneled back to him was so uncanny it was actually a bit unsettling. There was a reason he sat in the biggest office in the building and he never failed to remind you or deliver on the reason why. He had his finger on the pulse of the agency, its people and the city itself. In a manner that no one else did.

I settled further into my chair and explained. "Friday, I met with Customs Special Agent Ritchie Tavino, and he was rather adamant that U.S. Customs needed to get back in on money laundering cases because he feels that Washington shut them down and that they should be back in because they're the Treasury Department."

"Why are you meeting with U.S Customs?" he asked.

"Actually, I didn't arrange to meet with him. He wanted to meet with me and I hadn't seen him in a few years. I didn't know what it could be about, so I went," I said.

"Do they realize that we—or actually, more specifically *you*—are forbidden from doing outside investigations without the purveyance of the DEA due to our mutual aid agreement with the Justice Department?"

"Yes, I explained that to him Friday," I said.

"Then what makes U.S. Customs think we can just open our investigations to them and let them waltz in?"

At this point I was starting to wonder why he hadn't been swearing and was actually surprised at his lack of profanity.

"I mean for fucksakes, don't they think we need to follow our own fucking protocols and rules here or do they have their head so far up their egotistical asses that they think we'll just roll over for them? I'll bet this Tavino guy used that 'we're the fucking feds' attitude. didn't he?" bellowed Brunson.

I was quietly relieved to hear the profanity and nodded my head in affirmation.

"Tavino said their SAC might be reaching out to you." I said by way of warning to Brunson.

"Their SAC? You mean Dale Sorenson? Yeah, he reached out to me. I had a long talk with him. He tried to explain it all to me. I wasn't too impressed, to be honest with you. I'm not too impressed with him or with what they're trying to launch. I think because he's the SAC in South Florida he thinks it gives him some sort of emeritus status. Customs' reasoning is they're missing the high school dance because Principal Reno disinvited them. Now she's diverted her attention to catching smokers in the parking lot and they're hoping to do the watutsi with us in the sock hop and hope she won't notice.

He tried that bullshit 'we're the feds' with me. I told him to shove it up his ass," he said.

"So, we won't be doing anything with them. I guess that's good. Then I don't have to try to explain anything to DEA," I said with relief.

"Well, not so fast there. Actually, we are. We're going to do some introductory deals with them. I should say *you* will be doing some introductory deals with them. The Mutual Aid agreement says any cases you initiate must go through DEA. You're not initiating this case. I am. That little meeting at *La Caretta* was not for naught. Therefore, as your direct—and I might add, *only* supervisor—I'm telling you that Customs has a quick meet and greet set for three o'clock today. You call this Agent Tavino fellow and get onboard with them. This one we will be doing 'in house' and outside of the DEA agreement. I'll call Dale and tell him you're working with them."

"I never mentioned that we met at *La Caretta*, and you seem pretty familiar calling the SAC Dale," I said.

Brunson gave me a steely gaze. He held the gaze a tad longer than I was comfortable with. He ran his hand down the length of his necktie as if it would magically straighten the tie.

"Yeah, Dale. Special Agent in Charge Dale Sorenson. He's new to South Florida and did most of his enforcement career holding the pin flags on the golf courses of Hilton Head and Spartanburg. He's one of those guys who went to a decent university but had a shitty grade point average. Since IBM, Stanley Tools and any other fortune five hundred company wiped their ass with his resume and wouldn't look at him, he took some advice early in his life. He was advised to apply to be a federal agent and they hired him. Eventually he ended up the SAC in Columbia South Carolina, and now here he is, heading up the Miami office."

"You seem to know a lot about him," I said.

"I should. I'm the one who advised him."

He paused to take in the confused look on my face.

"What choice did I have? He's my brother-in-law."

Chapter Nine

THE NEWS THAT SAC Sorenson was related to Brunson had to sink in for a few seconds. Doubts started to fill my head. I didn't know if the whole Tavino meeting had been prearranged by Brunson or if it all came together just as they said. Either way this nepotistic slant was making me feel a little uneasy, because now it took on a personal aspect. And when it gets personal, mistakes happen, and things can get ugly.

"So Cade, since we are still without a lieutenant, consider this an agreeable directive for you to meet with Customs given to you directly by me. You will assist them in their money laundering case. Don't you worry about the DEA. Any issue with them and I'll handle them. Besides, those fucking half-wits have been asleep at the switch for the past two years anyway. Ninety percent of the time we do the deals, and they only show up when there's a seizure. They look good behind a press conference podium, but I don't have much recollection of what they look like out on the street."

I saw the proverbial dominoes stacking up and I just wanted to tiptoe around them as best I could. I didn't counter anything he was saying, nor did I add anything to his thoughts about the DEA. I was a little surprised by his attitude about the DEA. I was actually intrigued, because up until a scant six months ago when we had a lieutenant, it seemed that Major Brunson wasn't too plugged into the federal way, or our relationships with them. But then again, Brunson was not a man to be underestimated. He always knew more than he let on, until such time he wanted you to know.

"Cade, do you know what DEA stands for?"

"Drug Enforcement Agency."

"Bullshit. It stands for 'Don't Expect Anything.' I'm tired of doing the same shit with those fuckers. We're bringing in Customs. Let the best dog hunt on this. So be open today or tomorrow for this Tavino and his group."

"Okay," I said.

"Great. I don't see any need for us to carry on with this any further. Now how about you just wander on out of here. Thanks for not making my carpet wet."

"Make your carpet wet?" I asked as I was leaving.

"I heard you got stuck out in the rain Friday night. That's all, Cade. Goodbye."

Major Brunson's ability to gather information and then masterfully disperse it in small doses to keep you guessing was almost an art form. I left his office and went down the hall to the VIN offices. Ileana was still at her desk. I didn't see Gary at his desk.

"Hello, Ileana."

"*Aye coño,* Cade don't tell me *ju* are just getting here now!"

"No, I was here on time, I just didn't stop by," I said.

"Oh thank Jesus, because if *ju* had just been here now then *Broonsoon* would go crazy batshit."

Major Brunson said that whatever U.S. Customs had going on it was going on at three o'clock. He obviously knew more about this than me. That was fine with me, for the moment. The less I knew, the less the DEA could say I had a hand in the planning of this operation. This would all have to come from my immediate supervisor. I remembered exactly what he said in his office.

"So Cade, since we still have no lieutenant, consider this an agreeable directive for you to meet with Customs given to you directly

be me. You will assist them in their money laundering case. Don't you worry about the DEA."

"Where's Gary?" I asked Ileana.

"He stepped out to get that wheat grass *mierda* he drinks."

"I don't know if it's *shit*, Ileana. It's supposed to have some very healthy benefits."

"*Mierda, mierda, y mas mierda es un caca!*"

I grinned. *Shit, shit, and more shit, it's caca!*

She wasn't going to budge on her opinion of Gary's healthy intake of a wheat grass shot. I had other things I needed to get in order, mainly either reaching out to Ritchie Tavino or waiting for him to reach out to me. I decided that the less initiative I took in this inter-action, the better my defense would be with the DEA if they found out. It was still relatively early; I decided to see if Tavino would call me first.

"Ileana, I'm going to head out. I'll see you later."

"I'll tell Gary *ju* were here. *Ciao.*"

I got back in my car and decided to drive over to Nena's. At exactly the same corner I'd power-slid the Camaro through Friday night was a little breakfast spot—a cozy, unadvertised restaurant with darkly tinted windows. It was on the corner of Southwest 38th Avenue and Bird Road, right across from the Sherwin Williams Paint store. I'd frequented this little spot ever since rotating into VIN years ago. Just like there were bars in Vietnam that were friendly to American G.I.'s, Nena's was very friendly to many of us in VIN. No one ever asked any questions of what we did for a living, and always the service and food was spot on. I only knew it as Nena's because of the elderly woman in the back kitchen who everybody called Nena. I didn't even know if it had an actual name. It was just Nena's.

From the police station it was a short drive down Ponce DeLeon Boulevard. The only signage on the place was the address: 3791 SW 40th Street. Nothing denoted there was even a restaurant there. I pulled into the back parking lot of Nena's. I always parked in the back and always went in through the back door, which was a poorly mis-hung, hard as hell to open, mess of a door, protected just above it by a single aluminum awning. The front door had too much exposure on busy 40th Street. Once inside, there was a partition between the narrow hallway from the rear door to one communal dining room. So much wood paneling was on the walls that it would've made architect Mike Brady from *The Brady Bunch* proud for its functionality and overuse. Cars hummed by the front windows, but with the dark tint of the windows it was surreal. It was sort of like watching big metallic fish swim by in an oversized aquarium. There was a cocoon-like feeling of being ensconced inside. I didn't see Nena, but I could hear her shrill, squeaky voice somewhere in the kitchen barking orders and commands in high-pitched Spanish.

A gum-smacking, somewhat rotund waitress came by with a bored, but moderately pleasant demeanor and asked me in Spanish what my order would be. I get that a lot in Miami. Many people just assume I speak Spanish and always start the conversation in Spanish. Fortunately for me, my knowledge of Spanish is more passable than most and I usually get by.

"Huevos revueltos, tocino crujiente, tostadas cubanas y café con leche." Scrambled eggs, crispy bacon, Cuban toast and cafe con leche.

No sooner had I ordered than my cell phone rang.

"Hello?"

"Cade, its Ritchie."

"What's up, Ritchie?"

"Hey, I'm calling to let you know we're going to do an introductory pick up set for three o'clock today. Our SAC talked to your major and they're cool with it."

"Yeah, I had a meeting with him this morning," I said, not alluding that I knew that Major Brunson and SAC Dale Sorenson were related.

"Here's what we're thinking. They want to drop $150,000 to us and see if we can deliver on it. *If* we can. Which we will. Then they want to shuffle the rest of the seven million within twenty-four hours it hinges on us pushing their $150,000 down south. Since it's such a

107

small amount, we've preemptively started the process with our bank. Once they make the drop it should only be a few hours and we'll have it moved."

"Counting chickens before they're hatched, Ritchie. Are you sure you want—"

"Buddy, this is a slam dunk," Ritchie said, cutting me off. "We'll take the 150 back to Doral and have it in process. The guy we're dealing with is Chuco's main Miami guy, so we really need to make it look good."

"Have you set up the meet yet?" I asked.

"Three o'clock at a Cuban bakery called *El Brazo Fuerte*. It's on Southwest 32nd Avenue. You know where it is?"

"I know where it is, and it's not a good place. There's a big-ass wall across the street and there aren't any good places to set up and do takeaways. Plus, there's a school next door. Three o'clock, it's going to be full of kids, parents, cars and all kinds of shit. Ritchie, this isn't good, man. Why'd you let them set it? I mean seriously, see if you can change it. We got too many innocents in this one. Too many things that can go wrong."

"No can do. Chuco set it through his Miami guy."

"I don't care if he set it up through Wayne Huizenga and the entire Miami Dolphins team! This ain't good, Ritchie. It's been a while since you guys did these things. We can't set up for surveillance or counter-surveillance. The place will be a mad house with people and probably kids going into the bakery after school. Not good. Not good at all, man."

"Cade, this is a go. Our SAC wants it. We want it, and I'm sure your major wants it too. So let's just do it. Play nice. Pick up the 150 and get out. Keep your eye on the long game. We want the seven million. The way we got it set, we will be seeing that seven million in less than two days," he said.

"Where are we doing the pre-op meeting?" I asked.

"No need for a pre-op on such a quick, small amount. Two of our guys are out of play anyway. They're in court in Palm Beach. It'll be me and you on the inside and I'll have two more of us outside. We do this quick, and we're in and out in two minutes."

"You know this is totally not how we do business. I mean, totally. Ritchie, I don't like this at all."

The waitress put the breakfast plate in front of me, and as appetizing as it looked I was starting to crank up, and breakfast was the last thing on my mind. I was seriously beginning to think Ritchie had been inhaling paint fumes or something. His judgment and mind were clouded with his fervent zeal to get this deal done. I was boxed in. Major Brunson had already greenlighted this fiasco and I was stuck. If Ritchie was right, if we just showed up and did a pick-up, we could maybe minimize a lot of this. I still had some serious concerns about the school next door. This was absolutely not the way I would've set this deal up.

"Who is this big Miami connection?" I asked.

"Chuco says his name is Perchero. Chuco says we'll be able to pick him out easily."

"Ritchie, this is so wacked, man. You don't know anything about the guy doing the drop other than his name is Perchero, and somehow, some way we'll just *magically* recognize this guy. You know that Chuco's a complete liar and an untrustable little shit. Listen Ritchie, if we do this—and I say *if*—then going forward we get our ducks in a row, because this is some ratchety shit here."

"Cade, there is no *if*. There's only *when*—and when is at three o'clock. I know you and the DEA guys think and rethink everything. Listen, it isn't rocket science. We meet this guy, he gives us the 150. We don't care about take ways or where he lives. Chuco says if we make it go on down, then the seven million will be in our hands in two days, max. It's a hit and rip, practically."

"Okay, well since it isn't rocket science, then we don't have to get too cozy with this Perchero guy. Chuco doesn't need to know he's dealing with me. We weren't exactly square last time we saw each other, and I don't need that little shit weasel ratting me out from Colombia months from now when I'm back with DEA. So don't call me by my name or anything that can get back to Chuco. I don't trust that little fucker. Clear?"

"Yeah. Okay, I'll just call you 'Direct Deposit.' Happy now? Three o'clock at *El Brazo Fuerte* on three-two avenue. Let's be inside by two-fifty. Don't worry, Cade—we've done these tons of times in the past. This will be easy. Trust me. Okay?"

"2:50pm. I'll see you then," I said as I hung up the cell phone. I wanted to hurl it against the restaurant wall but instead just put it down on the table face-down. I started to eat the breakfast; the *café con leche* helped to calm me down a bit. The waitress came over when I was finished and checked to see if I needed anything else.

"*No gracias. La quenta, por favor.*" No thank you. The check please.

As she turned away, I called out to her.

"*Señora, como se dice en Ingles, 'Perchero?'*" Ma'am, how do you say in English, 'Perchero?'

She looked at me, puzzled for a second, then said, "*Perchero? Perchero*...um...coat hanger."

As I got in my car, I started running things through my head.

Coat hanger. A guy nicknamed "Coat Hanger." Why could he possibly have that nickname?

From Nena's it was a very short drive up Douglas Road to Southwest 16th Street. I decided to make a dry run while it was early and see what I could of the bakery. On the corner of 16th Street was the old dive bar *The Bushwhacker*. I turned at *The Bushwhacker* and continued east, passing houses on my right and the southern border of Woodlawn North Cemetery on my left. The cemetery was partially concealed behind scrubby ficus hedges and a chain link fence. Once I got past the first series of houses, the road became the community of Coral Gate, and that "big-ass wall" I told Ritchie about was now on my right side. It went the entire length of Southwest 16th Street to the intersection of Southwest 32nd Avenue. As I turned south, the wall also ran the length of the road on my right side. The entire way. Law offices, auto repair shops, and cafes ran the length of the east side, and as I neared *el Brazo Fuerte,* I could see the school. The sign out front was elevated on a pole, clearly identifying as a school. There would be no DEA trickery here with some storefront language school in an industrial park, like what befell Alvaro Dominguez's brother, Yordani. This school was clearly marked and the school was painted in a garish adobe red clay color.

"Jose Marti School #3."

Jose Marti School #3 was not only next door to *El Brazo Fuerte,* but they actually shared a common wall. I pounded the steering wheel once in frustration.

I was pissed at Ritchie and I was pissed at Brunson for allowing such sloppy undercover work to take place. Just like what I'd thought when I was in Brunson's office earlier and he revealed the relationship between him and Sorenson:

Either way this nepotistic slant was making me feel a little uneasy, because now it took on a personal aspect. And when it gets personal, mistakes happen, and things can get ugly.

After doing two additional slower passes in front of the bakery, I looked for a good place to park later in the day when we were to meet Perchero. Parking anywhere was going to be difficult. There were limited spaces near the school. The adjoining businesses had their own spaces filled, and it looked like it would stay that way for the rest of the day. The side streets were duplexes and apartments with regulated parking. Logistically this was not a good place to meet and was more than likely the reason Chuco and Perchero chose it. Directly behind the bakery were two identical two-story apartments, both of them with gabled roofs and open staircases to the second floor. The apartments themselves were protected by the roof eaves but were largely exposed to the elements with no interior hallways. A long asphalt lane bisected both buildings and there were dumpsters at the end of the lane. I chose to use that as the place I would park. I'd walk in from there.

Catty corner to the bakery on the side street was a smaller, but similar apartment building with an upstairs staircase landing. I figured if I got there early enough, I could walk over and use that staircase landing as a good vantage point to try a little counter-surveillance. I turned the Z28 around and drove south straight to the Sears department store at Douglas Road and Coral Way. Once again it was as if I was retracing my sloppy, wet, crazed drive of Friday night—only now I was driving well within the speed limits of the law. The Sears parking lot was fairly empty. I parked and went inside. Within minutes I found what I was looking for. I exited a few minutes later with a Spalding basketball, which I threw into the backseat. I stayed in the parking lot, picked up my cell phone and called the VIN office. After four rings Ileana answered.

"*Veen.*"

"Hi Ileana, is Gary in?"

"*Espere.*" (Wait.)

Soon Gary's voice was on the line.

"What's happening, Cade?"

"Does she realize that I really don't fully speak Spanish?"

"Dude, I don't think she realizes she doesn't fully speak English."

"Since we still don't have a lieutenant, I know you're doing a lot more admin stuff now. Do you have access to NINJAS?"

NINJAS was an acronym for Narcotic Information Network Joint Agency System. It was created just a year or so earlier and was a valuable tool for us in the VIN world. It was designed to avoid having undercover cops conduct cases with an adversary who, could also be an undercover cop. A secretive clearinghouse for the undercover operations in Miami. This basically kept cops from doing cops. An example would be if a C.I. and a bad guy were to come to me looking to sell ten kilograms of cocaine, but the bad guy was actually a Miami Beach undercover cop. Then he would put in the date and location and nature of the deal; in this case a ten kilogram deal. I, in turn, would also log into NINJAS and show myself as a buyer of ten kilograms of cocaine. NINJAS would work in the background and see the location, date, and nature of the deal and recognize a conflict. It would then warn both agencies. As the years progressed the High

Intensity Drug Trafficking Area (HIDTA) clearing house had started data tracking locations looking for trends on both sides for similarities. HIDTA was tracking the data to make sure the undercovers didn't do too many deals in the same location, which could leave us open to a link chart analysis by the cartels. Conversely, locations set by the cartel were also being monitored for frequency.

"Yeah, I have access. I just use the old lieutenant's username and password. I don't think they've figured out or even care for that matter, that he's no longer with us."

"Great. I need a few favors. Can you go into NINJAS and show me doing a pick-up for $150,000 at 1697 SW 32nd Avenue at 3 o'clock? Show just me there."

"No DEA?"

"For now, just show me. I'm not sure if DEA is in play on this one yet."

"Odd, but okay. What else?" he asked.

"Are you still filling in for us at the task force steering committees?"

"Dude, I'm busier than a hooker with twin beds. They got me doing that, all the financials, *and* monitoring the narcotic wire for HIDTA."

"When is your next steering committee meeting?"

"Wednesday. It's out at Blue Lagoon at the Hilton."

"Okay. When they ask for new business I want you to ask the steering committee if they have intel on a new player in town named Zeus. This guy might be responsible for a Miami homicide in the Grove, so make sure the Miami representative joins with you on the inquiry. Make sure they take the question back to their people. Miami needs to know what they can about this guy, the sooner the better. So make sure TNT and all the squads are aware Miami is looking for this Zeus guy."

"Got it. God of thunder and lightning kind of thing."

"Big G, this guy cranked seven rounds at a uniformed Miami cop last Friday night. No joking on this one. This Zeus is the real deal."

"Got it. I'm on it."

"Thanks, Big G. How was your wheat grass shot today?"

"Earthy."

"That's about what I expected it to be. Later."

With that I hung up. I made a call to C.C. and got her voicemail. I let her know I was just checking in and asked her if there was anything new. I checked my watch—just approaching noon. I was too far to go home, and I didn't feel like going to the VIN office and waiting for three o'clock. It was typical "doper time," which largely means hurry up and wait. Being in VIN had fostered a certain solo lifestyle mentality. Now that I was officially divorced from Gina that solo lifestyle was front and center for me. I didn't want to meet up with someone from the agency and get a quick bite to eat. Many of them didn't understand what it was I did. There was an oddness, an awkwardness. They either asked me multiple questions or they pretended to understand. Besides, I couldn't be seen in public sitting at table with them as they ate lunch in full uniform, or in full detective mode with their badge and gun presentable on their hip. Each detective would find a way to put the always squelching portable radio on the table as if it were a newly won bowling trophy. I preferred to be alone. It suited me. It suited where I was in my life now.

Alone.

Chapter Ten

I PUT THE CAR in drive and drove east through the Sears parking lot. I worked my way onto Coral Way. Just past Southwest 23rd Avenue. I pulled a U-turn and was fortunate to find a parking spot right in front of Maria's Greek restaurant. Maria's was situated in an ideal location, close enough to downtown Miami to service patrons there. It can service its own burgeoning neighborhood and northeastern Coconut Grove as well. It was also very close to the undercover Miami S.I.S office. Once again, I wondered if C.C. had made contact with S.I.S. about Zeus.

Maria's is wedged dead center in a long strip of shops. Many of these stores were cheap cell phone dealers. In the last eight years it seemed as though cell phone stores sprouted up like wild mushrooms. I walked into Maria's and was seated at a table just under one of the curved arches. Maria's had a distinctive Greek décor with curved edged smooth white walls. There was authentic Greek artwork and a wall-size map of Greece. The tables and chairs were all solid, dark wood. Maria was smart and had also installed decorative ceiling baffles that helped muffle the noise that bounded up from the beautiful bare tile floors.

I ordered the pastitsio, which came with some delicious green beans. I was madly coveting the Volken White Santorini beer, but I avoided it because I wanted to be as clear as I could for three o'clock.

I idled my time there, watching the take-out orders get bundled and ready to be picked up. Many of the orders were in sets of five. I could just imagine where those were going.

Divorce mediation.

Two attorneys, two warring spouses and one excessively, overly-paid mediator. I knew that routine all too well. At my divorce, Gina and her attorney were in one conference room, me and my attorney were in another and the mediator off by themselves. Two lives being ripped apart, two attorneys making big money, a mediator wracking in a good payday, all with a side of tzatziki sauce. Maybe I was just jaded, but each order of five that went out the door had me envisioning that.

The clock moved slow, but as it neared 2pm I left Maria's and meandered my way through the backstreets towards *El Brazo Fuerte*.

I came up the side street that was adjacent to the bakery. As planned, I turned into the apartment complex with the two identical two-story apartments, both of them with gabled roofs and open staircases to the second floor. A few older women sat in front of their units, and there was a smattering of tricycles and kids' toys on the common, exposed, upstairs open-railed walkway. Papers and crushed beer cans dotted the parking lot.

I drove straight to the rear dumpsters and parked on a weed covered spit of cracked concrete next to one of the most dented dumpsters I think I had ever seen. Nearly every dent had a different swatch of color paint in it. To the untrained eye it would seem that cars parking there kept hitting the dumpster. The probability of that was low. My guess would be each time they collect refuse from the dumpster and a car is parked there, the refuse truck operator lifts the dumpster to empty it and then makes sure to lay the dumpster back down on the parked car causing a lots of dents, scratches, and headaches to the car owners. A little message of, "Don't park so close to the dumpster."

It was after 2pm and I was willing to take the chance that the dumpster did not get emptied on this day or at this time of day.

I reached into the backseat and retrieved the new basketball.

Like a point guard on a team winning by fourteen points with only nine seconds left in the game, I casually brought the ball up through the center of the complex, bouncing it with every other step. The older Hispanic women just gave me a quick look, then went back to talking to each other. When I got to the street I crossed it and went straight to the apartment building catty corner to the bakery. On the outside staircase landing, I set the ball down and sat on it to watch the bakery and the avenue in front of it. Thin, scraggly palms and an overgrown pine tree both afforded me decent concealment. It took me about ten to twelve minutes to get a sense of the traffic light which was out of my sight. By counting the flow of cars and when they back logged and when they moved, I was able to determine the light at Southwest 16th Street was cycling every four minutes. When the cars would back up as far back as the bakery, I knew it took every driver in a row of cars one second each to react to a changing light. To be backed up to the bakery there must be at the minimum twenty cars waiting for the light. By the time the cars started moving from outside the front of the bakery, the light would have been green for twenty or more seconds. On a four-minute light, that only really amounted to three minutes and forty seconds of actual movement. With the school set to release its students in twenty minutes that time frame would be shortened dramatically.

If the two U.S. Customs agents didn't get in place soon they wouldn't be able to get in place at all.

Now that I had a traffic pattern somewhat established, I focused on the cars themselves. I was looking for the obvious single car with one lone male in it circling the block, looking for a space to park. Any affordable car with overly dark-tinted windows got my attention as well.

I checked my watch. 2:25pm.

A medium blue Oldsmobile Alero had driven by twice. It looked as though it had only one driver and the tints were dark for such an out of the showroom model. The Alero was Oldsmobile's newest model and rolled off the assembly line only six months ago. Ramon at the car rental dealership had a few, and called them *"viejo sedans."* Old man sedans.

After a few passes around the block I didn't see him anymore. Another car that caught my eye was a burgundy Buick Century. It too, had a lone male passenger. The tints of the windows weren't as dark as the Alero but the fact that it was a single male driver raised my interest. It too drove around a few times around the block. More cars started arriving in the area. There soon was an uptick in horn blowing and voices as parents were obviously jockeying to pick up their kids.

It was now 2:42pm and I needed to start making my way into the bakery.

I came down from the stairway landing and bounced the basketball a few times as I walked to the corner. I tucked the ball under my arm. From the corner, I scanned the street and spotted the Alero about halfway down the block south of me. If he wasn't a Customs agent than he sure had the federal agent look locked down. He was also in no position to see anything coming in or out of the bakery. More affirmation that he was either inept or too lazy to get here on time back us up.

Just across the street from me, in one of the angled spaces facing the wall, was an idling bronze-colored Mazda Millenia. The driver was Hispanic, black curly hair and a thin mustache. He also had on very distinctive Oakley Michael Jordan Iridium Leather sunglasses. I don't know sunglasses per se, but there had been a lot of talk about that style and brand of sunglasses and I recognized them from the hype. He looked ridiculous in the glasses, but he was doing what he was asked to do. I suspect he was counter-surveillance for Perchero; he was watching the bakery through his rearview mirror. He had an unobstructed view, and he was intently watching the bakery doors. Since he was backed in, I was able to see his license plate. It was Florida, license tag *RWB420*. I ran those numbers in my head so as to not forget them as I crossed the street to the bakery parking lot and headed for the front door. Parents and children were everywhere inside and outside of the bakery.

I surveyed the parking lot, bouncing the basketball. Each bounce represented three potentially innocent victims in that parking lot if this little fiasco went to shit. I bounced the ball eleven times. I looked like a parent or basketball tutor and no one paid any attention to me, including the Mazda Millenia. As I neared the doors of the bakery there were seven older kids there. They may have been brothers or sisters of the younger kids milling about. The school had a basketball court in front of it behind the gates. I put the basketball into the hands of one of the older kids and suggested they all go shoot some baskets next door. My suggestion was finalized with a "winner can keep the ball."

A free basketball and a dose of competition will do wonders. No less than nine of the kids peeled off and ran back to the school some with their parents following.

"*Oye regresa. Ven aquí. Oye! A dónde vas!*" the shouts sounded out. ("Hey, come back. Get over here. Hey, where are you going?")

That little maneuver cleared about fourteen potential innocents out of the vicinity of the bakery. I stepped into the bakery, making the assumption that somehow, some way Tavino was here, as was Perchero. I also assumed that since I had no idea what Perchero looked, like he wouldn't recognize me either.

The bakery is diabetes in a cinderblock storefront. Brightly lit glass display cases showcase row upon row of every type of Cuban and Latin pastry, cake, and baked good you can imagine. The creativity and presentation of these treats was astounding. The bright lighting glinted off the chrome framing of the glass cases and reflected back off the curved glass, literally creating mini prisms of light on the subdued, green-colored walls. There was a wooden map of Cuba on the wall, and between Maria's Greece map and this Cuban map, I was getting a gastronomical geography lesson today.

The bakery was slightly crowded and I could sense it was going to ebb and flow from a few patrons inside to many waiting out the door. The basketball competition helped greatly to reduce the bottle neck at the door, but that was just a momentary fix.

True to form, Tavino was not inside and with the exception of me, there wasn't a single male in the place who didn't have a child calling them "Poppi." That made me the first invitee to the party that I really didn't want to be a part of in the first place.

There was a small, three-chair bistro set deep in the corner with white painted wrought iron chairs and a small very thin, round, marble-top table. A black, rectangular napkin box in the center of the table housed those miniscule napkins which causes you to pull out an inch of napkins before you can get anything that has a marginal sense of absorbency. I had no choice but to wait. This was not my forte. I positioned the chair in a way which allowed me to face the entire bakery and simultaneously put the third attendee in a compromised position by allowing very little space for them to use the table. This would force him to keep his hands above the table and allow me to watch him more closely. Once again, I was assuming Tavino would be the next to arrive and take the other chair making my plan fall into place.

I sat there for about two minutes. No Tavino. I pulled out my cell phone. There were no missed calls and there were no text messages from him. I started to put the phone to my ear when two men walked into the bakery. They were both Colombian. The one in the front was about 5'10" and a little overweight. He kept his left hand in his pocket, and as he walked he eyed nearly every one of the bakery items in the cases. He had on a burnt orange shirt and black long pants. His boots were dust-covered, the left one hastily tied and the right one untied. He had small-set eyes and a very thin mustache. I don't think the mustache was intended to be miniscule, I just think there was a personal follicle challenge going on there, and he just couldn't grow a proper mustache. He had a full head of brown, spongy hair that looked like it had some remnants of sawdust in it. It was the man behind him that I immediately set my eyes on. It had to be Perchero. He was about 5'8" and very thin. His clothes seemed to hang on him. His belt was cinched nearly to the last hole on his pants. He wore a yellow shirt that looked like it had some sort of repeating small black bird pattern on it. His black hair was jelled into a side part and he had a dark black mustache, thin face, and brown eyes. His mouth was very small and his teeth seemed to crowd together most likely due to a narrow palate. The most noticeable thing about him was his shoulders. It was as if his collarbones and scapulas were too small. The seam of his shirt was just past the drop of his shoulders. It was what made his clothes look as though they were draped on him.

Small shoulders. Perchero. Coat Hanger.

They both sauntered over to me. I kept my stare affixed on both of them but primarily on the burnt shirt. I wasn't keen on his hand being in his pocket. I was seething inside that Ritchie wasn't present but I tried my utmost to contain my anger. As they neared the table, Perchero put his hand on the shoulder of his *compádre*. Burnt Orange stopped and Perchero stepped in front as they neared my table. Burnt Orange immediately turned his back to me. He was now standing only four feet away. He just stood there, looking at the front doors as he was now covering the rear. He kept his left hand still in his pocket. Perchero boldly stepped forward and in a Colombian accent said, "You Ritchie?"

From the sitting position and currently at a physical disadvantage I just locked eyes with him.

"We aren't even going to start talking until he takes his hand out of his pocket."

Perchero placed both hands on the table and leaned in and a little over me. I was already sizing up his Adam's apple as my first targeted punch. But that would entail me rising up and drawing my arm back; too much forewarning. I opted to casually wrap both hands around the napkin holder. One upward thrust and the metal can would smash into his throat. That would cause him to lean even more forward and I'd continue the metal cannister right across the bridge of his nose. Just as quickly, I planned to flip the table over, pushing him back and stand on the table with him under it. I'd draw my Glock and drop Burnt Orange and his unseen left hand right there in front of the *pastelitos* display. Perchero looked over his noticeably small shoulder at Burnt Orange and then spoke in rapid fire Spanish.

"Emiliano, estás poniendo nervioso al gringo. Saque la mano del bolsillo, pero vuelva a colocarla en un minuto. Quiero verlo retorcerse."

("Emiliano, you're making the gringo nervous. Take your hand out of your pocket but put it back in a minute. I want to see him squirm.")

The Spanish was spoken so quickly I could only catch the gist of it, but could fill in the rest. I did catch the front part where Perchero called him "Emiliano." At least I now had a name for "Burnt Orange." Emiliano smirked at me, pulled his hand out of his pocket and made a production of wiggling his fingers and opening and closing his fist at me in a defiant act of posturing. He then turned back facing the door with his arms crossed across his chest. It was at this moment that Ritchie walked in, looking a little frazzled. He saw me in the corner. Perchero had sat in the seat that I had wanted Ritchie to sit in and didn't see Ritchie come in. Ritchie side-stepped a few small children by the entrance and walked directly towards us. Emiliano simply said in Spanish, *"Otra pendejo."*

Another Dickhead.

Perchero sat back in the chair and just casually looked back briefly at Ritchie approaching. When he turned his gaze back to me, he said, "So Ritchie…"

To which Ritchie, who was nearly at the table, answered, "What?"

Perchero was momentarily confused as he watched Ritchie glide into the unenviable chair at the table and train his eyes on both of us. Ritchie leaned on the table with his left elbow, shrugged his right shoulder and said to Perchero, "Go on."

Perchero was a little miffed and motioning with his head at me said, "He said he was Ritchie."

"I never said I was Ritchie. What I said was we don't even start talking until *he* takes his hand out of his pocket. If he sticks his hand back in his pocket at any time during this meeting you and our mutual friend down south can take your cheesy intro 150 and find a new mover. Watching over your *otra pendejo* is not my idea of a fun afternoon spent. You hear me?"

"So what *is* your name?" Perchero asked me.

"You don't need to know his name. Just think of him as 'Direct Deposit,'" said Ritchie.

Perchero took slight offense to Ritchie's abrupt comment but he recovered quickly and motioned towards Emiliano.

"Well, you can think of my companion here as 'Overdraft Protection.'" Focusing his attention on me, Perchero said, "So since this isn't fun for you. What *is* fun for you, Mr. Direct Deposit?"

"Right now I should be at Melreese on the back nine, but instead, as a favor to Ritchie here, I'm sitting in this Cuban glucose mill for an amount of money I normally wouldn't even get out of bed for."

Perchero laughed as he pulled a pair of sunglasses from his front shirt pocket and started playing with them, opening and closing them as he looked down at them.

"Melreese? A big shot like you? I'd think you'd be at Riviera with all the high-class golfers."

"Riviera is a private club. That means everyone from the car valet to the golf starter has a record of you being there. That's all potentially subpoenaed information. Melreese is public. No record. Melreese is where I play with the people who also don't like records. No record."

"So our friend in Colombia says you need to drop a small matchbook to us and then if we get all the matches lit, you have some real firewood for us," Ritchie said to Perchero.

Emiliano looked over his shoulder at us and grinned and then turned back to watching the door.

"Perchero, time is money, and right now you're wasting both of ours. Where is the matchbook? We need to light those matches soon," said Ritchie.

Perchero motioned to Emiliano. "*Ve a buscar la bolsa y hagamos esto. Estos chicos son pingas.*"

Something like, "Go get the bag and let's get this done. These guys are dicks."

With that, Emiliano walked out of the bakery.

"I'm intrigued by Mr. Direct Deposit here. Tell me a little bit about yourself. I've been in this business a while and I've never heard of a mysterious gringo golfer who makes the wheels roll."

"This is a favor for a favor. I told you that already. You want to know about me? Seven years ago I was in Desert Storm in Al Busayyah, sitting in a hot fucking tent in front of a computer putting warheads on foreheads. It's even easier when they wear something bright," I said, looking at the departing Emiliano and his burnt orange shirt. "I saw all that cash on pallets in those other tents and said, 'That's the life for me,' and I've been pushing those minted notes ever since."

Still holding his sunglasses and giving his attention to them, with a pucker of his lips, Perchero turned his attention to Ritchie.

"If you can deliver like you say you can, there will be a lot of firewood to be delivered. It's October. Winter will be here soon. There are some very cold people who would be very happy to have that firewood. So, don't fuck this up."

Emiliano was back carrying a dusty brown knapsack with older rusted clasps. He casually dropped it on the floor near Ritchie. Perchero arose from his seat and put on his sunglasses. Both men wordlessly turned and left the bakery.

When they were gone. Ritchie started to pick up the knapsack.

"Don't. I'm serious. Don't you even touch that bag until we talk. Where the hell *were* you, Ritchie? What are you doing here? This is so wacked. No ops plan! I don't even know who you got on the outside. No takeaway. This isn't how we do business, Ritchie. You were late. Late to your own deal, and you left me alone with those two dumbasses. It could've gone real bad real fast, Ritchie. What the hell happened to you, man? You compromised me."

"Ah well, I'm sorry man. I didn't think the parking would be so bad."

"It isn't about parking. I told you this was a bad location and a bad time. I told you that."

"Well, it's where Chuco and them set it. I'm sorry. I should've called you or something and said I'd be late, but I didn't think these jack-offs would have been here on time anyway."

"Let me guess. You got a guy in a blue Alero and another one circling all of God's green earth in a burgundy Buick Century. That's all you brought. Tell me I'm wrong. Go ahead, tell me I didn't peg Abbott and Costello out there."

"Well pretty much, I mean—"

I cut him off right there my anger getting the better of me.

"Fuck you, Ritchie. You got one guy parked two blocks away and another circling because he can't find a space? They stuck out like sore thumbs. Did you just happen, maybe on the odd chance, to catch that counter surveillance in the Mazda Millenia with the Florida tag *RWB420*? Huh? You pull this careless shit with me one more time and you and your SAC can find another way back in the game because from where I see it, you lost your edge and suck at it."

Ritchie clasped his hands on the table and looked down at the weathered knapsack.

"We'll get it together, Cade. I'm serious, we know this run better than everybody else. We're going to take this back to Doral and get it in the system and get churning toward the seven million in a day or so. You'll see. We got this."

I wanted nothing more to do with this situation.

"Send over a count sheet. Tonight! You email or fax a copy of the count sheet *tonight* to our VIN office. I'm serious, Ritchie."

With that I stood up and waited for him to gather the bag off of the floor. We walked out with Ritchie carrying the bag. When I stepped outside, the burgundy Buick Century was idling in the bakery parking lot, having finally found an open parking space. The Mazda was gone and there was no sign of Perchero or Emiliano. I waited a few seconds, long enough to give Ritchie some protection as he threw the knapsack into the trunk of the Buick. He closed the trunk and gave me an appreciative nod of his head. He then sauntered next door to the school where he'd parked his pick-up truck. He and the Buick were down the avenue soon enough. About five car lengths behind them I saw the Blue Alero fall into line with traffic, and then the three of them were gone on their way to Doral.

I just stood there for a second, taking in the afternoon air, and then as traffic eased I walked over to where the Mazda Millenia had been parked. I looked at the now vacant parking space to see if the driver may have dropped a piece of paper or some other intelligence-gathering material. There was nothing there. I looked back at the bakery and tried to see it from the counter surveillance guy's perspective. With all the cars and minivans that had piled into that parking lot, he didn't have much of a view himself. The drop spot was such a disaster that the Customs guys and the counter surveillance guy for Perchero were all challenged with getting a good eye on the place. I felt a little more relaxed and comfortable that most of my own comings and goings would have been obstructed, or fleeting at best. Like I'd told Ritchie on the telephone, I don't need Chuco interfering with my future work with DEA.

I crossed the street and went back behind the bakery to the dual apartment buildings, past the same old women still in front of the open doors of their apartments, talking and gossiping. There were now a few small children running around the parking lot some on plastic ride-along toys and others just playing in small groups. My gamble that the sanitation company wouldn't come to empty the dumpsters paid off and my car was still parked there, dent free and unmolested.

I got in the Z28 and eased out of the weed-cracked concrete parking space and was soon leaving the apartment area. I debated going back to Maria's and downing a few of those Volken White Santorini beers but as much as I wanted them, I thought it might be better if I was closer to my own place. My cell phone rang as I turned south on Southwest 32nd Avenue. It was C.C.

"Hello?"

"Cade, are you busy?"

"No, I just finished something up a few minutes ago. What's up?"

"Well, we found Jamaal Boseman Cooper."

"Who?"

"Jamaal Boseman Cooper, the guy the Pinders called 'Jabo.'"

"Oh yeah, I'm sorry I caught the last name but—"

C.C. cut me off with her next comment.

"I'm with him now. Two in the chest and one in the head."

Chapter Eleven

ER WORDS THUNDERSTRUCK me. There was no avoiding the obvious. Miami had a trained assassin in their midst, and he was taking out young men.

"Where are you?" I asked her.

"We haven't given it an exact location yet but we're on Southwest 13th Avenue in the 800 block."

"I'm on my way. I'm near Coral Gate, I should be there in a few."

With that I hung up the phone, found the first turnaround spot on the avenue, and pulled a very quick and tight turn right in front of the Farmacia Julia. I accelerated past the bakery 16th street was purely residential with older established homes in the Shenandoah neighborhood. The manicured and tree-shaded houses were flying by in a blur. I knew it would be a crapshoot to cross the main thoroughfare near the 4pm hour, but I didn't care. There was a slight gap between a beat-up Impala and one of the Miami Trolleys. Municipal workers are always worried about losing their jobs. Well at least some of them are. I nosed the car in front of the trolley, causing it to stop abruptly. I couldn't hear the driver's profanity, but I'm sure it would rival Major Brunson's. Once I got partially across 17th Avenue, I turned north towards Southwest 8th Street or what is more commonly called, *"Calle Ocho."* Some of the taller buildings in downtown Miami were starting to loom over the encompassing tree line of the street. I slowed near the intersection of 13th Avenue. From SW 12th street north to SW 8th street the median on 13th Avenue is known as "Cuban Memorial Boulevard Park." The median was widened years earlier and along the four block stretch are walking paths in the median that are interspersed with various monuments and statutes. There are tiled walls and curved monuments with all types of homage to a courageous Cuban nation prior to Fidel Castro's rule of the Caribbean island. One of the statutes is a bust of Cuban General Antonio Maceo and is accompanied by a quote from him:

La libertad no se mendiga . Se conquista con el filo del machete.

Freedom is not begged. It is conquered with the edge of the machete.

I was able to get as far north as the 1100 block before the assembled police cars and crime scene tape blocked any further passage. I parked off to the side of the road. I called C.C and she answered on the second ring.

"I'm here in the 1100 block on the south side."

"I'll have someone come get you," she tersely replied and hung up.

Ten minutes later a young, uniformed Miami police officer came towards me from the crime scene. The name tape on his uniform said "Chiu-Montero." He had distinct Latin features with a slight touch of Asian. That clearly explained his last name. He lifted the crime scene tape and we walked wordlessly past multiple police officers and a few crime scene personnel. Countless residents and a few others were interspersed among the working investigators. This was a street of tightly connected homes and a constant stream of visitors. Keeping everyone out wasn't plausible. Many of the residents stayed within the curtilage of their own homes and allowed some of the visitors to stand with them on private property. It was a quick walk straight up through the median past multiple benches, places for reflection, low slung walls, and statutes all dedicated to the plight of a free Cuba and the Cuban exile experience.

As we neared the 800 block I could see for myself just how bad this scene was.

It was my first sighting of Jamaal Boseman Cooper. He was lying on his back in an entanglement at the base of a large Banyan tree. The tree was imposing and very large. Its gnarled roots were sprawling and interlocking. Jamaal Boseman Cooper was definitely inter-locked and intertwined within these large trunk roots. Six officers and detectives stood nearby, and C.C. was just off to the side writing in her binder. She kept looking up from the binder at Jabo's splayed body.

I made a point to not be too invasive. I walked a around the outside of the immediacy of Jabo's lifeless body. A few feet north of his corpse was a white alabaster statue of the Virgin Mary. She was barefoot, swathed in robes and wearing a veil, and she was holding the baby Jesus in her arms. The four-foot-high statue was on a double-pedestal base. At the base of the statue etched into the pedestal was in inscription, written in both English and Spanish.

"To the City of Miami: Motherhood is God's greatest blessing. Caballeros De La Luz 1957."

I looked up from the inscription and past the statue I could see Jabo's right leg draped over one of the largest raised roots of the Banyan tree. The rest of him was obscured by other roots. Automatic flash bulbs were broke through the approaching dusk with quick bright flashes as the crime scene technicians took photographs of the lifeless Jabo. In close proximity to the body was a white plastic bag with the readily identifiable green and yellow logo of the Caribbean chicken fast food franchise, Pollo Tropical. I edged a little closer towards Jabo. I could see more of him at the base of the tree. He was on his back. His legs and arms found final resting spots above and against the large, upraised tree roots. His shirt still covering his torso was a complete dark red pool of blood that nearly covered him from his shoulders to his belt line. His eyes were open and there was a distinctive singular bullet hole in his forehead. A minimal amount of blood oozed from that wound. I was reluctant to even think what the back of his head must look like. It was as if his body couldn't decide which holes to purge his life-sustaining blood from the most. I diverted my attention away from Jabo and took in the demeanor of the attending officers. Usually someone's saying something glib, or smiling about something unrelated. They were all pretty somber and quiet. C.C. closed her binder when saw me came over.

"Thanks for coming by."

I just shrugged as I ran my hand through my hair.

"I don't know. It's not my case, but after our times with the Pinders' I feel we have a little insight that many might not have. So, anything I can do to help. I'm here for you C.C."

She looked back at Jabo then turned to me with a forced smile.

"He was *blasted*, Cade. I mean just out and out blasted. We know the connection between him and Reggie was their job, but aside from that we got a local kid here trying to make ends meet, and another kid recently moved down from Baltimore and that's it. They were basically just kids. Young men in their early twenties."

"Any witnesses? Anybody see anything?"

"Look around. There are people everywhere. If they didn't see it happen they are sure as hell telling everyone that they *did* see it happen now. This time we have plenty of actual witnesses. Many who live on the street and some visiting the memorials here. They've all basically said the same story. Jabo was walking back from *Calle Ocho*, he was carrying the Pollo Tropical bag. Dinner for the night. Witnesses say an individual wearing a gray hoodie approached from the south. They met face to face here on the sidewalk median. Our most credible witness who swears she saw the whole thing, says the hoodie shooter just pulled a semi-automatic from the hoodie's hand warmer and shot Jabo once in the chest. Jabo spun toward the street, his back to the tree. The second shot was also point-blank into his chest, followed with a very quick shot to his forehead. Jabo was shot three times in a matter of a second or two. He was dead before he hit the ground. Our shooter then just casually kept walking north and turned east on *Calle Ocho*."

"Why do you say she's the most credible?"

"She's over there near Officer Chiu-Montero. She's the one with blood splatter on her blouse."

Officer Chiu-Montero and a detective were standing next to a middle-aged Cuban woman, who was visibly upset. She was wrapped in a heat retention blanket that had been provided to her by one of the officers. I knew she'd effectively had her life changed from this incident. Without saying anything to her I walked closer to them and stood off to the side. From where I stood I looked into her eyes—they were red and swollen from crying. I wondered how it was that she found the courage. This woman was probably laying flowers at a memorial and had her life upended. She was probably someone's mother and Jabo was someone's child. Right in front of the statute of the Virgin Mary and Jesus that celebrates motherhood, she witnessed a young man's life end.

C.C. was getting impatient to have the body covered and was insisting that the crime scene technicians hurry along with taking photographs. The technicians sped up their process, and it was only a minute or two more before they finished, and Jabo's body was quickly covered with a tarp. C.C. started asking the officers present to delicately convince the onlookers to move on. She knelt by Jabo's body as best as she could around the cumbersome tree roots. She reached under the tarp to retrieve his wallet, which investigators had earlier pulled from his pocket. They'd laid it adjacent to his hip. She went through his wallet and saw his RFS identification. He also had a driver's license, which permitted him to drive vehicles on the Miami International Airport property. There was pay stub in his wallet from RFS. Jabo was making just a little more than minimum wage; with taxes he was bringing home just a little over 200 bucks a week. A Miami Dade transit card and a worn, tattered Miami Dade library card were also tucked inside. C.C. surmised the library card was something he was using as a secondary form of identification. Recalling her own biracial years growing up, and with Jabo being African American, she was thinking many merchants and retailers must've often asked him for two forms of identification when he made certain types of purchases.

It was hard to tell what color his shirt was due to the saturated blood. It had rough sewn seams, making it look like it was worn inside out. She still noted for her report that it was beige. He was wearing dark blue Dickie pants and blue Nike runners. The crime scene technicians were now photographing the Pollo Tropical bag and its contents: a three piece chicken meal with white rice, black beans, plantains, and a dinner roll. The receipt was in the bag. Jabo paid cash and the receipt was time stamped at 3:35pm. His driver's license showed his address as 900B SW 13th Avenue, Miami.

C.C. looked up from where she crouched and turned her head ever so slightly to see the overgrown bushes across the chain link fence and white wrought iron gate of 900 Southwest 13th Avenue. The house was white with a Spanish tile roof. There were two garbage cans and two recycle cans. Each singular Miami residence was provided with one garbage can and one recycle can from the city. The presence of four cans was a clear indicator to C.C. of an efficiency apartment somewhere on the property.

"Jabo died just a few yards from the address he was calling home." C.C. said. Warring expressions of mourning and anger swept across her face. With only three months experience in homicide she hadn't fully cultivated that hardened persona yet. She momentarily seemed a bit overwhelmed with this young man's lifeless body at her feet and his chicken dinner just inches away.

I walked up to her and put my hand on her shoulder and whispered close to her ear. "Heaven helps the man who fights his fears. We can do this."

"I know. I know," she said. "We got this under control. I was just thinking something. I'm good."

She then went right back into focus mode. She gathered two uniformed officers and had them go to the Pollo Tropical restaurant just around the corner on *Calle Ocho*. "Interview all employees still on shift from 3:35pm. Secure interior and exterior security camera footage. I'll meet you at Pollo Tropical in about a half hour."

A crime scene technician was clumsily trying to put a yellow pop-up evidence marker over the three spent shell casings but the casings were all within the root system of the tree and the triangular wedges wouldn't stay upright. The technician started a different tact and thought to use a can of bright orange spray paint and paint a circle around each shell casing.

C.C. thankfully stopped him before he could start.

She put a hand on his shoulder and said smoothly, "That big orange ring will stay on the tree for months, if not years." She didn't admonish him but was stern in telling him to just catalog the location and forgo the actual marking of the location.

"Sciarotta," C.C. called out, "go to 900 over there and speak with the resident. See if our deceased lived in the efficiency. If so, get signed consent for us to search it. Make sure you have an English and Spanish consent form before you go. Once you get the consent signed, bring it to me—I don't want it getting lost. Then glove up. We may be searching the place."

Detective Joe Sciarotta was noticeably older than both C.C. and myself, and you could see he knew the necessity of case integrity. Although he was probably vastly more experienced in homicide than C.C., he didn't balk or grouse about being told what to do. I heard her mention the 900, and I quietly approached the address, looking at the ground for any signs of evidence the shooter may have left behind. I worked my way from further back thinking as if I was the shooter. If the shooter had been waiting for Jabo, he more than likely knew where he lived, and wanted to assassinate Jabo before he reached the sanctuary of his home.

I walked in the center median of the park down to the Jose Marti Memorial. My second run-in with the famed Cuban patriot today. By my estimation the wall would have been the furthest that the shooter would've stood waiting for Jabo to come walking towards home. The wall has white granite vertical panels that stretch across the center of the median. A large map of Cuba in black onyx is across the granite. Once again my second Cuban map in less than two hours. A new personal best for me. In the same black onyx, just below the Cuban map, is a quote from Jose Marti.

"La patria es agonia y deber..." The homeland is agony and duty...

What was actually more intriguing about the memorial was a plaque with a likeness of Jose Marti carved into it.

"Yo quero, cuando me muerta sin patria . Pero sin amo, tener en mi losa un ramo de flores y una bandera."

"I want, when I die, without a country, but without a master, to have on my tomb a bouquet of flowers—and a flag," I read slowly out loud.

I looked north towards the homicide scene. There were eight separate seating areas that the killer could've sat upon waiting for Jabo. Wooden angular benches, traditional park benches, and concrete sitting benches were interspaced within the very short distance from the Jose Marti Wall to where Jabo was killed. The walkway in the center wasn't straight, so some of the benches clearly would not have been tactically or visually advantageous. By standing in the center of the walkway I gauged which one of the seating areas afforded the killer the best vantage view of Jabo walking up the street. There's also a paved sidewalk that traverses the entire street right in front of the efficiency where Jabo lived.

It didn't make sense.

I couldn't figure out why Jabo would choose to walk in the winding center median park space if he was carrying dinner and possibly anxious to eat. The more I looked at the route the more it didn't seem right to me. There was a low mustard yellow wall surrounding the northern next door neighbor to 900 Southwest 13th Avenue. I looked at the house with the short yellow wall. The address was 852 Southwest 13th Avenue. The wall was purely decorative. It couldn't keep any small child, stray dog, or an accomplished assassin out of the yard. There was an even more fortified wall and fencing at the next door, north at 842 Southwest 13th Avenue. As I drew closer, I was able to see that the killer more than likely waited for Jabo at 852. The killer stood just inside the front yard at the corner fence line between 852 and 842. As Jabo neared his home carrying the bag, the killer stepped over the low wall and encountered Jabo on the sidewalk. The startled and scared Jabo moved towards the center of the street to evade the killer. The killer caught up to him on the edge of the park and with fatal precision, pumped three rounds into Jabo.

I walked back towards Officer Chiu-Montero who was still with the blood-splattered witness. I asked Officer Chiu-Montero to ask the woman in Spanish where she was when she saw the shooting. Officer Chiu-Montero recanted her story to me himself, telling me he'd already spoken to her. He didn't want to ask her to retell her story again to another officer. I listened politely, then I insisted that he ask her if Jabo touched her. With an aggravated twist of his lips, he asked the woman if Jabo did touch her.

She began to sob again. This time harder. She started to babble through her tears in Spanish as she shook her head yes.

Officer Chiu-Montero looked at me and then put both his hands on her shoulders. He told her to calm down and to compose herself. He asked her to explain how Jamaal Boseman Cooper touched her. Through her tears she relayed how she cleaned two houses in the neighborhood and she was in the center median waiting for a taxi to pick her up to go home. Jabo was walking when the gray-hooded shooter approached him on the sidewalk. Jabo darted to the center median but a tree blocked him from crossing it. He started to run forward but ran into her, the witness, and pushed her aside in an effort to protect her. The shooter closed the gap quickly—and that's how she got splattered in blood.

She was practically right beside him when he got murdered.

She was reluctant at first to say that Jabo had pushed her because she felt responsible for his death. She began to cry even more. She thinks if she had not been there, Cooper might have gotten away. I thanked her and Officer Chiu-Montero, then went back and stood on the sidewalk just outside 852 Southwest 13th Avenue. The residence was actually a two-story apartment complex—although the front building number said 852, it explained why the postal code jumped from 852 to 900 next door where Jabo lived. The multiple units inside were all separate addresses. Two lone Bismark palm trees stood in the front yard. Either out of laziness or convenience, the building owner had removed all the grass from the front yard and kept the entire front yard full of white sand. I crouched down to inspect the sand. Right up against the northern fence line in the white sand were multiple disturbed and scuffed footprints. Whoever had been standing there tried their best to obliterate their shoe impressions in the sand. I looked at the top of the low wall and found a small partial footprint with white sand granules within the impression.

I returned to C.C. She was still hovering over Jabo's body.

"You got a minute?"

"I got all the time in the world and not a minute to spare," she said ruefully.

"We can talk in a few then," I said.

"No, I got time. I'm just trying to maintain the lid on this. Already some of these jokers are talking serial killer. They don't realize that by FBI classifications, a serial killer is three or more victims. What we got here is murder and murder conspiracy being carried out by a very well-trained killer. Right now, as far as I'm concerned, anybody who works for Reliable Flight Services is a potential next victim or a potential killer."

Before I could answer her, Detective Sciarotta walked up with the consent-to-search form signed by the landlord. He brusquely butted in.

"When you're ready. Let me know," he said as he handed the form to her and walked away.

She put it in the back of her binder. It seemed that everything went into the back of her binder. This was her method of organization. She looked up at me.

"What do you have?"

I told her my theory about the killer waiting for Jabo to come home. I told her about the multiple places he could've waited within the center median park, but how none of them were ideal because of trees, parked cars, and the obstructed sight lines. Since Jabo lived at 900 Southwest 13th Avenue, that would be his final destination. I mentioned how the next apartment building at 852 had a very small decorative wall around it, but that the house next door had a classic six foot fence. I told her of my belief that the killer stood just inside the yard at 852, using the obscuring heightened fence post and fence line, and waited. The killer watched Jabo come down the sidewalk fresh from Pollo Tropical.

"The killer saw Jabo coming down the sidewalk, stepped on and over the low wall and confronted Jabo. Jabo ran into the street towards the median but was penned in by the Banyan tree and its roots. The witness was standing there too, waiting for a taxi to pick her up. Jabo pushed the woman aside, the killer closed the gap quickly and killed him."

"Cooper pushed the woman?"

"I used Officer Chiu-Montero as a translator and on the second interview she said she cleans houses in the neighborhood and was waiting for a taxi and saw it all. She feels responsible for Jabo's death because she thinks he pushed her to get her out of the way, and that gave the killer the time he needed to get close enough to kill Cooper."

C.C. glanced at the woman still wrapped in the blanket, and called out to Chiu-Montero.

"See if she'll come to the station. Arrange for psych services to meet you there. See if there's someone she can call who will bring her a change of clothes. I want her blouse, pants, everything she's wearing entered into property as evidence."

"Listen C.C., the whole front yard at 852 is white sand. The killer went out of his way to try and disturb his footprints in the sand. I think you need your crime scene people to go see what they can get from it. It looks like a partial sandy footprint is on the wall. Might be the right foot. If it is, he led with his right foot to push over the wall and catch up to Jabo. So we got a right hander here maybe."

"We got more than that. These were in Jabo's pocket," she said.

She opened her hand and inside was a Ziplock bag with odd-shaped screws with unusual, grooved slots in them.

Chapter Twelve

THEY WERE THE same oddly grooved slotted screws that both C.C. and I had found in Reggie Lamar's dresser drawer. There were about fifty of them in the Ziplock.

"You're going to be locked here, for the time being," I said to C.C. "You still have to search Jabo's room and get with your people about witness statements and whatever closed-circuit cameras you might have. Why don't you let me have one of those screws, and I'll go on over to Home Depot and see what I can learn. There's a Home Depot on *Calle Ocho;* by the time I get there and get done, you might be finished here and we can meet."

She reached into the Ziplock bag with her glove still on, and handed me one of the screws. It was shiny and the slots looked like little crooked, unconnected hash grooves in circle slot. Until these two homicides, I had never seen one of these before.

"Keep your phone on. I'll call you when I'm finished," I said.

The medical examiner van was just pulling up and looking for a place to park. I motioned to the driver that I was leaving and he smiled at me, relieved to be able to take my space as I pulled away.

Calle Ocho is one way west to east from where we were, so I backtracked, very similar to the route that I used to arrive at the murder scene. Home Depot was further west, about seventeen blocks away. I maneuvered through the side streets and as I pulled into the large Home Depot parking lot I noticed the Hotel 77 across the street. In the 1950's *Calle Ocho* was known by its original name, The Tamiami Trail. Little mom-and-pop hotels dotted the trail from the western fringe of the Everglades all the way into downtown Miami. The Hotel 77 was definitely one of the last bastions of that motor lodge architecture. Its single-story bungalow style was very popular back then.

I quickly parked and walked into the massive home repair store. I stood there momentarily getting my bearings and then saw an aisle banner that said "Hardware." I made my way to the aisle. One thing I learned years ago was to never wear an orange shirt when shopping in Home Depot. If you ever did, every patron in the place will ask you a ton of questions. I myself, still had my own questions. I saw a middle age man with an orange Home Depot apron around his waist. He clearly worked at Home Depot and was coming towards me.

"Excuse me, sir—"

"*Es no mi sextion,*" he said in a thick Spanish accent and kept on walking without even giving me the simplest of considerations.

I walked up and down the aisle at least six times holding the screw in my hand. I looked at all the diagrams, pictures, and slotted areas of screws to find a match to the one I held.

Nothing even remotely like the screw I was holding in my hand.

Two more Home Depot employees came down the aisle, both just passing by, but one said that they would call "Marcos," who apparently works in hardware, though he was not to be seen anywhere near hardware. Other customers started positioning themselves in the aisle, also awaiting the arrival of Marcos. I spied a young man coming around the corner, wiping his wet hands on his apron. I called out to him as he neared the aisle.

"Marcos?"

It was a gamble, but it worked as the young man looked at me like he was trying to recognize me from somewhere in his past. My calling him out by his name also alerted the other awaiting customers that Marcos had arrived, but it put me first in the "I have a question for you" sweepstakes. I closed the gap between us, holding my hand with the screw in it in front of me.

"I'm looking for this type of screw."

Marcos took the screw and held it up to the overhead lights boring down on all of us. He then held it closer to his eyes and fixed his gaze on the screw.

"We don't carry that type here," he said.

The other customers heard that and it became a free-for-all for his attention. As he handed the screw back to me and his attention was already being diverted by someone else, I was able to get one more question in.

"Have you ever seen one like that before?"

"No," was all he said, as he was led away by a woman hell-bent on getting half inch carpenter screws.

I called C.C. from my car.

"Hello?"

"Hey, I'm here at Home Depot and they don't carry this screw and the guy says he's never seen one like it before either."

"Well, that doesn't help us, now does it? Me and Sciarotta have finished up with Jabo's room. It was like a super bare efficiency one room thing with a small bathroom. No kitchen or anything. There really wasn't anything in there, and crime scene took possession of the Pollo Tropical camera footage. The M.E. loaded up Jabo about ten minutes ago. We're finishing up here."

"I'm still at Home Depot. You eat anything? Are you hungry?"

"I'm starved," she said with a weariness in her voice.

"There's a good Cuban place right near you. Do you want to meet me there?"

"Yeah. What's it called and where is it?"

"It's just west of you on *Calle Ocho* on the southside. It's called *El Exquisito,* right next to the old Tower Theater. I'm leaving now. I'll meet you there."

I was fortunate to find a parking space nearby the restaurant. I walked right past their own *ventanita* with its big yellow sign announcing "Cuban Coffee 75 cents." I went into the little Cuban café. C.C was sitting at a table midway down the left side of the narrow restaurant. The restaurant was a din of noise as sound bounced off of the tiled floor and the white ceramic tile which ran halfway up the wall. At the rear of the restaurant is a little cut-through doorway that leads to a bigger room in the back with canary yellow walls. Many don't know the extra room exists. I suggested we move ourselves back there to talk.

Once reseated in the back room, it was quieter, and we could talk. We sat there looking at the menu. I can't speak for her, but I was barely reading it. It was just a prop for me to hold while I collected myself, absorbing all the events of the day that had started in Major Brunson's office, to a complete shit show with U.S. Customs, and now another vicious execution of a young man. The waitress was very kind and even more patient as we both said we needed a minute before ordering. Eventually, I ordered the Monday special which was *Pollo Asado, Arroz, Potaje y Maduros* (Garlic Roasted Chicken, White Rice, Beans, and Sweet Plantains.) C.C. had no idea what I ordered and just said, "I'll have the same please." We both asked for two *café con leches,* although I knew I'd probably want another one as soon as I finished the first. The waitress collected the menus and we both just sat there, a little dazed and quiet. I started the conversation first.

"One of my guys will be meeting with the task force steering committee on Wednesday morning. He's going to ask about Zeus. If no one has any information, he'll offer as much information as he can to try and get them to do some heavy lifting on looking for Zeus."

"No one in Miami S.I.S. has ever heard of him. I spoke to Sergeant Brookings, and he told me that they haven't heard of him either."

"I know Brookings. He's a good man. So, let's think about what we do know about Zeus," I said.

C.C. snickered. "What do we know? The guy's a fucking phantom. He has no fear about killing in daylight and the proximity of any witness or potential innocent victim doesn't sway him. At all!" she said.

I nodded in agreement and let her continue.

"He knows the comings and goings of his victims. He knows their home base. He seems to not have any known transportation. He wears the same, or at the very least, an identical gray hoodie. Ballistics aren't back yet but I guarantee it's a Walther P-88 again. Same as Reggie."

"Have you learned anything more about the Walther P-88 since Friday?" I asked her.

She pulled out her binder and flipped a few pages until she found the section she was looking for.

"I spoke to our range master and our head firearms instructor. They both said basically the same thing—Walther tried to make the P-88 more suitable for law enforcement and the military in Europe. Specifically, Germany. It has a metal amalgamation called duralumin which they put in the grip to make it lighter. It has no safety mechanism, a modified Browning system and no traditional swing bolt lock. This gives it a better shot precision, making it ideal for an assassin. The problem with the gun is it can't hold up to certain pressures. It failed drop tests, the rear sights kept falling off, and after a lot of rounds are fired through it, the barrel can crack. It was in production for a short time, and then they tried to retool it as a compact version."

I nodded again at her due diligence. I was too tired to say much more. The moment hung between us and then I finally spoke up.

"Let's get back to Zeus. Aside from what you pointed out. If he works, he must be on the same schedule that both Reggie and Jabo had. I actually doubt he works. This guy is a machine. He has no fear. Let's not forget he was prepared to take on a uniformed Miami police officer, too. He'd probably have drilled right through your cleaning lady witness if he needed to. I'm glad he didn't. Whether due to Jabo's actions, or out of benevolence, but she was close enough to get blow back spray on her. She was closer to Jabo than I am to you right now.

You get it? If it is this Zeus guy, he covers his tracks literally, but has no fear of being identified. The hoodie's like a cloaking shroud for him. We're talking ice water in his veins. He is a cold stone killer."

The waitress put down two piping hot *café con leches* in front of us. It tasted very sweet and felt magnificent going down. I think the events of the past few days infused me with a sense of gratitude even for what many would consider the ordinary and mundane. I wondered if C.C. was experiencing the same feelings. She'd only been in homicide three months and now she was facing an elusive, phantom-like trained assassin. Even hardline experienced homicide investigators would be mulling this over twenty-four hours a day, seven days a week. These type of cases stay with you throughout your career. Whether you solve them or whether you don't. Some would say these are benchmark, but when you're tasked with cases like this, it's like trying to hold a venomous snake by the tail. You know might not be doing it right, but it's all you can grab at the moment. C.C. was in deep and she was going to need all the help she could get.

"Who on your team can you trust the most?" I asked her.

The question caught her by surprise. I took another chest-warming swill of the *café con leche* and was already looking to order another one, even though the one in front of me was only a third consumed. I waited for her to answer. I counted beats in my head to see how long it would take her to answer. On the fourth beat she cleared her throat a little.

"When you say 'trust,' what do you mean? I trust them all."

"No. I mean who's going to have you stay on the case until they run to your captain and say 'she's too new,' or, 'she can't handle a case this size?' Who's going to try and take this case from you?"

"Oh. I really don't know them at all too well. I was brought up when one of them went on light duty with an alleged back injury. At first they thought I would be temporary but then Insurance and Safety put surveillance on the guy and they have him on camera fixing his roof and going up and down ladders and stuff. He was removed from homicide, most likely on his way to being terminated.

I was already there so they said just keep her. So, I'm de facto by default, and by design the FNG."

"The FNG?"

"The fucking new girl."

I winced at the moniker

"So, a young black male gets gunned down on a rainy Friday night and you're at the office and no one wants to go out in the rain and deal with another kid killed in the hood?" I asked her.

"Exactly. That's why I hadn't even left the station yet when I got word you were chasing the train. When the shooter shot up Dominguez's car, it took on a whole other dimension, but they had already assigned it to me. It wouldn't have been politically correct to take it from the FNG."

"What if it was a fucking new *guy* instead of a fucking new girl?"

"They may have stepped in earlier. Now, with two kids dead and one of our units getting its front windshield replaced at the motor pool, they're probably seriously second-guessing themselves for assigning this case to me."

"Well, what would any of them have done differently? I mean, you're covering all the bases here. Ballistics, crime scene techniques, interviewing people, getting consent searches, separating witnesses, chain of custody. From where I sit, I think you're doing pretty good, but I'm going to ask you again: Who is on team C.C.? And who is going to get in your way?"

"Joe Sciarotta. He's near retirement and has a ton of experience, but so far he's done everything I've asked of him. He can be a little jaded and abrupt, he isn't the most pleasant person to be around sometimes—but then again, twenty years of scrubbing blood out from under your fingernails, and sticking measuring rods into bullet holes in people will make you a little unsocial."

"Okay. So, that's one for team C.C. Who else?"

"D.P. Hughes. He's dependable and has been pretty helpful so far.

He gave me a tour of the crime lab, introduced me to the crime scene techs. So, I'd say him."

"What does the D.P. stand for?"

She just stared at me like I had a third eye, and I realized it was a question she probably hadn't asked herself and it had never posed to her before.

The waitress put down two steaming plates of very aromatic garlic chicken with rice and beans spilling over the side of the plate. I asked for another *café con leche*; C.C. declined a second cup.

I let the question about D.P Hughes initials go.

"So that's two," I said between mouthfuls. "Anybody against you?"

She looked up from her plate and contemplated the question for a moment.

"I'd stop short of saying he's *against me*, but one of the sergeants. He seems…less inclined…to me being there. I think it's a gender thing. Women can't do homicide kind of thing. He assigned me a real masculine dark wood desk way in the back of the squad room behind a pillar. He asked me what I was going to do to feminize the desk and I told him I was going to put a 5'6" woman behind it. He didn't like that. His name is Tovar. Sergeant Roberto Tovar. I don't know if it's because I'm new or maybe it's a woman thing, but he can't be comfortable telling his dirty jokes and talking his misogynistic trash. I just think he doesn't care for me."

"What do you know about him?"

"I know he's a sergeant and he could get me removed faster than just a regular detective who might have heartburn with me. He does the evaluations and runs the squad. I think he's been married and divorced , like, twice. He used to be on the Robbery Interdiction Squad and they dealt with some pretty hardcore people then. A lot of bag 'em and tag 'em kind of stuff. He's tough, knows how to handle himself. He doesn't talk to me very much, if at all. I know he'd prefer me to be out of the squad so they could all quit walking on eggshells and not have to worry about offending the FNG. That's what they call me you know, right to my face. The FNG."

"Did that whole FNG thing start with Tovar?"

"Absolutely. He's the big leader in the group. Gets pretty much whatever he wants and he's not someone you'd want to cross. He was Special Forces or something in Desert Storm. I'm not sure how long he has been with us. Were you ever in the military, Cade?"

"Me? No. I actually had to make something up on the fly today, so I told some doper earlier that I'd served in Desert Storm just to get him to back down a little. But I've never been in the military."

"Tovar was definitely there, and I wouldn't be surprised if he's killed people before. I mean in war and all. He just has this iciness about him. I heard him talking to one of the guys about the best way to slit a throat. I mean, who talks about shit like that?"

My thoughts drifted quickly to what we know about Zeus.

"Let's talk about Zeus. You got a pen?" I asked her.

She once again looked at me as though I was a little touched. She had her binder with her always and she feigned consternation as she pulled out two pens.

"Black or blue?"

"It doesn't matter."

She found a clean sheet in her binder and wrote across the top of it, "Zeus Profile."

We started adding the characteristics of Zeus. For the next ten minutes, which for me was also over a second steaming cup of *café con leche,* we catalogued what we'd gathered about Zeus. We started based on the characteristics of the crime scenes. The profile was pretty extensive. It bordered on more emotional characteristics than actual physical characteristics. Descriptive terms like calculated, cunning, patient, efficient, trained, experienced, cold, determined, fearless, planner, and a few other terms went into the profile.

She then created a second page titled, "Victim Profiles." Both victims shared many similar traits. Age, gender, ethnicity, career, economic standing, living conditions, time of death, outside locations among them.

We then created a third profile. She titled it, "Potential Victims Profile," and in it we put down criteria related to the witness that saw Cooper get murdered today, as well what we could about Officer Alvaro Dominguez.

Both could've easily been killed by Zeus. He chose to let them live. Zeus actually went out of his way to spare killing Dominguez.

Once we'd stopped brainstorming on the profiles, she and I looked them over. It was very evident that Zeus had advantages on both victims and knew their routines and locations well. He'd definitely been studying them each for a while. He used the gleaned knowledge to make killing each young man as easy as possible. Zeus also had the advantage on the witness. With Dominguez he showed mercy in not killing him. C.C. looked at the notes and ran off a summarization.

"So, we have this very cold killer who isn't afraid to wear the same clothing to two different homicides, yet makes an effort to try and cover his footprints. He kills quickly and on the move. He's a skilled shooter. Two in the chest first and a third shot to the head. Mozambique is what you called it, right Cade? Quick. Deadly quick. No fingerprints on the spent cartridges and he's using a gun that has issues but is ideal for assassinations. He doesn't run—he walks. He walks right up on his victims. Then just as cool as can be, he walks away. He doesn't worry about cameras, he spares witnesses, and he went out of his way to not kill a cop in uniform. Both victims were in possession of Ziplock baggies with some sort of foreign screw that even Home Depot doesn't carry. Both victims were African American, and whether living with relatives or on their own, they both basically lived in single rooms. Both victims worked for the same aviation company. Both victims knew each other. We have no proof of Reggie ever visiting Jabo, but we know Jabo had visited Reggie. There's a good chance that Zeus may have military or police training."

"He could've killed Dominguez. But he didn't," I said, looking at her.

She slumped in her chair and then slowly mouthed the word, "Tovar."

Chapter Thirteen

And I'm depending on time, babe
To get you out of my mind
I guess it's one of those things

~ Runaway Trains by Tom Petty

"TOVAR?" I REPEATED back at her.

C.C. shrugged and looked down at her dirty plate.

"I don't know. I mean, Zeus could be anybody who has military or police training. It's just that by not killing Dominguez, it makes me think of the whole Thin Blue Line code of honor thing."

"I have a suggestion. We've got to start with someone somewhere. But it doesn't have to be you that does the first digging. It isn't too cool to be looking at your own people and if it ever gets out you are? You're toast. Let *me* look into Tovar. Let me see what I can find. Outside agency kind of thing. If anybody ever finds out, I'll play it off as we needed someone on our DEA squad. In fact, the less you know the better. Let's not mention it again. Okay?"

C.C. gave me one quick nod and then started looking around for the waitress.

"I got this. Why don't you go ahead and get going, get some rest. What are your plans tomorrow?"

C.C. stood up and gathered her notebook and bag.

"Thank you, and thank you for more than just dinner. Tomorrow? I'm gonna try to talk with some people at RFS at the airport."

"If I could make a suggestion, why not check with the people who contracted RFS? See if there are any other issues or concerns. How about a meeting with someone at the Miami Airport Authority?"

"Good idea. If I can get a meeting, do you want in?"

My initial instincts were to scream absolutely not. Then in the back of my mind I could hear Godfrey Pinder's voice.

"For us. Do it for us. Jump the curb on this one for us. Please."

"Yeah, give me a call. Go on home now—it's been a long day for you. Get some rest."

With a half-smile, she then walked out of the back room of the restaurant and was gone. I paid the bill and left. When I got in the car, I called my police dispatch from my cell phone. As luck would have it, I got Jeanie Rae again.

"Coral Gables Police and Fire, Operator J.R. Richards, how can I direct your call?"

"Jeanie Rae, this is Cade Taylor again."

"Cade, please tell me you're not doing something crazy again."

"No, I'm just sitting here Jeanie Rae, I promise. Can I have teletype please?'

She transferred me to the section of dispatch that handles the deciphering of information related to people and vehicles. Another operator answered the teletype line and I asked her to check the license number *RWB420* in the system. After a few minutes she asked me to repeat the number. I repeated the sequence of the license plate affixed to the Mazda Millenia from the bakery.

"Romeo, Whiskey, Bravo, Four, Two, Zero."

"I thought that was what you said, but I wanted to be sure. RWB420 not on file."

"No record of it all?"

"Sorry Cade, but as far as the system can see, that license tag doesn't exist."

I thanked her and hung up. The license plate obviously was real and did exist, but its owner, either through bribery or connections at the DMV, was able to keep ownership and even existence of the license tag out of the Florida system.

The Coral Gables Police Station was not exactly on my way home, nor was it too far out of the way. I decided to go by the station on the way home and see if Ritchie did fax or email the count sheet. The count sheet was going to be a decent indicator of what kind of credibility Perchero and Emiliano have. From what I'd seen earlier today at the bakery, my hopes weren't too high that they would be able to deliver seven million dollars in drug money in a few days. The ride back was uneventful from a driving perspective. My mind kept drifting to the image of Jabo sprawled across the Banyan roots and how close that witness came to having her own life snuffed out today. The exposure to violence this occupation subjects you to can be a little overwhelming sometimes. To reflect too much can be very bad for the psyche; to not reflect at all, even worse.

It had been a full day already, and here I was adding to the clock even more.

I decided to take Ponce de Leon Boulevard south from the trail and tried to decompress as I drove. I drove past the illuminated fountains near the Hotel ChateauBleu. The water cascaded down their marble sides and ornate basins. A few traffic lights later, I was pulling into the police station. I went up the hairbrained designed ramps and narrowly missed a fireman walking using the ramps as a fitness course. He was in his shorts and t-shirt and carried a radio in his hand, just in case the big fire of the decade should break out. He could respond looking like a middle schooler in P.E. class. I thought it must be nice to be in a job where the work summons you, instead of you seeking the work. When I had graduated the police academy I had a field training officer, who, upon my coming out of the police academy, had a few rules. The first rule was "no crime before coffee." The second rule was find a shady tree to park under and read the

Miami Herald. His famous quote was, "Fireman don't look for fires. I don't look for crime."

I used my credentials to enter the station building. I card-swiped my way into the VIN office and turned on the light. I sat at Ileana's desk. I never understood the whole conglomeration of family pictures on a work desk, but here I sat, surrounded by Ileana's own Kodak moments. The fax machine was behind her desk and tucked under a shelf that had a hefty volume of *Robert's Rules of Order: Newly Revised.* I was at a complete loss as to why someone challenged with the most rudimentary aspects of the English language would have that type of book behind her desk. There was a sheet of paper on the floor and one partially falling out of the fax machine. The paper on the floor was the standard government cover sheet. It probably spit out as soon as the wheels of the fax machine started spinning. Why people even used cover sheets was beyond me, but yet here it was. I crumbled the cover sheet up and threw it in the dented standard-issued army green garbage can—a former victim of Major Brunson's temper. I think his supply of undented cans was quickly diminishing. It seemed like every can on the third floor has a dent in it. Some have two. The sheet that was in the fax machine was the one I was looking for.

The count sheet.

The count sheet was going to tell me who was present when the currency was counted. It also denoted the day and time it was counted, more importantly, it would tell me the denomination of the bills and the exact total. According to the count sheet, S.A. Richard Tavino supervised the count, and he had S.A. Pedro Acevedo, and S.A. Johnny Slomianski with him. It took the three customs agents fifty-two minutes to count the money dropped to us by Perchero. There were some initials at the very bottom of the page that were circled. The initials were D.S. I assumed they were SAC Dale Sorenson's initials. If they were, then he obviously signed off on the authenticity of this count sheet.

Immediately there were some issues with the count sheet.

The final amount counted by the U.S. Customs Agency was

$145,500. That meant there was $4,500 missing from the reported dropped amount by Perchero. That $4,500 equates to a 3% loss.

I could almost assuredly guess that Perchero carved out a 3% commission for himself, when in fact it was a complete package he was supposed to be sending down. No commission. That was something Ritchie would have to take up with Chuco, because if Perchero decides to carve 3% out of the seven million there'd be a $210,000 shortage.

In looking more closely at the count sheet I was beginning to have my doubts these jokers actually had seven million to be moved. The denominations on the count sheet told a different story than what you would expect from a criminal operation that could control and move seven million dollars. I read down the list of denominations:

- 6,800 ten dollar bills
- 3,000 twenty dollar bills,
- 2,800 five dollar bills,
- 3,500 single bills,

This was not good for many reasons. The most glaring issue was the shortage. The cartel expects exact amounts to be sent down south to Colombia. They don't contract with me or my undercover agents at the DEA to move money for them and then have the amount we are contracted for be short. Being short on your contract in the money laundering world either smells of theft or ineptitude. Either one will cancel you out of the business or even out of your eternal life. The other issue with the count was the actual denominations of the bills. When an experienced money launderer sees such crappy bills it is a huge indicator of what we call "money on the downside." I can confidentially assume the bills in the count were torn, ripped, crumbled, and dingy. All over South Florida and the Caribbean bills circulate and recirculate again—it's street money. Hands—as in lots of hands—touch those bills. From Haitian tire sellers in a flea market in Port Au Prince, on up to a bellman at a posh South Beach hotel. The small bills mingle and get pushed into hands, wallets, stripper G-strings, and school cafeteria cash registers. It's common money. It isn't refined. It's symbiotic of street drug sales. Small bills borrowed, begged, conned and stolen to help a street user keep their drug habit going. It's shit money. Money on the downside of the economic scale.

Perchero and the human shadow he brought with him were bit players in a much bigger theatrical production. They weren't even worthy of a credit at the end of the movie. These clowns couldn't move seven million dollars in two to three days from now. No how. No way. Ritchie and SAC Sorenson were being duped by a short con man in Bucaramanga.

I took the count sheet and made a copy of it, sticking both in my assigned mailbox on the shelf.

I could use a drink. It just one of those things. The events of the past days weighing on me. Gina and I would have been celebrating our wedding anniversary today. Instead, I was rubbing short shoulders with Colombian jackasses and standing over another young man killed way too early in life.

Once out of the building, I opened my trunk and checked my go bag. It still had a few changes of clothes in it. I grabbed my Hartford Whalers baseball hat and put it on, tucking it low over my brow, and pushed my hair up behind my ears under the hat. I walked down the parking ramps with my bag. The fireman would have long since finished his fitness regime—I wouldn't be seeing him. I cut across the street using the westside back alleys of Ponce de Leon, rather than using the street itself. I kept walking north, past one stinking restaurant dumpster after another. Many of the highly coveted restaurants in Coral Gables had their rear kitchen doors wide open, or at least were open with a screen door. Each one resembled the next one, and the next one after that one, with steam, noise, voices in different languages, chefs on break in the alley smoking cigarettes, and indiscernible bustle spilling out into the alley as I passed. When I got to Miracle Mile I crossed the crosswalk near the Starbucks and walked north past Houston's Steak House, where many of their clientele were waiting outside the wood and glass doors for a table. I weaved through them, my head down and bag tucked over my shoulder. They'd have no idea I was a cop. To many of them I'd look like a guy on a bender.

Premature thinkers, they were.

Three blocks up on Ponce de Leon I crossed over to eastside of the street on the corner of Alcazar and Ponce de Leon. On that corner there's a triangular three-story building. On the top of this triangular building is a four-sided square turret with windows that overlook the boulevard. From the turret looking west towards Lejeune Road, the large red lighted bat from the Bacardi building can be seen. Green creeping fig shrouds the triangular building in thick vines, its tendrils like tree branches. The creeping fig knows no boundaries; even the Spanish tile roof has the vine affixed to it. Tall arched windows on the ground floor are protected by black awnings like massive bat wings. The same blistering sunset rays that bake the police station every afternoon stand no chance with these awnings. The interior is always cool. The second and third floors have French-inspired wooden framed casement windows. The name of the building is barely legible due to the green vines.

Hotel Place St. Michel.

I went in through the Alcazar Street side entrance. The heavy doors have a beautiful arched transom window above them, with three teardrop glass inlays in the transom. The transom window is designed to flow well with the arched ceiling. Meticulously maintained marble floors gleamed against the dark cherry wood doors and frames on each side of the hallway. The arched ceilinged hallway lead to a reception area and the hotel lobby. The lobby has a staircase that's wide at the bottom but tapers as it leads upstairs. The elevators are just around the corner from the stairs and are framed in multiple French Moroccan tiles. Just off the stairs is a front desk, where I found a very attractive attendant.

"Welcome to Hotel Place St. Michel."

I looked around the French-inspired lobby and then at her name tag.

"Hello Monica. I just got in and was wondering if you had any vacancies tonight?"

"A one-night stay? Let me see the computer here."

She punched a few keys, then asked if I had a car and if I would need parking as well. I told her no and she confirmed that they did have vacancies. I tried to negotiate a rate as a walk-in, but she was pretty firm on the nightly rate. So, 144 dollars later I was checked into room 202.

The hotel was originally called the Hotel Seville in 1926, but had been completely renovated and reformed as the Hotel Place St. Michel in the early 1990s. Monica handed me an actual key for the room. It was nostalgic having an actual key rather than a card reader or fancy electronic digital lock. I chose to take the stairs, since the elevator entailed using an actual elevator operator to man the vintage lift. I turned the key in the room, threw my go bag on the desk and then turned and walked right back out. I went downstairs and headed straight to the bar.

The place was nearly empty except for a couple in the corner. She had a glass of white wine in front of her and he had a pilsner glass of beer in front of him. He was looking at a tourist brochure. I sat at the end of the bar. If a crowd came in, I didn't want to be penned in on either side. I also didn't want to feel obligated to give up my middle seat to help accommodate a mixed party of people. I was looking for solitude and quiet. The bartender came over; his name tag said, "Arturo."

"Hello, Arturo. I'll have a Jameson, neat please."

"Right away, sir," he said in a very clipped accent.

I looked at the young couple in the corner still trying to figure out where they were and what was the difference between Alhambra Circle, Alhambra Court, Alhambra Plaza, and South Alhambra Circle. George Merrick, the founder of Coral Gables, sure had a twisted sense of humor naming the streets of the city after nearly unpronounceable Spanish towns and regions. He took his twist-iness further, deciding that street signs were undesirable. Instead, he chartered that all street markings be corner "curbstones" no higher than two feet and two feet long. Outside of the business district, each corner has only these street level markers. God forbid the grass grows high or someone parks in front of one of them.

The Jameson was set in front of me on an embossed napkin. I mentioned to Arturo that if the couple in the corner needs help with directions to let me know.

"You are familiar with the city, beautiful?" he asked me.

"Yeah. When I was a kid I resurfaced tennis courts all over here. Now I own a pool liner company, so I've spent a lot of time in Coral Gables ."

"Excellent. I've only been here two months. All I know is that to get to work I have to turn at the Burger King on Lejeune Road."

I turned my attention away from the confused love in the corner and started thinking about my own confusion about love. I lifted the shot of Jameson and said a very soft toast to a dissolved marriage on its anniversary that had ended officially a few months ago, but for all intents and purposes was over before I knew it. The pain of the divorce was like an unhealing laceration. Just a little salt in the wrong place or an errant scratch and you could find yourself back onto a pretty bad infection. That's where I saw myself at the moment.

The sip of Jameson was mellow and smooth with a spicy, woody, vanilla undertone.

I'd been afflicted with the "curse of the provider;" I'd been too busy working and being pulled away by my cases to see that Gina was learning all too well how to live without me. Eventually, she not only learned to live without me, but was happy to be living without me. I became a physical reminder each time I walked through the door of the life she didn't want. As I was going through the gut-wrenching divorce and trying to keep a lid on my percolating unhappiness, I tried to maintain a focus on my cases. I found myself totally adrift on the inside all the while projecting a hardened exterior. I was foolish to think that the department would not find out I was in a ruinous marriage. I was equally foolish to think that I could maintain a sense of secrecy about it all. Her lawyers started filing one motion after another. Many of them were sent to the police station. Her scheister lawyers feigned shock and ignorance, saying that the station address was in the court system as my address, when they in they knew my residential address because it was our marital home. We lived there for years as husband and wife. It was all such bullshit.

I continued sipping the Jameson quietly by myself, ruminating the deplorable state my life had become. I was driving a car I didn't own. I was living in a condo I didn't own. I was untethered in the world. There was no bonding agent in my life. No sticking point. Nothing was holding me in place. I had hardened myself to the world. I reasoned that if I was the flame then I can't be burned. Six months ago I'd started a relationship with someone but she'd already committed to taking a job not only out of the area, but out of the country. Long distance relationships just aren't feasible in a real-life adult world. I'd be in my bed and she'd be in hers, and we'd both know that one of us was in the wrong place. The rules of long distance relationships should be the same as those posted at public pools: walk, don't run. And no diving in headfirst, even if the water looks deep enough. If I dove too early at this point in my life, I'd crack my skull beyond repair. I was thinking even wading in the water was too much for me. I had to taper it back once she moved.

So, for the past few months I'd been going it solo, just trying to stay in the groove with work. After the little clown convention today with Ritchie, I was beginning to wonder if maybe the VIN lifestyle had run its course for me. I was doing deals with agents and agencies that I thought understood the necessity for operational safeguards, yet they cut corners, putting themselves, innocent people, and yes, most notably me, at risk.

The smoothness of the Irish whiskey was burnishing my hard edges. I motioned to Arturo for another.

As he dutifully poured me another, he cautiously asked me if I'd parked my car on the Alcazar side of the building. Arturo was good. It was a very subtle way of finding out if I was a potential drunk driver without offending the clientele.

"No tengo llaves." I don't have keys, I said.

"¿Tu hablas español?" You speak Spanish? he asked me.

I shrugged in a half-assed yes, maybe no, possibly maybe, sort of way.

The second Jameson was easy and straightforward. It tasted even better than the first one. My mind kept lingered on the thought that maybe after eight years in VIN, it was time to put this lifestyle away. There'd just been too much of a compilation of losses versus wins—and each loss was resonating more and more. I thought about the young detective that Brunson had admonished this morning for writing a traffic citation. Maybe driving a "career-ending white, stuck-in-patrol blue" car wasn't such a bad idea. You handle your calls and you go home. I'd gain more control of my life when the job's over. The distrust, betrayal, and subterfuge winds down dramatically.

I could tell people who I really am, not that I'm Cade Daniels, pool liner company owner.

People could get to know who you really are—who I really was—and I wouldn't have to always keep reminding myself who knew exactly what about me.

I was closing in on a decade of undercover work in Miami, Florida. The fact that I'd survived this long was either a testament to extreme luck, or just enough luck to get by. People who escape a burning airplane crash, or an F5 tornado talk about "extreme luck."

What if it isn't extreme? What if it's just enough luck to get you through? Either way, sooner or later I'd be looking at diminishing returns. You can only roll the dice for so long before the dots conspire against you.

In many ways this whole VIN lifestyle was a daily, if not hourly gamble. Playing the odds on successfully making a case, all the while hoping a trigger-happy Colombian doper doesn't decide to make you another statistic.

I had seniority in the department. I could choose my shift and days off. Commit to appointments and be where I say I'll be, and not be pulled away all over South Florida, New York City and Los

Angeles on a moment's notice. But losing those "perks," I could live a more normal lifestyle—and in doing so, maybe have a normal relationship in my life.

I was deeply somewhere in my mind when I broke from my Jameson-enhanced fugue. I noticed the guy with the brochure map standing near me, talking to me.

"Excuse me. I'm sorry to bother you, but the bartender said you know the area."

I looked at him, a little perplexed for a second, then replied, "Oh yeah. Sorry. I was thinking about something. What do you need?"

"My wife and I want to go to the Biltmore but the map is… confusing. It looks like I have to go to Desoto Circle or something."

"Yeah, Desoto Circle off of Biltmore Court, but it's easier if you aren't from here to just go south on Lejeune road and turn right on Anastasia Avenue. Stay on Anastasia until you run into it."

"Thank you so much. We just got into town and this is so different and new to us."

"Where are you from?"

"Athens, Georgia. I'm an ER Physician and my wife is a nurse practitioner."

"Let me ask you something, Doc. You ever get tired of all the uncertainty and surprises that come through the ER door every day? I mean, would you rather have the stability of being a family doctor with less stress?"

I think it was more question than he was anticipating. At that moment he may have actually secretly wished he hadn't spoken to me. He gave it a brief mulling-over. "I do it because I'm good at it," he said. "Everyone starts at the family doctor level of skill and knowledge, but the ER is where I'm better suited because my abilities and experience is a furtherance of the family doctor's level. I do it because many think they *can* do it, but realize it's a specialization—not just in knowledge, but in emotional absorption. I can absorb it all pretty well."

Emotional absorption. I hadn't thought of it in that context before. Maybe I was better suited for VIN because I had emotional absorption capacity. His words made sense to me in an odd way.

"Well, I hope you both enjoy your time in Miami. When you get to the Biltmore, go to the Biltmore Bar. It's adjacent to Palme d'Or, off the lower lobby. Look for a bartender named Deanna. Tell her Cade sent you."

He thanked me and then he and his wife quickly left the bar and went on to find more lofty pursuits at the Biltmore Hotel, leaving just Arturo and I in the bar. He politely refilled my shot glass with another pour of Jameson. My third. I loved the feel of the little glass in my hand and the sip of it was as wondrous as the prior two. I was achieving my goal of getting a decent buzz on. My plan was to stay in the city tonight; not worrying about driving, and traffic. I could look forward to waking up later than normal. It was all worth giving sweet looking Monica $144.

I thought about what the out-of-town doctor had said. I began to realize that with all the pitfalls of being VIN in Miami, I'd cultivated a certain emotional coat of arms. I began to rationalize that the concepts of a "relationship," and normal hours and days off were just an illusion. People are challenged regardless of all the blessings or misfortunes that come their way. We all just have to navigate our own way through the morass and carve out the life we want with the tools and people we have in our lives. Airline pilots get called away from their families. Even plumbers get called away for extreme situations. It's just the way of the world. There is no normal, and whatever you think is normal is just something you don't fully know.

"I do it because many think they can *do it but realize it's a specialization—not just in knowledge, but in emotional absorption. I can absorb it all pretty well."*

I'd worn a uniform and had driven a "career-ending-white, stuck-in-patrol blue" car, but I too had a skill set and knowledge gleaned from my time in VIN that most did not have. My ability to absorb the emotional aspects of VIN had already been tested and retested plenty of times. I needed to get my head back in the game.

Archie Manning played for the New Orleans Saints. He ran for his life every Sunday in Tulane Stadium. He had no real receivers and a crappy offensive line, but he hung in there every Sunday. I needed to hang in there. I needed to hang in there, especially now. We had no lieutenant, I was being pulled from the DEA task force to assist U.S. Customs, and now C.C. was up against a trained assassin. Now was not the time to take my ball and go home.

Gina was gone. I'd told myself that over a hundred times. She would not be coming back. Not now. Not ever. I needed to face facts. I needed to move on. *Completely* move on. In the dark confines of this isolated and unpopulated bar I pored over some of the events in my life lately: Godfrey Pinder asked for my help, C.C. needed help, and Brunson was getting pressed by his familial obligations. I'd find a way to get around Ritchie's corner-cutting ways and make it work, and it all started because I went to back up a lousy cop who called me a pussy.

After downing the third and final shot of Jameson, I got up and left a fifty on the bar, which was more than enough to cover the drinks and still leave Arturo a hefty tip. I trudged up to room 202.

It was time to get busy.

Chapter Fourteen

I SLEPT RESTFULLY IN the hotel. I woke up knowing it was a wise choice to stay in the hotel for the night. The condo was so far away from the city, and I wanted to have a few drinks last night. It was a good, common sense thing to do, and I felt more at ease knowing there would be no heavy commute. The shower felt great—I stayed in the hot water as long as I possibly could. Coming out of the shower, I checked my cell phone, and there were no calls. That was a very good sign. I retrieved some clothes and underwear from the go bag and threw my clothes from yesterday in, along with the Hartford Whalers hat, then got dressed rather quickly. I called The Gables Juice Bar from my cell phone and placed a take-out order for a colada of Cuban coffee, and a PMS smoothie for Ileana. The PMS did not stand for what many might think. It actually stood for Pineapple, Mango and Strawberries. I ordered a mixed veggie juice for Big G, and an egg white, turkey and cheese English muffin for myself. They said the order would be ready in twenty minutes. Regardless of what you order or where you order in Miami it's always "twenty minutes."

Grabbing the old-fashioned room key, I headed down stairs. I left the key at the front desk and stepped out into the amassing traffic on Ponce de Leon Boulevard. The vehicle traffic was moving nicely until a block north. All the Pilates moms, and tennis lesson moms dropping their kids off at Coral Gables Elementary School were why it started to back up. Nothing is more dangerous in South Florida than the *"Latinasportautilius."* These primarily Latin mothers in their oversized dark SUVs are fierce in the morning as they shove little Luca, Jose Manuel, or Carolina out of the car and speed off to their yoga or pottery class. I turned south and walked to Miracle Mile, then cut across Ponce de Leon at the Starbucks. I went back down the same alley as last night. At Almeria Street I turned and went to the Gables Juice Bar. The tiny café was crowded with people waiting for orders, but I was able to get my order quickly. I was out and around the corner in the alley, and within a block I was at the bank of elevators at the rear of the police station. I took the elevator up to the third floor and went right into the open VIN office.

Ileana was the first person I expected to see, and my expectations were exact as she was dutifully at her desk. I presented her with the smoothie.

"*Aye* Cade, *ju* are always so thoughtful. Thank *ju.*"

My next stop was Big G's office.

"Big G. Here's a mixed veggie drink from Gables Juice Bar."

"Damn bro, you're alright. I don't care what all those people say about you."

"Well, like I always say, it's best to have your own opinion than go with the masses," I replied.

"My opinion of you is worse than the masses' anyway, why sink to the common denominator when I've already surpassed that level? Know what I'm saying?" he joked.

I reminded him to ask at tomorrow's steering committee about cases with a player named Zeus on anybody's radar screen. We chatted about the comings and goings in the department, then I sat in the vacant lieutenant's office and ate the English muffin sandwich, contemplating how my day might unfold. First and foremost, my reason for being in the office early was to see Major Brunson, and to brief him about what happened with Tavino and Perchero yesterday. As soon as I finished the sandwich I picked up the phone and dialed Charlene's extension. I asked if she could squeeze me in when the

Major had a free moment. She told me to come down. I grabbed a copy of the count sheet and the colada.

I walked into Major Brunson's office, said good morning to Charlene, and offered her a hit from the colada, which she gladly accepted. She told me to go on into his office. I left the colada with her as a lovely welcoming gift for whoever had the misfortune of visiting Major Brunson this morning.

Brunson's office door made a *swoosh* as it rubbed over the carpet. Major Brunson was sitting behind his desk, signing a stack of papers that I'm not even sure he was taking the time to even read.

"Have a seat, Cade. I'll be with you in a minute." He continued signing documents and papers, stopping to glance up at me and said, "I hear it went off without a hitch yesterday."

"I can assume who you heard that from, but from my perspective, this is a complete mess."

He stopped signing papers and put down his pen. He leaned back in his chair, looked out the window, and then back at me.

"Explain yourself."

"Explain myself? I think these guys at Customs need to explain themselves."

"Like how?"

"For starters, like the fact they set this meet up in a bakery at the exact same time as the school *right next door* was letting out for the day."

"I thought the Colombians set the location?' he answered.

"Exactly. You have any idea how many thousands of ways this could've gone bad yesterday? Kids and parents everywhere. Nowhere to set up surveillance, nowhere to prep for a takeaway. It was a logistical mess."

I purposely omitted that Ritchie Tavino was late to his own meet. I also intentionally omitted that Customs didn't have an adequate amount of agents as back up.

"Okay Cade, I get it. The world didn't spin exactly the fucking way you wanted it to, so because you had to cram into a *pastelitos* factory, you got your panties in a wad. From what I hear the pick-up went flawlessly, and we've already sent the money down to Colombia. They're happy with the trial run and want to drop seven million more. Sounds like it went pretty damn well to me. Anything else?"

"Anything else? How about these Colombians are playing us?" I said.

"What do you mean?"

I put the count sheet in front of him. He picked it up with a "What's this?"

"It's the accountability sheet of the currency that was picked up." When he didn't react, I kept explaining. "It's the record of what was supposed to be picked up and what the full accurate amount of the currency we actually did pick up was."

"Looks like it's all here to me," he said.

"Minus a $4500 self-deducted commission by their courier," I pointed out.

"That's a Customs problem."

"No. It's a we-have-a-problem. I'm in this, too. That makes Coral Gables and you in this, too. This is a shortage that wasn't expected by the owner of the money. We'll look like we're either incompetent or thieves. This will affect their relationship with us going forward."

"Cade, from a Coral Gables perspective, I see a very short future here. We're here to light the Customs rocket and then stand back and watch it go. After we do the seven million, I don't give a shit what they do."

"Look at the count. Look at the denominations. They don't have seven million," I said.

"What? What the fuck are you saying? Because some bozo skimmed a $4,500 bonus for himself, they don't have seven million still to move? What makes you think that?"

"They set the meet for after three in the afternoon. These guys are working guys. They aren't money launderers. One of them had saw

166

dust in his hair and dirty work boots on. They picked him up right off the job site somewhere. The money was in an old canvass satchel with rusty latches. It's probably been sitting in a public storage locker for weeks or longer. Look at the money. It's shit money!"

"Again, I say what? It's all here minus the little turd's cut."

"This is money on a downward slide. It's crap. It hasn't been refined. These guys are pure bottom feeders. These bills are small bills. This is street money. Street drug sales, fenced goods, illegal bovine steroids, winnings from *Bolita*, shit like that."

"What the fuck is a bolita?"

"It's a form of lottery played off the losing numbers in the Florida lottery. The Cubans play it every week both here and in Cuba. Listen, it doesn't really matter. What matters is these guys couldn't move a couch let alone seven million dollars. This is what we call 'money on the downside,' the remainders of a larger parcel. These guys are grabbing the crumbs like scavengers. It's like picking up all the oranges that fell off a truck at the state turnpike weigh station, and calling yourself an orange grower. These guys are scrap collectors. Their key man in Colombia has a history of being a distrustful little asshole."

"Well, couldn't that bigger parcel possibly be the seven million?"

"Is it possible? Yes. Is it plausible? No. I'm telling you, this whole Customs thing is not sitting well. They want back in this business in the worst of ways, and they're going about it in the worst of ways."

"We have committed ourselves to seeing it through. If they set the next deal for seven million and Customs calls for you, you're going. You are going! End of discussion," he said.

I was standing by the window and I looked down at one of those "career-ending white, stuck-in-patrol blue" police cars. All of the thoughts from last night of putting the VIN lifestyle behind and being a regular guy who shows up at a regular time and goes home at a regular time flooded back to me. I turned back to Brunson who was just looking at me for an answer. I knew he was being pressed because the new Customs Agent in charge in Miami was his brother-in-law.

I thought of my initial reaction when I first heard that SAC Dale Sorenson was related to him.

Either way this nepotistic slant was making me feel a little uneasy, because now it took on a personal aspect. And when it gets personal, mistakes happen, and things can get ugly.

I turned away from him again to look down at the patrol car, and just acknowledged his comment with a simple, "Okay Major." Then I left his office.

I went back to the VIN office, poked my head in to check if any subpoenas or mail had come in, then went outside, got in my car, and drove down to Scotty's Landing. I parked again in front of Miami City Hall. I walked through the same cut-out chain link fence and cut across the marina parking lot.

The employees at Scotty's were still in early morning set-up and preparation for the day. This time I caught Santiago's eye as he was working. I walked out past the last table at Scotty's and continued across the short grassy strip to stand on the flat sea wall looking out at Biscayne Bay and the spoiler islands. The bay was calm, the marine traffic and noise nearly nonexistent. The sun glinted off the water and it was looking to be a beautiful fall day in Miami.

Within five minutes Santiago was standing beside me. We both watched the water in silence. neither of us saying anything.

"I need you to run a one-nineteen on someone," I said, staring straight ahead.

"You want a records check? Why don't you just do it yourself?" he said.

"I need distance. Not just from me, but from Miami. I need *extreme* distance. Use one of your contacts at the *Nassau Guardian* newspaper. Have them ask Miami P.D. for the personnel file of one of their sergeants. The guy's name is Roberto Tovar. You got it? Tovar. T-O-V-A-R. The guy might have been Special Forces before the police department."

"I got it, but you do know what you're asking for? This type of thing costs just as much as a *politico*."

I turned my attention from the water view and looked directly at him.

"I know. When you get the information call our VIN office and leave a message with the secretary. Tell her that you're an attorney from Collier County. I don't care what name you use just say Collier County. I'll come find you."

With that I turned away and walked silently back through Scotty's. Within two minutes I had the T-tops off, with Miami City Hall in my rearview mirror.

Traffic on Bayshore Drive was light and it was just a few minutes until I was once again ensconced in the leafy canopy of Main Highway. At Douglas Road, I turned south in front of the toney and walled section of DeGarmo Estates. Once I was in Coral Gables, I picked up the cell phone and called the VIN office.

"*Veen,*" said Ileana in her accented English.

"Hi Ileana, is Gary there?"

"*Coño,* Cade. *Ju* were just here."

"Yeah, I know I forgot to tell him something."

With an air of exasperation in a 'how dare you interrupt me from my *telenovela* attitude,' she put me through to Gary's direct line.

"Dude, I don't care how many smoothies you buy her. Once she's done with the smoothie, she's done with you, too," said Gary as he picked up his line.

"I know, it's like I'm feeding the beast. That's why I'm calling you, too. Can you go into the C.I. files and look for a C.I. for me? His name is Fermin Rivacoba. I'm on my way to meet him at the Hungry Bear Sub Shop across from Miami Dade South College."

"We don't call it south or north anymore. We just call it Miami Dade College. I think those '*I AM MDC*' parking pass stickers we see on cars secretly stand for 'I don't use turn signals.' What's this guy's name again? Fermin what?" he asked.

"To me it's still Dade South. His last name is Rivacoba."

"You want to hold on or do you want me to call you back?"

"I'll hold. I can't risk disturbing Ileana if we get disconnected."

I kept driving south. I was now on Old Cutler Road. I was approaching Kendall Drive when Gary came back on the line a few minutes later.

"Hey, you there?"

"Yeah, go ahead," I said.

"Okay, I got his file. Fermin Rivacoba, C.I. number K291. You haven't done anything with him in about six years. What do you need?"

"Gary, please look up the exact address for Hungry Bear Sub Shop across from Dade South and show me meeting with him in the NINJAS system. For objective, make it related to the meeting I had yesterday at 1697 Southwest 32nd Avenue. Make sure you link this meet with yesterday's meet in the comments section."

"You…uh, by yourself again, Cade?" he asked with a suspicious tone.

"Yes. Once it goes through NINJAS without any conflicts please fax a copy of the no conflict page to Special Agent Ritchie Tavino at U.S. Customs. His numbers should be in Rivacoba's file. Ritchie should remember him from when we used to work with him at Customs. Make sure you get that faxed to him."

"Okay, just confirming you'll be at Hungry Bear Sub Shop on Southwest 109th Court? Right?"

I was passing Kendall Drive and if I was going to be at the Hungry Bear Sub Shop, I should've turned west from Old Cutler, but instead I continued driving south.

I had no intention of meeting anybody at the Hungry Bear Sub Shop. Especially a low-producing informant I hadn't seen in six years who was hovering near death in a hospital a good twenty miles away.

"Yeah. I'll be pulling up shortly. So set the meet for ten minutes from now. I know it's short notice, but I don't expect any conflicts," I said.

"You got it. Just keep me in mind when you go by Gables Juice Bar."

"Always. Thank you, Big G."

I continued south and was reluctantly chiding myself for choosing the Hungry Bear, because I was actually craving a decent sub. By the time I was deep south on Old Cutler Road I called Papa Ricco's.

"Yeah, can I get a pick-up for a Kitchen Sink?" which was basically an Italian sub with an eye-catching name.

I gave him my info and he said, "Be ready in—"

"Twenty minutes. See you then."

I was enjoying the low humidity of the Miami autumn. I turned west and went to Papa Ricco's. In just under twenty minutes from making my turn I was back on Mitchell Drive heading east straight to the condo at Paradise Point. It was a little before one o'clock. I was thankful to have missed all the school zone traffic that I'd traveled through. In an hour the region, which is overrun with public and private schools, would be teeming with school buses, small private jitneys, and the ever-present *"Latinasportautilius."*

I was happy to be back at the condo.

I brought in my go bag. Hungry as hell, I grabbed an Amstel Light from the refrigerator, and the Kitchen Sink sub. I headed up to the third floor outside deck, where I sat in the overstuffed, incredibly comfortable chaise lounge, and dug into the sandwich and beer. Afternoon drinking wasn't usually a problem in VIN. At the moment I didn't have anything lined up, and besides, I'd lost count of how many times I had to meet dopers, informants, and every person in the legal profession in a bar. The view from the deck was splendid. The blue sky seemed to lock lips with the blue waters of Biscayne Bay all the way to the horizon. A few boats glided out in the bay, and the slight rustle of the palm trees that were just about at the height of the condo were the only sound I was attuned to. I looked at my cell phone. No messages. That was good, but I knew it wouldn't last. I expected a call from Ritchie soon regarding the fax about Fermin

Rivacoba. I finished the sub and the beer and was contemplating another chilled Amstel Light when my cell phone rang.

"Hello."

"Cade. It's Ritchie. Hey man, what the heck is up with Fermin? I just got the fax. I haven't thought of that guy in years. What does he have to do with yesterday?"

"Oh hey, Ritchie. Yeah, I know you guys have been out of it a while. Fermin and Chuco were going to be restaurant partners on a place in Miami Lakes, but something got in the way. He said it was permits and licensing. I took him at his word. But I wanted to see what he knew about Chuco since their last failed venture."

"What did he have to say?"

"He said Chuco has gone pretty far in the business and he knows that Chuco wants to get back to Miami. He thinks Chuco wants to invest in Miami real estate and then get back to Colombia. I asked him if he had the juice to do that. He said he heard that he might, but that he's been letting some mopes run his show here, and he doesn't trust them."

"You mean Perchero and that cigar store wooden Indian he brought with him?" asked Ritchie.

"I'm assuming that's who he was talking about. Listen, Fermin's also in a jam with another group and he wanted to relay some information, but only if he could get paid real quick. I had to make an executive decision. I settled at a flat $4,000. No points. No complications. When we do the seven million, I'll need 4k right off the top immediately. Add it to the count and we'll leverage it as a C.I. expense. He's documented and he did work for both of us. You got that new SAC, just push it through, Ritchie. You guys want in and I have to bend the pipe to squeeze you through it."

"Yeah. Yeah. I don't care. So, what did he say?"

"He said he thinks that Perchero and Emiliano are playing behind Chuco's back. Fermin doesn't know we're looking to do a seven million pick up. He just thinks that whatever these two are saying, cut it in half, and cut it in half again. He says they're complete bullshit artists. He says don't trust these guys. They were there when he and Chuco were trying to get the restaurant going, and they were constant naysayers about everything. He cautioned that any dealings with them usually end up being fucked up. I took that to mean a possible rip. If these guys are looking to rip us, we need to be prepared."

"I don't think they're looking to rip us. I mean they are delivering to *us,* for Christ sakes."

"I'm going in this alone, Ritchie. I got no DEA and no Gables with me. I'm depending on you to have this fleshed out. Make sure your guys have long weapons or MP5's."

"When this goes we'll have Pedro Acevedo and Johnny Slomianski with us again. Acevedo has a Steyr AUG he carries in the trunk. I'll be sure he has it when this goes."

"Steyr AUG? I thought they were outlawed by Forty-One?"

"Well, Steyr AUG made some changes and Bush's ban no longer applies to the new, modified version. Acevedo saw it at Glynco. He liked it. He's the only one in the Miami field office who carries it."

"See if you can get Slomianski to carry something bigger, too. We are talking seven million here. Plenty of people die in Miami every day for a hell of a lot less," I said

"Did Fermin have anything else to say?"

"He just said that Chuco has been out for a long time and he's roaring to get back into legitimate business with real estate and other ventures. It stands to reason why he's willing to sell out family and friends for eleven and a half percent of seven million. Once he gets some legitimate business going he can pick and choose who he wants to throw under the bus. You know, if he's willing to go in deep for seven million, he'll do it again."

"Exactly!" he exclaimed. "That's why we're willing to pay the high points, because we think he's going to be a cash cow."

"Just be sure he isn't a *vaca,*" I said.

"I just said that. A cow. A cash cow."

"No Ritchie, a *vaca* is just a cow. In the Amazon, when a rancher wants to move a herd of cows across a river, he sends a diseased or old cow into the river first. While the piranhas feed off that cow, the rancher moves the rest of the herd slightly upstream. With a guy like Chuco, you guys could all be high-fiving, having 'Miller Time' six months from now over a $350,000 seizure, while Chuco moves a couple million elsewhere in Miami. Fermin says don't trust him, and I believe him."

Chapter Fifteen

WHEN I HUNG up from my call with Ritchie, I gave some thought to what I had said. I used the phony meeting with Fermin Rivacoba as a way to convey my feelings and concerns about any deals we may have now, or in the future with Chuco. It was a good way to get my point across about a need for more firepower and for more adherence to the protocols and mechanisms we'd set in place years ago to help insure the undercover's safety. Unlike what's portrayed in television and movies, seven million dollars doesn't fit in a slim Samsonite briefcase. Cash is bulky and cumbersome. It's weighty. It can be moldy, wet, dirty, or fresh from the U.S. Mint, pristine. Either way, seven million will take up some space. If Perchero and Emiliano are the rock bottom feeders I think they are and *if* they actually have seven million dollars you can bet your last burrito it'll be in small. stinky, nasty, torn, worn bills. That means I'd have to lug and tug some sort of bag or suitcase across God's green earth. I like to have my hands free, not trussed up carrying someone else's old luggage. Ritchie needed to hear it from me conveyed from a third source that Chuco was not to be trusted. We need to be thinking defensively of a rip or some other cash caused calamity.

I think I sold it pretty well. Ritchie assured that long weapons would be with our backup. I'd ideally like to have more than just

Acevedo and Slomianski there. To me, they were just like Abbott and Costello. If you can't get to a meet in an adequate time and find a good parking spot, then as far as I'm concerned, you're a little low on the competency scale. What was going to be, was going to be. Major Brunson was quite clear about that.

"We have committed ourselves to seeing it through. If they set the next deal for seven million and Customs calls for you, you're going. You are going! End of discussion."

Somehow, some way, my life was continuing to career and spin without me asserting any control. Trying to gain mastery of my life was like trying to grasp smoke. I'd gone from being detached to a DEA task force to now breastfeeding U.S. Customs back into the money laundering world. Operational concerns and my own safety concerns were being dismissed to appease familial relations. Ritchie was so rabid to get up and running, he was clearly missing signs he should be reading. The clientele we were dealing with had a history of skimming, scamming, and skirting the truth. I was not only dealing with a guy with shoulders like a coat hanger, but his oversized babysitter as well. Having a Customs agent who fell in love with a previously banned gun he saw on a gun range didn't make me feel any more comfortable about the space I was in.

Once again I found myself assessing if the VIN life was still in the cards for me. I was actually beginning to wonder what cards, if any, was I actually holding?

Then there was C.C. A novice homicide detective pursuing a highly trained killer who had no compunction turning a marked Miami police car into Swiss cheese. The very same killer, for all she knew, might be sharing her squad room coffee maker with her every day. Whoever this Zeus was, he was one seriously lethal individual.

Maybe I should start carrying a larger arsenal in the Z28, too.

If C.C. and I were to come up against Zeus, why should we think he's only carrying the Walther P-88? Zeus might be even more heavily armed. He's well-versed in tactics and weaponry, and most likely has a Special Forces background. Zeus could prove to be a formidable foe for both C.C. and I together. A guy like Zeus could take us both out before we could even comprehend what was going on. Zeus used the Mozambique Drill with obviously practiced accuracy.

The Mozambique Drill is intended to render the target to immediately be stopped or more precisely, to be killed. The first two shots into center mass of the upper body are designed to be lethal. If the target is still alive, the third shot is a more precisely aimed, difficult to make head shot. Many factors such as body armor, the individual being under the influence of drugs, or the failure to hit vital organs, can make the body shots less than effective, necessitating the third head shot. The third shot is designed to guarantee instant incapacitation by impacting the brain right through the medulla oblongata. That third and final round usually is delivered to the area between the eyebrows and upper lip. The fatal triangle.

I found myself staring off toward the tree line west of the condo, deep in thought about all of this, when my cell phone rang. It was C.C.

"Hello."

"You up for a field trip? Do you need your permission slip signed?" she said by way of greeting.

"What do you got?"

"I took your advice. I was able to secure a four-thirty appointment with the chief officer in charge of public safety and security for Miami International Airport. I was wondering if you wanted to meet there. We could see this guy together."

"Sounds good. Where at the airport?"

"Concourse D. He said to park in the Dolphin parking lot, go as high as at least the eight level, and look for the covered pedestrian walkway. Take the walkway across to the terminal. If you're on time, I'll wait for you by the bank of elevators."

"I'm deep south but I should be able to make it. In case I'm late, what's this guy's name?"

"Marshall Ellinport, Chief Security Officer in charge of public safety and security for Miami International Airport. I kid you not, that is how he answered his phone," she said.

"Think he'll validate parking?"

"Like I said before, being cheap is not a very endearing quality," she said.

"Okay, I'll see you there."

Dilemma time. Do I brush my teeth and head out the door, or do I grab another Amstel Light for the road and swish some mouthwash in the parking lot? I opted for the safe route and decided the Amstel Light, or any other beer for that matter, could wait for later. I took in the view looking north as though it would give me a glimpse from southern Miami Dade County all the way to Miami International Airport. It was just a deep and continuous tree line that stretched as far as I could see in nearly every direction except out towards the bay.

I went back downstairs. I restocked the go bag with clean underwear, jeans, and a few shirts. I kept the Hartford Whalers hat and the jacket in the bag. Go bag in hand, I left the condo. I started the engine of the Z28, pausing to listen to the RPMs take stock of themselves. I headed north on Southwest 67th Avenue and stayed north on the avenue, crossing U.S.1 right past the Big Cheese Restaurant. Passing the neighborhoods, their affluence and lack of affluence viewed from my windshield, changing and morphing constantly. At Tamiami Canal Road I turned east and drove on the curving road all the way until merging onto Northwest 7th Street before turning north on Red Road. I drove under the Dolphin Expressway and across the railroad tracks. I turned a hard right on Perimeter Road. The road is called Perimeter Road because it literally is just barely outside the airport boundary line. It's used by fuelers, long transport truckers, airline catering trucks, and any commercial vehicle that services the aviation industry. There are plenty of civilian vehicles, but most people stick to the expressway, which was parallel to my right. The scent of Jet A aviation fuel seeped in through the car's air conditioning. All kinds of ground activity could be seen as the commercial jetliners parked at the concourse gates and were being serviced by ground crews.

On the other side of Perimeter Road were railroad tracks and very thick, tall saw grass. An Atlas Cargo 747 Jet rumbled from behind up to me. Its mammoth wheels lifted off the ground just as it was nearly astride my moving car. The runway was still about two hundred yards away on the other side of the chain link Cyclone barbed wire-topped fence. The inertia and energy of such a large aircraft seemed to shake me and the car. The big 747 was airborne in just a few seconds and steadily climbed into the eastern horizon, its huge engines pushing it up higher and higher with each passing second. It went from being a colossal white, navy blue, and gold airplane thundering next to me to a mere speck in the sky in a matter of a minute or two.

I followed the road as it curved toward the large fuel farms. The fuel farms have giant round cylindrical silos filled with diesel fuel, gasoline, and Jet A aviation fuel. The faded orange approach light towers to Runway Thirty were just off to my right. Seeing the towers only about twenty feet above the road prepared me for the shrieking inbound American Airlines A-300 that roared directly overhead. I do know light travels faster than sound, and the shadow of the aircraft as it flew directly overhead blanketed the car and the road with a fast-moving airplane shadow. It created a brief umbra as it momentarily eclipsed my car with me in it. The sound of its cowlings, engines, and thrust reversers reverberated right through me, clear into my sternum.

Try as I may, it was nearly impossible to keep darting my eyes from the road to the landing airplane. I kept looking for the tell-tale white smoke that comes up as the wheels, stationary in landing, are forced into full roll rotation, leaving deep black swatches of melted rubber on the runway. Just as those passengers on the American Airlines A-300 were probably hearing the standard intercom announcement, "Please use caution when opening overhead bins as items may have shifted during the flight," I was approaching the entrance to the Dolphin Parking Garage.

I went up the ramps, taking note of the tire marks on the

sidewalls of the elevated ramps and quietly wondered who in their right mind can't drive up a ramp without grinding their front end and tires against the retaining walls? On the eighth level I found a parking space next to a wood-paneled minivan. I don't know what's worse: driving a minivan or driving a minivan with wood paneling? I exited my car and took the covered pedestrian walkway C.C. had mentioned across the congested airport roadway below. The roadway was a sea of cars, taxis, luggage, people, hugs and "see ya laters." I relaxed for a second on the air conditioned moving walkway. When I got to the terminal side, I saw the bank of elevators—but I did not see C.C. I stayed in front of the bank of elevators and then C.C. came out of the ladies' room, wiping her hands on a paper towel.

"So, you made it after all," she said.

"Anything to help the cause," I said. I was secretly wishing Godfrey Pinder hadn't been so insistent that I assist on the murder of his nephew, Reggie LaMarr.

"I think it's this way," she said as she led me through a large wooden door with a placard above it that said, "*Landside Operations.*"

Inside was a long hallway with deep blue carpeting. Various office suites lined either side of us as we walked down the hall, some with their office doors open, others closed. The hall opened to a circular room where a secretary sat behind a desk. Her nameplate said Diane Ford. C.C. spoke first.

"Hello. Are you Ms. Ford? I'm Detective Clay from the City of Miami Police Department. I believe I spoke to you on the phone about seeing Mr. Ellinport."

The woman was very pleasant and replied that Mr. Ellinport would be available in a few minutes. She offered us refreshments and showed us a comfortable place we could sit while we waited. Major Brunson's office had *Law Officer* magazines in his waiting room; Marshall Ellinport had *Aviation Today*. I was starting to wonder what kind of magazines a proctologist had in their office waiting area when a smooth dark wooden door opened and man poked his head from around the doorway.

"Detective Clay?" Before she could answer he had already widened the space in the doorway and was turning back to go inside.

The office was nicely appointed. A large window overlooked the D concourse—most notably gates D-4 to D-9. I imagined that on certain summer days Ellinport could watch the heat rise up from the massive stretches of concrete, and by midday see dark, heavy, moisture-filled clouds move in, drenching the airport with torrential rains. One of the first things that caught my eye aside from the view, was a framed photograph of Ellinport shaking hands with Forty-One. Ellinport looked a little younger and the inscription said, "*To Marshall, Thank you for everything! George W Bush.*"

Marshall Ellinport greeted both C.C. and I at the midpoint of the office. He shook both of our hands. He had a slender build and wore a non-descript navy suit and a light blue tie with a tiny white diamond geometric pattern. He had rimless glasses which I noted when he turned slightly were bifocals. He directed us to a small seating area off to the side of his desk. C.C. started the conversation by telling Ellinport that we were there to discuss an investigation being conducted by the City of Miami Police Department. He held his hand up in a manner that suggested she refrain from talking any further.

"Before you go on, I want to let you know a little about myself. I was the SAC for ATF in Oberlin Kansas. My office oversaw three states from Oberlin to Fort Morgan, Colorado and onto Ogallala, Nebraska. So I've dealt with plenty of investigations and police matters. Two years ago I retired from the ATF. I took this position here as Chief Security Officer in charge of public safety and security for Miami International Airport."

I was willing to bet he liked to say that title a lot. ATF was the acronym for The Bureau of Alcohol, Tobacco, and Firearms and Explosives. They chose to keep the explosives part out of their acronym because it just was a tongue twister to try and say it, and to try and explain it was even more cumbersome. They could also be called the Alcohol and Tobacco Tax and Trade Bureau, as it seemed the majority of their work was compliance and taxation. They collect

Federal excise taxes on alcohol, tobacco, firearms, and ammunition. They assure strict compliance with permitting, labeling, and marketing requirements. Basically, they contend with alcohol, tobacco, firearms, and explosives. Ideally, a better name would be The Agency of Fun and Danger.

If his whole career was overseeing Oberlin, Kansas and the equally desolate neighboring cities, regardless of whether you cross state lines or not, it wasn't something that, as I sat in his office, convinced me he was the best candidate for this position in Miami. Ellinport seemed to be highly inflated with his relatively new position here at Miami International Airport, airport code MIA.

"So I can assure you that if anything involving your investigation has an MIA angle to it, I and this office are willing to assist you any way we can. Why don't you tell me as much as you can or perhaps feel comfortable sharing with me, and I can see what we here at the office of the Chief Security Officer in charge of public safety and security for Miami International Airport can do for you."

There was that title again.

C.C looked at me briefly as if to say *"Okay I'm going into the deep end without my water wings."* She then started talking.

"Well, once again, I am Detective Cynthia Clay from the Homicide Division of the Miami Police Department. With me here is Detective Cade Taylor from the Coral Gables Police Department."

Ellinport held his hand up again. I was beginning to think this was going to be an ongoing thing with him.

"Coral Gables? Isn't that a different jurisdiction?" asked Ellinport.

"We have mutual aid agreements and there may be a Coral Gables component to our case and by talking with you we hope to maybe affirm that theory." She fibbed effectively sidestepping the hand in the air while simultaneously appealing to his *"I worked cases in three states"* ego.

"Mr. Ellinport, we have had two homicides in the City of Miami that have clear connections to each other. We think both homicides were committed by the same person or persons. Both victims were young African American males in their early twenties, they both were killed by gunshots we think from the same weapon, and they were both killed in the same manner."

"The connection to MIA is?" he asked

"Both victims were employed by a contractual company that does work here at MIA. They were both employed by Reliable Flight Services. I'm sure you aware of this company they are commonly known as RFS."

"I know RFS. If it were up to me I would terminate all third party vendor contracts. I would have the airlines service their own gates and aircrafts with their own personnel."

"Why do you say that?" she asked.

"It helps with the span of control. If you are working for a company with a decent health plan, other benefits, a 401k or even a pension you are more likely to stay with that company and adhere to company policy and protocols. Companies like RFS have incredible employee turnover, their employees often fail unannounced drug tests, their background checks are very sketchy, they fight each other in the workplace, argue with our personnel, disregard airport rules, the list goes on. There is just a whole assortment of issues when you hire outside agencies and people to do a job your own people could do but won't do because of a union clause, or some other work infringement. Did you know that flight attendants do not start getting paid until the actual cabin door closes?"

That made me think of Katie Eighty and her unpaid drives from North Bay Village to MIA. It also explained why flight attendants are less than agreeable to assist placing luggage in the overhead bin or other issues.

"Our victims also knew each other and they were killed within a week of each other."

Ellinport reached into his inside pocket of his jacket and pulled out three business cards. He gave one to each of us and then flipped the third one over and held it in his left palm. He produced a pen from his shirt pocket with his right hand. Using the back of the business card he asked C.C what caliber of gun was used to kill both LaMarr and Cooper.

"Our victims were killed with a Walther P-88. We are having a hard time finding any ownership records of this type of handgun."

Ellinport looked at C.C over his glasses briefly and then wrote something on the back of the third card. It was a name and a phone number with a 925 area code.

"This is the phone number for our Walnut Creek, California lab. Ask for Special Agent Robert Ainsle. Tell him I asked him to look into your P-88 issue."

Even though retired from the ATF Ellinport still referred to it as *"our lab."* I am sure C.C appreciated the help.

"Whatever level you're looking at to find any information that can help you with the Walther P-88, you're still steps behind just going directly to our lab or to a guy like Robert Ainsle."

C.C thanked him for the tip and for helping that portion of her investigation along.

"May I ask you the names of the RFS employees who were killed?"

"Our first victim was Reggie LaMarr the second victim was Jamaal Boseman Cooper."

Ellinport was now writing on a yellow legal pad. He scribbled some notes.

"Are you two available to come back tomorrow? I might be able to have more information that would be helpful to you then. I am also going to ask my direct boss to be present as well. I like to keep it as transparent as I can."

Spoken like a true fed. In the federal agencies you don't get ahead by doing the right things you get ahead by not doing the wrong things. Consult the manual. Call Washington. Wait for approval. It is the methodology that all of these guys have.

"Who would that be?" asked C.C

"We have a multi-tiered supervisory structure here. At the top is the Aviation Director, followed by the Deputy Director and then the

Chief of Staff and Senior Policy Advisor. Those are the three above me. I'd like to have Chief of Staff and Senior Policy Advisor Suezie Chanin-Galperin be here for our meeting tomorrow. "

He then stood up and moved towards the open door. He called out through the open door towards Diane. "Can you get Ramona on the phone and find out if Ms. Chanin-Galperin has any openings tomorrow for about 30 minutes to meet here with me and these two detectives?"

He sat back down and we three engaged in small talk while waiting to hear if Ms. Chanin-Galperin was available for a meeting. It only took Diane a minute or two to get back to Mr. Ellinport. Ms. Chanin-Galperin was available from 11:15am to 11:45am. Mr. Ellinport set the meeting up and asked Diane to add it to his calendar.

"I should have checked your own calendars but getting any of the top tier people together here at any given time is nearly impossible. So I do hope you both will be back here at 11:15 tomorrow. I do think we may have something that can help you, but I need to have Ms. Chanin-Galperin here. It's a policy thing and she and I will need to discuss what we can divulge about our own affairs here before talking with you. I'm sure you understand."

That just didn't sit right with me. In hindsight I should have been more diplomatic but Ellinport was already rubbing me wrong playing the emperor's new clothes card by telling us to use his referral at the ATF lab and constantly reminding us what his capabilities were as long as he was given permission to demonstrate those capabilities.

"You know we aren't here because someone slipped and fell in one of your bathrooms. This is homicide. We are here because of two murders. Is there something you can tell us now rather than have us sit on ice until tomorrow? I asked him

Looking more at C.C then at me he simply reiterated. "I'm sorry but I think we can be of more assistance tomorrow. Now if there isn't anything else I can help you with, we can reconvene here tomorrow at 11:15. I thank you both for coming in."

"Hold on. Maybe there is something you can help us with. Have

you ever heard of an employee or better yet somebody named Zeus?"
I asked him directly.

Ellinport sat back in his chair and rubbed his chin with his hand
for a second. He looked at me. He then looked at C.C and then he
looked back at me.

"Zeus? Yes I have."

Chapter Sixteen

C.C IMMEDIATELY LEANED forward in her chair. I kept my eyes locked on Ellinport. It was my subtle way of saying *"We aren't leaving until you say more."* Ellinport broke from my gaze and stalled a bit brushing mysteriously absent crumbs and lint from his desk ink blotter.

"Tomorrow would be a better time to talk about what the office of the Chief Security Officer in charge of public safety and security for Miami International Airport can do for you."

There was that title again. The redundancy of his inflated version of himself and his silk-plant-adorned office was becoming trite.

"Listen," I said. "You might have been the SAC in some corner of the United States in a fly-over state, but this is Miami, *amigo*. We do things a little different here. She and I aren't going to wait until tomorrow because you're worried about saying something out of turn. Zeus. What do you know?"

He maintained the party line to a degree.

"Tomorrow would be a better time to talk about all of this—but what I *can* say is that there have been times that employees of RFS abruptly quit. When we interviewed them they expressed a fear of this character Zeus. I have never seen him. I've gone through as many of the employee lists as I can get my hands on and I haven't found anyone named Zeus. I found Zekes, Zacharys, and a Zadie, but no Zeus. Whoever he is, I suspect he's running a smuggling ring here using RFS employees and other MIA personnel. I don't have any full proof, but I hope that by tomorrow I can open some things we're looking at internally here, and share them with you. So, it *is* tomorrow at the very earliest…*amigo!*"

I felt C.C.'s hand on my arm and was subtly reminded by her grip it was her investigation, and I should follow her wishes. If we needed to wait until tomorrow, then that's what it would be. I couldn't decide if Ellinport was like many other feds and ex-feds I'd encountered or if he was actually a stand-up guy. It made no matter, because like I mentioned, it was C.C.'s investigation and I didn't want to jeopardize it. I rose from my seat and started for the door, pausing just long enough at Diane Ford's desk to overhear Ellinport tell C.C. that, "maybe you could teach him some manners before tomorrow." C.C. caught up to me midway down the blue carpet hallway. We walked out together towards the bank of elevators.

"Is it always like this with you? Seriously, Cade! You need to forestall your need for immediacy," she admonished me.

"Look, I know I can appear to be a little rough around the edges—"

"A little rough? You're a stone sharpened into a spearhead. Cool it down a bit."

There was no point in arguing with her.

This job.

My divorce.

The life I was leading was doing nothing for my personality appeal. I tried to be agreeable, warm, and friendly, but inside it was a whole different thing. I was like a broken window on a dark, wintry January night. Sometimes I feel like I don't belong around people. Like I belong to all the wasted minutes that didn't happen. Time haunts me with the teasing notion of what could have been. Lost moments never to be reclaimed. I have recurring thoughts about who I could have been—maybe a better husband, or a better detective? It's as though neither one would allow the other to thrive.

One had to win out. Gina was gone and I was still carrying a badge, so we can see who won out.

But was it really a win?

The VIN lifestyle isn't like anything one could possibly understand unless they'd lived it themselves. Trying to understand the way grays and dark blues look alike when light and darkness mix, and how they combust under my skin becoming a robust storm is unfathomable to nearly everyone. You won't see the storm, but you will hear the synchronistic cracks. Everything in my life seemed within reach, but unattainable. Like forever trying to grasp smoke.

"Seriously Cade, the guy is doing us—actually he's doing *me*—a big favor. It's almost five o'clock. What good is it to badger him now? So we wait until morning. It gives him time to prepare, and guess what? It gives us time to prepare, too. Look at the upside. It can't always be a *now* thing ."

"So, we are in a wait-and-see mode here. Starting with our first wait tomorrow morning," I said.

C.C. sat on a faux leatherette bench across from the elevators, and I gingerly sat with her. I was hoping that whatever she had to say would be short; I didn't want Ellinport coming out of his trophy office to go home and see us sitting there like two school kids outside the principal's office. C.C. opened the binder that she carried with her always.

"You were right about the partial footprint from the white sand on that low wall at Jabo's murder scene. There were some partials in the sand as well. Our crime scene techs have sent what they got off to the FBI shoe lab in Quantico."

The FBI laboratory maintains a footwear database that's a computerized reference collection of more than 14,000 shoe outsoles from hundreds of different footwear manufacturers. "We were confident that they'd be able to match Zeus's shoe." she said

I nodded my head in agreement, knowing full well that the FBI shoe impression laboratory was top notch.

"There's still more I want to show you. We have more surveillance photos of our shooter, Zeus. It seems that he got off the train at the Coconut Grove Station."

She produced a barely decipherable security camera photograph of a person in a gray hoodie exiting a Metrorail train. So by the time I'd been able to get underway to pursue the shooter on the train, he was already getting off at the next stop.

"So I was chasing an empty train."

"Well, it wasn't *empty*. There were people on it. It's just that that our shooter wasn't on it. He got off at the first stop. But I can assure you, we all appreciate your efforts. Really, we do."

"You seemed none too happy to see me on that train platform when I first met you."

"Well, you take some getting used to, Cade Taylor."

"What about now?"

"Now? I like you more. Yes, I like you more than the first night I met you on the train platform," she said, cheeks pinkening.

I suggested we take the conversation somewhere else, away from the vicinity of Ellinport's office. We got up from the bench and headed to the Dolphin Parking garage. We'd parked just a few cars from each other.

"Are you hungry?" I asked her.

"I'm always hungry."

"Do you like Austrian food?"

"Is it like German? Because I've never had either," she said giggling.

"Really? You've never had German or Austrian food before? Well, why don't you follow me and we'll change that."

She smiled and nodded her head in agreement.

The drive from the airport to the restaurant is short, but rush hour traffic in Miami can make any trip into a long trek. The southbound exit ramp from the airport eclipsed a lot of the traffic. Once we were past the expressway entrance ramp it opened up a little more. After we crossed Southwest 8th Street, it was a very quick drive south. I turned east at the same Burger King on Alcazar Avenue that Arturo the bartender uses as a marker for his trips to work at the Hotel St. Michel. A few storefronts down from Burger King was the restaurant, Mozart Stube. The place was a tiny tucked away café with an authentic Austro-German menu. All entrees are made to order. I pulled past the restaurant to leave the parking space directly in front for C.C. Getting out of the car, she remarked how quaint it was, and how she had no idea the restaurant even existed.

"A little Coral Gables secret," I said.

Inside, the restaurant was painted in a light lemon chiffon color with dark wooden benches and tables. Dozens of pictures, steins, German and Austrian soccer banners, adorned the shelves and walls. The restaurant is dimly lit, despite a large panel of windows framed with red gingham curtains overlooking the avenue. Viennese waltz music was playing, which to me was a direct indicator that the owner wasn't present. He's a blues afficionado. When he is onsite, you'll hear T-Bone Walker, Lightnin' Hopkins, Blind Lemon Jefferson, or Big Bill Broonzy playing on the music system. Nonetheless, C.C. was very taken by the attentive service and great food. She had an entree of salmon filet in a riesling cream sauce. I went with the staple *Schweinebraten* with *Spätzle* and *Jägerschnitzel*. I ordered a Bitburger beer and she had white wine. Over dinner, we talked about Zeus.

"I heard what Ellinport said about Zeus being part of a smuggling ring. That tells me he has some permeance here. He's more than likely the top of the money line on this." I said

"What do you mean by that?" she asked.

"He has the most to lose here. He's protecting a criminal enterprise. But rather than get someone else to do the henchman work, he's doing it himself. He's an accomplished killer. He more than likely derives pleasure out of killing those who transgress against him. It's also a good way to keep everyone in line. We both know he has deadly skills. He doesn't linger or gloat; he's quick. He doesn't fear law enforcement. He doesn't fear being seen by witnesses. This guy is not to be played with. I can't stress that enough. I'm willing to bet

Reggie had no idea what he was getting into. After Reggie was killed, Jabo was probably starting to look over his shoulder at shadows."

"Do you still think he has Special Forces training?"

"Some sort of training. Could be Special Forces. Could be a survivalist. It could be law enforcement. The fact that Zeus had the option to blast Dominguez and chose to leave him—pardon the James Bond pun—shaken and a little stirred, has me concerned. This person has a respect, to some measure, for the working cop or enlisted soldier. Don't delude yourself into thinking that badge on your hip means anything to him, though. If it's a choice between him and you he'll take you out if he can. You cannot give this type of person an inch of opportunity. People like him know how to kill with shoelaces and bent spoons. You hear what I'm telling you?" I said.

"I hear you all too well. What do you think of the screws that both victims had?" she asked me.

"My guess is since they both worked near airplanes those screws are probably aviation related. Home Depot doesn't carry them and the guy at Home Depot said he'd never seen them before. We need to find the manufacturer. I'd suggest you check with George T. Baker Aviation School by the airport, see if any of their instructors can shed some light on what those screws are."

"That's a good idea. I can do that on the way to Ellinport's office tomorrow. One of the things that was surprising to me was that Zeus exited the train at the very first stop. It doesn't make sense to me. Zeus kills Reggie and then he walks south to get on the train, and then takes it only one stop north before he gets off?"

"That one I can't figure either," was all I could surmise.

There was a moment of contemplative thought between us both and it was apparent neither of us had an answer. I shifted the conversation.

"What's the demeanor of your squad room?"

"Most of the homicide guys know I have my hands full. They don't actively offer assistance, but they will step in on things whenever I ask. D.P. Hughes has been helpful whenever I've asked for something.

Sciarotta is laying low. He's laying real low. He's planning to go out of town for the Dolphins and Jaguars game, which for the life of me, I can't see driving all the way to Jacksonville to watch a football game that's on Monday Night Football. "

"That is a long drive for a nationally televised game. Don't you find that odd?" I said.

"It just seems like a lot of effort, and the drive is murderous," she said.

"Was he already in the leave book prior to these murders ?"

"No. That's what's so peculiar. It's like he decided right after Jabo's scene to take off to Jacksonville."

I recalled exactly what C.C. had told me about Sciarotta:

"Joe Sciarotta. He's near retirement and has a ton of experience, but so far he's done everything I've asked of him. He can be a little jaded and abrupt, he isn't the most pleasant person to be around sometimes—but then again, twenty years of scrubbing blood out from under your fingernails, and sticking measuring rods into bullet holes in people will make you a little unsocial."

"Does anyone else find it weird to travel so far to watch a nationally televised game? Is he a diehard Jaguars fan?"

"No! In fact, he's a Dolphin fan. To me, that makes it even crazier. He put in papers for Monday the 12th and Tuesday the 13th. I guess he'll be driving back from the game on Tuesday. He put in his papers the night of Jabo's murder and Tovar approved them."

"Does Tovar usually easily approve papers for leave?" I asked her.

"No, not usually. I mean he can't deny a lot of the leave requests but there's always some mini lecture about having 'enough coverage in case we have a big drug shooting like Dadeland' and stuff like that. Tovar knows deep down he can't keep any of us from taking earned leave. He likes to have as many homicide detectives on-call as he can. He's been up my ass over this case."

"How so?"

"Just keeps asking for status updates and wants to know where I am in the investigation. What progress is being made. He seems to have a very active interest in the progress of this case. He doesn't talk with too many of us. He seems to talk with Sciarotta the most. Have you found anything about him yet?"

I just looked at her and didn't answer. I adhered to what I told her in the *El Exquisito* Cuban restaurant.

"In fact, the less you know the better. Let's not mention it again. Okay?"

There was a brief lull in the conversation while she looked at me over the candlelight. I'm certain she knew the reason for my silence and she changed direction in the conversation.

"Tell me a little about you, Cade. I don't know much about you outside of what I've heard"

"What have you heard about me?"

"Our guys in S.I.S. say you're solid. Sergeant Brookings and Johnny Morris were very complimentary about you."

"So you did some checking on me?"

"A little," she smiled sheepishly as she swirled the wine in her glass.

"Well, there isn't much to say. I've been with the Gables about eleven years, and the past nine of them in some form of street narcotics or VIN unit. "

"Are you married?"

"No. I'm divorced. You?"

"I'm not married. Came close once but when I went into the police academy he couldn't handle his fiancé, soon to be wife, soon to be whatever, being a cop. So we ended it. Well, actually *he* ended it. I have a lot of nieces and nephews and my family keeps asking me about a boyfriend or getting married like it's something you just choose off a shelf at the supermarket."

She put her glass down and said " I'm sorry to hear you're divorced. That must have been difficult. How long ago was that?"

"The divorce took some time to grind its way through the system, but I've been divorced officially a few months. The process started last year, before Christmas. At least that was when she moved out."

"She moved out?"

"Yeah. I came home and noticed a few of her things gone. I called her. She said she wouldn't be coming back. That was it. I mean, that was really it. I never really heard from her again after that unless it was through her attorneys."

There was that familiar awkward silence where one person doesn't know what to say. They also don't know what to think. What kind of monster must I be to make my wife want to move out and never come back? Or what kind of woman was she? It's a damned if you do, damned if you don't turn in the conversation. It felt like I had seen it a hundred times or more the past six months although very few people actually ever spoke to me about the divorce. I learned a quick way to help the inquisitive person who strayed too far into the personal quagmire to know how to get back out.

"It takes two people to ruin a marriage," I softly said, motioning to the waiter for a refill on the Bitburger.

"Do you really think that?" she asked me.

"Not entirely, but in this case, it seems to be the best answer. When people ask, I simply say, 'My ex-wife chose to live a life that didn't include me.'"

"Does that make it any better? I mean for you?" she asked.

I looked at her and started to speak, but at that moment the waiter placed a frosted stein of Bitburger on the table. I held my tongue for the moment and simultaneously reformed my thoughts.

"Does a Band-aid really make a cut better? No. It's a protective barrier. The wound will heal on its own. It might scab over. It might scar. It might be totally unnoticeable to the naked eye. But you'll always know that there was a cut there, whether people can see it or not. It's like a cancer patient—when they're first diagnosed, no one can tell they have cancer. They carry their disease on the inside. When chemo makes their hair fall out, they then wear their disease on the outside, and everyone can see. So when you ask if it makes any better for me, I think the question is does it make it any better for you? Because I know the severity of the cut."

"I didn't mean to offend…."

"You didn't offend. I just remember when I heard about coworkers going through divorce I was always just like, 'oh well is he still going to the Marlins game?' I had no idea what it was like. No idea at all. Tell me about this guy from your academy days who couldn't handle your career choice."

She wasn't expected to have to contribute to the show and tell portion of this conversation and she was briefly caught off guard. She lifted up and then put her napkin down on her lap as she thought about what to say.

"Um, his name…his name is Ernesto," she stammered, more quietly than I'd heard her speak before. I felt a twinge of guilt that I'd unnerved her. "And he was a law student at the University of Miami. There was always a lot of debate and argument between us. Not at first but as I went through the police academy it seemed to be all about the law, probable cause, search and seizure. You'd think that one class on constitutional law made him one of our Founding Fathers. He liked to throw case studies at me. Constantly. So and So versus Ohio, So and So versus Arizona. He said whatever I was learning in the police academy was totally wrong, that they were programing me to be a jack-booted government thug. The negativity became too much. I continued getting up every morning and going to the academy and he gave me an ultimatum: quit the police department or quit him. Actually, I guess it wasn't much of an ultimatum, since he quit me. That was eight years ago. I think deep down he was just scared of something happening to me, and he couldn't handle that thought."

"So, whatever happened to him?" I asked her.

"He's an attorney in Wellington. You know, way out in western Palm Beach with the private airstrips and polo grounds? I figure he spends his weekends at the Wanderers Golf Club, shaking hands and making connections."

"He went to UM for law school? It seems every judge and attorney in Miami went to the University of Miami Law School. If you ever go to trial in Miami and you don't have a UM lawyer you might as well just plead out. Those guys are as thick as fleas on a mangy stray dog. You can't tell me those attorneys and judges don't talk cases and things at the alumni tent at Hurricane football games. I don't believe it." I said.

"A little jaded there, Mr. Taylor?" she said with a smirk, becoming more comfortable again.

"Maybe just a tad," I said, chuckling as I took a healthy swig of the frosty Bitburger.

The waiter brought C.C. another white wine and I mentioned I'd be ready for another Bitburger in about five minutes. I saw C.C. try to conceal her reaction to me ordering a third beer. I suppressed my initial comment about people judging others, and figured I'd let the conversation between us carry on and see where it went. The restaurant was now empty except for us.

"Has there been anybody since your divorce?" she asked as she looked down at her wine glass, running her finger over its rim.

"There was one woman. She'd already committed herself to a job far away, so our time was nicely spent, but it was also short."

"Do you miss her?"

"I don't know what I miss anymore. I'm learning not to get too attached to things. It keeps me from missing them when they aren't in my life anymore. I also don't have expectations. Expectations lead to disappointments. I miss what she brought to my life. It was a crazy time for me, when I felt like I could trust no one. She brought some stabilization to me and all the things that were swirling around me. I miss the calm with her. It was like a refuge in some ways."

"Don't you think that by not allowing yourself to get attached to people and things you're depriving yourself of some of life's joys?" she asked.

"I'm also missing out on the heartaches and disappointments. I know I'm on a deep descent into disconnection. I like it there. At least right now, I like it there."

"Encasing your heart in armament keeps pain out, but it doesn't let your heart leap. It doesn't let your heart wander. Hearts are wild things—that's why they're in cages," she said.

The waiter was now tableside with my third Bitburger. I slipped him my Chase credit card. C.C. protested, or at least protested enough to make it look legitimate, but I was thinking of a few more libations somewhere else where there are no disparaging looks from across the table. Tobacco Road came to mind and so did Bryson's Irish Bar. As I was thinking of the next watering hole to go to, C.C. snapped me back to the current moment.

"Cade. Thank you for dinner…again. Thank you for also letting me see a little more of you and get to know you a little better."

I looked across the table at her. In the soft light of the restaurant and the illumination of the table candle, I started to see her real beauty. Her eyes were soulful, thoughtful, and a swallow you whole deep brown. I could see myself and anyone else except Ernesto getting lost in her beautiful eyes. She had a blaze of beauty that had a radiance to it. Her dark black hair had a natural curl that framed her light mocha features. Her lips were full and lush, her teeth white and very straight. When she spoke, she used her hands in an expressive manner that drew me into the conversation. They drew me into *her*. She rested her elbows on the table and leaned closer across it towards me. She could see through me, it seemed. With a shy smile, she asked me what was I thinking.

"I think Ernesto is a serious dummy."

Chapter Seventeen

W<small>E STEPPED OUT</small> into the early evening, an awkwardness between us as we stood there.

I had been warned years earlier about the entanglements of getting involved with people you work with. Technically C.C. and I were not coworkers. This was hopefully going to be a temporary thing, but with Zeus out on the streets somewhere I just couldn't risk the complications that can come from getting involved with someone like her. I needed to focus and not let three Bitburger beers cloud my judgment or fill me with an unrealistic assumption. I mean, who was I kidding? It was just dinner. I needed to keep my ego in check and stop thinking that someone like C.C. would be interested in me.

"Every time I call you, you say you're deep south. How far south from here do you live?" she asked.

"It's pretty far. It's actually nearly a straight line from here but with the bay and all, you have to wind pretty far down Old Cutler Road."

"Oh, because I was thinking if it wasn't too far, maybe you could meet me for breakfast before I go to George T. Baker in the morning. I need to repay you for all these dinners."

"That's kind of you, but not necessary," I said.

She was standing close to me, looking up at me with those incredibly alluring brown eyes. I took a deep breath, stepped back a foot or two, and looked over at her car. She picked up on my reticence, and answered me with the chirp of her car unlocking from the remote in her hand. I opened her car door and as she swept past me to get inside, I caught a faint whiff of her perfume.

"What is that you're wearing?"

"Pearl by Element Edition I. Do you like it?"

"It's very nice."

We stayed in the open doorway a beat longer than necessary and she finally said with a tinge of exasperation, "I'll have to wear it more often." With that, she drove off.

I just stood in the road watching her drive away. I felt like a fool. For the briefest of moments there was no Zeus, it was as if it was just she and I.

Shaking off the moment, I got in my own car and headed south on Lejeune Road. Upon passing Bird Road I gave some serious thought about stopping into the Lejeune Casa bar. Not many people knew the actual name of the bar. The lime green building's only identifier was a three-foot tall vertical neon sign glowing the single word, "Beer." It was a serious drinker's spot. An enormous oval bar top fashioned from deep, dark wood was its sole feature. Nothing substantial adorned the walls except extension cords for the wall unit air conditioners. The irony of the bar was that it was directly next to an Alcohol Anonymous meeting room. Patrons of both establishments on more than one occasion were stunningly surprised as they walked in through the wrong door from the alley parking lot. Rumors of a shopping complex being built where the bar and our nearby city motor pool stood were always in the air. The shopping complex would encompass four to five city blocks. A lot of little buildings, gyms, and even an old undercover office we used in VIN would be demolished to make room for it. I personally didn't see how they could do it. The rumor was nothing but an acknowledgement that the space could be better, but with no conviction behind the plan. It, and every part of it, would never change.

The neon sign for Lejeune Casa called out to me but I plowed on by and went home. The drive was uneventful, and the moon was coming up over the bay as I pulled up to the front of the condo. The car lights splayed across the deep dense green vines on the staircase.

Shit! What was wrong with me?

I immediately put the car into reverse and whipped out of the space and then drove swiftly towards the point where the complex terminated at the bay. I'd allowed myself to get careless.

Zeus may not know who I am or anything about me—but there was still a chance that Tovar, or maybe even Sciarotta *was* Zeus.

I could be next up on a hit list.

I chastised myself thoroughly. I slowly and cautiously drove back to the condo. I'd need to start cleaning myself each and every time I went somewhere. Clean my trail and make sure I'm not being followed. Carelessness could get me killed. This time I eased slowly into the parking spot in front of the condo and checked my mirrors. I carried my keys in my clenched left hand, each key sticking through my fingers like a five-finger sharp medieval morning star. In my right hand I carried my Glock held close to my side. I holstered my weapon once I was inside and the door was closed and locked.

I opened the refrigerator and found what I was looking for. The soggy cardboard on the bottom of the six pack of Amstel Light made a slurping sound as it was relieved of its place on the glass shelf. The condensation from the shelf acted like a binding agent. Before closing the door, I snatched a bottle opener conveniently kept in the built-in holder for eggs. I deemed the holder better suited for limes and lemons than eggs. It also was a logical spot to keep a bottle opener. I walked past the upright bar and the Julio Larraz sculpture of a portly bearded man in his underwear holding a bent barbell over his head. The sculpture sort of represented getting older, but still getting it done to me. The eclectic array of art in the condominium was primarily by South American or Caribbean artists. Grabbing a pint glass from the counter near the stairs, I headed upstairs, through the master bedroom, and out onto the oversized deck. The deck faced due east out over the tree line, the wide expanse of trees in the moonlight, and the dark Biscayne Bay were my only companions.

The night was still early by Miami standards, and occasionally I'd hear a boat come in through the channel or the soft undiscernible voices of my neighbors from their outdoor decks and terraces. I deluded myself that by drinking the first beer out of the pint glass there was some form of control and refinement. By the second Amstel I was chugging it from the bottle and kicking myself for letting another potential amorous situation slip away. I knew it would complicate things. I told myself that over and over. I reminded myself of professionalism. I reminded myself that I had a job to do and I couldn't let my personal feelings for C.C., or anyone for that matter, get in the way. I told myself that over and over. It was around 3am when the very last remnants in the beer bottle I was holding spilled across my lap, waking me up. I'd finished the entire six pack and fallen asleep on one of the chaise lounges. I hated myself for passing out but was secretly relived it happened when I was alone and at home.

I took my soaked pants and underwear off, then ripped off my shirt as well. I left the wet garments in a heap on the deck. Smelling like a brewery, I went inside and pushed the bed covers aside to slip into bed and into a deep sleep.

I woke up from a dream of sitting in an open-air outdoor stadium, and it was really hot. When I fluttered my eyes open, the window shades and valances were open, as was the door to the deck outside. The condominium's air conditioning was laboring to keep the bedroom cool with the open door. The morning sun was streaming in hot, right on me. I was sweating, and the heat from the sun was making me feel unsteady.

Or maybe it was the nine beers from the night before.

I stutter-stepped leaving the bed and got a glimpse of the deck outside: I saw my clothes and the empty Amstel Light beer bottles. In college I had a guy in my dormitory who liked to revive himself from his drunken state by turning on all three showers in our communal bathroom. Each shower had a partial partition between them. He would crawl under all three partitions and lay on the floor of the shower for an hour, trying to revive back to normalcy, all three showers streaming water down on him. It seemed stupid at the time. But now, I wanted to do the same. Luckily for me, this opulent condominium had a large, tiled shower that could easily hold three people in it. The shower also had dual heads. I turned both heads on and closed the glass door letting the flow of the water and steam build up. After a few minutes, I opened the door and crawled into the shower. I laid on the expensive Italian tile, replicating my college classmate. I must have dozed off because the water had gotten colder. I knew I was depleting the hot water heater. I went out exactly like I went in—on my hands and knees. I grabbed one of the fluffy towels off the towel bar and dried myself from a sitting position, like some sort of uncouth toddler.

In short order I was upright, wrapped in a towel and beginning to act like a grown man. With a mouth full of toothpaste, vigorously brushing my teeth, I took a visual inventory of myself in the mirror. *Much better.* I went out to the deck and retrieved my clothes, threw them all into the washer and then quickly got dressed. I collected the six beer bottles and put them in the recycling bin. I called the VIN office. After three rings Ileana answered.

"*Veen.*"

"Hi Ileana, it's Cade."

"*Coño*, do *ju* think I don't know *jur* voice *ahora*, Cade?"

"Well, it's such a pleasure to talk to you too, Ileana. I'm calling to tell you I'll be with Miami today most of the day, but I'm expecting to hear from an attorney in Collier County any day now, so let me know please if he calls."

"What's *de* name of the attorney?"

I wasn't expecting her to ask me that. She rarely keeps up with the actual comings and goings of the VIN unit.

"I'm not sure. It's a public defender, so if they say Collier County I'll know. Is Gary there?"

I asked her about Gary so she wouldn't have the opportunity

to ask me anything more about the attorney from Collier County. Thankfully, she's not the type to normally probe or proactively call me seeking information, unless Major Brunson or someone else directs her to do so.

"*Espere.*" Wait.

Gary's relaxed voice picked up on the line after about fifteen seconds.

"Yo, dude."

"Good morning, Gary. I just wanted to remind you about asking around at the steering committee if any other agencies have heard of a guy named Zeus."

"Yeah, I got it, dude. I'll let you know."

"Thanks, Big G. I'll be at the airport the mid-morning part of the day so I can zip over to Blue Lagoon if you need me."

"Cool. I'll let you know. Either way I'll get back to you."

"Thanks, Big G."

I hung up the phone and continued getting dressed. I wasn't too impressed with Ellinport and didn't foresee this meeting being the center point of my day, so I threw on some jeans, a long sleeve black polo shirt and a pair of Cole Hahn driving loafers. My hair was still a little wet from the shower and I gave it a once go-over with the towel. I grabbed a pancake holster and once I had it on, I holstered my Glock. I kept the polo untucked and put on my badge, which I had on a nighthawk chain. The chain and badge were also concealed under my shirt. I grabbed my keys and gave the condo a quick once-over, confident I hadn't forgotten anything.

I drove out through the Paradise Point gate. On the way out I stopped at the gatehouse and the guard stepped out of the gate to meet me. I mentioned to the guard that a termite company would be by later to tent the condominium for termites. I instructed him that unless it was the termite company to not let anyone in saying they were there for 6211 Paradise Point Drive. He wrote it down on a clipboard. I thanked him and drove off. There was no termite company which meant I should have no visitors at all. I was proactively setting trip wires, in case Zeus was out there gunning for me.

My drive to the Dolphin garage at Miami International Airport was smooth and easy as I timed it after all the school traffic had died down. I was a little early when I pulled into a parking space on the eighth floor. I had time to take the elevator downstairs and find an airport café that had Cuban coffee. Being armed, I didn't want to risk going downstairs amongst the flying public. Someone might see my gun under my shirt and alert the authorities. So I decided to just stand on the enclosed overhead walkway. I looked down at the cars coming and going into and out of the airport. I imagined some of those drivers picking up and dropping off friends and family for a myriad of reasons. People fly for many divergent reasons. Some fly for business. Other passengers are flying for pleasure, long-awaited vacations, unexpected funerals, or anticipated sporting events.

That got me thinking about Sciarotta.

A flight to Jacksonville is so inexpensive that it outweighs the benefit of driving unless the drive provides an opportunity flying doesn't. Like no traceable record of your coming and goings. It's also 347 miles of opportunity to dispose of a Walther P-88 handgun, especially if you dissembled the gun into six to eight parts along the way. Maybe having the public records check on Tovar should expand to include Sciarotta. That's what I was thinking when I saw C.C. walking toward me. She was dressed in a pair of dark slacks and a form-fitting blue blazer over a patterned blouse. Her hair hung low and natural. Her curly, long locks were very eye catching. She looked very attractive. The closer she drew near me the more attractive she seemed to become. She smiled at me as she drew near. I could actually smell her Pearl by Element Edition I.

"Good morning Mr. German Restaurant Man. Are you ready for the big reveal from Ellinport? "

"As ready as I'll ever be."

We entered through the glass double doors. I stole a glance at her in the reflection of the doors, in awe of how attractive she actually was. Before long we were walking down the long hallway with deep blue carpeting. We followed the carpet to the hallway to the same circular room from yesterday where Secretary Diane Ford sat. She asked us to wait in the same comfortable chairs as yesterday. I noticed her glancing at us intermittently as she did her work at her desk. Finally she spoke.

"Are you both police officers?"

I looked at C.C. and she looked at me. I half shrugged at C.C. as if to say that it made no difference to me.

"Yes, we are," said C.C.

"You are way too pretty to be a police officer," she said to C.C.

Diane Ford looked at me as if she was trying to find something nice to say.

"I don't think I've ever seen a policeman that looks like you."

I assumed my longish dark hair, goatee and earrings were not something she was used to seeing by watching *Law and Order* and *NYPD Blue*. I gave her a smile and pretended to start reading an *Aviation Today* magazine. Diane continued her commentary to both C.C. and I.

"My brother-in-law Todd, he was a deputy for the Ontario Sherriff's Office. It's near Rochester, New York. He retired about two years ago."

"What does he do now?" asked C.C.

"He moved to central Florida and he builds decks and does home repairs for all the widows in the Villages."

C.C. looked at me and in a hushed voice with more than a bit of sass she said, "You should think about retiring and being the handy man in the Villages. Maybe in more ways than one." I met her gaze over the magazine and slid the magazine even higher, burying my face even more in it. She started laughing.

At that moment Ellinport appeared from the interior of his office. He greeted us both and just like yesterday, he widened the space in the doorway and turned back to go inside.

"Good morning, one and all," he said as we entered his office.

I thought it was a peculiar greeting, but then again, it was a way for him to welcome us both when he might not be too enamored to have me in his office. In a reenactment of yesterday's meeting, we settled into the same seats across from him. Off to the side was a TV on a portable stand, and a VCR on the shelf below it.

"I trust you both had a restful night. We're just waiting on Chief of Staff and Senior Policy Advisor, Suezie Chanin-Galperin, to join us."

I was now firmly convinced that Marshall Ellinport lived in a world of titles and status quo.

Small talk ensued as we waited, mostly between C.C. and Ellinport. I passed the time glancing around the office at the various plaques and certificates on the wall, some of them dated more than two years ago. They were obvious hold-overs from before Ellinport took office—a fact I'm sure he thought many wouldn't notice. The ambient noise from the airport was still partially audible although the thick windows, and walls did muffle out most of the sound.

The intercom buzzed and Diane Ford announced that Chief of Staff and Senior Policy Advisor, Suezie Chanin-Galperin was on her way in. Ellinport immediately stood up as if royalty were about to walk through the door. Suezie Chanin-Galperin wasn't royalty but she sure carried herself with a high measure of confidence and competency. Ms. Chanin-Galperin came into the office with a very commanding presence. As she crossed the threshold all eyes, including C.C.'s were on her. She was noticeably attractive, at about 5'8,"tall with thick, long, reddish brown hair that was layered and went halfway down her back. She wore a linen long sleeve shirt with wide cuffs that were prominent under her dark navy jacket—a jacket that was failing in its attempt to conceal her generous bustline. Her dark navy pencil skirt had vertical gold piping, highlighting her bare legs that were tanned and highly toned from an obvious adherence to a strict fitness regime. She had on a pair of black Salvatore Ferragamo Vara, shiny, low-heel pumps. She seemed to glide across the blue carpet as she first shook Ellinport's hand, and then turned her gaze on me and C.C. She had piercing green eyes. She looked directly at me and said, "You must be Detective Taylor."

I stood, and I shook her hand.

"How did you know?" I asked her.

"Percentage guess. I was going to either be fifty percent correct or fifty percent wrong."

She extended her hand and greeted C.C. very warmly.

"Homicide. It's a rough job I'm sure, but as a woman I am so proud to see another woman leading the charge," she complimented C.C.

Ellinport suggested we all take seats. He went through the motions of explaining to Ms. Chanin-Galperin the reason that C.C. and I were in his office, and he recanted the events of our meeting him yesterday. He made a point to say why he didn't want to continue discussing MIA events without Ms. Chanin-Galperin present. Inwardly, I knew that a person of her importance wasn't going to go into any meeting blind and she had already been briefed. Ellinport's spiel was for C.C. and I. When Ellinport finished, she sat further back in her seat, nonchalantly crossed her long legs, and held a French manicured hand up by her chin as if to signal Ellinport to start the show. Ellinport straightened the lapels of his jacket and continued to speak.

"Detectives, I asked you to come back today because I wanted to confer with Ms. Chanin-Galperin before advancing our conversation any further. With her consent to speak freely and share with you what we can to assist your investigation, we're prepared to present a few things we've discovered here during our own internal investigation. RFS is not our most cherished third-party vendor, and it was in our investigation of them that we stumbled upon what we think will be of assistance to you."

Chanin-Galperin listened impassively, and I wondered when the superfluous rhetoric was going to end and we could get on with it. Ellinport continued.

"We had heard that name Zeus mentioned by a few workers,

most notably RFS workers, who stated in their exit interviews that there was a close-knit smuggling group operating here at MIA. What we have been able to determine is that they themselves, are not smuggling anything. What they *are* doing is stealing what we think is drugs or money from drug couriers."

"So, what you're saying is that these guys are ripping off drug couriers from commercial flights. That naturally led to the untimely deaths of our two victims," I interjected.

"Exactly," Ellinport said, pointing a finger directly at me.

Ellinport got up from behind his desk and closed the blinds to the window behind him, dimming the room. He remained standing.

"Let me show you something. Here is surveillance video from September 23rd. We set up hidden cameras on the concourses and had flight control purposely reroute all Miami to New York flights to these gates where we had the cameras set up. LaGuardia, Newark, JFK, it made no difference. The A-300s we had sent to other gates, but DC-9s or 727s we had come to our camera-set gates."

"Why is that?" asked C.C.

"The A-300s are cargo loaded by what we call 'cans.' Luggage is put into these very large aluminum containers—cans—that are sitting on dollies. That's done in the cargo luggage receiving area at airport ground level. When the cans are full, they're connected like a train to a tug that takes them out to the aircraft. Once within the safety zone of the aircraft, high lifts are waiting that will pick up a can from the dolly. The high lift raises the can up to the aircraft cargo opening and a series of rolling ball bearings within a track system enable the can to be pushed onto the aircraft. The load master knows the weight and balance of the airplane and the cans are loaded onto a similar track system of ball bearings and rails within the aircraft. When the can's in place, there's a foot lever that the RFS worker kicks up to lock the can in place."

Both C.C. and I nodded in understanding. Chanin-Galperin obviously knew this already but politely sat through the explanation.

Ellinport continued as he started fidgeting with a remote control for the VCR.

"The 727s and DC-9s are loaded by hand. What that means is the ground crew—in this case, RFS—uses their employees to load the airplanes. The tugs come out with loaded luggage carts attached to the back of them. An RFS employee drives a conveyor belt up to the aircraft cargo opening. The conveyor belt is actually attached to the vehicle he's driving. The driver raises the conveyor belt to the aircraft cargo opening. One to three employees walk up the raised conveyor belt and go into the cargo hold of the aircraft. The other RFS employees remove the luggage from the carts and start sending them up the belt to the employees inside the belly of the airplane. As the bags reach the top of the conveyor belt, the RFS employees… well, I'd like to say *place,* but more than likely they throw the bags to the back of the cargo hold of the aircraft until it fills up. It piles up towards the door opening. When the plane gets to its destination the process is reversed as the plane is unloaded." he explained.

"So why Miami to New York flights?" asked C.C.

I spoke up and answered for Ellinport before he could speak more.

"Like he said, they aren't controlling their own product movement. They're ripping off drug dealers who are using drug couriers to mule money or cocaine from Miami to New York and back. Most likely, it's cocaine going up and money coming back. Reggie and Jabo may have just ripped off the wrong guy—and his name is Zeus."

Chanin-Galperin finally spoke. "Why don't you show them the video?"

C.C and I looked at each other and then at Ellinport as he started pushing buttons on the VCR remote control. The imagery came in with a static wave and then the time stamp was seen in the bottom of the screen: 9:20am September 23rd, 1998.

I recognized Reggie on the screen by his distinctive green Pumas. He was standing with a crew of six other RFS employees. It seemed that two were Latin, and the rest African American. C.C. leaned in very close and I could hear her softly say, "Jabo." The crew seemed to be just conversing and hanging out. From the corner of the frame the conveyor belt driver pulled up. Two of the guys broke from the others. The carts of luggage had been unhitched from the tug. They pulled it up to the conveyor belt like it was a big tug of war, with both RFS employees leaning way back as they pulled the cart train of luggage. Jabo pulled his knee pads up which had been around his ankles, and started walking up the incline of the conveyor belt.

Ellinport stopped the tape just as Jabo was entering the opening of the airplane.

"So, as you can see here on the tape, this is one of your victims. We had already identified Jamal Boseman Cooper. This identification was done prior to your coming in and telling me he was deceased. RFS hadn't seen him in a few days. RFS assumed he'd just quit his job without informing them. That's fairly common. That's why they thought the same of Reginald LaMarr. I spoke with their supervisor this morning. I informed him they were actually deceased although I didn't elaborate. Now *here* is where it gets interesting."

The tape showed one of the RFS employees start the conveyor belt. Jabo was on his knees in the cargo hold of the airplane, just inside the opening. The other RFS employees, including Reggie, started loading suitcases on the belt and sending them slowly up to Jabo. The suitcases were upright so that Jabo could grab them by their handles. As the suitcases rose up to Jabo, he would grab them and throw them into the cargo hold of the airplane. The suitcases were spaced apart enough on the conveyor belt so that Jabo had time to grasp each one and "place" it in the cargo hold. For about three minutes we watched suitcases of all sizes, colors, and styles go up the belt, and Jabo dutifully grabbed each one and put it behind him in the cargo area out of sight of the camera. One suitcase did fall off the belt, which caused the fairly efficient operation to temporarily stop.

"There! There it is!" said Ellinport with enthusiasm.

C.C. and I studied the screen trying to see what he was talking about.

"Just like you said, Marshall. It's the angle," said Ms. Chanin-Galperin.

Both C.C. and I struggled to see whatever it was they were talking about. Ellinport rewound the tape back about forty seconds.

"These guys, they lift bags all day. They can tell a lot by the feel of them. They can tell by the weight. They can tell by how many locks or what kind of locks a bag has on it. They have a feel for it, and some of these guys are very good at it. Reggie LaMarr was very good at it. Reggie was very good at figuring out what bags might have kilos of cocaine in them or loads of money. Watch the tape now and I'll take you through it."

Ellinport started the tape again. Suitcases and bags were placed on the conveyor belt in a straight line. Ellinport pointed at the screen and then said:

"See how the bags are all in a straight line? Now, watch this brown one here. Reggie puts it on the belt at an angle. That's the signal suitcase. Now, watch as the signal suitcase goes up the belt. Just as it reaches Boseman Cooper, he knocks the one in front of it off the belt."

The video clearly showed Jabo reaching for the bag from the cargo hold and mishandling it, causing the suitcase to fall to the tarmac below. Reggie immediately stopped the conveyor belt. The rest of the crew, as if in intentional slow motion, stopped what they were doing. Reggie slowly and casually walked around the equipment to retrieve the fallen bag. Upon retrieving it he made a very deliberate production of wiping the sides of the bag to brush grit and dirt off of it. One of the other RFS employees approached Reggie and offered to help. Now both Reggie and the worker were looking at the bag. Jabo, from the very beginning of when the bag fell was notably out of camera range. He was deep in the cargo hold of the aircraft.

"LaMarr and this other fellow are buying Cooper time. Cooper's in the baggage hold using lock picks and universal keys to try and open the bag that Reggie identified as possibly being loaded with cash or cocaine," said Ellinport.

On the video Cooper could now be seen gesturing and yelling to the crew members on the ground. He's holding a beige pouch with a leather band at the top of it.

"The mail? You have got to be kidding me? I don't believe it," said Chanin-Galperin.

"Believe it," said Ellinport.

C.C. and I looked at each other and then back at the video. Jabo was yelling down to one of the crew members and he appeared to be angry. Reggie stepped up as peace maker. Jabo leaned out of the cargo hold and softly dropped the mail pouch to Reggie, who caught it, then casually walked over to and climbed aboard an unhitched tug. He started the engine and then drove off out of the camera view. The rest of the crew continued to load bags on the conveyor belt and send them up to Jabo, who continued to load the airplane until there were no more bags to load.

Ellinport stopped the video. He opened the blinds and let the room fill with light. Chanin-Galperin sat still, but was obviously none too pleased with what she just saw.

"What was it that we just saw?" C.C. asked.

"Reggie LaMarr identified a piece of luggage as being potentially filled with cocaine or cash. He let Cooper know which bag it was by placing it an angle as it went up the conveyor belt. Cooper saw the angled bag coming towards him and he purposely mishandled and dropped the bag in front of it. Reggie stopped the conveyor belt to get the fallen bag. Cooper pulled the angled bag inside the baggage hold and worked to open it while they stalled on the ground, retrieving the fallen bag. I think he had crammed an empty mail pouch down his pants and when he found what he was hoping to find in the suitcase, he then transferred the money or the cocaine to the mail pouch."

"What is the purpose of the mail pouch?" asked C.C.

It was Chanin-Galperin who spoke next.

"As airmail began crossing the country successfully in the mid-1920s, railroad owners complained that this government-sponsored enterprise was cutting into their business. They found a friendly ear in Congressman Clyde Kelly of Pennsylvania, chairman of the House Post Office Committee, who largely represented railroad interests. He then sponsored a House resolution known as the Contract Air Mail Bill. Part of the bill is that mail must come off of the airplane first. So what this Cooper guy was doing was yelling at his colleagues that they missed a mail pouch, when in fact he *created* the pouch and its contents himself in the cargo hold. The guy on the tug, the one you call Reggie; he's in on it. He takes the missing mail pouch and whisks it away to, presumably, the U.S. mail facility at concourse B. Although my guess is he never made it there."

C.C. started to say something again and I'm sure she was going to mention finding the mail pouch at the Pinder residence in Coconut Grove. We were sitting close enough for me to push my foot on top of hers and keep her from speaking.

"My guess is the drug couriers and money movers aren't reporting any of these losses to any of you. If it's been going on for a while, it might even be factored in as the cost of doing business. But someone was getting ripped off and complaining. I think the greed factor surged here, and that's how you were brought in. When they started miscalculating kilos and cash, they didn't want to come up empty-handed—so they started taking watches, cameras, and jewelry. Am I right?" I asked.

"Exactly. We thought we had a baggage theft ring here. It was through observation and surveillance that we saw this pattern of falling bags and missed mail pouches. From the flights where no one reported any losses, I was able to deduce that we had a bigger problem than just watches and cameras. It's a lucrative way to get in the cocaine trafficking and money laundering business without incurring nearly any of the risk. If these guys hadn't gotten greedy, I would not have pieced this together," said Ellinport.

"So Zeus may have killed our victims because they endangered the true meaning of their criminal enterprise by being greedy," said C.C., wide-eyed.

Once again, I put my foot on top of C.C.'s and lightly pressed.

"Is there any need for guys like Reggie and Boseman Cooper to remove panels in the interior of the aircraft?"

Ellinport looked at Chanin-Galperin and shrugged.

"The turnaround time of the aircraft from coming into a gate and leaving a gate is pretty tight. I don't see how removing any panels would benefit them. Are you insinuating that they're secreting contraband in the airplane panels?" Chanin-Galperin asked.

"No. I was just wondering since they have such easy access to the airplane, what if they find something too big to put in a mail pouch? What if they have stash locations in the airplane where they could hide the contraband until the plane returns?"

"I see your point of view, but I can assure you as Chief of Staff and Senior Policy Advisor, it's impossible. These airplanes move around the country, if not the globe, like chess pieces. It's all predicated by Flight Control and Scheduling in Dallas. We never know which exact airplane is going to be here and these planes go through an ABC check system: 'A' check is every four to 600 hours of flight time. The plane is brought in and a minimum ten- hour maintenance is performed. Progressively through B, C, 3C, and D checks, the aircraft is nearly dismantled and reassembled. As contract employees, they'd never have the capability of even knowing where an airplane will be an hour from now; let alone days or weeks later," said Chanin-Galperin with a sophisticated air of unquestionable authority.

"This has been an insightful meeting. We have a better idea why our victims were murdered, but we still have no idea who Zeus is," said C.C. Chanin-Galperin stood up and adjusted her pencil skirt. My cheeks grew warm as she clearly caught me trying to be nonchalant as I watched her shapely legs cross and uncross as she stood.

"Marshall. Thank you for allowing me to see the back end of this investigation. You have put so much work and effort into it. Detectives, I am needed on Concourse E for an event, but please, feel free to continue working with Mr. Ellinport. My office is always available to you both. Detective Clay, once again I'm enamored by your ascent at the Miami Police Department, and Detective Taylor it was a pleasure meeting you as well," she said with a cool smile before leaving.

Ellinport reached into a drawer and pulled a small box out.

"Detective Clay, I'm sure there are people you answer to. Here is a copy of the tape you just saw. I'll continue to see what I can learn about this Zeus fellow, but with the deaths of LaMarr and Cooper there have been no more complaints of bag theft or item loss. As of now, I think I've taken this as far as I can unless more complaints come in or I hear of anything related to Zeus. I am sorry—I wish there was more I could offer you at this time," he said.

Ellinport asked C.C. if she'd called the phone number for the Walnut Creek, California lab. C.C. explained that with the time difference from east coast to west coast she hadn't done it yet. In front of us, Ellinport picked up his phone and called the Walnut Creek lab. He had Special Agent Robert Ainsle on the phone after a few connections. We listened as he relayed the information about the Walther P-88 and asked Ainsle to send a list of all registered owners of the Walther P-88 in Palm Beach, Broward, and Miami Dade counties. C.C quietly asked if he could add Monroe County to the list. Ellinport asked Ainsle to add Monroe County as well. They had a friendly banter about the ATF and then Ellinport hung up.

"Agent Ainsle said to expect the information as early as the end of the day today. It's a simple process of inputting the model and caliber and the geographical location and any legal owners of that type of firearm will populate the list. Then he just needs to send the list to you. Keep in mind these are the *legal* owners. Anything illegal will not show up."

We both shook his hand, and we both expressed our appreciation, she and I left his office. Out by the elevators, C.C. looked at me and asked me why I didn't want to mention the mail bag at the Pinder house or the bags of screws both victims had. I explained that it was just better if we held that back for now. I reminded her that there were cameras in Reggie's footlocker as well as the cash in the mail pouch. There would be plenty of time to return property later to Ellinport. Our focus should be on finding Zeus.

Chapter Eighteen

A S WE WAITED for the elevator I called Gary, who was at the task force steering committee at the Blue Lagoon Hilton. The Blue Lagoon corporate and hospitality area was a seven minute drive from the airport. Gary picked up the phone and sounded as though he was walking when he answered.

"Mr. Cade. What can I do for you, sir?"

"That's quite a greeting there, Big G. I'm just calling to see if you heard anything from anybody about Zeus."

"Nada. No way. No how. No one has heard anything about him. It's as if the guy doesn't exist. There was mostly talk of a Jamaican posse up in Miramar called the 'Reload Posse,' because every time rivals come against them, they better be prepared to reload—because as the Broward Sheriff's Office said 'there will be bullets flying.' The Law Enforcement Trust Fund is pretty healthy for all agencies in the task force. They set an agenda for next month and that was about it."

"So the LETF was the only real big issue. Are you going back to the office?" I asked.

"Eventually. Going to lunch right now. There's a new place on the circle in Miami Springs called Harvest Moon. Very healthy, my kind of place, or at least that's what I'm told. I'm going to check it out."

"I don't know Miami Springs too well. I only know Bryson's Pub."

"Yeah, well go past Bryson's Pub. I mean, if you can. Just stay on that road. That's Curtiss Parkway. It will lead you into this big circle. The restaurant is supposed to be there on the circle."

I looked over at C.C. as he was talking and motioned with my finger to my open mouth, and she understood it meant let's get something to eat. She nodded her head up and down.

"Cool. If you get there before me, get a table for three. I'm bringing someone with me," I said.

I hung up with Gary and explained to C.C. who he was, that he was very health conscious and that he wanted to try a new place for lunch in Miami Springs.

"I'll follow you," she said as she got into her car.

We both left the airport and took the Lejeune Road north exit. The grittier maintenance side of the airport was on my left as I passed bars, Chinese restaurants, hotels, and gas stations on my right. I turned north on Curtiss Parkway and I must admit I did give a sideways glance at Bryson's Irish Pub as I passed it. I don't think they had neon in 1948 when the pub first opened, but the green neon which I think is on twenty-four hours a day, was evident even in the October sunshine. The two-lane road bisected through a golf course parking lot and then developed into a wide median with trees and bushes throughout. At the circle, I saw the Harvest Moon on my left. The place looked like a gas station. As I parked adjacent to it, I saw that it was indeed a recently converted gas station. Gary was already seated at an outdoor table under a patio umbrella. The remnants of the once-functioning gas station were evident with the pumping islands, bay doors, and garage area all intact. In what must have been the gas station office was a nook created where patrons ordered their food from a chalkboard menu. Gary was most pleased with himself.

"The guy wanted to buy a gas station but the tanks deep in the ground are inverted and nonfunctional, so the guy got screwed on the sale. In typical making-lemonade-out-of-lemons, he's turned this place into a healthy restaurant with a killer menu. I ordered the veggie melt with carrot juice," Gary said with a grin.

C.C. walked up to us just as he was finishing.

"Big G this is C.C. She's homicide with Miami. C.C., this is Gary he works as an analyst in our VIN unit. I call him Big G."

Gary got up from his seat and shook C.C.'s hand.

"Homicide. Wow. I'd be happy to lay in a chalk outline for you," he said in a semi-off-putting but endearing way.

Gary explained that you order off the chalk board and then they bring it to your table. The place had only been open as a restaurant less than a year and was still finding its way. There were only five tables. I was thankful that Gary secured one for us. C.C. ambled over towards the narrow door that was once the gas station office. I started to follow her when Gary grabbed me by the arm and said quietly in my ear, "Dude. She is *smoking* hot."

"Let's keep it professional, Big G. Let's keep it professional."

I caught up to C.C. just inside the tiny space, reading the chalk board. All the menu items were written in bright orange, blue, green, and yellow chalk. When it came time for her to order she ordered the Middle Eastern salad with a bottle of water. I ordered the Caesar chicken melt also with a bottle of water.

"This time I'm paying," she said as she wedged herself between me and the cashier. She handed the cashier a twenty. I wasn't going to argue with her, and I continued to look at the menu. The script in the colorful chalk was very eye catching. I noticed at the bottom of the menu chalk board a very small section that said, "Today's Scripture."

Behold, I have given you authority to tread on serpents and scorpions, and over all the power of the enemy, and nothing shall hurt you. ~ Luke 10:19

I read the scripture twice more. C.C. was holding both of our bottles of water. She asked me if I was coming, breaking me from my reverie. I went back outside with her and we sat down with Gary, who was wearing a pair of stylish Perry Ellis sunglasses.

"So no one has any information about Zeus from the steering committee?" I asked.

"Dude, it's like all they really cared about was how much money was in the LETF. The more drug money you guys seize, the more they think they're CEOs of some international company or something. They're freaking cops, for crying out loud! But to hear them say how healthy their LETF's are, and what they hope to spend it on… It's like watching kids playing grown-up."

I turned the attention and the conversation to C.C.

"C.C, did you come up with anything about the screws from George T. Baker Aviation School?"

"Actually, I did. I spoke to a guy named Matthew Walton. He's a senior instructor in metallurgy and tensile strength. I showed him the screws and he said they're European manufactured. They're made of a combination of alloys designed for *interior* aviation and not *external* aviation. I left him a few of the screws in case it helped him to figure what their purpose was."

"Wait, what screws are you talking about?" interrupted Gary.

"The two guys we think Zeus killed were both in possession of these screws that we've never seen before. I took them to Home Depot and the guy there said he'd never seen them either," I explained.

C.C. interjected, "It seems that when they manufacture aviation screws there are different tensile strengths and torque require-ments because of the pressure, altitude, and temperature changes the airplane goes through in flight. External screws and bolts have to withstand all of that repeatedly; interior screws and bolts not as much. But to retool the machinery to go from external to internal is a tremendous endeavor—so they just notch it down a little for the interior screws and bolts. So, the panels and floorboards get *these* type of screws, as does the galley, cockpit doors and things like that."

"Basically, you're saying these super strong screws and bolts on the outside of the plane cause the manufacturer to make interior screws and bolts that are stronger than the average hardware kinds," said Gary.

"Pretty much yes. Since both Reggie and Jabo had these screws, there *has* to be an interior thing connected to either their deaths or the smuggling operation they were in. They have slotted heads that most American screwdrivers won't fit."

"Wait. The victim's name is *Jabo*?" Gary said, adjusting his sunglasses. "Too cool."

We both just looked at Gary, me knowing we may have inadvertently help him nickname his firstborn surfing son, if and when that should ever occur.

"I'm only guessing," I said, "but I bet that a large aviation company like Airbus manufactures their own screws. I say Airbus because they're a large European—actually a Dutch—aerospace company, that make the A-300 and other types of airplanes that American and others are flying. Maybe we can get a deeper answer from someone at Airbus."

C.C. and Gary both thought that was a good idea. Our lunches arrived and we enjoyed the autumn sunshine and the tasty meals. Gary raved about the carrot juice. Gary and I caught up on some of the comings and goings in the department. Since the VIN unit was currently without a lieutenant, Gary's role as a financial analyst has also increased to having more exposure to some of our operational situations. Conversation turned to the ruthlessness of Zeus. Gary's ears perked up when he heard some of the details of the Jabo's and Reggie's murders, but we were interrupted by my cell phone ringing.

Ritchie Tavino.

I excused myself from the table and walked a few steps away and took the call. "Hello."

"We're on for tomorrow. Wear your big boy pants."

"Okay. What's going on?"

"Chuco himself just called. It sounds like him and Perchero are having a little disagreement."

"Disagreement? Like what?"

"Are you ready for this? Perchero knows that he needs to push the seven million on us and he's trying to hold Chuco to a storage fee— two percent storage if it goes past Friday. Chuco told him to drop it all to us by tomorrow, and he's pissed because he thinks Perchero is trying to strong-arm him at the eleventh hour. He also thinks that Perchero is disrespecting Chuco's position in the cartel. On the side, Chuco told me if he wasn't looking to carve out his portion, he'd just send a security team up here from Colombia and put them all six feet deep in the Everglades. So, he wants us to meet with Perchero tomorrow. We seize the seven mill, and he says put it all on Perchero. At first he wanted to keep him removed—now he says pin it on them and fuck 'em."

"This is sounding way too personal, Ritchie. I said it, and Fermin Rivacoba said it, too. I don't think they have seven million. Perchero and that lump of a human, Emiliano, look like amateur players."

"From the start I didn't care if we made an arrest or an indictment. All we want to do is get the engines going again. Your Major Brunson and SAC Sorenson don't care either, as long as we make the seizure. If we take Perchero down tomorrow it just builds an even bigger wall for Chuco to distance himself from all of this. We've got a big fish on the line—and we can reel in even bigger fish," said Ritchie.

I looked back at the table where C.C. and Gary were talking and laughing animatedly. The other tables were filled with patrons enjoying their lunches. I thought how ironic that here I was, a few feet away, talking about a seven million dollar drug money case. Only in Miami, and only in Miami frequently.

"Have you set the meet yet?"

"Seven million is going to take some time to count. We set it earlier than our normal times. Ten in the morning tomorrow. S&S Diner at 1757 Northeast 2nd Avenue."

"The S&S can be really busy at that time, and it's tiny," I hissed.

"Yeah, but it's got a big L-shaped parking lot in the back. We're going to pre-meet up at the Ace Hardware down the street at eight-thirty."

"The Ace Hardware? The one with the naked woman painted along the entire length of the building? Man, you sure can pick em,' Ritchie. This is getting more and more odd with you, Ritchie."

"I know. Right? I thought it would be a good set-up spot. What a better way to start your day off banging bad guys and taking in seven million dollars than under a sixty-five foot long naked woman? So, we'll all meet you somewhere in the parking lot between her ankle and her boob," Ritchie quipped.

"Ritchie. It's *seven million dollars,* and they're pissing off the owner of the money already. I had suggested long weapons before. I'm telling you now, you and your guys need to heed that advice. Something just isn't right with these guys."

"Cade, we got it covered. Acevedo will have his Steyr AUG, and Slomianski will have a Colt SMG. We got this covered. I got another call coming in, I gotta take this. Tomorrow. Eight-thirty. Naked woman, Ace Hardware. See you there." And he hung up.

I pulled the phone down from my ear and looked at the call duration timer.

One minute and forty-one seconds. That was all it took to learn that a Colombian drug trafficker intends to rip off his own cohorts by having seven million dollars seized, and he has amplified the situation by throwing his own drug couriers under the slow-rolling asphalt truck of justice. To make it even more Miami, I and the agents of the U.S. Customs Service employed by this great nation of ours, are meeting in a parking lot of a national hardware chain that just so happens to have a sixty-five foot long painting of bronzed naked woman lying on her stomach painted on the wall.

Damn, everything has become erratic.

I gazed up at the sun, listened to the sound of birds and a smattering of traffic, and just thought how absurd this life I was leading was becoming. I'd left a table where we were discussing a cold, calculated professional killer to take a call about a seven million dollar drop in less than twenty-four hours. One that I felt necessitated stronger firepower.

This isn't normal, I told myself. *Normal people don't live like this.*

I watched C.C. and Gary, and seriously contemplated whiling the afternoon away, throwing back a few Jamesons at Bryson's Irish Pub, right down the same road I was standing on.

As I walked back towards the table, I was just in time to hear Gary regaling C.C. about his times at F.I.U. I sat back down with C.C. and Gary and finished the remnants of my Caesar chicken melt.

"Dude, everything okay?" asked Gary.

"Yeah, it's all fine. Remember that NINJAS input you did for me yesterday at the Hungry Bear Sub Shop?'

"It was yesterday, of course I remember."

"When you get back to the office can you input another one for me? It's for tomorrow at 1757 Northeast 2nd Avenue at ten in the morning. Add it as an addendum to the others so that it's clear they are connected. This one is for an undetermined amount in a pickup with U.S. Customs. Make sure you also put Major Brunson on it, as well. Don't input any of it until you're ready to leave the office today. I want this to go in as late as possible."

"Why is that?" he asked.

"Did you see U.S. Customs at the steering committee meeting today?"

Gary thought about it for a second and then it hit him.

"Oh a dance with a girl from a different school. I got you."

C.C. cocked her head, perplexed, and looking at me for some insight. I explained what NINJAS was and how it worked. She was also curious why we would set up deals and cases in her city but not inform her S.I.S. I also explained how as a multi-jurisdictional task force, we tended to operate all over the tri-county area, even in New York and Los Angeles sometimes. I told her that if ATF Agent Robert Ainsle gets any ownership information on the Walter P-88 and she needs help with addresses, or even if the list is super long, she could call me. I would help her with it. We discussed amongst ourselves, wondering if it was worth trying to get someone at Airbus who could help us understand the exact reason for the screws, and if any of us had any connections with Airbus. With Miami's large aviation industry there had to be Airbus people in the area who could put us in touch with someone knowledgeable of the machinery and screws.

It was getting near 1pm and I knew that tomorrow would be a very full day. Even if everything went without a hitch there would be people to process, vehicles to impound, currency to be transported and then counted. Ritchie was correct. Seven million is a lot of money and it could be a full day out at Doral, assisting Customs with the seizure.

When we got up to leave, I hung back as Gary and C.C headed off towards their cars. I went back into the little restaurant space to get a bottle of water to go. Then I saw it again.

Behold, I have given you authority to tread on serpents and scorpions, and over all the power of the enemy, and nothing shall hurt you. ~ Luke 10:19

I didn't have anything lined up specifically for the rest of the day and was reluctant to check in with my DEA task force and get pulled into something that might stretch into the night, effectively compromising my sleep and readiness for the morning. I made the decision to just lie low for the rest of the day. I'd go home and tidy up the condo. I'd finish the laundry I'd started and just be off the radar.

Then my cellphone rang. It was the VIN office. It couldn't be Gary, there was no way he was back in Coral Gables that fast.

"Hello?"

"Cade. Major *Broonsone* wants to see *ju* at two."

"Okay, Ileana. Thank you. I'll be there."

"*Bery* good, then I will tell him to see *ju* at two."

Since it came from Ileana, that meant Major Brunson wanted to see me at two-thirty. I looked at my dashboard clock and decided it was if I got there by two, I might be able to slip in early, the Major's wrath be damned.

Most people have no idea that the life of a cop is often spent driving. Either back and forth continuously between set places, or just aimlessly in a designated patrol zone. Cops drive. When they aren't driving, they're preparing to drive. Cops know entire large metropolitan cities like no other. They can tell you shortcuts you never imagined, where particular gas stations are, they even know where specific potholes and dips in the roads are in a thriving city of millions of people. Driving back to Coral Gables was an autopilot thing. I was very soon pulling into the station. Rather than drive up the climbing winding ramps, I chose to park in the private parking garage across from the front doors of the station. Spaces were always available. The only notable tenant in the building was the Consulate of Guatemala. I walked across Salzedo Street and in through the front door.

In the lobby of the station was a twenty-four hour police officer-manned booth. It was encased in bullet proof glass with large circular cutouts so that the officer inside could be handed papers, licenses, and anything else from a visiting resident. It made no sense having the bullet proof glass if someone could reach their hand through a portal hole and still shoot a gun at the officer, who by the way, would need to find a separate portal hole to fire back if he could. They called the booth the P.O.D.—an acronym for Police Operations Desk. There wasn't a lot of operations coming from that desk. It was a frontline place for the officer to tell the wandering public that we didn't take reports for lost cellphones in Miami Beach, or some other inane thing that had nothing to do with Coral Gables. Truthfully, it should have been an acronym for Police Officer on Display. The uniform desk officer looked up from reading the *Miami Herald* and yelled through the bullet proof glass.

"Cade! You still work here?"

Out of the 160-person Coral Gables Police Department, that was a continual comment from at least 140 of them, due to the fact that for the last five years I'd been detached to the DEA task force focused on large cocaine trafficking and money laundering cases. I was rarely in our station. Within that time, there had been such a surge in hiring and attrition that there were some Coral Gables police officers who had never seen me.

"I've never worked here. I'm just employed here."

I went straight to the bank of elevators, since the impressive wide center staircase in the lobby only went to the second floor. I pushed the elevator button. I then remembered that elevators in public buildings are a great place to be elevator-pitched or drafted to do things by superior officers. I turned on my heels and headed for the fire stairs. These stairs are tucked in the corner near the door that adjoins the lobby to the fire department. Just as I entered the staircase, I heard the elevator doors open in the lobby. I heard someone inside the elevator say, "How the hell did we end up in the lobby?"

The cool, institutional, flat-gray painted steps and banisters could've been any staircase in any city in America. They were industrial to a fault with remnants of sloppily poured concrete along their sides. Never underestimate the quality construction of a government's lowest bidder. I went up to the third floor, crossed over the open-air interior hallway and then through the double doors, which led me to an interior hallway where Major Brunson's office was. I gingerly opened the door and saw Charlene. She looked up at me from her desk. I mimed tapping my wrist asking her what time, as in what time was I supposed to be there. She looked at the day planner on her desk.

"It really doesn't matter. Ileana has thrown off the calendar already."

Her answer was audible enough for Major Brunson to yell from his office out to Charlene.

"What now? Who am I supposed to be seeing now?"

"Actually, you have a half hour until Detective Taylor's appointment but he is here now."

I felt my shoulders dip slightly as I knew that my early arrival would necessitate sitting in his outer office for a half hour or being admonished for being early.

"Send him in," was all he said. No profanity or kicking of a waste basket. I was truly surprised. I walked into his office and he was sitting behind his desk squeezing one of those bright orange stress balls. I sat down across the desk from him. He kept squeezing the orange stress ball.

"My wife got this for me," he said, looking at the stress ball. "She said she wants me to live a long time. What kind of demented woman would want to spend a long time with me?"

It was one of those personal rhetorical questions that to even try to answer would not bode well for me. To cede with his wife would be akin to calling her demented; to agree with him would affirm his own intolerance. I just sat there and simply muttered a very low question.

"Do those things really work?"

"For fucksakes Taylor, do you think they work? Do you think it's done anything for my sterling fucking demeanor? It's not like I'm the kind of guy you want to ever put on a speaker phone. "

With that, he opened a desk drawer and tossed the bright orange ball into it. It bounced against three other stress balls in the drawer.

"I know. She thinks if she keeps buying me these balls, I'll keep using them. Soon I'll be able to fund my own fucking juggling school with these soft little bastards." In typical Major Brunson fashion, he transitioned very quickly to why I was now in his office. "I asked you to come by so that we can be on the same page about the pick-up tomorrow. I'm assuming Customs called you?"

"Yes, I spoke with Special Agent Tavino about an hour ago."

"Well, Special Agent in Charge Sorenson is not only a tremendous pain in my ass, but he's also very excited to see this go. I spoke with DEA Group 6 on Monday and told them you were helping us inventory our property room and storage areas, so if you're wondering why you haven't heard from your DEA group, that's why."

Inwardly, I didn't appreciate him randomly calling my DEA group and having me out of pocket with a made-up story about inventorying our property room. I was none too pleased at how easy it was to put me out onto the sidelines and that everyone at DEA would just believe the story.

"Cade, do you have any more trepidations about this pick-up? Before you answer, keep in mind I don't give a hairy rat's ass what you think about these ass clowns having seven million or not.

Seven million would be nice, but I just want to get Sorenson and his crew back in so that I can shut the door and let that party carry out on without us. So, with that said—are there any more goddamn concerns that you haven't already brought up before?"

Faced with that kind of question there really wasn't much I could say. I just glanced towards the window, the sun filtering in, then back at Major Brunson.

"It is what it is. Let's just get it done and move on."

I left the building pretty much the same way I came in. I took the interior stairs and rather than deal with the desk officer. I went through the door that adjoins to the fire department. I cut across the completely empty fire lobby, past the wall of pictures of long-ago retired firefighters. There sure was a lot of mustaches and sideburns in those days. I was in my car and heading back to the condo within minutes. I was almost there, just crossing Southwest 144th Street when my cellphone rang. It was C.C.

"Hello?"

"Well, that guy Ainsle at the ATF lab in California is very quick."

"Did he give you a list already?"

"He sure did. Monroe, Miami Dade, Broward, and Palm Beach. Sixty-seven registered owners."

"Even from your own research, you saw that the Walther P-88 wasn't a very popular gun."

"Yeah, sixty-seven people in four counties is a very small percentage," she said.

"Are you going to start with Miami Dade? How many are in Miami Dade?"

"Thirty-two. Yeah, I'm starting with Miami Dade."

"Are you going to do it alphabetically or by zip code?"

"I don't know yet. I think I'll just start with the easiest one first?"

"What does that mean?" I asked.

"Roberto Tovar."

Chapter Nineteen

ERGEANT ROBERTO TOVAR of the Miami Homicide unit owns one of the sixty-seven registered Walther P-88s in Miami Dade and the neighboring counties. This was a coincidence of extreme magnitude. He definitely has police experience. We believed that he had prior military experience.

The boxes in my head were starting to be checked. The arrows were starting to point in the right direction.

I still had not heard from Santiago about the background check he was doing on Tovar.

"Tovar can wait for now. I mean, you know him. I know what we said in the restaurant. The other sixty-six should be checked for violent criminal histories and such, wouldn't you say so, too?"

"That's what I'm actually doing. I'm going to do a little process of elimination, but don't think that I don't have Tovar at the top of the list in my head. I'm working two related homicides and he hasn't even mentioned that he owns the exact same type and caliber gun that was used in the murders? That's a convenient omission. Now I got Sciarotta making an impromptu visit to Jacksonville to watch the Dolphins play on Monday night when he could just stay home and watch the game. Sounds like a gun drop to me."

"You think Sciarotta is going to take Tovar's Walther P-88 and scatter it, whole or in pieces, somewhere along the east coast?" I asked her.

"The thought has certainly crossed my mind. If they are in this together, for whatever reason, it makes total sense."

"Just keep checking on the other registered owners for the moment and try not to let Tovar know you have that list. So far we have no other homicides and it may just end with Reggie and Jabo. Has anything come back on the shoe impression in the sand at Jabo's murder?"

"The only thing the FBI says preliminarily is that they know it's a Nike brand. They're now searching through the Nike databases and the hundreds of types of shoes they have."

"Wonderful. A major sneaker brand. That may take some time to get the actual type and model of shoe. I'll be out of pocket most of the day tomorrow. Let's you and I circle back either later tomorrow or Friday."

By the time we hung up, I was cruising through the gate at the Royal Harbour Yacht Club. I continued through Paradise Point and continued right past my unit, scanning all parked cars for anybody in them or any inconsistencies. I drove to the end of the point. I backtracked my way back to my unit and pulled up in front of the condominium, sitting there for a moment, digesting what C.C. had just said about Tovar.

I gathered my things and went inside. I tidied up a little and made sure the deck was completely back in order. I took the laundry out of the washer and put it in the dryer. The continuous hum of the dryer was nearly hypnotic except for the few coins that were clanging out of rhythm with the rest of the tumbling laundry. I grabbed two Amstel Lights, and decided a little fresh air would be good for me. I made my way out the front door. I walked west toward the guard gate along the tree-shaded lane. Just prior to the guard gate, I turned left down the asphalt path adjacent to the tennis courts. I walked the entire length until I got to the small, but very nice private beach.

There was a sand volleyball court there and a large chickee hut.

No one was there. Chairs faced the bay at the water's edge. I sat down in one of the comfortable white Adirondack chairs and popped open the first beer, looking out across Biscayne Bay directly at Chicken Key. To my right as far as I could see was uninterrupted mangrove coastline. I knew that just around the point was the entrance channel to the Deering Estate, but from where I sat it felt as if I was the last man on earth, with the last two beers. The bay water gently lapped at the white sand beach making nary a ripple.

I recognized that had I not followed Dominguez, there was a very good chance that fifty percent of what had consumed my last few days would have been none of my concern.

I never made an out-and-out promise to Godfrey Pinder to find Reggie's killer—but I didn't fully say no either.

I was starting to loathe the cozy family ties Major Brunson had to the SAC at U.S. Customs. It must be nice to direct from the "biggest office in the place" and not have to worry that it's you in harm's way. Ritchie was in such a high fever to get this deal done. Aside from what he said, it hadn't alleviated my concerns at all. I watched him slipping more and more into casualness about this deal. I mean, he actually hung up with me to take a call from someone else. We're talking about seven million dollars and agents with long weapons, and he takes another call! Ritchie was just in this downward whirlpool of carelessness, and taking me with him.

I wondered if SAC Sorenson hadn't been related to Major Brunson, would they still have sought me out to do this deal? Was I brought in because I'm good at what I do, or was I brought in because Sorenson could get Brunson to *make* me do it? I remember exactly what Ritchie said at *La Caretta* last Friday afternoon.

He'd been gauging how receptive I was to join up with him and the Customs agents. Testing me to see if I was still a collaborating guy or if I'd been jaded from my time with the DEA. He was measuring me to see if I was available and agreeable to broaden my case log and lend a hand on helping this established agency get reestablished in the money laundering business.

Grasping Smoke: A Cade Taylor Novel

"So do you need my DEA group or do you need me?"

"Both. But right now we want you."

It wasn't about the DEA at all. It was about me. They can't control the DEA, but through Brunson they can control me.

This wasn't going well for me in many ways. I'd been backed into a corner.

With a heavy swig of beer, I looked out at the serene scenery. So calm.

My life had become an overturned table.

I felt like everything that I'd laid out neat and tidy was now scattered, upside down, ruined, and unusable. The disintegration of my marriage to Gina was the focal piece of my ruinous state. I tried my hardest to recognize that my feelings about Gina just couldn't afford to be in my future, so they needed to remain in my past. Sometimes our past has a way of pushing into our present, and barges into our future. The reason why your rearview mirror is so small compared to your windshield is because what's in front of you is so much more important than what's behind you.

Gina was behind me. Like it or not.

As for me, I was so deep in her past that I wasn't even visible in her rearview mirror. She moved on quickly and with neither a care nor concern, jettisoned me out of her life. I was just an asterisk in her timeline. I didn't matter. I was inconsequential.

They say time heals. Time taunts me with the screeching memories of what might have been. As I see successful marriages in and out of the police department, I'm reminded how big a failure my own marriage was. Time has no business in police work. Regardless of the need to document exact times for report writing, time really doesn't matter in police work. The knife was plunged, the trigger pulled, the cars collided in a time and space before the police were even notified. They'll continue to do so long after I am no longer in this job. We document the decrepit, the detrimental, and the depraved.

It was the same with the agency. It could just as easily have been me instead of young detective Johan Williamson getting the lecture about being moved to the patrol division. Dismantling cocaine distribution channels and seizing drug money was a common occurrence; or so it appeared to those who weren't actually doing it. Gary said it—these police majors and chiefs all think they're corporate CEO's now that they're flush with the seized drug money. But many of them are so stupid they couldn't count to twenty-one unless they were naked.

When I was first assigned to Customs before they were shut down, my first seizure was $285,000. Chief McIntyre and a few others came out to the scene and raved about the seizure. We are now talking *seven million dollars,* and everyone thinks it's just a normal course of business. These things don't happen without some work. The ease that Chuco presented this gift-wrapped case, and the fact he was willing to have Perchero and Emiliano take the fall, says either a ton about his own greed or his ardent necessity that may be tweaked and cloaked with panic. Chuco and Ritchie want this to go so fast and so soon. That, to me, is a red flag. SAC Sorenson is so new to Miami, he's still using a map to find his way around town. It had potential disaster written all over it.

When this is over, I'd love to put in my own papers and take some time off.

I'd taken a little time last February, and I did make my way to Toronto for a few days in May, but it had been some time since I took a breather. Carrying a badge in Miami can be wearisome. I sometimes feel like we invent crime here in Miami and then patent it and sell it worldwide. It's a modern-day Casablanca with nefarious criminals, wayward politicos, warring factions, and burgeoning crooks, all here laundering drug money, getting documents forged, arranging contractual murders, planning coups, and creating alibis.

A mullet jumped, breaking the surface of the water, and snapped me from my blue funk. Soaking in the warm sunshine on and taking in the splendid view, I reminded myself that no one put a gun to my head and told me to be a VIN detective in the nation's most dangerous city for VIN work. I signed on for it. I was here by my own volition. Like Ritchie said:

"We're on for tomorrow. Wear your big boy pants."

I'd worn big boy pants plenty of times before. Tomorrow would just be another day of donning big boy pants. Acevedo would have us covered with his Steyr AUG and Slomianski would have a Colt SMG. We should be better prepared and ready than Perchero and that moron Emiliano. It's a few bags or suitcases. *It should go quickly,* I reasoned.

I opened the second beer and tried to focus on the positive rather than the negative or what could go wrong. The second beer was just as refreshing as the first. I wished I'd brought down a six pack. But no—I needed to be on my game tomorrow, and had to get up early to beat traffic. The S&S Diner is quite literally across on the other side of Miami in the northeast section. I savored the second beer and the view and calmness of the bay. After a while I went back to the condominium. I checked my go bag and made sure that I had clean clothes, rain gear, a Hartford Whalers baseball hat, some toiletries and whatever else I thought I might need. I checked the springs in my magazines. I removed the bullets from the magazines. After giving the magazines a rest of about an hour without any bullets I reloaded. I inserted a fresh magazine into my Glock. I had a piece of neoprene sleeve from a wet suit that I'd cut at the calf which I placed on top of the go bag, with my Glock beside it. I put the go bag by the front door.

The night wore on and I tried to watch some TV, but there were just mindless shows like *Dateline NBC*, *20/20*, and *The Nanny*. At 10pm the NLCS game between the Padres and the Braves was coming on but I didn't care that much about baseball and couldn't see any reason to stay up and watch it. I climbed into bed and set the alarm for 6am. I don't really know why but one of the last things I thought about was the scripture from the restaurant.

Behold, I have given you authority to tread on serpents and scorpions, and over all the power of the enemy, and nothing shall hurt you. ~ Luke 10:19

I was surprised how fast I fell asleep.

The alarm shocked me awake at 6am; I thought it was a smoke alarm for the briefest of moments. Then I remembered and quickly turned it off. I turned on the local TV news to get an idea of what the weather was going to be. While waiting for the traffic report, the morning weather woman came on. In Miami, most men, and I suspect a few women, have to watch the weather report in the morning at least twice. The gorgeous, buxom, short-skirted women they hire to report the weather are such a distraction that rarely is what they're saying ever initially heard. I was too busy getting ready to go into the shower that I didn't pay much attention and once I heard the high would be eighty-eight degrees, I turned the TV off. The shower was rejuvenating and the temperature was ideal. I stepped out onto the upper deck and took in the view as I toweled myself dry. I made a mental note that if I ever owned this unit to have an outdoor shower installed on the deck. I got dressed in a pair of light gray Dockers Marina slacks with a slight flair at the bottom cuffs. I grabbed a pair of tan Sperry topsiders and a dark blue polo shirt, which I kept untucked. I went to my go bag by the front door and slipped my Glock into a quick release tan pancake holster. I threaded the holster onto one of my sturdier and thicker belts, then put on the belt. I checked myself in the mirror—no noticeable bulge where my gun was tight against my side under the dark polo. I grabbed the neoprene sleeve from the cut wet suit. I wiggled and tugged the sleeve over my left foot and pulled it up to the top of my ankle above my hem line and partially up to my calf. It felt like it took a few leg hairs with it. I then grabbed the two spare Glock magazines and pushed and wedged them between my leg and the neoprene. I then put on the top siders. I checked myself in the mirror again and there was no noticeable bulge of the spare magazines attached to my leg. I grabbed my go bag, walked out and locked the condo. I opened the trunk of the Z-28 and threw my bag in. I then slowly eased back from the driveway and then started the very long commute across Miami to the Ace Hardware parking lot on Northeast 2nd Avenue. The commute was stop and go and U.S.1 was a virtual parking lot in some places. It was very slow going. Thankfully, I'd built in enough time to accommodate all these delays. I left the condo at 6:40am, and it was now nearly 8:15, and I was just making my way to Northeast 2nd Avenue. I drove past the Franklin Court Apartments with its old New Orleans-style architecture. The Ace Hardware was just ahead of me on the left hand side. Bypassing the actual front door of the hardware store, I pulled into the parking lot on the northside of the building.

There she was. Sixty feet of painted, languid, naked woman lying on her stomach on a beach somewhere with a small Cesena 172 airplane flying in the distance just above her heels.

Special Agent Pedro Acevedo was already there in the parking lot waiting. There was no sign of Slomianski or Ritchie Tavino. I was not surprised. We still technically had ninety minutes until go time, but it was the little things about Ritchie and his crew that were getting under my skin. I had serious doubts Acevedo had ever seen me, since his surveillance position at the Cuban bakery *El brazo fuerte* was so far away. He looked up at me from his blue Alero as I drove in the parking lot. I waved at him as I drove past and parked a few car lengths away.

I got out of my car, and Acevedo exited his car.

"You Cade?"

"You Pedro?"

We shook hands and exchanged some pleasantries. He seemed like a nice enough guy. I asked him how long he had been with Ritchie's group. He said he'd transferred in from Tampa about a year and half ago. I asked him how he liked Miami.

"It's different from Tampa, but I grew up in Miami. I went to Miami High. The whole nine yards. When I joined Customs they stuck me in Houston and I've been working my way home ever since. Tampa was close, but now I'm here with family, so it is much better," he said with a very slight accent

Slomianski pulled in, still driving the burgundy Buick Century. He also found an abundance of parking spaces at this early hour. I was wondering if a psychologist would have an opinion regarding where we each chose to park in proximity along the painted naked lady. Slomianski got out of his car and joined me and Pedro.

"Johnny, this Cade Taylor. Cade, this is Johnny Slomianski," said Pedro by way of introduction.

"So, we going to make this thing go or what?" asked Slomianski.

"Looks that way. We're just waiting on Ritchie to show up," said Pedro.

Up close you could see that Pedro Acevedo was a little more home-grown than Slomianski. Acevedo was clean-shaven and had short, but very thick black hair. He was about 5'10" and seemed to work out enough to keep a tone physique. He wore blue jeans, light blue Nike runners, and a beige button down, short sleeve shirt. Slomianski was in dark pants and black, low ankle boots, a cranberry red, long sleeve shirt rolled up at his forearms. A faded military tattoo peeked out from under his right sleeve. His brown hair was a little long and shaggy. His unkempt mustache was fuller on one side than the other. I asked Slomianski the same question I asked Acevedo.

"I was raised in Stevens Point, Wisconsin but I've been in the Miami office for three years. My wife and kids are still in Chicago. That's where I was stationed for thirteen years. I've been trying to get transferred back ever since I got here."

"That must be tough," I said.

"It's not so bad. I got a big bump in pay coming here, we get a ton of overtime, and I fly back nearly every weekend on Midway Airlines."

It was very obvious we were now waiting on Ritchie to show up. At around 8:40 Ritchie pulled into the parking lot.

"Johnny. You ever see Ritchie on time for anything?" asked Pedro.

Slomianski watched Ritchie park his truck and said, "He's always in so much of a better a mood than the rest of us who wait for him."

Ritchie bounded out of his truck in brown cargo pants and a lavender polo shirt. He was all smiles as he walked over and joined us.

"Cargo pants, Ritchie?" I asked him.

"What? I figured we'll be moving some big boxes or suitcases," he said.

"You don't want to spook these guys from the beginning, do you?" I asked.

"We'll be inside the diner. They can't see shit. Besides, by the time we get to their car we'll just be ripping them anyway. Chuco said put it on the dumb one. I know—which one, right? He says the cardboard cutout big dummy lives just off the Gratigny Parkway somewhere. We'll say we were following him since Monday, put it all on him."

The other two agents nodded their heads in agreement, but I wasn't in favor of the idea. I didn't think it insulated Chuco enough, but I also didn't give a shit if Chuco lived or died, so I just stayed quiet. Like Brunson said:

"Cade from a Coral Gables perspective, I see a very short future here. We are here to light the Customs rocket and then stand back and watch it go. After we do the seven million, I don't give a shit what they do."

"Okay, it's getting near 9 o'clock. Cade and I will be inside the diner. Pedro you cover the avenue from the north, and Johnny, you stay here and cover us from the south."

"What about the Mazda Millenia?" I interjected.

"Oh yeah, keep your eye out for a bronze Mazda Millenia with a Florida tag of *RWB420*. The tag isn't on file and Cade thinks it may have been counter-surveillance on Monday."

Now he was talking directly to Slomianski. "You and Pedro be on Tac 9 and if you see anything hinkey, including the Millenia, you call me and hang up. If I get a hang-up from any of you, then Cade and I will know something's up outside the diner. Aside from that, you guys go get something to eat or coffee or whatever—just be in place by 9:30. Cade, you want to ride over with me?"

Acevedo and Slomianski took advantage of the half hour to get settled in and both made a bee-line for their cars. I climbed into the passenger side of Ritchie's truck.

"Ritchie, is that it?"

"Is what it?"

"Is that your ops plan? 'Be on Tac 9?' Do these guys know where the nearest hospital is? Have you cross-checked with NINJAS? Did you let Miami P.D. know we'd be out here? I mean, seriously guy, this is super wonky."

"Chuco assured me these guys are wusses. No guns. No guts. It's going to be easier than any pick-up we've ever done before. They're gonna go down, and the big guy is getting it pinned on him. Chuco will start raising holy hell from Colombia about the two of them and put more attention on Perchero and the big guy."

He was already pulling out of the parking space and driving the short two blocks north to the S&S Diner. We were lucky and got a parking space directly in front of the diner. I was liking that. If these "wusses" did have guns, the truck could be a strong barrier between them and us, or any innocent patrons in the diner.

The S&S Diner opened in 1938. It is pure Miami history. Large Art Deco letters read, "S & S Diner" in red above the front door that partially wrapped around the octagonal front entrance. It is on a corner, but the corner isn't a street but a small alleyway that leads to the same L-shaped parking lot in the back that Ritchie had mentioned. Across the front façade of the restaurant are floor to ceiling windows. Inside, patrons sit at the long horseshoe counter, with nearly all of them having their back to the street. All the delicious entrees come out through a kitchen window in the back. There isn't a single table or booth in the place—everything is done at the counter. Old and young, black and white, blue collar and white collar, criminal and prosecutor; they all rub elbows at the tight counter. Many a time a patron will slide over from his red vinyl swivel stool to make room for a larger party. Plates jostle and cutlery changes constantly. It is a great place to be left alone as you eat in a communal setting, if that made any sense.

The diner was packed. Luckily, we found two of the last empty counter stools together in the very back of the horseshoe by the window where the food is passed out from the kitchen. I have no idea who the cook was, but occasionally I would see a black hand passing the plates out. I saw one of the counter waitresses lean into the window and call her "Mardochée," so I'm almost certain she was Haitian. The guy next to me in workout clothes was eating a trembling six-egg white scramble. Across the counter from us a woman who looked like a law firm secretary was digging into a heaping plate of pancakes. I ordered the three-egg scramble special, as did Ritchie.

The interior of the S&S is designed to evoke all the time periods the diner has withstood and thrived. Kitschy photographs and memorabilia crammed all along the walls. There are so many of them that the picture frames actually touch each other where they'd been haphazardly nailed to the wall. Just above me was a poster of Charlie Chaplin and child actor Jackie Coogan from the movie *The Kid*. There were pictures of Marlon Brando from *The Godfather*, and Paul Newman with Robert Redford from *Butch Cassidy and the Sundance Kid*.

The diner's bank of glass windows cover the entire length of the southside wall and continue along the front. Ritchie and I squeezed in the back with the wall of pictures. It was a good tactical place because as much as Ritchie kept talking, I kept scanning the windows looking for Perchero or Emiliano to show up. The clientele inside the restaurant bustled and changed in a constant flow of movement. People who had a coveted seat graciously got up from their stool and offered it to a waiting patron. It is a rare sight to see civility in Miami, but those who had already eaten knew the value of the stool and relinquished it so others could sit down and enjoy, too. They also did it voluntarily before a counter waitress moved them along. Newspaper sections were left behind and patrons picked up and passed multiple sections of today's *Miami Herald*. A lone TV in the diner was placed just above the kitchen pass-through window. The news was on—Art Carlson, anchoring for Channel 10. The sound was turned down, so I had no idea what the news stories were. although there was some footage of fire trucks and the crawl under the pictures said North Miami Beach. I found it ironic that the television studio was just a mile away on Biscayne Boulevard and here we were, watching the news. Well, *some* people were watching the news; I kept my eyes roving from the front doors to the windows. I expected to see Emiliano and Perchero come sauntering by the windows from the back L-shaped parking lot. Ritchie devoured his eggs and bacon. I took my time eating, trying to extend our time so we could stay on the stools.

"What's our clock?" I asked him.

"9:55" he answered.

I put in an order of pancakes to go, to stall for more time. I watched the waitress put the ticket into the slotted window. Just as the ticket left her hand and laid on the windowsill, I heard a faint double whistle. I looked towards the front door and Emiliano was there, with the door open. He was wearing a black t-shirt with some script writing down the length of each long sleeve. He was also wearing green cargo pants. He motioned to us to both come outside. Ritchie briefly looked at me and very quietly said, "What do you think?"

"Well, you're not the only dickhead in the place wearing cargo pants," was my reply.

Ritchie laid a twenty down on the counter and we started to walk out moving sort of sideways through the narrow passage of patrons. A waiting couple saw us get up and started to move to get our stools, causing an even slower momentary passage for us. We all wedged past each other. By now Emiliano was gone from the open door and it was closed. We got to the door and Ritchie started pushing it open.

I was right behind him when his cellphone rang once and then abruptly hung up.

Chapter Twenty

You can never explain
Like when an angel cries
Like runaway trains.

~ Runaway Trains by Tom Petty

TOO LATE NOW. It was showtime.

Ritchie stepped out onto the cracked and heaving pavement just outside the front door. It was as if each cement mason was worse at his job than the one before him. I followed closely behind him. The sun was bright. I shielded my eyes with my hand, looking for Emiliano. Ever the charmer, he low whistled again. He was standing in the open doorway of a blue 1998 Lexus ES 300. The car was running. It looked like Perchero was sitting in the driver's seat. The Lexus was parked just a little north of Ritchie's truck. Emiliano was holding a large canvas zip bag—not a duffle bag, but styled in the cargo duffle bag family. Parked across the street and facing south, was the same bronze-colored Mazda Millenia. The same driver I'd seen at the bakery was behind the wheel, watching what he could of us from across the street.

"*Para ti, para ti,*" For you, for you, Emiliano was saying, motioning with his head to Ritchie.

Ritchie split away from me and slowly started towards Emiliano. I stayed where I was just off the front end of the truck, watching Perchero as much as I could see of him through the rear window of the Lexus. Ritchie made his way hesitantly towards Emiliano, who was holding the bag with both hands across the front of his body.

"*Para ti, para ti,*" Emiliano said repeatedly. Occasionally he stole a glance across the avenue at the Mazda Millenia.

"Hey, Mr. Direct Deposit, don't be so rude, come here. I want to show you something," shouted Perchero from the partially opened driver's window.

I could see Perchero looking at me in his side view mirror. Perchero's request caused Ritchie to stop walking. He looked at Emiliano and said, "I can tell from here you're light."

"*Luce?*" Light? was Emiliano's response.

"The rest is in the trunk and backseat. Come on, let's get this done, gentlemen. I'm feeling exposed here," Perchero yelled.

I quickly stepped out from between the truck and the Lexus, in case Perchero had any ideas of throwing the car in reverse and pinning me between the two vehicles. I walked on the street side of the Lexus, tentatively up towards Perchero. I kept my eyes focused on his face as he intently watched me approaching in his sideview mirror. At this point Ritchie was standing directly in front of Emiliano and they had the bag between them. Emiliano was forcefully pushing the bag at Ritchie.

"*Aquí, es para ti. Tómalo. Entra,*" (Here, it is for you. Take it. Get in.)

As I cautiously approached the driver's side window, I intentionally stayed close to the body of the Lexus, and positioned my right leg against the seam of the driver's door. If Perchero tried to jump out quickly or even open the door, I'd feel it before I saw it. I was trying to see his hands, but they were in his lap, just out of my view. Ritchie and I were directly across from each other and Emiliano had his back to me. He was trying to put the bag in Ritchie's hands while simultaneously saying, "Take it. Get in." Perchero briefly took his eyes off me in the rearview mirror to turn towards Emiliano and the open passenger door.

It was at that moment I heard Ritchie yell "Gun!"

I instinctively lowered my body and reached for my Glock, my eyes frantically searching for wherever the gun was that Ritchie just screamed out about. My pulse quickened immediately. It happened in a millisecond. Emiliano had pushed the bag up into Ritchie. He got frustrated and after trying to get Ritchie to take the bag, he pulled a cheap Lorcin Model L9mm. He was holding the gun in his right hand, and still pushing the bag.

Seeing the Lorcin Model L9mm, Ritchie pulled his Sig Sauer 9mm and fired two rounds right through the bag at Emiliano.

The percussion of Ritchie's two shots were startingly loud. My head yanked across the car and I saw one of his rounds ripple the roofline of the car. It looked like a mini eruption from inside the interior of the car. It didn't penetrate the roof, but made a cystic-looking bulge.

The backside of the bag blew out and fragments of money fluttered across the front seat of the Lexus like confetti from a circus cannon. How Ritchie missed Emiliano, I will never know. His two rounds went up into the bag of money, blew two huge holes in the back of the bag and lodged themselves somewhere in the roof line of the Lexus. Emiliano was startled and most likely didn't know if he'd accidentally discharged his gun or if he was being shot.

Perchero leaned away from the gunfire, towards the driver's door and towards me.

Perchero was holding an Ingram Mac-10 with a large suppressor and extended magazine. The weapon without the adornment of the suppressor and extended magazine, would have been a compact and very lethal firearm. He tried to stick it out the half-open window, but the suppressor made it awkward. A hot, bright flash of a twelve to fifteen round micro-burst sprayed across the avenue in a wild, crazy pattern. Although suppressed, the flash still caused me to blink rapidly.

It took a brief moment to realize he was trying to actually shoot me.

The window being only half open impeded his ability to wield the weapon effectively. The Mac-10 has extreme blow back, and Perchero wasn't able to get his left hand over the top of the gun. The weapon rose up as he fired, narrowly missing me, as hot empty shells fell on me and I'm sure on him too.

I dropped flat onto my back in the street, pulling my Glock as I went down, and threw my entire right leg hard against the bottom of the driver's door to pin it shut. Concrete hard against my back, I lifted my head. I held my Glock tight to my chest with both hands. Using my torso like a turret, I shifted my weight to my right and shot four rounds into the open driver's side window. Perchero ducked hard to his right against the car seat, trying to avoid my rounds. From the ground I could see a spiderweb-like explosion of his front windshield, showering glass particles all over me. My focus was to shoot Perchero but he kept leaning into the right side of the car, out of my vision. I don't think he or Emiliano expected me and Ritchie to be armed. I fully extended both my arms from my prone position and made sure to shoot a single round and obliterate the side view mirror so Perchero couldn't see me. Across the car, Emiliano fell back into the open passenger door, pulling the bag on top of him. He was still holding his gun.

"*Conduce. Conduce. Lárgate de aquí!*" (Drive. Drive. Get the fuck out of here!)

A jolt went through my leg as Perchero shoved the transmission into gear. I wriggled away from the Lexus towards the back, hoping to get to the perceived safety of the truck behind the Lexus. If Perchero cut the wheel, he'd have crushed me with the back tires. Ritchie had stepped back and yelled, "Federal Agent! Stop right there!"

Perchero gunned the Lexus and the car lurched forward, passenger door hanging open. Emiliano splayed across the seat facing out and fired two rounds at Ritchie. Both bullets ended up in the roofline of the diner. Ritchie fired two more rounds; the first blew out the back window of the Lexus. His next round went right through the rear tire, blowing it out immediately, sending the car skidding. Emiliano curled himself in just as the open door was crushed shut when Perchero sideswiped a metal telephone pole. I rose to my feet and retreated to the passenger side of the truck.

"Ritchie, let's go, let's go. You okay? Get in the truck. Let's go!"

"I swear to God I'm going to kill those motherfuckers," he said as he jumped in to the driver's seat.

I snapped my head around to the diner, where the entire clientele had been pressed against the glass, watching us. When the bullets started flying, they all scattered to the back of the diner. None of them could have known for certain if we were cops or not.

I'd thought of cranking some rounds into the Mazda Millenia's front grill to disable the radiator, but I needed every round I could save. Out of the corner of my eye I saw Johnny Slomianski in the burgundy Buick Century, tearing north up the avenue with a roving blue light on his dashboard. He drew abreast of the Millenia and cut the wheel hard, smashing his left front quarter panel directly against the driver's side of the Mazda. The collision was violent enough to lift the Millenia and nudge it up and onto the curb.

Ritchie had the truck started and Perchero and Emiliano were still visible driving north. Slomianski was out in a flash and he butt-stroked the already dazed driver through the open window with the back of his Colt SMG. Looking back towards the fleeing Lexus, I could see Pedro Acevedo in the Alero. He too, had a blue light on his dashboard. He was bearing down from the north straight at the Lexus.

I didn't even have the driver's side door closed and we were tearing away, chasing Perchero and Emiliano. In a second it was shut and I'd reached down and pulled a fresh magazine from the neoprene sleeve. I extracted the partially spent magazine from my Glock, quickly put it lengthwise across my mouth, and bit into it. I held it across my mouth with my teeth and I hard slammed the fresh, fully loaded magazine into my Glock.

Like I said. I needed every round.

Perchero didn't know where he was. His rear tire was shredding into chunks of rubber that were flying off like black rocks tumbling down a hillside. Strips of steel were unbanding from the tire and breaking off in wire shards, sending the car sliding and bucking all over the road. Perchero must've seen Acevedo coming at him. The Lexus wavered as Perchero was obviously wondering where to go.

We were now drawing very close to him. I was certain Ritchie was going to ram the back of the Lexus. Perchero turned the wheel hard to his left and bounced over the opening in the curb, crossed the sidewalk, and went right through the open ornate gates of the City of Miami Cemetery. The Lexus was shuddering and heaving through Miami's oldest cemetery; a ten acre resting ground for members of every important pioneer family in the city. It's a fully-fenced piece of land with a singular road. Perchero gunned the engine and tore down the palm tree-lined center asphalt path, right past the first of two circles of monuments. Ritchie breeched the same open gates and we both realized the same thing: Perchero had stopped near the second circle of monuments and headstones. The Lexus looked empty.

"Hold up!" I yelled.

Ritchie slammed on the breaks, the seatbelt making my breath catch even as it kept me from smacking into the windshield.

"Ritchie, we don't know where they are. It could be a trap. We can't stay like this inside the truck, we're sitting ducks. Have Acevedo block the gate behind us and hold there in case they try to backtrack."

Ritchie leaned out the driver's window and told Acevedo to take a point position at the gate and to block it with his car.

"Put it in drive and just slowly let it idle us forward, then give it very little gas. You cover from your seat to the left side, I'll cover the rest," I told Ritchie.

Ritchie stayed in the driver's seat and opened his door a crack. I stepped out of the truck and kept the door open. Leaning my left shoulder against the door, I used the door as a tactical shield. The truck began to roll very slowly. I was in a tactical firing position, scanning from the front of the truck to the far right. As the truck rolled I did cross-over steps, keeping my Glock pointed in front of me. Sweat rolled down my back and I was acutely aware of my breathing.

Focus on the front sights. Breathe in…and out. In…and out.

We were slowly approaching the first monumental circle. The palm trees were casting shadows on us as we crept past each one. The cemetery was eerily quiet. There were patches of untended grass and a few headstones were toppled. Others were crooked and long-ago weather affected. The center island we were coming up upon was the final resting place of pioneer Julia Tuttle and her family. Off to my right was a mausoleum. I kept scanning and moving with the barely rolling truck. I snuck a glance behind me and saw Acevedo had blocked that gate and he was out of his car, scanning in front of him with the Steyr AUG.

Then Perchero came into my line of sight, running north to south about fifty-five yards in front of us. He let out a rapid burst from the Mac-10. The rapid-fire bullets bounced off a few tombstones and ricocheted in our direction. He kept running and I peeled back and behind the truck to have a better shot at him as he cleared Ritchie's front side. It was then that Emiliano popped out from near the Burdine mausoleum on my left. He came charging at our truck, firing from his 9mm and yelling in Spanish as he ran towards us. The first two rounds lodged themselves into the front quarter panel of the truck.

"*Chinga tu madre!*" Fuck your mother.

I held a low crouch at the rear of the truck and had just put my front sight on him when it was actually Acevedo who got the first shot off. From behind me and to my left side, he fired a single round from the Steyr AUG. He hit Emiliano just above the right knee. The torque of the spiraling round made his leg swing like a wooden toy soldier's. It blew his leg completely back as if he'd slipped on ice. Emiliano fell flat forward. The round literally took him off his feet. He screamed in pain with his face flush in the high grass of the cemetery. He still held the Lorcin 9mm in his right hand and attempted to get up using his four extremities like rigid stilts. He looked like a baby giraffe at a

Serengeti watering hole as he tried to get his coordination through his pain. I could see the sweat soaking his shirt. His right leg was a bloody mess, he had both knees locked and both his arms splayed out as he tried to rise.

"Stay down and drop your weapon!" I yelled at him. His head was down. He was struggling to get his four limbs in concert and get himself upright.

Ritchie kicked open his driver's door and turned in his seat. He held the door open with his right foot and he leaned on his left hip. He took aim at Emiliano. The truck was still slowly moving forward, with me at the tail-end just behind Ritchie.

Emiliano started to push off with his arms and tried to aim his gun at us.

Ritchie fired one round that went right through the top of Emiliano's head. His head exploded. His entire body just collapsed right then and there. There wasn't any twitch, any sound, or movement. He was dead. Face down, gun in his hand.

Watching it happen was surreal. I told Ritchie in a wavering voice to put the truck in park. We knew Perchero was somewhere in front of us and he'd already crossed to the southern part of the cemetery. We'd need to go look for him amongst the tombstones and mausoleums.

Slomianski had run up the street, and was beside Acevedo with his Colt SMG. I waved both of them to join me at the rear of the truck. They tactically leap-frogged the tombstones and made their way to the rear of the truck. Slomianski told me he'd secured the barely-conscious Mazda driver by taking the car keys and handcuffing the driver to the steering wheel. Ritchie got out of the truck, looked over at Emiliano's dead body and simply said, "Motherfucker."

"Let's split up. One long weapon per team," I suggested.

"Pedro, go with Cade. Start from the front here. Johnnie, you and I will go south and work the fence line. We should come together somewhere up above. Remember this guy's got a Mac-10 and he's shot at us twice already. He makes the wrong decision for any reason, put him in the dirt," said Ritchie.

Acevedo just looked at me and nodded. All four of us were sweating profusely. Pedro and I started to move as a two-man search team. He kept the Steyr AUG in the ready position. He pointed off to the left. I held my Glock out and covered the right, just a step behind him. We tactically searched with me keeping my left hand on his shoulder. If he moved in an aggressive manner, I'd feel his threat assessment before he'd have to say anything to me.

We moved slowly amongst the gravestones and monuments, between those that were toppled over, others with long, deep cracks in them. Some of them large enough to hide the diminutive Perchero. The graves weren't in any rigid order or linear designations. It was a morass of stepping forward and side-stepping to make any progress. Slomianski and Ritchie were already out of our eye line. I could hear my breathing in my head as we approached every large gravestone cautiously. Perchero was small and wiry. I reminded Acevedo to look up, in case he'd climbed atop one of the mausoleums or was in a sea grape tree.

We started to approach a maintenance building that had a Spanish-style roof. I wasn't feeling very good about this; neither was Acevedo.

I tried the door to the shed. It was locked. I let out a breath.

We continued weaving through the tombstones and gravesites until we reached a small walled section with black wrought iron gates. The gates had the Star of David on them. This was the Jewish section of the cemetery. There was also a black section somewhere in the cemetery, still delineated but overgrown, from its creation in more segregated times.

I caught a flash of movement off to my right and signaled with my left hand by tugging on Acevedo. Pedro split a few feet away from me and we moved amongst the Poinciana trees deeper into the cemetery. All was still and quiet but for the breeze blowing through the Poinciana trees.

That's where I first saw Perchero.

He was sitting on the ground, panting nervously, his back against an old large headstone. The Mac-10 was about six feet from him, lying in the high grass.

"Right there. Don't you fucking move!" I yelled at him. My Glock was raised and in shooting position. Acevedo was moving to my left to avoid a cross fire.

"Go ahead, shoot me, motherfucker! Shoot me!" Perchero yelled back.

"Let me see your hands. Let me see your hands!"

"Fuck you. Shoot me. Get it over with," he screamed at me.

"Let me see your hands. It's over. Give it up."

Perchero just continued to sit there in the shadow of the Poinciana trees against the dirty, neglected, and cracked tombstone.

"You don't get it, do you?" he shouted back.

"*Manos arriba.* Hands up!" I called out again.

"You don't get it. You have no clue, you stupid gringo fuck. They're going to kill me anyway."

I was up against another gravestone with a clear shot at him, but I still couldn't see his hands. Acevedo had a clear shot as well and was focused on Perchero's head through the sights of the Steyr AUG.

"Who's going to kill you?"

"After today, I'm already a dead man. So shoot me. Because if you don't, then they're going to kill me."

I could hear sirens in the distance getting closer.

"It doesn't have to be this way. Let me see your hands. Give it up, man," I said.

"I can't go to jail. The cartel's got people inside. They'll kill me in jail. I'm dead either way. After today I got no hope. They're going to kill me anyway."

Perchero and I locked eyes. He saw me staring down my Glock at him. He'd have noticed the sweat beading on my forehead, the intensity in my eyes, the rigidness of my grip, even the discoloration in my trigger finger as I tried to keep from pulling the trigger and was refraining ardently from killing him for trying to kill me. He smiled a little.

"Mr. Direct Deposit, no records right? Keep it off the record."

With that he pulled a Bersa Thunder 380 up from his lap and put the small Argentine handgun to his temple and blasted a bullet right through his brain. His right eye and the whole right side of his face and head were horrifically misshaped. He slumped over and a steady stream of dark crimson blood trickled out of his mouth. The right side of his head at first pumped a few spurts of blood, then just became a bloody gaping hole with singed skin where the bullet tore through his brain. The gravestone behind him was splattered with parts of his skull, scalp, sinuses, and brains in a diverse wild pattern of displacement. Perchero's remains sprayed across the gravestone and smeared down it where he slid to the ground. As he finally came to rest on his side, I could make out the bloodied inscription on the gravestone:

"I have given you authority to trample on snakes and scorpions and to overcome all the power of the enemy; nothing will harm you. However, do not rejoice that the spirits submit to you, but rejoice that your names are written in heaven." Luke 10:19-20

Chapter Twenty-One

ACEVEDO AND I looked at Perchero's lifeless body. We just stared at him. Neither of us said a word. He didn't look at peace as most people wish for when someone dies. He looked just as anguished, only now he was dead. Still staring at Perchero's lifeless body, I called out over my shoulder to Acevedo.

"Pedro, call Ritchie on the cell. Tell him we're okay. Tell him and Johnnie to stand down. Tell him to have Johnnie stay with the other body and that I want him to meet me at the Lexus. Stay here for a minute 'til the cops show up."

I thought of the irony or premonition of that inscription. I turned away from it and holstered my Glock, then made my way amongst the graves to the center road. A minimum of fifteen City of Miami patrol cars were outside the cemetery gates. Acevedo's car had the entrance blocked and I'm sure it infuriated many of the officers, most of which were milling around the graveyard. I could also see Ritchie holding a cellphone in one ear and his Customs badge high up in the other hand. He was walking towards the officers and talking to the cops simultaneously as to whoever he had on the phone.

I went over to the Lexus. Both the driver's door and the passenger door were open. Fragments of glass spread across the seat. The car had a sense of disarray and panic still in the air. It smelled like feces; one or both of them had shit their pants. The backseat was empty and there were multiple flex cuffs in pre-arranged loops on the floor. The bag was still zipped but there were two baseball sized blow-out holes in the back.

I unzipped the bag. It was filled with rubber-banded stacks of twenties and a few stacks of fifties. The bundles weren't faced, and the rubber bands were different colors and widths. I grabbed a bundled stack of fifties and tore the rubber band off. I quickly lifted my pants leg and shoved the loose fifties deep into the neoprene sleeve on my ankle. I shoved a sizeable, but unnoticeable amount into the sleeve, and zipped up the bag just as Ritchie came walking up. He was hanging up the cellphone as he approached me.

"You okay, bro?" he asked.

"Yeah I'm okay. Perchero wacked himself in front of me and Pedro."

"I just spoke to Pedro. He told me that. Miami wants him to move his car."

"Fuck Miami. His car is part of the crime scene. That's where he was when he shot the ugly one. They can work around and go around his car. There's a lot of scenes to process. This is going to be a seriously long day."

Ritchie looked over the Lexus, noticing the bullet holes and the frayed bag of money.

"There ain't no way there's seven million here," he said.

"There never was. I kept trying to tell you that. These guys were barnacle builders, hoodlums. There never was seven million, at least not here, Ritchie. Chuco has been pulling your dick through this whole thing. I kept telling you that. I took a small stack out of the bag for Fermin Rivacoba. Remember we already talked about his commission? Whatever shit money is in here, just leverage it that way in your paperwork," I told him.

By now the cemetery was crawling with uniformed Miami officers. Suits and ties were starting to show up. "What do we tell Miami?" asked Ritchie. I gave it a very brief thought and replayed the events in my mind.

"We don't tell them anything." I said "They had a shooting in their city. That's all this is. Perchero killed himself. That's a witnessed suicide. That's a Miami case. Anything else is Customs C.I.D. Emiliano's death was you and Pedro—that's your own C.I D. investigation. Our discharging of our weapons is under the purveyance of your C.I D. We tell Miami the bare minimum. We need to debrief the guy Johnnie handcuffed. Let's get Miami to help, and see if they'll tape off all the cars, and both areas where the bodies are. Get your C.I D. out here pronto, before Miami and FDLE start acting all huffy and puffy. Go have Johnnie get that guy so we can have a post interview with him here before some jackass Miranda's him."

Within thirty minutes it was absolute pandemonium. TV news trucks outside of the cemetery. Miami police officials wandering everywhere. A uniformed Coral Gables lieutenant had arrived on the scene too; he'd be assisting with the shooting investigation that pertains to me. Three separate Miami Crime Scene teams were taking pictures and measurements. Emiliano and Perchero were now under tarps. Preliminary news reports that were filtering their way to me from the Miami cops were saying that it was a robbery at the S&S Diner gone bad. The media was going to have to do a serious *mea culpa* on that one in about an hour.

Johnnie had walked the Mazda Millenia driver up the street away from the car, and now Pedro, Ritchie, Johnnie, and myself were standing over him as he sat on the back step of the cemetery maintenance shed. He had a big knot on his head and a bloodshot eye from where Johnnie had hit him with the Colt SMG. His wrists were raw from struggling to free himself from the handcuffed steering wheel. Johnnie was holding a 35mm camera. In our debriefing of him, which quite honestly did entail Ritchie threatening to shoot him in the head, we learned his name was Livan Cancio. He said that the plan was for him to photograph Perchero and Emiliano meeting with me and Ritchie. Once sufficient footage was obtained of us four, Perchero and Emiliano were going to kidnap both of us. Perchero was going to tell Colombia that the full seven million was delivered to us. Emiliano had access to an abandoned warehouse in the industrial section of Miami called Medley. They planned to kill us in the warehouse, encase our bodies in concrete, and put them in the rock pit behind the Medley warehouse. As far as Colombia would know, we'd have stolen the seven million—but actually, Perchero and Emiliano were going to keep the money. They'd send the pictures to Colombia of us four meeting, as proof that Ritchie and I took the money.

It made sense now why there were flex cuffs in the back of the Lexus, and why Emiliano kept looking over at the Mazda and had gone from saying, "take the bag" to "get in."

Inwardly I was losing track of how many factions in this equation were trying to rip each other off. Chuco wanted to rip off the cartel by having us seize the currency and blame Perchero and Emiliano. Both of them were going to rip off Chuco and blame Ritchie and me. It's money and cocaine. It's volatile and without rules or trust. This business has a filthy underside to it that rarely do people ever see. Today two men died over seven million dollars, but somewhere else in Miami Dade County, others will die today for a hell of a lot less.

"Once Clinton put Janet Reno in as U.S. Attorney, she all but shut us down. She thinks money deals are unethical."

I was recalling the conversation I had with Ritchie at *La Caretta*—and at this point, I couldn't argue with Janet Reno.

More suits and technicians swarmed the cemetery. This was going to be a very long day indeed. Crime scene tape was strung around the Lexus, Ritchie's truck, and Acevedo's car. Two portable tents were erected over Emiliano and Perchero's bodies. Lights and generators were being wheeled in, and three tow trucks were staged outside the gates. Miami Homicide was now arriving. I saw C.C. off in the distance. At least two other male investigators were with her.

A white extended van pulled up. It was full of the windbreakers. Regardless of the temperature outside, these guys always wear windbreakers. Five men and two women exited the van wearing identical blue windbreakers that said "CID Treasury" across their backs.

I looked around for a comfortable place to sit, since I knew it would be a long day of questioning. I looked over at the Belcher mausoleum with its doublewide steps and Greek pillars and decided I'd just sit there and let the interviews begin. The first person to interview me were two of the C.I.D. investigators. I took them through the process from the S&S Diner, on into the cemetery, and finally to Perchero's suicide. The question and answer session took about forty five minutes in total.

I'd fired my weapon but I never hit Perchero, so my involvement— although substantial—wasn't going to be nearly as involved as Ritchie's and Pedro's. The uniformed Coral Gables lieutenant was Charlie Maddalone. Lieutenant Maddalone asked for my Glock, which he put into a foam, rubber-lined case. He needed to take my gun back to the station to make sure it was functioning properly. At the station they'd test fire it, dissemble and reassemble it to make sure there were no manufacturing issues with the handgun that may have led to an accidental discharge or other mishap. He in turn gave me a different Glock from the case, which I holstered. The policy was they could ask you for your weapon in an investigation, but they could not leave you without one. He also said he was pretty sure Major Brunson might be coming by as well.

C.C. and the two Miami investigators were talking to Pedro off in the distance.

Minutes later Major Brunson stalked towards me. I decided to just stay where I was on the mausoleum steps.

"Taylor, I got a pretty good idea of what the fuck happened here already. You okay?"

"Yeah, I'm okay."

"So these fucking dumbshits were going to try and take you and Tavino hostage and *kill* you?"

"Apparently so."

"You sure you're okay?"

"Yeah. I'm okay. But we need to clean this mess up a little more."

"What are you saying?"

"I'm saying when DEA Group 6 finds out this all went down, they're going to want explanations from you, and it's not going to be pretty."

"Taylor, I told you I'd handle those morons—"

"That's not it. We got maybe five or so million dollars still out there in the wind. Their accomplice, Livan Cancio, says its back at the dead guy's place off of the Gratigny Parkway. He gave up the address. I think a call from you to DEA Group 6 with that address would save our asses on this. They can go hit the address. We seize the five million, which was coming our way anyway. Now we fuck that little fucker Chuco who set this up, and you tell SAC Sorenson that's just how it's going to be."

"Speaking of Sorenson, that's him over there," said Brunson with a wave of his head.

I looked over to my left where a guy was wandering around in a light yellow button-down shirt and brown slacks. He was talking with three of the windbreakers.

"He looks like a dentist," was all I said.

"He's too fucking stupid to be a dentist," said Brunson.

I handed Major Brunson a slip of paper with the address that Livan Cancio had given up. By calling DEA Group 6 and providing them this information, it changes the narrative of the story. We were helping Customs, and it went bad, but we found a stash address that will be an easy seizure location. As far as the DEA is concerned, this was *mana* that fell from the sky. Brunson walked away with the address and started making a cellphone call, while I took in the sights and sounds of an active multi-crime scene.

In the cool shade, I laid my head back against the pillar and caught a little sun on my face that darted between the wavering Poinciana tree above me. I knew that the commotion would eventually settle into a cohesive flow, but for now it was a lot of mini huddles as Miami and C.I.D. settled it out. I wasn't concerned. Eventually, it would go like I said it would. Miami would get Perchero's "attended" suicide, and everything else would fall to C.I.D. Treasury. C.I.D would be very thankful to Miami for securing scenes and gathering what evidence they did in the form of shell casings, diagrams, and pictures, but in the end it would all come down to C.I.D. Since SAC Sorenson was pushing for this the whole way, it would quietly stay in their own house. Even though I repeatedly warned Tavino it smelled like a rotten set up, Customs would probably reward him and his team. Acevedo and Tavino would get some sort of citation, and there'd be a unit commendation in the near future for them, I was nearly certain.

I just continued to sit there, slightly bemused. I wasn't giving a lot of current thought to Perchero having tried to kill me twice with a Mac-10, or that Emiliano came charging the truck like a crazed rhino, firing at us. There'd be time for that later. Right now, I was just looking at the gates, and Acevedo's blue Alero, wondering how I was going to get back to my own car past the thick gauntlet of onlookers, and media. My moment of quietness was broken.

"You Taylor?"

I looked up at who I was sure, as C.C. described him, was Sergeant Roberto Tovar. He was about 5'10" with a very firm, fit build. He had a long sleeve, white shirt rolled up to his elbows. The sleeves had military precision to them in their tight and equal position on his arms. He wore dark, creased slacks. He had sporty sunglasses with a thin gold frame across the top of both lenses, and a gold Miami police badge on his hip beside his Glock sidearm, which was in a tight high rise holster.

"I'm Sergeant Tovar, Miami Homicide. I need to ask you a few things."

I just nodded, pulled my knees up towards my chest and wrapped my arms loosely around them. He asked for my full name, and how long I'd been with the Coral Gables Police Department. I answered all of his rudimentary questions. When he wanted specifics about the shooting, I deferred. He asked how it came to be that I was at the S&S Diner.

"Based on information provided by a law enforcement source, I was at the S&S Diner."

Nearly every question was answered in the same way. This seemed to frustrate and anger Tovar, and push him to unimaginable points of exasperation. I explained that it was an ongoing C.I.D. investigation, and that I'd already given a statement to C.I.D. I didn't want to compromise the C.I.D. investigation by providing conflicting statements. Anything he needed to know he could get from them. I was more than willing to talk about Perchero's suicide, since I was a witness, but anything else was not a Miami situation. As much as I wanted to help him there was nothing to help him with. Miami wouldn't be handling the incidents. His ire with me got the better of him, until he finally called over C.C. and the other investigator.

"Detective Taylor, you're familiar with Detective Clay. With her is Detective Hughes. Detective Hughes is assigned to the suicide. Since this is *not* a C.I.D. case, but a Miami case, I hope you'll be more cooperative with him than you were me. I must say, I am very disappointed in your attitude and refusal to say anything other than, 'based on a law enforcement source.' D.P., he's all yours." With that, he stalked off.

C.C gave me a raised eyebrow. Detective D.P. Hughes, who C.C. had mentioned earlier, stepped forward and introduced himself again. He proceeded to ask me about Perchero's suicide. I took him through all the events, starting with me and Pedro Acevedo teaming up and searching for Perchero in the cemetery, and ending with Perchero blowing his brains out. C.C. listened attentively. Any questions related to Perchero killing himself, I gladly answered. D.P. Hughes was intrigued by Perchero's fear of going to jail, and that the cartel had people inside the corrections system who would kill him. I elaborated that since he was trying to rip off the cartel today and pin it on me and Tavino, he knew the cartel would make an attempt on his life because of his transgression. D.P. Hughes told me they'd already spoken to Acevedo, and he said the same thing. I already knew they'd spoken to Pedro because I saw them talking when Sergeant Tovar was trying to talk to me. One of the Miami Crime Scene technicians came walking by and D.P. stopped him and asked him to test my hands for gunshot residue, commonly known as 'GSR.' I knew they'd get around to that eventually. The technician went over to a large orange case and donned some latex gloves, then came back and swabbed my palms and fingers with a solution. The swabs were put into a plastic bag and sealed with red evidence tape. D.P. then excused himself and he left with the technician. He wanted the technician to take additional photographs of the suicide location from the back of the gravestone Perchero had been resting against. D.P. wanted Perchero's perspective in his final moments as me and Pedro confronted him. That just left me with C.C.

"Are you sure you're okay?" she asked me.

"I'm okay. I'll be fine. I'm still kind of processing the day's events here."

"You don't look like you're okay."

"Thanks. I'll keep that in mind next time a guy blows out my hearing shooting a Mac-10 at me."

"I mean, seriously Cade, this has been a big event here. We could very easily be processing your homicide back at the S&S Diner."

"This, I'm fully aware of. I'd just like to get out of here. I've given my weapon to the Gables, I've given my statement to Treasury C.I.D., I've given my statement to you guys. Why I am still here?"

Before she could answer, Ritchie came walking over.

"Special Agent Ritchie Tavino, this is Detective Cynthia Clay from Miami Homicide." I made the introduction from my sitting position, knowing that any thought I had of leaving just got put on hold. Ritchie nodded once at C.C. and then looked back at me.

"It's okay. She's cool. We're working on something else together, you can talk in front of her," I told Ritchie.

"Chuco's been blowing up the U.C. phone. I'm not answering him. I'm sure he's blowing up Perchero's phone, too. DEA must've been watching these jokers unbeknownst to us, because they just hit the address of off the Gratigny, and it looks like they might get a major score."

"Holy shit, no way?" I said in mock surprise.

"How do you think we should play this?" asked Ritchie.

"Give it sometime before you call Chuco. I mean, really make him sweat on this. Say that they never showed up and tell him his reputation is shit. Tell him you're doing everything to keep him in play, but your SAC wants his balls. Cut him totally out of his commission of whatever's in the Lexus. As far as he knows, we never even seized that money. Tell him your new SAC is so pissed that he wants his snitch file dropped all over Colombia. Tell Chuco you're doing all you can to prevent that. When he finds out DEA hit the stash location, accuse him of selling the deal to DEA over you. Tell him you talked to DEA, and he's blackballed. He has no choice but to only work with you. Tell him that to do so he needs to come up with at least five million in seizures at a standard six percent in the next two months, if he wants any chance of ever getting back in the business," I said.

"Sounds like a plan. Hey, for what it's worth thank you for today, man. Thank you."

"We'll talk in a few days, Ritchie. Right now I'm just looking to cash my ticket out of here and go home."

"I wish I could leave too, but I'm gonna be here a while longer. Let's talk in a day," he said as he walked away.

"How about you? Do you need to be here for anything else?" I asked C.C.

She looked around. "I don't think so. D.P. has the suicide, he's got both statements from you and Acevedo. Other than that, like you said, this is a C.I.D. scene."

I stood up and brushed the small twigs and leaves from my pants. I looked at the teeming throng of onlookers and media outside the gate. I didn't feel like walking through, or even past, any of them. I looked west in the opposite direction; the gate was locked, but there were nobody there. Adjacent to the west gate was Miami Fire Station Number 2. I turned to C.C.

"Can you call Station Two and see if anybody has a key to the gate? I'm sure those guys walk in here sometimes for exercise."

Within five minutes she had a fireman in a gray jumpsuit at the gate with keys in his hand. We trekked past the Lexus, and just kept going west past all the activity. We were putting the commotion behind us with each step. The fireman looked bewildered as he stared past us at all the activity. We just thanked him and quickly turned south on North Miami Avenue. It was a very short walk to 17th Street where my car was parked, directly under the sixty-foot woman's boob.

"Where are you parked?" I asked her.

"I'm back up by all the people at the gate."

"You want a ride to your car?"

"No. I'm okay, actually. I'm a little concerned about you. Maybe you shouldn't be alone right now."

"I live way down south."

"That's okay, I like to drive."

"Why don't you give me a little time to get cleaned up and stuff. Its three o'clock now, how about around 6:30, my place? I'll text you the address," I said.

"Great. I'll pick up a pizza," she said.

I took a deep breath in the quiet of my car as I watched her walk away, until she was out of my sight. I started the car and eased south into moderate Miami traffic. Halfway home I reached for my cellphone in the glove compartment. There were a lot of missed calls. The first was Ritchie, probably telling me he'd be late for the meet today. I deleted most of the call history. Whoever it was that had been calling, if it was still important I'm sure they'd call back. I texted my address to C.C.'s phone. Then listened to a voice message from Ileana at the VIN office.

"Cade, attorney Phil *Jacksoone* from Collier County called. He said *ju* have his number."

I slightly smiled. Santiago had obviously done his part.

My calm and serene condo at Paradise Point welcomed me, and I felt very grateful to just have a place to come home to.

I went upstairs to the master bathroom, and turned the hot water on in the large jacuzzi bathtub. I lifted my pants leg and pulled the wad of cash from the neoprene sleeve and put it into a pair of boots in my closet. I took the spare magazines out of the neoprene sleeve and stripped the rest of my clothes off and threw everything, including the sleeve, into the hamper. I slipped slowly into the warm water of the tub and let it fill to a pretty good depth. With the jets purring, I let myself think about the day. But the tub was so invitingly sensational that I felt myself dozing asleep in the hot, bubbling water, the trauma of the day flitting in and out of my mind.

Chapter Twenty-Two

I MUST HAVE BEEN in the bathtub for well over an hour—my hands were all pruned and wrinkled. It was just past 5pm, and the autumn sunlight was still filtering through the master bedroom from the deck. Feeling a little wobbly, I dried off and changed into a pair of jeans and a long sleeve turquoise shirt. I put on a pair of Nike runners and fell into one of the oversized lounge chairs in the living room for a while. I really wanted to go down to the private beach, but knew by the time I got down there it would start getting dark, and if I was being honest with myself the idea of walking anywhere sounded exhausting. Instead, I went out on the deck with an Amstel Light and watched the day's fading rays across Biscayne Bay.

I wondered if there was anything I could have said or done to stop Perchero from killing himself.

I understood his fear all too well; he'd tried to rip off the cartel. There were enough incarcerated Colombians who, for the right price, would gladly give Perchero a brutal death in jail. As he tore away from the S&S Diner, he had to have known his plans for the day, if not the rest of his life, were about to go right down the rustiest drain he could ever imagine.

The sun was pushing across the sky, leaving dusty pink and purple soft reflections in the clouds. Sunset wouldn't be official until at least 7pm.

Ritchie had handled himself well. It was fortuitous that he'd seen Emiliano's gun and yelled it out. One more step, and I'd have been square with Perchero's car window.

A lot of things went right today, I thought to myself. *But a lot of things went wrong, too.*

Ritchie still should've had more people covering the drop, and he should've listened to me when I told him it had all the markings of a rip-off. His philosophy that they were dropping money to *us*, that it couldn't be a rip-off, was obviously tragically flawed. The whole remembrance of just a few hours ago made my eyes well with tears and I saw a slight tremble in my hands.

Before I could dwell on it anymore, I went back inside the condo to clean up—but was actually satisfied with the cleanliness of the place. I'd done a decent job the other day tidying up. I pulled another Amstel Light from the refrigerator and texted C.C., telling her if she was still thinking of dropping by to pass on the pizza and I'd just order it from here.

"Mushrooms and green peppers," was her text back.

I called Papa Ricco's and placed an order for a medium mushroom and green peppers plus a large cheese pizza for delivery. I also called the front gate and told them to expect the pizza, as well as C.C. I carried the Amstel back out to the deck and plopped into a deck chair to watch the clouds glide by. I could hear the now-wild colorful macaws as they flew about the expansive FP&L property. I say 'now-wild' because once Hurricane Andrew blew the Metro Zoo aviary to shreds, the macaws escaped. Now, nearly seven years later, they were wild all over southern Miami Dade County. They loved burrowing nests in old dead Royal Palms. Lying in the chaise, downing the beer, I zoned out a little from the events of the day I distanced myself from my thoughts like a macaw escaping the zoo. After about forty-five minutes the Papa Ricco's delivery guy knocked on the door. The pizza smelled delicious. I paid him and watched as he made his way down the stairs and into his car. As I started to close the door, I saw C.C.'s Dodge Intrepid waiting for him to pull out so she could pull in. When she got out, she immediately noticed me standing up above her. I just sort of shrugged and lifted the pizzas up for her to see.

"Good timing," I said as she walked up the steps to the front door.

"You said you lived pretty far down south, but this place is *way* south, and it's *gorgeous*."

"Thank you, but it's not mine, I'm just staying here for a while. I hope you're hungry. The pizza just got here."

"I know, I saw the pizza guy pull out, remember?"

My cheeks got hot, and I realized for the first time I was actually nervous around C.C.

My manners had practically gone out the window; I'd neglected to ask her what she wanted to drink. I ran through the litany of what I had to offer, and she asked for a white wine. The owner of the condo had nearly every type of alcohol in the place and I found a chilled bottle of 1993 Chateau Latour from Pauillac France and popped it open. She'd already opened the pizza boxes and was asking me where the plates were. Coming from a guy who usually ate pizza from the box in front of the TV or on the deck, I had to think for a second where the plates actually were. Luckily, on my first pull of an overhead kitchen cabinet, there they were, making me seem like I knew where they were all along. I poured the wine in a crystal stemmed glass and we took the plates, pizzas, and drinks up to the deck, just in time to see the majestic sunset begin to take shape. I pointed out Chicken Key, and she could just make out Sands Key way in the distance. Her dark eyes reflected the sunset colors as she grew mesmerized by the view.

With each bit of the delicious pizza, the sky took on a more pinkish, cotton candy hue, with purple and tangerine orange mixing in. A sense of calm washed over me, not for the first time that day— but this was different. The colors of the sunset mixed with the pizza and now my third Amstel Light, were ending the day much better than it started. Having C.C with me, actually having anyone with me was a step in the right direction. But her being here especially with all that had happened today was a colossal relief.

We talked for a while about the mess the day had become. I told her about Ritchie, that I'd *warned* him, reliving how we were outside the diner when the shooting began. C.C. said she and her squad got the call that there'd been a robbery in front of the S&S Diner and that there was a man down in the street. I smirked, realizing they were probably talking about me laying down to avoid getting shot by the Mac-10. She said when their marked units arrived all the patrons in the diner were in the street screaming about the cemetery, further confusing everyone. Then the calls started coming in about shots fired from somewhere inside the cemetery and people running with rifles.

"I'm sure we caused quite a stir for your officers and dispatchers."

"Tovar blew a gasket. He cleared out the whole unit and had us hit the scene. He thought this was another shootout in the streets— which it was— but it took him awhile to realize that aside from the suicide, there really wasn't anything for Homicide to do. At first, he was really pissed at you, I mean he was *furious*. As the facts became more clear, he began to understand better and begrudgingly felt that in spite of it all you were a tough nut to crack and and kept your cards close to your chest rightfully so."

I didn't say anything to that remark. I just took a healthy swig of beer and looked out at the sunset. Fact was, I always kept my cards close to my chest. If you'd asked Gina, she'd say I kept everything close to my chest—my feelings, my fears, my traumas, my hopes—if I allowed myself to hope for anything. Gina once said that I lived in constant survival mode, which wasn't really living at all. I was languishing in life, what many psychologists refer to as the middle child of mental health. Not feeling anything to high or to low just existing. I was tractor driving over the feelings of my life plowing them under and pushing them down deeper.

Here I was, looking for peace by staring out at the same sunset, searching for calm in the waves, in a home that wasn't my own, with a woman right beside me that wanted to share it with me. And I was still hiding when I asked my next question.

"Anything new on Zeus?"

"It's been super quiet, but I got a bit of break about ninety minutes ago!" she exclaimed, sitting more upright and turning toward me, wide-eyed. "Remember that instructor at George Baker Aviation School, the one I spoke to, Matthew Walton?"

I nodded between bites of pizza.

"Well, he called me today, said he'd been giving some thought to what we discussed, and he remembered that one of his former European students had gone back to Belgium and left his European tool kit behind."

"Okay."

"He tried some of the tools on the screws, and they fit!" she said, waving her hand around with the pizza in it. She had sauce on her cheek, and I couldn't help but smile at her enthusiasm. "He called them Torq-Set screws. I'm going to meet with him in the morning and also pick up the tool kit, too."

"So Reggie and Jabo had these European screws called Torq-Sets that need European tools to be able to screw them in and out."

"Apparently so."

"Well, that's interesting. Now we just need to see what parts of the airplane they had access to that uses Torq-Set screws," I said.

"Zeus has been quiet," she said through a mouthful. "I wonder if the killings will stop with Jabo and Reggie. If they do, this trail is going to colder by the day. I hate being new in the unit and having unsolved homicides. Tovar has been giving me very little support and he seems to always be talking off to the side with Sciarotta."

"Tovar still hasn't mentioned that he's a registered owner of a Walther P-88. I mean, he knows from looking at the reports that this is the type of firearm Zeus is using, and yet he's opened nothing about it to you as far as assistance or insight?" I asked her.

"Zip. Nada. Nothing," she said.

I poured her another glass of wine. She seemed to be soaking up the peace and quiet of Paradise Point, and I was savoring the company. Soon, we slipped into conversation about things unrelated to our careers. I opened another Amstel Light and was at that point losing track of how many I'd already had. I think she was too, as most of the bottle of wine was now empty. She told me she'd never really gotten down this far south unless it was on elementary school field trips to Metro Zoo or the Gold Coast Railroad Museum.

I filled her glass again. "Ever spend any time in the Florida Keys?"

"I'm not sure," she said with a giggle. "I think as a kid I did some glass bottom boat thing? But I'm not sure."

The night was turning into one of those splendid South Florida nights where the darkness fights for the fading light to capture your attention. In that same fading light, her beauty flourished. In my Amstel Light-fueled thinking, I was captivated by her thick, dark hair, full lips, and her brown seductive eyes, which were mesmerizing to me. The slight mocha coloration of her skin was enchanting. Couple all of that natural beauty with the allure of being a strong, proud, woman and I was finding myself very drawn to her.

"Why are you looking at me like that?" she said with a devilish smile.

"Like what?" I said as I drew closer to her, as if magnetized.

"Like that!" she said, giggling again.

"I was just thinking your ex-boyfriend Ernesto must miss you something fierce."

"You want to see what he's missing?" she said hoarsely, and stood up from the chaise lounge.

She reached out and took me by the hand and led me back inside the condo. She sauntered right to the master bedroom and sat very demurely on the edge of the bed. I stood in front of her, and she reached up and began to unbutton my shirt. As she undid each button she leaned forward and planted small, soft kisses on my chest, kissing me lower on my chest and abdomen.

I pushed her back slightly and started undressing her. Within a few seconds, her blouse was off. Dropping to my knees, I undid the top button of her slacks and unzipped them, while she fell back on the bed, offering her legs to me as I pulled her pants off. Now just in her matching lavender bra and panties, she squirmed back on the bed, pulled back the covers, and slipped underneath.

Her body was exquisite. She had the most delicious curves.

I kneeled with one knee on the bed, and she shimmied more to the center, making room for me. She reached up and started to unbutton my jeans. I'd already discarded my shirt on the floor. Her grasp on my jeans started to waver a bit and I could see in the advancing moonlight, her eyes were starting to flutter and she was having trouble focusing. I started to help her with my jeans and her hands fell limply down on the bed. She was fighting to keep her eyes open and losing that battle.

I stood there with one knee on the bed and watched her rather quickly slip into a blissful sleep. I half-smiled to myself and made a mental note to go easier on the wine next time. She was comfortably tucked into my bed and I gently eased off so as not to disturb her. I went into one of the spare bedrooms. It was one of the rooms in the condo that I had barely spent any time in. I climbed into the bed. The full day's events and the Amstel Lights helped me nod off and soon I was in a deep sleep myself.

I slept through the night and awoke to the smell of freshly brewed coffee. I didn't normally drink American coffee, choosing my caffeine to be the highly potent Cuban coffee. It didn't take long for me to recall the events of last night and I searched the floor for my shirt as I slipped my jeans on. I went downstairs to find C.C. pouring what I assumed was her first cup of coffee. When she saw me enter the kitchen, she said, "Oh my God I'm so embarrassed."

"Embarrassed? Embarrassed about what?"

"Well, it's not like I fall into bed with every man I've known for less than a week, and then conk out on top of that to boot."

"If it makes you feel any better, you're not the first woman I've seen do the loop-the-loop with her eyes before snoring."

"Oh my God! Was I snoring?"

"I have no idea. I went into the other room and I was out."

She held her coffee mug in both of her hands and took a sip. I think if she could've hidden behind the mug she would have. She seemed a little sheepish about last night.

"What does your day look like?" I asked her.

"Me?"

"Yes you, it's only you and I here in the kitchen," I said, chuckling. *When was the last time I chuckled?*

"I'm going to meet with Matthew Walton at George Baker Aviation School, learn what I can about Torq-Set screws, and give him a property receipt for that Belgium student's toolbox. I'm going to keep tracking ownership records on the Walther P-88, and see if I can find a way to get Tovar off the top of my suspect list. What about you? What does your own day look like?"

"Me?"

"Yes you, you goofball."

"I'm going in for an after-action debriefing, try to keep them from putting me on some sort of administrative leave, since technically, I didn't shoot anyone. I'm going to freshen up real quick upstairs. I'll be back down in a few."

I went upstairs and washed my face and wet my hair down, brushed my teeth and changed my shirt. I went into my closet and pulled the loose fifty dollar bills out of my boots. I threw them into a shaving kit. I grabbed the loaner Glock. I started to head downstairs when I noticed that C.C. had done me the courtesy of making the bed. I thought that was very kind of her.

When I came down, she was pretty much ready to head out the door herself. We had an awkward moment of seeing each other off as I locked the condo. She had already started down the stairs and was on her way to her Dodge Intrepid. By the time I was at the bottom of the stairs she was starting to pull out. She waved one last time at me with a big smile. Then she was on her way and out of my sight. I got in the Z-28 and started the engine. I opened the shaving kit and I started counting the cash from the stack I took out of the Lexus. I counted $4,450. I sectioned off $450 and put the rest of the money in the shaving kit, which I stored it in the car's center console.

I left Paradise Point and drove west on Coral Reef Drive. At Southwest 75th Avenue I turned into the parking lot of Saint Richard Catholic Church. I pulled up under the angular overhang and left the engine running as I went to the church's front doors. To the right of the doors was a brass plate with a slot in it, embossed with the words, "*For the Poor.*" I pushed the $450 in the slot and got back in the car to plot the best route to the Coral Gables Police Station.

There really wasn't a set time that I needed to be at the police station, but I know what these things entail. I just wanted to see if I could sit down with Major Brunson and get it over with.

Ileana glared at me as I entered the VIN office. "*Aye* Cade, *coño es son tine ju* will try not to give me a heart attack *por favor?*"

"How do you think I feel, Ileana? The main thing is I'm okay, and we are all okay. Can you please call down to Charlene and see if she can get me in to see Brunson?"

Surprisingly, she actually did it without any pushback. Charlene told her to send me down. I walked down the hallway to Major Brunson's office and rapped on the door frame very lightly, Charlene told me to just go in. The Major's door was open and he was sitting behind his desk, his black Tony Lama boots visible underneath.

"Cade, pull up a chair," he said with surprising civility.

I sat down and looked at him across his desk.

"Do I look like a guy who got very little sleep?" he asked me.

"No."

"Well, I can assure you I am very fucking sleep deprived. Sorenson faxed the preliminary C.I.D. reports and other related papers to my home last night."

"Couldn't that have waited until you got in the office this morning?" I asked him.

"How the fuck am I supposed to know? He's my wife's dipshit brother and I've been stuck with him ever since. The guy is as stupid as an Arizona mule. The goddamn fax kept beeping and chirping all night. I finally unplugged the fucking thing at 1:30am."

I just pursed my lips and wondered how long was I going to have to be in his office before he turned his wrath on me.

"First things first. The Lexus was towed to our motor pool. The car is paid for and after we replace the windshield, rear window, passenger door, tire, and side mirror—good shooting, by the way—we'll go to work on the interior. We're going to keep it, under the asset forfeiture rules. So we got a fairly new Lexus coming our way. There was $340,600 in the bag in the car. Both Dale and Tavino were sorely misled to think there might even be two million in it. DEA Group 6 hit the address off the Gratigny Parkway and found five million six hundred thousand in a closet. The dumbshit left a wrench with the money so one of the DEA guys got creative and went out to the garage and checked one of those Craftsman upright fucking tool chests and found an additional million inside of it. So the total haul from the house was six million six hundred thousand. Add that, plus with what was in the Lexus, and we're in the seven million dollar ballpark." he said.

I nodded my head, agreeing with the math.

"So, we're going to reverse the wheels on this. We'll endow Customs $400,000 and they'll cut that little Colombian fucker completely out. They're going to tell him to create five million in business in the next two months at a measly six percentage points per deal, or they're going to drop his snitch file all over that Godforsaken fucking country."

I wasn't about to tell the Major that the plan he'd just laid out were my instructions to Ritchie nearly verbatim, so I just acted like I was hearing it for the first time.

"Lieutenant Maddalone recommended remedial firearms training for you since you fired four rounds that didn't hit the suspect. I reminded him of the circumstances. Magically, he changed his recommendation to just keeping his fucking mouth shut and giving you back your gun in a day or so."

"Thank you," I said.

"You okay with that skinny fucker blowing his brains out in front of you?"

"We make choices in life and he chose to do that. His choice, not mine," I said.

"Cade, as far as I'm concerned, you're not on any restrictions. Yesterday was a shitbag mess and you did well. I sit in the biggest office in this place for a reason, so don't worry about anything. The C.I.D. reports from Treasury have all but cleared you and Tavino. You got nothing to worry about from our side of the house."

I started to get up to leave.

"I'm serious, Cade—two fucking assholes dead and we got seven million dollars. I'd say that's a pretty good Colombian scratch-off ticket."

I looked at the Major and nodded my head as slightly as I could in an appearance of agreement and went out to the outer office where Charlene was.

"Charlene, do you have a manila envelope please?"

She reached into a drawer in her desk and handed me a clean legal size manila envelope. I walked out and down the hallway. On a desk in an open vacant office was today's sports page from the *Miami Herald*. I took it and went to my car.

It was nearing 10:30am.

I drove down towards Coconut Grove. I went to Miami City Hall. I parked in an open space at the large circle in front. I opened the center console of the Z-28 and pulled the $4000 from the shaving kit and shoved the bills into the manila envelope. I then slid the manila envelope into the sports page, which I left on the passenger seat. I exited and locked the car. I made that same walk across the parking lot and through the chain link fence opening of the marina docks. I walked into Scotty's Landing.

Santiago was there. He was behind the bar, apparently doing inventory of the alcohol bottles. He looked up and saw me. I met his eyes.

I went into the men's room. I put my car keys on top of the urinal. I started urinating in the urinal. Santiago came in and started urinating at the urinal next to me. Staring straight ahead I said, "I hear this might be Phil Jackson's last year with the Chicago Bulls."

"I heard that, too," he said.

"I saw it in the sports page of the *Miami Herald*. Unfortunately, I left it in my car."

I zipped up my pants, washed my hands at the sink. Santiago stayed at the urinal. I left the bathroom.

I found a table close to the water, yet still under the green and white canvas sun-shading awning. Although the sun did peek through on occasion, I wasn't overheated. I could handle it.

The same waitress, Alicia, came over to my table. I had my order ready before she could even hand me a laminated menu.

"Alicia, I'll have the grouper sandwich and fries, please."

She narrowed her eyes, clearly trying to remember where she had seen me and wondering how I knew her name.

"Anything to drink?" she asked.

"I'll have a beer. Let Santiago choose for me."

Immediately I saw the lightbulb of recognition go off in her head.

"Right away," she said as she turned to make the long walk back to the kitchen.

I chose to sit with my back to the restaurant and take in the view of the bay. The sun was able to slide occasionally under the green and white canvass and the warmth felt good on my face as I sat there with my eyes closed, listening to the current gently lap against the seawall in a smooth, rhythmic lull. It was about fifteen minutes of peacefulness when I sensed someone near my table. It was Alicia, placing down the magnificent looking sandwich and fries in a plastic basket on the table, along with two very chilled Kalik beers.

"Need any tartar sauce or cocktail sauce?" she asked.

"No, thank you."

The first Kalik tasted terrific as I continued to take in the view.

Just like before, the sandwich was enormous and fried to perfection. The lettuce and tomato on top of it was very fresh and all in all it was a great lunch. I thought of nothing else but that sandwich for just a few moments. Halfway through the sandwich I started in on the second Kalik, enjoying the golden deliciousness of the fries nearly as much as the grouper. Midway through the pile of fries, I saw my car keys in the basket. Retrieving the keys from the fries, I wiped them down with a napkin and stuck them in my pocket. I finished the beers and my lunch, and left a twenty on the table for Alicia because I wasn't sure if Santiago had comped the meal.

Having left the restaurant, I got in my car, and inside the same sports section was a thick white envelope. I opened it to find the file on Sergeant Roberto Tovar.

I didn't think the City Hall parking lot would be the best place to read the file. I started the engine and drove west through Coconut Grove and down Main Highway. I took Main Highway around Sunset Circle and continued south on Old Cutler Road. The overhanging canopy of Banyan trees cast light and shadow on me through the T-tops. I pulled into the small, nearly empty parking lot of Fairchild Tropical Gardens.

I opened the file.

OFFICIAL FILE:
SERGEANT ROBERTO TOVAR
City of Miami Police Department

Basic, rudimentary things were in the front of the file. He attended a private, Catholic high school in Miami, Immaculata-La Salle. His grades were passable but far from Magna Cum Laude material. He graduated in 1982. From high school he went to Barry University, another Catholic school. He lasted one year at Barry University. He took mostly required courses. Looking at his transcripts, he wasn't setting the world on fire academically, and it looked like he was setting himself up as business major. He left Barry University in the late spring of 1983 and joined the U.S. Army. His first deployment was basic training in Fort Leonard Wood, Missouri. I looked through his basic candidacy file and couldn't see any reason why he didn't stay on the east coast at Fort Benning or Fort Jackson, but somehow, he ended up in Missouri. There wasn't much in the file that told me anything about his basic training but in turning the pages I began to see what he was angling for in the U.S Army. Somewhere along his military career he ended up in a unit under the command of the U.S. Army Special Operations Command (USASOC). He had a speeding ticket in his file from the Fayetteville, North Carolina Police Department in 1985. Fayetteville is right next to Fort Bragg—and from what it looked like, he may have been Delta Force. The ticket was placed and noted in his file by Commander Richard Stenbers from the Delta Force Command Division.

I looked up from the file. Sergeant Tovar had been Delta Force in the Army. He was in North Carolina from the fall of 1983 to 1986. In those three years he completed correspondence and satellite courses from East Carolina University and received a Bachelor's degree in Humanities. He also was accepted into and passed the very intense Survival, Evasion, Resistance, and Escape (SERE) training course. The curriculum is rigorous and includes outdoor survival techniques, urban escape, survival methods, combat survival, general survival, evasion resistance and escape, special survival situations, and jungle, arctic, and desert operations.

"You are definitely the real deal, Sergeant Tovar," I mumbled to myself.

His military file showed a few commendations, but I suspect due to confidentiality concerns there are a slew more that weren't documented. He was one of those guys who'd been to twenty different countries, six of which he entered with a passport; the others had no idea he was ever there. I recalled what C.C. had said about him when we were in the *El Exquisito Café*:

"...I wouldn't be surprised if he's killed people before. I mean in war and all. He just has this iciness about him. I heard him talking to one

of the guys about the best way to slit a throat. I mean, who talks about shit like that?"

Upon receiving an honorable discharge from the military, he moved back to Miami in 1987. He applied with the Miami Dade Police Department and the Miami Police Department.

Both agencies offered him a job, but he chose the Miami Police Department over Miami Dade. He had the requisite three letters of recommendation, but what caught my eye was one of the letters of recommendation was from one of his neighbors.

Joe Sciarotta.

The same Sciarotta had been employed by the Miami Police Department. He wrote a glowing letter of recommendation for his neighbor, Roberto Tovar.

My interest was very piqued that Sciarotta and Tovar knew each other prior to Tovar being hired. Now Tovar was Sciarotta's direct supervisor.

In looking at his police file, Tovar had no issues in the police academy, and was selected as class leader for his Basic Law Enforcement (BLE) class. There was a notation from the police psychologist who mentioned that *"considering the applicant's military background, he may find the rigors of police work unsatisfying and beneath his skill level and experiences."*

Tovar transitioned through his three months of being field trained and was assigned to the patrol division in Overtown. He and his squad members had a considerable number of use of force complaints against them.

Overtown wasn't the easiest sector, but the use of force complaints were an inordinate amount.

He transferred from uniform patrol to a street narcotics group. C.C. had said it was a robbery interdiction group, but she was mistaken—it was actually a street narcotic unit.

Five months in the unit, he and four of his street narcotic detectives were brought up on a wrongful death case. A local drug dealer named Rogelio was heard threatening the life of one of the detectives. Tovar and four of his coworkers located Rogelio sitting in a parked car. In the course of arresting him someone stood on his back, compressing the lungs of Rogelio, who died on the scene of "respiratory distress." Tovar and his coworkers were sued civilly. The state attorney at the time was none other than Janet Reno. Her office turned it over to the medical examiner's office for assistance in filing charges. The medical examiner detected traces of cocaine and rotenone in Rogelio's system, both of which can be respiratory inhibitors. The state attorney's office saw that as their political out and didn't file any criminal charges. It was left to a civil jury to decide how much culpable negligence there was. The City of Miami settled for one-point-two million with Rogelio's relatives.

Tovar went back to patrol and was placed where his chances of getting into any trouble were minimized—the very southern tip of Brickell Avenue and the Powell Bridge on out to Virginia Key. That quiet police sector afforded him the opportunity to study for, and subsequently pass, the sergeant's exam. After his supervisory probation period ended, he was assigned to Homicide in 1993, and that's where he's been ever since.

The rest of the file was mostly unit commendations, a few letters from citizens thanking him for doing things like driving an elderly woman to a medical clinic, and for his efforts in searching for a lost and recovered child. Things like that. There was a letter where he specifically endorses Joe Sciarotta to be officer of the month for his work in Homicide.

Most of the information in the file was very much what I expected. I didn't think it was worth $4,000, but this type of information as Santiago says, falls in the category of "politicos." The main thing is, it keeps C.C. insulated from investigating not only one of her coworkers, but her actual direct supervisor. It also answers the question about Tovar's Special Forces experience— which was sizeable.

The big surprise was that he and Sciarotta knew each other before Tovar even got hired. Now Tovar is Sciarotta's supervisor.

Tovar also has narcotic experience.

He owns the exact model and caliber handgun that Zeus used to kill those young men.

Tovar still hadn't mentioned anything about the firearm to C.C. He'd lent zero assistance to her in her investigation, but she said he huddles often with Sciarotta.

He approved leave for Sciarotta to go to Jacksonville to watch the Dolphins play a Monday night game. A game that was on national TV. Why make that very long drive? It would be an ideal opportunity for him to dispose of his buddy's Walther P-88 somewhere along the way.

I closed the file and slipped it back into the sports page. I actually got out of the car and put the whole thing in the trunk. Not the most secure place for it, but it was better than having it across my front seat. I looked at the clock on the dashboard—it was nearing 1pm.

The Glock I was carrying was exactly like the one that Lieutenant Maddalone switched out for mine. I saw no reason to rush that process. I was sure I'd hear from him in due time; besides, it was Friday and he most likely wouldn't be done with my Glock's testing and examining until at least Monday.

It might be time for a little mental health vacation and just start my weekend a little early. A sunset from Burdine's bar in Marathon Key might be just what the doctor ordered.

I looked at my gas gauge and decided that I'd just use the U.C. Chevron credit card and fill the car up; maybe grab a change of clothes, and some cash from an ATM in case I decide to stay down in Marathon.

As I was formulating all of that, my cellphone rang, and it was C.C.

"Hello?"

"What the hell did you do?" she growled at me.

"What are you talking about?"

"Tovar! He's going off the rails like a runaway train. I mean, he is fit to be tied, he's so pissed."

"Pissed about what?"

"Some reporter from the *Nassau Guardian* filed a public information request to get his complete file. He just found out about it. They requested it a few days ago and now the assistant chief is up his ass asking him a ton of questions. Tovar has no idea why any newspaper, let alone one in the Bahamas, would want his file. He is literally furious and stalking about the office."

"Well, I don't know what to say about that."

"Really, you have no idea?"

I remembered the conversation we had the *El Exquisito Café*:

"We've got to start with someone somewhere. But it doesn't have to be you that does the first digging. It isn't too cool to be looking at your own people and if it ever gets out you are? You're toast. Let me look into Tovar. Let me see what I can find. Outside agency kind of thing. If anybody ever finds out I'll play it off as that we needed someone on our DEA squad. In fact, the less you know the better. Let's not mention it again. Okay?"

"C.C., I just rolled all around Northeast 2nd Avenue yesterday, avoiding a Mac-10. I got better things to do than wonder why some newspaper wants Tovar's file."

I hated to keep the truth from her, but at this junction it seemed prudent and protective to not reveal to her what I'd learned yet. If Tovar was blowing a gasket over a reporter looking into his file, imagine how he'd be if C.C. accidentally let it slip that she was a reason for the inquiry.

"Well, I just thought that maybe—"

"Did you ever meet with that instructor, Matthew Walton?" I asked her, throwing her train of thought in another direction.

"Oh my God, yes! I got the tool kit, too. It's really weird how another continent can be so different from our own. The screwdrivers that are needed for these Torq-Set screws have a really weird curve to them. I'll show you next time I see you. Walton was really informative. Let me read from my notes... The Torq-Set is what they call a cruciform screw drive used in what he called, '*torque-sensitive applications.'* It's designed to hold more firm and steadfast. The Torq-Set head, as you know, is similar to a Phillips screwdriver. They both have a cross with four spurs, or offshoots. But as Walton explained, In Torq-Set the lines are offset from each other, so they don't align to form intersecting slots across the top of the head. It wreaks havoc with USA tools. Because of this, a regular Phillips or flat-blade screwdriver will *not* fit the head. That's why the guy at Home Depot was probably wondering what the heck you were holding. According to Walton, the Torq-Set is used in military and aerospace applications. Airbus and Embraer aircraft use them a lot. Walton started giving me all the technical jargon. He said the applicable standards that govern the Torq-Set geometry are governed by the National Aerospace Standard. He wrote the codes for me, he said they are—and I quote—"NASM 33781 and NASM 14191" for the ribbed version. The ribbed version is also known as ACR Torq-Set. Whatever that means."

Tovar, Torq-Set, Treasury C.I.D., I was just a little tired of it all. I could hear Marathon Key calling me in my soul. I just wanted to get off the phone. I'd put the phone in my trunk if the day wasn't so early still. I needed a break from it all. The realization that a guy with small shoulders tried to put multiple holes in me yesterday was starting to set in. It was Friday and time for me to pull the plug.

"C.C., that's real good work. That might explain the Zeus connection to Reggie and Jabo even more. Those screws are obviously aviation designed. Those guys must have been accessing, or storing something that's held by those types of screws. I'd like to see those tools later. Are you going to keep looking into the P-88 ownership files?"

"Yeah, I guess so. I just hate doing it at my desk. I mean, Tovar is on the warpath over this Freedom of Information 119 request for his file."

"I'm sure he'll simmer down over time. C.C., let me take care of a few things and I'll get with you later," I said, becoming more and more antsy.

"Okay. Let's talk later," she said.

When we hung up I realized that I could use a little time at Anne's Beach in the Middle Keys. I needed to get a decent beach chair and at least one towel. Rather than drive home, I'd just swing by a CVS Pharmacy and get an inexpensive Brazilian beach chair and a beach towel. There was a CVS at U.S.1 and Kendall Drive. There was also a Bank America ATM a block away. This would be real convenient. I could jump up on the 874 Expressway and be on the turnpike in a few minutes. Southbound and down.

I made the drive to the CVS, and as luck would have it, everything I needed was there. I chose a blue and white striped little Brazilian beach chair. The CVS is so close to the University of Miami, they had the university's mascot Sebastian the Ibis beach towels. I grabbed a green and orange one off the shelf. I made my purchases and was happily putting the items in my trunk next to my go bag when I heard my cellphone ringing in the car. It was C.C. *again!*

"Hello."

"Cade, they just found Ellinport murdered.

Chapter Twenty-Three

"**W**HAT? YOU HAVE got to be kidding me," I blurted.

"I wish I was. Believe me, I wish I was. I'm on my way there now."

"Where's 'there?'"

"3691 Northwest Twentieth Street."

"How did this happen?"

"I don't know much yet. It seems he didn't show up to work today and that secretary, Diane Ford, got worried. She had a welfare check done on him. Some guy they sent over saw him from the bridge."

"The bridge?"

"Yeah, he lived right off of Douglas by the Tamiami Canal. Look, I don't know much more than that right now. I should be there in about fifteen minutes."

I looked into my open trunk at the gleaming new beach chair and the beach towel, and I just slammed the trunk.

"I'll be there in about a half hour," I said as I hung up.

I sat in the car for a minute and tried to settle my mind. Three minutes ago, I was thinking my day would be down at Anne's Beach with a sunset, capped off at a multi-level tiki bar. Now my entire day was turned upside down—again—with a single telephone call.

I started the car and recalled C.C. said it was off of Douglas Road and the Tamiami Canal. 3691 Northwest 20th Street. I just figured I'd work my way to Douglas Road and figure it out once I got to the Tamiami Canal. When I arrived, I saw just before the bridge rise, that the street was one way. I decided to drive in against the traffic direction and quickly made the turn into the curve where the house sits.

Two marked police units from The Miami Police Department were already at the house, and enough Dodge Intrepids to stock a small Dodge dealership. The entire property was a sight unto itself. The most distinguishing feature was a monstrous forty foot high cathedral-like brown cedar shingled A-frame.. The A-frame front was one enormous frame, minus the glass with crisscrossing brown support beams. The north side was completely open. The entire structure straddled an open concrete boat slip. It had at one time probably been used as a boat slip for a tall, masted sailboat. From the slip it was just a few drawbridges and you'd be in the Miami River, and then out in Biscayne Bay in under fifteen minutes. Attached to the A-frame was a simple, flat-roofed house with matching cedar shingles rimming the entire flat roof in a four-foot wraparound. The Douglas Road bridge over the Tamiami Canal literally abutted the property line. Where the bridge rose to its highest point, the A-frame still towered over it. It also towered over the Bertram Yacht Factory on the other side of the canal. A six-foot wooden fence ran the full length of the property and practically hid the little house from being seen from Northwest 20th Street, but there was no hiding the A-frame. Palms, and even a few banana trees were planted in front of the fencing to try and soften the towering aspect of it all.

I got out of my car. I saw that the wooden fence was broken at the locking mechanism. Someone had forcibly pushed the door in. One of the hinges was twisted. The door precariously hung on the bottom hinge. Stepping through the damaged door, I looked to my left. The left side of the property closest to the rising bridge was where all the activity was.

I slowly walked past the A-frame, feeling its height rising above me. Through the beams I could see investigators and uniformed officers standing closer to the sea wall at the canal. I walked to the west side of the A-frame and the boat slip. A section of Bermuda grass about twelve feet wide was between the rising bridge and the A-frame, and extended all the way down to the sea wall where the investigators and police were gathered.

C.C. was the only investigator that I recognized. There was a body under a thin yellow tarp. Lying in the grass was an overturned lawn chair and a fishing pole, as well as a bucket, probably filled with brackish canal water and live shrimp. Once C.C. saw me, she met me on the side of the A-frame.

"Thanks for coming," she said.

"Is that Ellinport?' I asked, looking past her at the body under the tarp.

"Yeah, it's him. Based on lividity and rigor mortis we think he might have been killed last night around ten o'clock. Looks like he was sitting in the lawn chair and fishing when he was killed."

"Any connection to Zeus?"

"Two in the chest and one in the head. I'd say so."

The news that Ellinport was most likely another Zeus assassination was a little too much to wrap my head around. "Tell it to me from the beginning, please."

"Ellinport was renting this house to be close to the airport, in case he ever needed to respond for something. Because of the fencing and its location, neighbors didn't have anything to say to the uniforms when they did an area canvas. Nobody heard anything. Many of them had their air conditioners on, plus the traffic on the bridge is a steady source of noise, so the neighbors are a little sound aversive, if you get my drift. Ellinport didn't show up for work, and Ms. Ford got concerned because that's not in his nature, according to her. She had one of the fuelers drive over and check on him. The fuelers leave the airport two to three times a day to fill up at the fuel farms, so he had no problem doing her the favor. The fueler's name is…" She flipped through her binder, "Benito Santos. He tried to make contact but couldn't get past the gate. When he started heading back to the airport, he took the Douglas bridge. Since he was sitting high up in the truck, he looked down and saw Ellinport on his back covered in blood. He pulled over by Bertram, ran back up the bridge and called 911 from there. Our arriving officers broke through the fence and could tell that Ellinport was dead. He'd been dead for a while."

Past C.C. I could see about twenty Bertram yacht employees standing at the back of the factory, watching all the police activity from their side of the canal.

"Two in the chest and one in the head. So, he's fishing and Zeus must've come up behind him," I said.

"It looks like he got up from the chair at the last moment and confronted the shooter—or as we think, Zeus. When he got shot he fell and his foot knocked the chair over. He died there on his back," C.C. said.

"You said the patrol officers had to break through the fence gate to gain access. Yet Zeus was able to enter and exit without going through the gate. He didn't access the property from the water or Ellinport would've seen him. If what you say is correct, then Zeus came right through here, walked up and startled Ellinport. Come on out to the street side with me for a minute."

C.C. followed me through the broken gate. We stood on Northwest 20th Street, and looked at the house. We were near the curve of the one-way street. The gate and fencing made the house look very fortified. I looked towards the bridge and I noticed that there were four different electrical and telephone boxes on the edge of the property. As the bridge started to rise there were some palms on the property, but on the other side of the palms was a small concrete utility shed with a louvered door. Large, twelve-inch plastic conduits emerged from the electrical and telephone boxes, affixed with heavy metal strapping to the concrete section of the bridge. Two of the conduits had a ninety-degree bend in them that ran the full length of the bridge and spanned the canal.

"Come over here with me," I said to C.C.

I led her to the concrete shed and looked at the doorknob.

There was a smudge of a footprint on the doorknob where someone had stood on it, then propelled themselves, up to the roof. We went behind the shed. We found multiple toe scrapes and shoe impressions on the conduit piping. We both walked back into the side yard where there was a small shed on the inside of the fence. Shed to shed, Zeus used the conduit as a foothold, and holding onto the lower part of the bridge, he basically walked the conduit over the fence.

"I think your crime scene people are going to get a lot of forensics from all of this," I said to her.

After she took it all in, C.C. called over to two of her crime scene technicians. She told them to get ladders and check the roof of both sheds for handprints or shoe impressions. She also told them to check the conduit for any evidence as well. After talking with the crime scene techs, C.C. and I started trying to figure how all of this came about and why Zeus chose to kill Ellinport. She mentioned that Sergeant Tovar was meeting with the legal attaché for the Miami Police Department in attempt to find out why a newspaper in the Bahamas would want his file.

"He's barking up the wrong tree on that one. Anyone can get a copy of any of our employment files as long as they file the proper paperwork and pay the required ten cents a page per copy fee."

"No. I know that, but it just strikes me as odd that this has a Zeus hit all over it and neither he and Sciarotta are here."

We were standing near the broken gate when a black Ford Explorer pulled up. Two men got out of the car. The driver was about 6'2" and he was in a gray suit and tie. He had aviator sunglasses, a well-trimmed mustache, and a full head of wavy brown hair. He also had an ATF badge on his belt. The other man was in a full Class A City of Miami police uniform, and he had three stars on his collar. His gold badge and the medals on his chest glinted in the South Florida sun boring down on us. C.C. whispered to me, "Assistant Chief, David McAndrew." It was McAndrew who spoke first.

"Are any of you Detective Clay?"

"I am, sir," said C.C.

"Detective Clay, we've never met, I'm Assistant Chief McAndrew. I wish we were meeting under different circumstances. This is Special Agent, Gregg Chapman from the ATF. Although Marshall Ellinport was retired from ATF, he was still one of us. We want all the horses pulling this wagon."

"Yes, sir," she said.

McAndrew and Chapman both looked at me in my jeans, Wayfarer sunglasses, long hair, goatee and earrings.

"Chief, I'm Cade Taylor. I'm a detective in the VIN unit with the Gables."

"VIN. Well, that explains things a little. Do you work for Teddy Brunson?"

"Yes sir, I do. I just saw him this morning, in fact." I turned towards Agent Chapman. "Agent Chapman, I am sorry for your loss," I said.

"Detective Clay, we're getting information that Marshall Ellinport assisted you recently through our Walnut Creek California lab. Is that true?" asked Chapman.

"We have two ongoing homicide investigations involving contractual airport workers. Both victims were killed with the same caliber handgun. Mr. Ellinport put me in touch with your lab to help me find ownership records in the tri-county area," she said.

"So, he did in fact assist you with your investigation?" he said again, more like a question than a statement.

"Yes, he did. He was also aware of who our two victims were and had his own internal investigation started involving our victims," she said.

Inwardly, I cringed.

"Anyone else that was aware of Ellinport's internal investigation?" asked Chapman.

"Suezie Chanin-Galperin," C.C. said.

"Who is she?" asked Chapman.

"She was Ellinport's supervisor. She's the Chief of Staff and Senior Policy Advisor for the airport."

"Hang on for a second. Detective, help us get up to speed on this whole thing. Kindly tell me and Agent Chapman how all of this connects to your investigation of two current unsolved homicides," asked McAndrew.

C.C. went back to that rainy night a week ago and spent about eight minutes informing both men about her case. She didn't mention her suspicions of Tovar. When she was done talking, both men quietly soaked it in for a moment.

"Detective Clay, you have your hands full with this one. If this Zeus, as you call him, is out there, then anyone related to, or with knowledge of this case is in danger. I'm going to see if we can get Ms. Chanin-Galperin to agree to consensual police protection," said Assistant Chief McAndrew.

He then turned his attention to me. "Since you have such a strong working knowledge of this case, I think it best if Detective Clay continue to work the homicide investigation and I'd like to see if you would augment our detectives providing dignitary protection on Ms. Chanin-Galperin. I'll put in a call to Teddy, see if he'll loan you to us for a few days."

"Well, actually—" I started to say in protest.

"Detective Taylor," he said, cutting me off, "I am very much aware of what happened yesterday in my city involving you. Yes, *my* city! I'm also aware there will be some down time as your agency, our agency, and Customs C.I.D. do their after-action reports. I have a homicide detective out on leave and another homicide sergeant in Internal Affairs for cursing at our legal attaché today. We're momentarily depleted of our resources. There will still be homicides and natural deaths to be investigated. So for a few days I am asking you to assist us with a little protective custody. I said from the beginning—I want all the horses pulling this wagon. Ellinport was a federal agent. Zeus has crossed a line that we can no longer put on a back burner. This is now our biggest priority."

Checkmate. I was surprised to hear that a homicide sergeant was in Internal Affairs for losing his cool with the department's legal attaché. I assumed, as I'm sure C.C. did too, that it was Roberto Tovar.

"If you can clear it with Major Brunson, then I'll help out until you get fully staffed," I said.

"First things first: Where is this Chanin-Galperin lady right now?" asked Chapman.

"I assume she's at work at the airport," said C.C.

"I'm having two of our agents meet her at the airport. I'm going to push heavy on them to be persuasive with her. If it goes as I intend it, one of our agents will ride home in the same car with her followed by my other agent. Once they get to her residence, we'll set up a schedule of round-the-clock protection coordinated by Miami P.D. Is she single or married? Do you know?"

Both C.C. and I replied that we knew nothing about her, and that we'd only met her once. Chapman excused himself and went back to the Explorer to make a series of cellphone calls. McAndrew busied himself talking to C.C. about her case. He revealed to her that it was Sergeant Tovar who was in a little "timeout" for being testy with the legal attaché. McAndrew predicted that by late Monday or Tuesday, Tovar would be back at his normal position in Miami Homicide.

McAndrew asked me if I knew Brunson's direct extension. I replied that I did not, but I gave him the direct line to the police department. Within a minute he was walking away with his cellphone pressed against his ear and I heard him say, "Teddy, it's Dave, how ya doing?" It was now just C.C. and I by ourselves, standing in front of the house and A-frame boat shelter.

"Tovar let his emotions get the better of him. You're going to be alone on this for a few days. They'll have me and a few of your other people babysitting Chanin-Galperin. I hate this shit. We had a prominent arms manufacturer who lived in Coral Gables get threatened by the Russian mob once. I had to stay with his wife and kids for a few days until he got back from Japan. It sucks." I told C.C.

"I'm confident we will get some forensics from those sheds and the conduit, and I hope some of it breaks this open." C.C. said.

Assistant Chief McAndrew walked back to us after he was done talking with Major Brunson. He let me know that I was now officially on loan to the Miami Police Department. Agent Chapman exited the explorer about forty-five minutes later and said his agents made contact with Chanin-Galperin. She was obviously very sad over Ellinport's death, and she also readily accepted the offer of police protection.

"My agents said she's really scared, and was visibly upset and shaking. One of my agents is driving with her to her residence with the other following. Her address is 2624 Taluga Drive in Coconut Grove."

"Taylor, how about you head over there and set up with her? Until we get a schedule in place you might be with her until 7am tomorrow. I hope to get relief for you at midnight, but I can't guarantee it," said McAndrew.

I noticed that once I was on loan to Miami I was no longer Detective Taylor but just "Taylor."

I know the Grove really well, but I had never heard of Taluga Drive. Based off the address, it must be near Southwest 27th Avenue. I pulled C.C. away, out of earshot.

"I'll be heading there in a minute," I said over my shoulder to McAndrew. "C.C., do you have those tools from that Belgium avionics student? I'd like to see them."

C.C. took me to her car and opened the trunk. Inside was a black metal box. She opened the box and showed me the tools, demonstrating how the Torq-Set screws interlocked. The handles of the screwdrivers were odd; they had clear, elongated Lucite hexagonal handles with ridges on the side to help with gripping the tool. I remarked how strange the screwdrivers were. After being shown the tools I said goodbye to McAndrew, Chapman and C.C., got in my car and started driving towards Coconut Grove. I used my cellphone and called the Coral Gables Police Station. I asked the desk operator to check the Bressler's directory and tell me where 2624 Taluga Drive was. After a brief hold while she searched, she got back on the line and told me it was off of Southwest 17th Avenue. Well, that made little sense to me, but she had a map in front of her and I didn't. She said the easiest way would be to go west onto Wa Kee Na Drive and make my second left. *Wa Kee Na Drive?* I thought I knew my way around Coconut Grove, but I'd never heard of that street either. I thanked her and hung up. I zig-zagged my way east and south from Ellinport's house. At U.S.1 and Southeast 17th, I turned south and followed the directions given to me right to the house.

The first thing I noticed when I pulled up was a dark blue Chevrolet Blazer with a man sitting in it. I pulled up to the front of the house and effectively pulled in nose to nose with the Blazer. As I got out of my car, he in turn got out of the Blazer.

"I'm Cade Taylor, I'm with the Gables," I said holding my badge up and out the open door as I stepped out.

"You're Taylor? They told me you'd be coming. I'm Special Agent Holcomb with ATF."

"Your mother named you Special Agent?"

"It's Phil. I'm Phil Holcomb."

"Hi Phil," I said as I shook his hand.

"Special Agent Adrienne Tooley is inside."

I took a moment to get acquainted with the house from the outside. It was incredibly impressive. Two stories and probably built in the 1930s. It had an extremely rough stucco exterior. The house came to a blunt point at the very end of Taluga Drive where it intersects with Opeechee Drive; the front door was on Taluga, but the house ran nearly the length of Opeechee Drive. Five steps with a curved decorative border led to the front door, which jutted out of the house. There were wide framed windows on either side of the door, with another above it. The roof looked like it was flat, with decorative miniature block stacks that broke up the visual monotony of a long, flat roofline. The stacks were framed heavily just like the windows. The house looked very large from the street. I was wondering about the possible security breaches there might be as Agent Holcomb suggested we go inside. I sensed his cloaked urgency—it was obvious that once I arrived, he and Agent Tooley could clock out and start to enjoy their weekend.

We went up the five steps to the heavy wooden door and he knocked loudly. No windows in the door and the side windows were a single row of frosted blocks. Already, I wasn't liking this set up. After a moment or two, there was the sound of feet approaching the door.

"Who is it?" a female voice said.

"Adrienne. It's Phil. The Gables guy is here."

After a series of clicks and clacks as the door locks turned, it opened. We stepped inside and she closed the door behind us. Introductions were made.

"The primary is upstairs. I'll go get her and tell her you're here, then Agent Holcomb and I will be leaving," said Agent Tooley brusquely.

I took the time to look at the inside and think about possible security issues. The front door was odd in that it opened out and from the left, causing exposure of more of your body to let someone inside. The door was very thick and reminded me of a neighbor's door as a kid that was planed from Honduran hardwood. The floors were a highly polished dark Dade County pine. Stepping through the front door I saw there were red, blue, and green geometric patterned tiles covering the foyer. On either side of the foyer were porthole windows about six feet high. I thought they might lend themselves as good vantage points to see out. The living room had a fireplace on the right side—which meant a chimney. Directly across from the fireplace and within just a few steps of the front door was a French door leading outside. A small partial wall broke up the room and could provide a quick hiding spot if necessary. On the other side of that wall was a curved arch that from the street looked like a turret. It curved all the way to the second floor, and on the ground floor it served as a raised porch for the French door and all of the windows of the curved feature. Directly across from the curved windows was a narrow, but impressive mahogany staircase with white painted sides and gorgeous curling banisters. Eleven steps led up to a landing. I counted the stairs in case I needed to use them in the dark. Behind the staircase were two narrow doors. Both of them were a deep mahogany as well. I didn't venture any further in the house. From what I could see it was richly appointed with some very eye-catching artwork and plush couches and chairs. The amount of windows and doors would make securing this house highly problematic.

Special Agent Holcomb and I were standing by the stairs when both Special Agent Tooley and Suezie Chanin-Galperin came into view as they rounded the staircase from the landing. Chanin-Galperin was behind Tooley, and from what I could see of her, she was as attractive as I remembered her. She was wearing a tangerine-colored blouse under a cream-colored jacket and cream-colored slacks.

"Oh, I know you," she said when she saw me.

"Good to see you again. I wish it was under different circumstances," I said.

Special Agent Tooley was anxious to get relieved from her assignment and she was rather quick about handing Chanin-Galperin to me. She said a few customary words, then both she and Special Agent Holcomb were soon out the door and on their way.

I looked at Chanin-Galperin. "Do you feel like a football that just got punted?"

"They were so insistent about getting me home and locked down. Now they seemed like they couldn't wait to get out of here." she said.

"It's the release of responsibility. Those two are not the Secret Service, but whenever the President visits a location they have a 'wheels up' party as soon as he leaves. Once the wheels of Air Force One are up and he's in the air, he's no longer their responsibility—he's Washington's problem. So the Secret Service agents all party at a bar somewhere and call it a 'wheels up' party."

"Is that how you feel about me? Someone else's problem once you're gone?" she asked me with a smirk.

"No. The Miami Police Department will have a more coordinated effort. You'll be seeing the same faces."

"If I remember, you aren't Miami. You're Coral Springs or something," she said, narrowing her eyes and waggling her finger as she tried to recall.

"Coral Gables," I clarified for her. "Miami has requested that since you and I had a prior meeting, that I be loaned to them for this assignment. I'll be here either 'til midnight or on into tomorrow morning."

"Oh my, that's a long time," she said.

"Yes it is, Ms. Chanin-Galperin."

"Please call me Suezie. Marshall was big on titles, but especially considering this arrangement, I prefer you just refer to me by my first name."

"That's fine with me. Please just call me Cade," I said.

"Marshall. I didn't know him too well—a lot of staff meetings, ribbon cutting ceremonies and stuff like that but to think he was killed… It's just so *incomprehensible*. I mean, I had *just* talked to him the day he died, before he left to go home. None of this makes any sense."

I listened to her patiently.

"Does it make sense to you? You're a cop. Is this how things go? Is this normal? I mean, to think this person has killed *all these people*, and now you think he wants to kill *me*? I will admit—I'm scared. I am very scared," she said quickly, low, as if she worried someone was watching at that very moment.

"Well, it's not so much a question of does it make sense. It's more a sense of progression. How this case is progressing. Let me try and tell you what I can, and hopefully it will help you with your fears. C.C., the female detective you met? This is her case. As you already know from Ellinport's presentation, two young men who worked on your ramp were killed. Ellinport suspected, as do we, they were involved in a drug rip-off ring. They were ripping off drug and money couriers. They got greedy and started taking watches, cameras, and such from regular passengers. The drug couriers weren't going to report *their* losses to the authorities, of course. But regular passengers will, and did. We think the drug ringleader is named Zeus, and that he killed both young men for bringing attention to his drug operation. He killed Ellinport because he also knew. As of now, you're the only other person who has any knowledge of this, so the Miami Police Department thought it prudent to give you what we term 'dignitary protection' until we either catch this Zeus guy, or we figure out how many other people knew about Ellinport's investigation."

She sat in a chair across from me in the living room, watching her own hands in her lap. She nodded as a way of conveying she understood me.

"You said you are pretty new to this job. How long have you worked at the airport?" I asked.

"I was hired in May, but we'd been here in Miami since last January of '97."

"We?"

"Yes, me and my husband Aharon. I should explain better—I'm a widow. My husband passed away in March," she said.

"I'm sorry to hear of your loss. May I ask, was it expected?" I asked her.

"No. It was a great shock. I still think about it, and him, every day. Aharon and I are both Jewish. As in we're from Israel. Aharon worked for the Israeli government as a lobbyist. We were married six years ago. When he got assigned by the Israeli government to the state capital in Sacramento, we moved from Tel Aviv to the United States. We were practically newlyweds and California was a wonderland to us," she remembered with a smile. "He was busy meeting and working with California legislators, and I got a job at the Sacramento airport. We really enjoyed California. In January of '97, he got transferred to the consulate here in Miami, and we moved here, and closed on this house in early February. Aharon loved Miami. He went to the consulate every day and didn't have to endure the long hours of a state government when they're in session. It was a nine-to-five existence. It gave us time to explore Miami. He loved the water, and the weather here so much. He took up SCUBA and he was so happy diving and being in the water. He loved spear fishing. I was fortunate to get the position at MIA. It was glorious. I miss him every day—but every day I put on a brave face, and go to work, and thankfully my days keep me busy. I'm able to put my hurt behind me."

I was so moved by her story. It was just heart-wrenching to hear of two people whose lives were in front of them, awaiting them to plunge into and indulge in it together. Now one of them was no longer here. Not by choice. Not a divorce like mine. Her story was truly very touching.

"Do you mind if I ask you how he passed away?"

"Aharon Galperin was a very outdoors type of a man. He loved exploring, and nothing was off limits. It could be kayaking a raging gorge, SCUBA diving in Key Largo, or camping in the Golan Heights on Mount Agas and Mount Dov. He was fully invested in the adventure of outdoor life. Last March we went back to California. Aharon wanted to see a California condor in the wild. He was developing a love for ornithology, and turning his interest to bird watching. That was brought on from us living here, seeing all the different types of birds. So we took a trip to California. We camped in the San Rafael Wilderness Region. It's down near Santa Barbara. It's one of the few places that the California condor was being reintroduced after nearly being extinct. It was about three in the afternoon and he was certain a condor was circling below us in a ravine. He asked me to go back to the tent and get a different pair of binoculars than the ones he had. When I came back...I couldn't find him anywhere. I'll never forget as long as I live the *silence* when I called out his name repeatedly. It was like he vanished. I mean, it just shakes me to my spine even now, retelling it."

"I'm sorry, I should have not asked you."

"No, it's okay. I had to hike up a hill to get cell reception, I called 911, and about forty minutes later a ranger pulled up in a truck. I told him I couldn't find my husband, he got on his radio and asked for more rangers. He called for a 'possible rescue recovery team.' When I heard...that my knees buckled, I fell against his truck." She stopped, closed her eyes to gather herself. "About two hours later, a helicopter spotted Aharon's body at the bottom of the ravine. They rappelled some rangers down and they brought him up in a basket. Seeing the shroud-covered body of my precious Aharon in that basket as the helicopter cleared the top of the ravine... Well, it sent me into hysterics."

The room got quiet, and I just felt so bad. I'd pressed her to tell her most gut-wrenching experience of her life, and while she was terrified of being hunted down. It sounded to me like a part of her died that day in the San Rafael wilderness. She took in a deep breath, then exhaled.

"Aharon is buried in Israel in the Sanhedria Cemetery. His mother and brother and I wanted him to be home. I thought it best that I also return to Israel, but when I came back to this house after the burial, when I saw it filled with all our stuff and memories even as small as they may be, well I decided at the last minute to try to stick it out here in Miami. I 'pulled myself up,' as you Americans say, 'by my boot straps.' I've been here since. I know one day I'll be with Aharon but for now, it's only me."

"I'll never be able to tell you how sorry I am to hear of your momentous loss. I am so sorry."

"Thank you," she said.

There was an awkward silence for a few seconds.

"Suezie, can I ask you to show me the rest of the house? I'd like to have a better understanding of the layout so I can do my job better."

"Yes, of course."

We got up from our chairs in the living room and she showed me the two doors behind the stairs. One was a coat closet; the other, a small half bathroom. Moving through the house it became apparent that it was one continuous, streaming room, separated only by archways framed in thick crown molding. The next space was more of a den and outfitted as such. It also had a French door on the left side that led out to the same circular turret-type patio. To the right of the den was a narrow entryway into the kitchen. The kitchen was functional, but in need of an upgrade the cooking area was small. The side-by-side refrigerator was stainless steel and so near the entrance that one door, when opened, blocked all access to the kitchen. The breakfast nook off of its east side had another French door to the side yard.

This house was as I first thought, a security mess with all the windows and doors.

After she showed me the kitchen, the last room in the long chase of rooms was a home office with beautiful built-in bookshelves on both walls. This room also led outside via yet *another* set of French doors. I noticed a discoloration in a perfect square peeking out from the plush Moroccan carpets. I made a mental note that it either a closed off heating vent or possibly a floor safe.

She took me to the ornate, but narrow, stairs to show me the rest of the house. The first landing featured a window and on either side were custom built-in shelves adorned with multiple books. The spines of the books were a multi-color reader's dream. In another time and place, I might have liked to flip through them. I couldn't say when the last time I read a book was.

Each side of the landing was another three-step rise to the actual second floor. I had never seen a staircase like this before. I was very intrigued by its design and architecture, meant to accentuate the curvature in the turret. Looking directly across the staircase opening and the landing was a small cubby space adorned with more gorgeous built-in bookshelves. Picture frames and little objects like vials of different beach sand from around the world were displayed throughout it—memories of life with her husband. A narrow set of French doors led out to the balcony on top of the turret. She opened the doors and we stepped outside. From this vantage point I saw the yard was a hodge-podge of planted fruit trees, flowering bushes, and tropical plants. There were thick concrete borders poured around flower beds and the yard looked as though it had been once tended well, but was on its way to a disappointing disarray of plants.

"I have professional landscaper coming out later next week to give me some ideas and bids on how to make this all a lush garden again," she said. The breeze gave me a faint scent of her hair. Lovely, like cinnamon. It reminded me the rest of the country was experiencing autumn leaves falling while we were still sweltering in heat.

We went back inside and she made a point to go back to the stair landing as if to not miss showing anything in the house out of order. To the left was a deep mahogany door leading into a small vestibule that opened to one of the front-facing upstairs rooms. The room was all angles as it followed the lines of the windows and construction over the front door. It seemed to be just window after window with streams of separating stucco in between each window. The stucco's only purpose was to support each window frame. I did notice the floor was an off-white Saltillo tile, whereas the rest of the house was wood floors. I wondered if they had ever had a roof leak or moisture issue that necessitated for this room to be tiled.

The next room had wooden floors, covered in a lot of bins and boxes. There was an odd assortment of things in the room: a kayak paddle, large tubes of maps and charts, fishing poles, Hawaiian spear fishing slings, SCUBA tanks. It was nearly impassable with all the outdoor equipment and boxes. There was also a wooden desk in the room with thin spindly legs.

"This is where I store all of Aharon's things. I just feel so conflicted. I mean, I never come in here. I get all teary and sad," she said her eyes gloomy and swimming with moisture. "This was everything that meant anything to him. His nautical charts, his fishing equipment, his telescopes…everything that was him is in here. I just can't part with it at this time. I know one day I'll be in a better place and I will donate it or something, but for now I just moved it all here where it's out of sight."

She opened the door out to the landing of the second floor. It was simply three rooms which were all interconnected, leading in a

180-degree curve right back to the staircase landing. Relief emanated from her as she closed the door behind us as we stepped out to the landing. There was a laundry room on the right with a tiny square porthole window and a bathroom tiled completely in white.

The master bedroom was the last room. It was appointed in beautiful lemony-type colors with large closets and a plush wingback chair in the corner. The bathroom was very feminine with lavender, heather, and yellow daffodils in vases, and exotic soaps and bath oils aligned along the bathtub and shower.

"Well, what do you think?" she asked me, now that the tour was over.

"I think you have a very lovely home that has a lot of you in it. From a security perspective, this can be a very tricky situation here. There are just so many points of entry. It seems that almost every room has a French door that leads outside. The foliage and trees now darken the place at night, and it's poorly lit outside, except for that miniscule streetlamp. But I'm more concerned about the windows and doors. I will tell you in advance, expect to see me tonight and each night constantly checking and rechecking the doors and windows."

We went back downstairs, and she sat on one of the plush couches in the living room. I took a comfortable chair across from her.

"So, what was it like growing up in Israel?"

She thought on it a few seconds and then she answered. "You live two beats behind the rest of the western world. Because of Jewish customs and religious holidays, a lot of things we see and hear from the United States come to us two to three days later. Take for example, Casey Kasem's Top Forty. We'd hear that mid-week or even a week later. He was probably already compiling a new list by then. We'd see American television shows months, if not *years* later after all censorship of anti-Zionism or anti-Semitic comments and scenes were cut out. The streets were always full of people and cars; they all seemed to have their own course of energy and direction. If you can think it, you can do it in Israel. Just lots of teeming people and movement. Whatever country Israel was friends with that year, those were the cars we'd see on the road. Fiats, Volvos, Chevrolets, they all just blended in. The hardest part for me wasn't an Israeli society, but my actual family."

"How so?"

"There were just the four of us. I have one sister. Dayana. She's four years younger and still in Jerusalem. She's a pediatrician. In my house you were either a doctor, a lawyer, or a failure. So, you can assume how my parents felt about my career choice. There was a lot of pressure to go to med school. I rebelled. I smoked pot, wore short skirts, and took plane trips to Istanbul to shop and explore the markets. It just drove my father crazy. He was an attorney who specialized in corporate litigation. My mother was a very happy homemaker, who I think deep down, was also very happy to see my father leave for work every day. One day, I'm trying to figure out where I'm heading with my life, I'm sitting at a café on Bograshov Street. It's a pretty big street that goes from the beach into the center of Tel Aviv. There's a lot of shopping and cafes and restaurants. Anyway, I'm sitting outside and Aharon walks by. He then stops and comes back to my table. He tells me, 'I'm doing it wrong.' I wasn't doing anything but having a *sfenj* and a latte." She laughed to herself.

She noticed my brief confusion.

" A *sfenj* is like a donut. So I said, 'I'm doing what wrong?' He said I was sitting wrong. I told him, 'I always sit like this,' and he said, 'Not anymore. Now you sit with me and that makes it right.' He pulled up a chair and we started dating immediately and were married rather shortly after that."

"That's quite a whirlwind romance. When was the last time you saw your parents and sister?"

"At his funeral. They gave me as much support as they could, but there was very little that anyone can say. It was so sudden and so unexpected, we were *all* still in shock. It was good to see Dayana again. She and I picked up right where we left off. She was a great comfort to me. One night we stayed up playing *semordnilaps* just like when we were kids. Which I must say is much easier in English than in Hebrew."

"What is *semordnilaps*?" I asked her.

"You don't know what a *semordnilap* is? They're words that can also be read backwards, but the backwards spelling forms an entirely different word. Like swap would be paws, peels would be sleep, evil would be live. Get it?"

"I do now," I said, feeling the grin spread across my face. "You actually play a game like that? It must get a little intense at times, with all that concentration going on."

"Nonsense. We've been playing *semordnilaps* since we were kids. She actually challenged me. Can you imagine that? My little sister trying to use all her medical terms and I still beat her. We opened a lovely bottle of French Chardonnay and had a good old time."

"Well, I just learned a new word." I said.

She looked at me a bit pensively for a second and then ran her hand through her hair, brushing all of it away from her forehead.

"You know Cade, I woke up this morning and none of this was in my plans. How could I have possibly imagined any of this? How does this all work anyway?"

"I understand the imposition this must feel like. Miami P.D thinks it a credible threat to your life, and that's why this has been thrusted upon you. I think you should know that you don't have to be in every room with me or that my being here should keep you from doing your day-to-day activities."

"So, if I want to go to Bikram Yoga, I can go?"

"I will go with you and try to find a place where I am able to keep you safe but not be overbearing to you or anyone else at the yoga studio."

She seemed to think about that for a beat.

"I know it's part of your job, but I really abhor any guns around me, especially in my house. I know you aren't prepared for this today but if this goes for a few days, is there a way you can carry your gun less visibly? Maybe a gym bag or something? I keep getting glimpses of it under your shirt and it frightens me."

I tried to smile to reassure her. "Unfortunately, the gun has to be with me at all times but as we get more intelligence on this killer, Zeus, and the case takes more shape, perhaps we can migrate to a gym bag type-thing—as long as we're both in the house and all the doors are locked." She gave me a tight-lipped smile in reply. "Are you hungry? The City of Coral Gables is buying, although I'd suggest we order in at least this first night."

After some discussion she decided on ordering Chinese food. I made the call and placed the order. She busied herself watching TV while I checked and rechecked all the doors and windows to make sure they were secure and locked.

The Chinese food arrived and we ate together in her breakfast nook. Over spicy green beans, Mongolian beef, spring rolls, and chicken lo mein, we talked a little more about Ellinport, the June Gloom fog of the California coast, her dislike for figs, and my tenure with the police department. After we'd eaten and stored the leftovers in her refrigerator we returned to the living room. She took the big plush couch again. I sat in the same large comfortable chair. She poured herself a healthy splash from a Paul Beau Hors d'Age Cognac decanter. I declined her kind offer to have a drink with her.

"Teetotaler?" she asked me.

"No. I'm working."

"So, you're not married?" she asked, nodding at the lack of a wedding band on my hand.

"No. Not anymore."

"Divorced?"

"Yes, I am divorced."

"How long have you been divorced?"

"I don't know if that really has any bearing on where I am now."

"You're a very secretive man, Cade." she said with mock consternation.

"There's a big difference between secretive and being private." I sighed. "Okay, it's been about four months now officially, but we were separated last Christmas. It's one of those things that I know better than anything, and still find myself confused by. I guess she just wanted a life that didn't include me."

"A life without you?"

"A life without me, yes."

"What does that mean, exactly?"

I hadn't been asked that before and it was becoming apparent that Suezie subscribed to the Socratic Method of dialogue. She answered my questions and asked her own in a way in attempt to stimulate critical thinking. She wanted every bit of information she could get, verbal and nonverbal, so she could make very educated judgments. Her eyes glittered with intelligence.

"It means that she wanted a life that didn't include me, but included someone else."

"Oh, I see," she said. "What did you do after you got divorced?"

"I just kept doing what I do. I had cases to work, some informant issues I had to work out with the Miami Dade Police Department. I recognized that sometimes you just have to eat the shit sandwich that was made for you and go on."

"Didn't you feel a sense of liberation? Didn't you want to drink a beer in Dublin? See the Aurora Borealis in Iceland? Run with the bulls in Pamplona?"

"Run with the bulls? I've been running from bullshit my whole life," I said with a little more bite than I intended to.

"Do you ever get lonely, Cade?"

"I think there is a difference between being lonely and being alone. I don't know. I'm not some simpleton, but I just don't give it too much thought." I said.

Was I supposed to tell her that I drink enough beer to pass out on my deck? Was I expected to reveal that a few Jamesons poured neat made me feel a little straighter, a little more upright from the heaviness of my life? I curbed and curved away the oncoming busses that life seems to continually drive and assault at me to my core. Here I was, sitting across from this absolutely stunning woman and I was trying my hardest not to show how much of the décolletage peeking out from under her blouse I'd been noticing.

Am I supposed to hide the fact that every time she moves or stand I see her amazing figure and I feel something tingle from my spine to my spleen?

I had no problem veering away from a one-night stand with "Ms. Life Preservers are Under Your Seat Katie Eighty," but Suezie was unlike any woman I'd ever encountered before. She was attractive, worldly, intelligent, and in many ways, vulnerable like a small child.

"I feel lonely. I do," she said. "It's not a differential between alone and lonely for me. I miss the nearness of a man in my bed, arms around me while I cut carrots in the kitchen, someone to open my car door. I do. Maybe I've said too much, but I do," she said.

My palms were getting a little moist. I started rubbing them absentmindedly on my thighs as I sat in the chair.

She smiled at me slyly. "I think there's more to you than just you. I don't know. You have a certain magnetism that's actually very attractive. I noticed it when I first walked into Marshall's office. Oh, and for the record, I did notice you looking at me."

"What? Looking at you? I don't think so."

"You are hopelessly conventional. Yes, you did. I can tell when a man is interested, and you were definitely interested. Tell you a little secret? I was very surprised, but actually very happy to see that you were my bodyguard when I came down the stairs this evening. Can I call you that? My bodyguard?"

"If you'd like. As for noticing you a little more than normal at the airport…well, sorry."

"Don't be. I was quite flattered. You know how long it's been since a man—any man—showed an interest in me? They hear or know of Aharon and they think they can't compete. Your noticing me was purely natural, and I quite frankly enjoyed it. There was a certain rawness to it."

I felt like a high school kid busted for appropriately having inappropriate thoughts.

"I just told you that I find you attractive, Cade. Did you hear me? Do you find me attractive?"

"I think you're very attractive," I admitted.

She looked down at her drink, then up at me. And she truly was drop dead gorgeous. It was at that moment that we both heard a loud *thud* against the front door.

Chapter Twenty-Four

"**S**TAY HERE. DON'T leave this room and don't get up until I come back for you. Even if you hear me call you from another room. Don't get up until you see me. Understand?" I said as I rose from my chair.

I unholstered my Glock and quickly peeked around the corner crown molding. *Clear.*

I then moved swiftly through the house as I scanned in front of me, holding my Glock in the firing position. I braced myself against the front door. I could've sworn I heard a loud *thud* come from the door, but now it was quiet. This house. Too many windows and too many doors.

What if the loud noise was designed to pull me away from Suezie while Zeus enters the house from a different door or window?

Keeping my gun pointed at the front door, I started stepping back from it.

Then I heard a distinct knock. I stepped closer, but not fully against the door.

Using my best authoritative voice I called out, "Who is it?"

"Officer Carmen Reyes, Miami P.D.," was the quick response.

"Hold on just a second," I said.

I didn't have time to call Assistant Chief McAndrew or Agent

Chapman to get answers about relief or change of shift. I leaned forward, turned the multiple locks on the front door, and opened it just an inch or two. Then I very quickly backed into the room where the staircase was, and positioned myself straight up against the wall facing the door. Taking my Glock in my left hand and steadying it on the doorframe, I bent my elbow at a complete ninety-degree angle and held it at hip level. The Glock was pointed right at the door. Only the gun, my left eye and a small portion of my forehead would be visible to the person entering. I closed my right eye and kept my left eye focused on the door.

Zeus was a trained killer. His deadly skills and the potential to mimic a female voice were not to be taken lightly at all.

Whenever you partially open a door, the natural inclination of the person on the other side is to either slowly push it open and step in, or slowly open it, stay on the threshold and call out again. Officer Carmen Reyes did the latter. She pushed the door open slowly and called out:

"Hello? Hello? Miami Police. Hello?"

I saw her in full uniform. She was in what we call the "fatal funnel." Totally framed by the doorway. It makes it almost muscle-memory-easy to shoot someone standing stationary in a framed door. With only my left eye I could completely see her in full uniform; she didn't see me at all. The uniform was fine, but uniforms can be stolen from dry cleaners and parked cars. I focused on her radio, her weapon, the wear and tear on her belt, the building entry IBM reader card attached to her pocket, those to me were the indicators that she was an actual police officer. I quickly slid completely behind the wall and holstered my weapon before I stepped out as if nothing was amiss, and greeted her.

"Sorry. I was getting my phone charger. Hi, I'm Cade Taylor from the Gables."

"I'm Carmen Reyes. I'm your relief."

She most certainly looked like a Miami police officer. She was

Latin and a little thick, with a streak of gray creeping into her hair in a singular, one-inch streak. I figured her to be about forty years old.

"Who sent you? Was it Assistant Chief McAnderson?" I asked, purposely mispronouncing his name as a little test to see if she was who she said she was.

"It's Chief McAndrew," she corrected me.

"Oh yes, you're right. Sorry. I just met him today."

I noticed a small vinyl bag with a broken shoulder strap behind her on the porch.

"Come in. Please come in," I said to her. She turned back to get her bag, then stepped in, closing the door behind her. She looked up at the ceiling and then around her.

"I misjudged the steps and my bag hit your door. I hope I didn't startle you," she said.

"No, not at all. Wait here a second I will go get the homeowner." I said

I called Suezie, the homeowner. I wanted to eschew the ATF and Dignitary Protection jargon of calling Suezie "the protectee," "the principal," "the primary," or even, God forbid—"the target."

Back in the living , I found Suezie on the floor between the couch and the chair I'd been sitting in. She was visibly shaking and there were tears in her eyes.

"Suezie, it's okay" I said softly. "It's a Miami policewoman who will be with you the rest of the night. She seems very nice. Her name is Carmen. Come on, why don't you come meet her?"

I extended my hand to help her up. She reached up to me, worry furrowing her brow, and grasped my hand. As I pulled her up, she threw her arms around my neck and squeezed me close to her.

"Why do you have to leave? Why can't you stay here tonight? I feel safe with you. I don't want someone else."

She tightened her embrace and I was torn between hugging her back and pulling away. She felt so wonderful in my arms. I could feel all of the essence of her pressing against me. It felt so *right*, like this was where she belonged all the time. It didn't seem fair that I had to choose between the feeling of holding her or doing my job.

Regaining a small measure of composure, I pulled away from her desirous embrace just as Officer Reyes stepped into the room. So much for following directions about waiting near the front door.

"Ms. Chanin-Galperin, I'm Officer Carmen Reyes. I'll be with you until six in the morning. You can call me Carmen if you'd like," she said as she stepped further into the room.

"Oh, yes, I guess…sorry, this has all been very confusing and it's made for a very long day. Carmen, you can call me Suezie."

We were standing now in a triangle as I spoke to Carmen at length about the vulnerabilities of the windows and doors. She gave a brief description of her experience; she had spent a large portion of her fifteen-year career in the vehicle Accident Investigation Unit also known as AIU. She had an AIU pin on the pocket cover of her uniform. Inwardly, I recalled my first impression of the AIU pin as meaning "Asshole In Uniform." I kept that inside joke very inside within myself. The more Carmen spoke, her personality and warm kindness began to show more and more. I was confident that Suezie would be in good hands for the night, and I think Suezie started to calm down too.

I asked Suezie to excuse me and Carmen for a moment and I walked with Carmen back towards the front door. I asked her if she was fully briefed on the lethal, dangerous capabilities of Zeus. She had a rudimentary understanding, but I implored her to be as careful and cautious as possible. I gave her my assessment of Zeus and the uncanny ability he had to not only kill, but kill so efficiently. I told her how Zeus was responsible for shooting Dominguez's car.

What I didn't tell her were my suspicions of Tovar.

She provided me with a schedule of the shifts for the next three days for protecting Suezie. There would be four of us working in six-hour shifts. Although it was 10pm, starting at midnight the schedule would go into effect. Carmen would be with Suezie from midnight to 6am, then a Miami Economics Crime Detective named

Matt Burns relieved her until noon. ATF Special Agent Adrienne Tooley would be back here relieving Burns, and I would then relieve her at 6pm and stay until midnight. Two Miami detectives, one ATF agent, and I would be the security detail through Monday. Assistant Chief McAndrew negotiated a fast one as he kept *all* of his homicide detectives out of the security detail and augmented his need with two outsiders—me and ATF. A rather nifty move, and another reason that explains why he was assistant chief.

"Carmen, since there are only four of us scheduled for this detail, and especially since you have the graveyard shift—pardon the expression—and since Zeus can be *anybody*, I'd suggest you don't open the door for anyone other the three of us working this with you. I wouldn't take any chances. I know *I* won't be opening the door for anybody from *any* agency who might be just stopping by to check in or ask a question. Not unless it's cleared, from at the minimum, a lieutenant's level first," I said.

I was trying to checkmate Tovar or Sciarotta. I had no idea if Sciarotta had left for Jacksonville yet and either one of them could very easily be Zeus. They could *both* be Zeus for all I knew. They could be working in tandem, especially if the theory that C.C. and I shared was correct—that Sciarotta would be taking the Walther P-88 with him to Jacksonville and disposing of the gun in some obscure canal, or in pieces, along the way.

Zeus was a trained killer. This I fully believed. Whether it was personalized training, or some sort of military or law enforcement setting, he was trained and he knew how to use a gun.

I got the feeling that Carmen thought I was being a little dramatic, but she wasn't the one who saw Reggie's green Pumas sticking out from under that rainy-wet tarp. She wasn't the one who saw Jamaal Boseman Cooper dead in the tree trunks. She didn't see Ellinport toppled back over his fishing chair; and she most definitely wasn't the one who made a promise to Godfrey Pinder.

Zeus was out there somewhere. He was the real deal and not to be taken lightly at all.

I thanked her for the schedule. Since we were by the door, I simply called out a goodbye to Suezie—it would avoid any awkwardness. She rounded the corner and stopped near the staircase.

"Thank you, Cade," she said. "Will I see you again?" she asked expectedly.

"Yes, they have us on a schedule. I'll be here at 6pm tomorrow."

Suezie looked at me as if she was thinking something.

"Don't forget a gym bag," she said, "and wear slacks. Just in case we decide to go out for dinner."

I said good night to Carmen, who then closed the door behind me. I heard the multiple locks click into place. I stood there for a second, looking out at the street. I cringed at the way that must have seemed to Carmen. *"Just in case we decide to go out for dinner."*

We.

Carmen must've raised an eyebrow at the way that sounded.

The street was deathly quiet. *Deathly quiet,* I admonished myself for thinking. I looked up at the moon. It had been a full moon on Wednesday now it was a waning gibbous, nearly full. The moonlight deftly found ways to dance and filter through the rustling palm trees and majestic Poinciana trees. The shadows and light wrestled for their own imprint on the nocturnal landscape. I turned back to look at the house from the street. I imagined what the house would look like to Zeus. *How would Zeus see the house? What would Zeus see?* From his perspective, where were the breaching points? Where would he park? I stood in the wavering shadows and just took in the enormity of the house. There was a guest cottage type-place in the back that I hadn't seen before. Damn, that should have been mentioned by either Agent Tooley or Suezie. I made a mental note to inquire about that next time.

I walked to the corner and saw how in the dark, the large stucco house looked like a moored battleship. It had such an imposing linear length to it. From the outside you couldn't see that it was just one continuous strand of a room, only broken up by the case molding and archways. A light came on in the master bedroom. I assumed

Suezie was up there. I thought about her undressing in that lemony colored bedroom. I walked back to my car and sat there for a moment having thoughts about my thoughts. I drove back to Paradise Point, all the while thinking of the best way to keep Suezie safe from Zeus.

Pulling into Paradise Point I cautiously adhered to my own safety protocols and drove first past my unit to the end of the road at the point by the channel in the bay. I then turned around and looked for any vehicles or people I didn't recognize. I pulled up to my unit and exited with my Glock drawn and in my hand. I unlocked the front door. For some odd reason, it felt like I hadn't been home for days.

I took a shower and wrapped in a towel, stepped outside onto the deck to take in the light of the moon as it reflected off the bay. I looked in the direction of Coconut Grove and stared east for a few minutes. I put on some gym shorts and the first t-shirt I could find in the top drawer of my dresser. I went back downstairs and picked up the bottle of Jameson from the bar and a shot glass. I went back upstairs. I went back out on the deck. I sat in one of the lounge chairs and poured a shot, had a few sips and contemplated my day. I thought about what that Georgia emergency room doctor had said to me in the bar at Hotel Place St. Michel what seemed like years ago.

"I do it because many think they can do it, but realize it is a specialization—not just in knowledge, but in emotional absorption. I can absorb it all pretty well."

I was beginning to doubt my own ability to absorb it all. The events of the past week had come at me like a runaway train. All speed and fusion. I wasn't so sure how much of this directed commotion I could handle. Suezie had touched a deeply driven down emotion in me when she talked about an empty bed, and having someone with you in the kitchen as you prepped a meal. I'd repressed those yearnings for so long, ever since my divorce from Gina. Now, I felt my absorption rate was getting stretched thin. There was a loneliness to me, and to how I spent my days and nights. That repressed loneliness was gurgling and bubbling to the surface.

The VIN lifestyle is not for the faint of heart. It's not a clean business. The denizens of Hollywood movie studios who portray money laundering as bespectacled, meek accountants in offices accepting new, shiny, slim briefcases full of cash have it all wrong. Nothing could be further from the truth. Anyone who doesn't believe me could just go ask Perchero. Ask him right through that gaping bloody hole in his head. Look him right in his ravaged brain and tell me if you see a Hollywood version of this life? My life was nothing but a dizzying carousel of cocaine, money, guns, death, and misery.

I started in on my second shot of Jameson, only this one I threw down like a frat boy at his first party. Right down the hatch. The effect was immediate. The tingly sensation of release and relaxation settled over me. The moon acted like a clarifying light—or maybe it was the Irish whiskey starting to course through me—but something was out of place.

Something was tugging at what remaining sensibilities I was trying to numb. I couldn't put my finger on it. I kept looking at the moon's reflection on the bay, hoping the rippling light and breezy chop of the water would somehow extend my mind. I wanted to arrest this feeling I had that something wasn't right. Slowly, almost minutely, it started to dawn on me.

All along I had C.C. believing that Zeus had respect for law and order. He was more than likely a former Special Forces trained operative, an ex, or even current, law enforcement officer. Zeus let Miami Officer Dominguez live. But he viciously killed former ATF Agent, Ellinport.

It went against the grain. It chafed. It didn't feel right. It leaned hard on the boundary of the profile. It bowed the construct. Dominguez was doing his job and he was innocent of any knowledge of a group ripping off drug and money couriers at the airport.

What if Ellinport *wasn't* innocent ? Or had Zeus, as Miami P.D surmised, gotten wind of Ellinport's investigation and now Suezie was in the sights of a well-used Walther P-88?

How did I get sucked into this disaster anyway? Had I not taken it upon myself to follow that marginalized example of a cop Dominguez, I wouldn't even be in this throat-tightening mess of a case. C.C. looked like she was in way over her head. To come from data management into an all-male homicide squad couldn't be easy. I felt that she was getting really pressed on this.

"That's what they call me you know, right to my face. The FNG."

"Did that whole FNG thing start with Tovar?"

"Absolutely. He's the big leader in the group. Gets pretty much whatever he wants and he's not someone you'd want to cross. He was Special Forces or something maybe in Desert Storm.

Tovar. I can just imagine him coming unglued over the request for his official employment file. He sure fit the suspect possibility list. I saw his file. He has all the training and knowledge behind him to be a very good assassin. He fits very well into the situation in so many ways: Former narcotics detective sued civilly in a wrongful death case; He had homicide and narcotic connections; He had an ally in his unit. I'm sure many of C.C.'s colleagues in Homicide didn't even know the Tovar connection to Sciarotta forged before Tovar was hired.

Then there was Godfrey Pinder. I let him tug on my emotions and draw me into this case.

"For us. Do it for us. Jump the curb on this one for us. Please."

Either way, what brought me here was not what was keeping me here now. I was in. All in. C.C.'s ass was on the line and Suezie's ass was in the line of fire. I *needed* to be all in, and I needed to find Zeus before he found his next victim. Suezie or otherwise.

Chapter Twenty-Five

THE CHIRPING OF my cellphone is what woke me up. Before answering, I wondered briefly if the developers of cellphones knew that between the alarm and incredibly inconvenient telephone calls, their devices woke more people up then they could of ever imagined. I have such a distaste for the vile intrusion the cellphone has brought to my life. It just kept ringing and my opinion of the telecommunications industry was not going to stop it from ringing. As I reached for the phone on the nightstand, something hard pressed against my leg in the bed—the Jameson bottle. I'd deal with that and how that happened later, but first I answered the call.

"Hello."

"Hey there mister, got time to talk?"

"Oh hey, C.C., what's going?" I said as I tried to sound coherent and awake.

"Did I wake you?"

"No…no. I've been up for a while." I lied just like everyone else does when someone asks that question, as if sleeping was some sort of scourge.

"Want to meet me for a bagel and we can talk?"

"C.C I live—"

She cut me off pretty effectively.

"—pretty far down south. I know. I know. Can you meet me at Roasters and Toasters in thirty minutes?"

"You know, the last time you called me on a Saturday I ended having my life turned upside down. It's only been a week actually so you can understand if I say yes, but with a strong measure of hesitation."

She laughed, bright and loud. "Well, if seeing me in my underwear in a week's time constitutes you having your life turned upside down, then I'll take that compliment. If you're talking about our case with Zeus, then I don't know what to tell you," she said.

"Where are you now?" I asked her.

"I'm just getting off 95 onto U.S.1."

"Okay. I'll see you there, but can you stop somewhere and get me a *colada*?"

"You want Cuban coffee?"

"I want a lot of Cuban coffee. A *colada* please. I'll see you there."

I hung up the phone and then looked at the half-filled bottle of Jameson against my leg in the bed. Drinking is good. Going to bed is good. Going to bed with a bottle of Irish whiskey is not good. I looked towards the door that led out to the deck. The door was closed. I saw that as an improvement. Nonetheless, I must have had a few snorts, more than likely, straight from the bottle before closing my eyes last night. This was not acceptable behavior. I was gravely in need of getting my act together. Numbing my heart strain over my divorce and beating back the demons of VIN with alcohol wasn't the answer. Maybe alcohol was going to be my continual wrong answer. I just needed to have more right answers than wrong answers to avoid failure. I deluded myself with this flawed logic as I got out of bed and I trudged off to the shower. There was an expression that was often heard in law schools:

Students who make A's make great judges.

Students who make B's make great attorneys.

Students who make C's make great money.

I was feeling a little on the C+ side of the phrase.

The shower would need to be quicker than I'd prefer for a sobering effect, but it sufficed, and I was dressed and leaving the condominium within twenty minutes.

Roasters and Toasters was a New York style deli restaurant in Pinecrest, across from the Dadeland Metrorail Station. C.C. was already sitting at a booth, her back to me. I saw her as my eyes also skimmed across the deli case loaded with bagels, tuna salad, chicken salad, and large black and white cookies. She was wearing tight workout pants with an odd logo on the top; I shamelessly caught a glimpse of her rear as she got up to greet me. She was also wearing a white sweatshirt with the words *Sweaty Betty* in off-white across the chest.

"Here's your *colada*," she said with a proud flourish as she handed me a small white paper bag.

"Thank you so much," I said, sliding into the booth as she sat back down across from me.

"What kind of pants are those you're wearing? I've never seen that brand."

"They are called *Lululemon*. They're a new brand—I call them Lu Lu's. You can only get them at Bloomingdales in Aventura."

I was listening, but I was more intent on taking the thin plastic lid off the *colada* and trying not to spill any of the potent Cuban caffeine rocket fuel. The lid came off with a *pop*, surrounding the whole table with the escaping aromatic blast of the coffee.

"You realize I'll have to order something extra here? Just so I don't piss off the waitress for bringing in my own coffee," I said.

Within a minute the waitress came by and she filled C.C.'s empty cup with piping hot coffee. C.C. ordered the western omelet special with an All the Way Bagel, toasted well. I ordered two breakfast sandwiches—eggs over medium with cheddar cheese and bacon on plain bagels. The waitress looked at the *colada*. I ordered a hot chocolate, too.

"You caved in like house of cards on that. Are you really going to drink hot chocolate?"

"I happen to like hot chocolate." I defended choice.

"It's like being with a third grader with you sometimes," she said.

"Since we're sharing another Saturday morning working—but not working—any development on Zeus?" I asked her as I eyed the piping hoy Cuban coffee

"Our crime scene techs were able to get some shoe impressions from the top off the shed at Ellinport's. To the naked eye, they think that what they got off the piping on the bridge matches those same impressions. Those impressions were sent last night to the FBI shoe impression lab and they were asked to be compared to the ones we got at Boseman Cooper's murder scene. One of our techs thinks they are Nikes."

"So, you're making progress on that." I asked as I took my first eye opening sip.

"Cade, thank you again for that whole entry point theory at Ellinport's; it really explained a lot."

"We're in this together. We will figure this out, one way or the other. Everyone makes mistakes. Zeus has already made a few small ones, and there will be more." I said as I nodded my head slowly up and down. " What happened to Tovar that he got jammed by your department?"

"Oh, you won't believe this. He goes into the legal liaison office and starts demanding to see who's in charge. He wants to know all he can about the Freedom of Information records request. There are four people in that office—most of them are interns from the University of Miami Law School. They see this guy they've never seen before, all ranting and raving. One of the interns calls down to the lobby and asks for an officer to come up. Tovar's completely out of line. He's calling all the legal attachés something spelled with a G in Spanish that means worms."

"*Gusanos,*" I interjected

"You speak Spanish? I'm surprised."

"No, I don't, but go on." I said

"So anyway," she goes on, waving her hands, "Tovar's calling them all these names in English and Spanish and it's getting *heated*. He's still demanding to see who's in charge. Well, we got this new legal attaché from Florida State University, and I guess she worked in law or something in Tallahassee. Her name is Suzanne Cummings, and she comes walking in and she sees all this." C.C. giggles a little. "She shits a *kitten*, and in turn demands that Tovar leave immediately. Tovar rips into her and then—he did it."

"Did what?" I asked.

"He called her the C word," she said in a hushed tone, eyes wide.

"By the C word, I assume it wasn't her last name, Cummings," I said.

"No. It wasn't her last name."

"So, all these witnesses most of them female, hear this and he's written up. Suzanne Cummings wants to push it even further and she's trying to add a hostile work environment component to it. So he's temporarily relieved of duty until Internal Affairs is done with it."

"Like I said, everyone makes mistakes. Your Assistant Chief McAndrew made it sound like it was no big deal."

"Well, he's either woefully misinformed or just as misogynistic as Tovar is." she said firmly.

"This doesn't help us in any way. You realize that, right?" I said.

We briefly held our conversation as the waitress placed the food on the table. Chocolate shavings in the whipped cream at the top of the hot chocolate formed a happy face. C.C. looked at the hot chocolate.

"Seriously. A third grader."

After a few bites she asked me, "What do you mean this doesn't help us?"

"I mean that with Tovar relieved of duty we have no way to know where he is. He's totally unaccounted for. The guy's in the wind.

Plus, he's angry. If he and Sciarotta are connected in any way to these homicides, they'll try something sooner than later. Sciarotta's more than likely going to head up to Jacksonville tomorrow for the Dolphins game on Monday. I'm not saying Sciarotta is part of these murders, for all we know Tovar might just be using him to pass the gun to someone else. He could be an innocent messenger. Who knows? But if Tovar *is* Zeus, then we have no idea when or where he might turn up."

C.C. thought about that for a second.

"I know it was you who got Tovar's file pulled." she said eyeing me suspiciously.

"What you need to know is that *you don't know*. You work for Miami and with him. I don't. I told you that if anybody ever finds out, I'd play it off as that we needed someone on our DEA squad. I also said the less you know the better. Remember the part where we said 'don't mention it again?' *This is that part!* Here and now. All I'll say is that Tovar does have extreme high specializations from the military. He's very capable of all of these homicides. *All* of it."

She looked past me out at the traffic flowing on U.S.1 . I could see her thinking. I could also see her reflection in the mirror behind her. She looked pretty and natural. I on the other hand probably looked like a neglected junk yard.

"Who's the A-slash while Tovar is out?" I asked her.

"D.P. Hughes is acting sergeant while Tovar is out. We're down to the bare minimum here. Sciarotta you know is on leave, Tovar is looking at suspension, D.P. is now supervising the squad, and as of yesterday, I'm working only Zeus and will be until we catch him. I've put the ATF address checks on hold for now. Most everyone I looked into that has a Federal Firearms License and are either collectors or historians interested in owning handguns from different eras."

"Is that how you see Tovar? A collector?"

"No."

"Neither do I." I was nearly done swigging down the colada.

The waitress dropped the check on the table, and I could see people standing by the door waiting for tables to open up. I grabbed the check.

"Let's go outside and we can talk some more."

I paid at the register and left a tip on the bill. Outside we sat on a bench near the parking lot, taking in the Saturday morning sunshine.

"You and I are stretched here," I said. "I'm stuck doing dignitary on Suezie Chanin-Galperin at night, you're chasing paper on Zeus when we should be finding a better way to catch this guy. You got two people now in Homicide that are out of play, and your biggest ally, D.P. Hughes, is supervising the ongoing unit. So in many ways, he's out of play, too. We both think Tovar is a good suspect." I counted off on my fingers, "He has working knowledge of the case, he's been less than helpful, and we know from the ATF—may I remind you, *not* from him—that he owns the same type of gun that's been killing your victims."

She nodded her head in solemn agreement.

"I told you we wouldn't talk about the one-nineteen request on Tovar, but I will say this to you: He didn't come from a robbery inter-diction unit. He came from a street narcotic unit where they killed a street dealer named Rogelio. He has Special Forces training that surpasses nearly anyone I've ever seen before, and he and Sciarotta knew each other before Tovar was hired by you guys."

She stared at me, scanning my face for any trace of exaggeration.

"You're' kidding me," she said.

"I would love to be wrong on my suspicions of Tovar, but I can't just eliminate him. There are too many puzzle pieces that are in his box. Believe me when I say it—if Tovar is a stone cold killer, he wouldn't be the first cop I've known who was and had everyone fooled."

"I wish we had more people in on this with us," she said.

"Why do you say that?" I asked her.

"Because we could set up surveillance on Sciarotta and have

Palm Beach County or the Florida Highway Patrol pull him over on I-95 and toss his car, see if he has the gun with him."

"Sciarotta has a badge—and one that he's had for a long time. It's unlikely another cop would do that to him. He'd smell it out real quick," I said.

"Every department has that one guy who would write his own mother a ticket. We just need to have our guy act like that departmental blowhard," she said.

"Well, there's no way we can pull that off without some upper level help, so you can just put that idea aside. At least for now," I said.

"How did babysitting go last night?" she asked me.

"I basically had her once ATF passed her off. She has a pretty wild background. She grew up in Israel, got married to an Israeli and moved to Sacramento where they lived for a few years and then he got transferred to Miami so they moved here. He died in a hiking type-accident in California last year. She's a widow."

"Her husband died hiking?"

"She said he was getting into bird watching and they were in the San Rafael Wilderness Region in California, and he must've slipped and fell into some ravine."

"She didn't see him fall?" she asked.

"No. He sent her to get a set of binoculars and when she came back he was nowhere to be seen."

"So, *she* is Suezie Chanin. He must be the Galperin? What was his first name?"

"Aharon. It's spelled A-H-A-R-O-N. I saw it scribbled on boxes of his stuff in an upstairs bedroom. He was a real outdoorsman kind of guy, liked to fish, hike, all that stuff."

"I can think of a lot worse assignments that spending nights with a beautiful widow."

I picked up on her sarcasm really quick.

"C.C., we need to put all that kind of talk on the side and focus on what we do know. You have a very dangerous assassin in your city who now fits the FBI classification as a serial killer."

"Zeus fits the classification in the category of three or more victims, but the personal gratification aspect seems lacking here. He's killing because his drug courier rip-off business is being affected by the actions of his victims."

"C.C., do you know what the FBI stands for?" I asked her.

"Federal Bureau of Investigation."

"No. It stands for Famous But Ignorant. We might be able to use this three-or-more theory from Quantico to our advantage. If we have no significant movement on Zeus by Wednesday, why not drop a dime to the FBI that a three-or-more player is in Miami. Let's see what resources we can shake out of the FBI tree. Meanwhile I'll go back to Ritchie Tavino and let him know that we have a guy in Miami who's been ripping off the cartel on courier drug and money runs on commercial flights in and out of Miami. I'll have him get the word to the cartel that they're being ripped. Let's attack this from two sides. Let's see what the FBI can do with the investigation. Let's see what the cartel can do with the enforcement, and see who finds our guy for us first?"

"Cade, you're a genius!"

"Not too bad for a third grader, huh?"

"I think it's brilliant," she said, eyes lit up. "Let's squeeze Zeus from both sides. The good guys *and* the bad guys. I like it. By Wednesday we should have our shoe impressions report back from the FBI, and I'll be done with all the names on the ATF list."

"Okay. It's your case, and I agree—I think Wednesday is a good day to switch it up. It'll give us some time to do our own work and then start applying pressure on Zeus from both the FBI and the cartel."

"What time do you have to be with the enchantingly beautiful Ms. Chanin-Galperin?"

I let the adjectives of Suezie's beauty slide off and let C.C. know of the schedule that had been created by her agency. She said she knew both Miami police officers Matt Burns, and Carmen Reyes. The only person in our detail she didn't know was ATF agent, Adrienne Tooley.

"What are your plans for the rest of the day?" I asked her.

"I was wondering if maybe you'd want to catch a movie with me. This new one, *Saving Private Ryan* with Tom Hanks is supposed to be pretty good. There's a one o'clock showing at the Falls Shopping Center Theater. That's not too far from here, right? You should be able to catch it and still get to your detail tonight."

"The Falls is further south from here. It's at least another forty or so blocks." I picked up my phone and called the Dadeland Movie Theater line. It was playing at 12:50 pm almost directly across the street.

"Let's take my car. It's across the street in Dadeland and starts in twenty minutes."

She got in my car and we waited for the light that leads out of the parking lot to cross U.S.1 to change.

"You must feel odd going to the movies with a third grader. Maybe we can get a children's admission."

Chapter Twenty-Six

THE MOVIE WAS long. Two hours and fifty minutes. Including previews and crowds I wasn't exactly *rushing* to get C.C. back to her car, but it was getting close to 4pm. Our time at the movie was very nice. I don't even know if I'd classify it a date, it was so spontaneous—at least for me it was. She did sit close to me. And when she said she was cold halfway through the movie I did put my arm around her. I don't know. I wanted to kiss her and I think she wanted me to kiss her but when I went to drop her off, just as we got to her car, D.P. Hughes called her cellphone. She switched gears quickly, fumbling in her purse with her phone in the crook of her ear as she searched for something for him. I glanced at the clock on my dashboard. She stepped out of the car and gave me the universal "one minute" symbol, holding her finger up as she pleaded with me with her eyes. I shook my head slowly no and gave her back the universal "I'll call you symbol." I had to get home and get changed.

With a wave, I pulled away.

I drove back to Paradise Point, and forgoing my own protective protocols a bit, pulled right into my parking spot. I still exited my car with my gun in my hand. I could smell the theater popcorn on my clothes.

Dashing up the stairs, I unlocked the front door and went right upstairs to change clothes and shower. I chose a pair of black slacks and a long sleeve, off-white linen guayabera shirt. I grabbed the same quick release pancake tan holster I brought to the meet with Perchero, and slipped my Glock into it. I threw it into a gym bag and went downstairs. I caught sight of myself in the mirror and was momentarily struck by how absurd I was being. I took off the guayabera, folded it neatly and placed it into the gym bag. I grabbed a mint green polo from the closet and put that on. The dashboard clock said 5:15pm as I was passing the guardhouse at the community entrance.

Traffic was light, as was to be expected on a Saturday afternoon. I pulled up in front of Suezie's house at 5:50pm. ATF Special Agent Tooley opened the door and met me with a bored, but inquisitive look.

"Ever feel like you're just keeping a seat warm for someone else?" she asked me.

"I have no idea what you are talking about," I replied.

"All she's done is talk about you. I'm glad you're here because I'm ready to make like a tree and leave."

"Okay. Anything I need to know?"

"We went shopping at Mayfair and she bought a ton of clothes. We went to the Crepe Maker for lunch. She's napping upstairs. The end."

"I get it. I guess I'll see you tomorrow," I said.

"Not if I can help it. I'm going to see if Chapman will get someone else to take my place."

She leaned a little closer to me and quietly said, "She's kind of bitchy and superficial if you know what I mean."

I just half-smiled at her and realized that Agent Tooley had very little dignitary experience and was letting the personality of the "homeowner" get to her.

"Anyway, she's all yours. Either me or someone else will be here tomorrow. Later."

With that she pressed past me, went straight to her car and got in and closed the door. She gave me a half assed wave. She pulled a U-turn in the street and was gone. I stepped inside and closed the door behind me. I locked all the locks on the front door and quietly walked around the ground floor, rechecking all the locks on the French doors. In the living room, I sat in the same chair as I did the night before and just idled the time for a while. After about twenty minutes, Suezie came down the stairs.

She was wearing a moderately long t-shirt and what appeared to be nothing else. It left very little to the imagination. Through the sheer fabric I could see traces of her areolas and nipples. The shirt barely covered her upper thigh and there was a lot of her muscular tanned legs visible. She saw me in the living room, and feigned embarrassment. She turned quickly and went upstairs, all the while explaining she thought that Agent Tooley was still here instead of me. She came back down five minute later in a modest white terry-cloth robe that covered significantly more of her. She once again apologized sheepishly. I told her to not give it another thought. She looked past me at the clock on the living room armoire.

"I usually go to Firehouse Four for happy hour on Friday, but all this commotion put the kibosh on that last night. I asked you to wear slacks because although it isn't happy hour on Saturday, they have a great house band. I was hoping we could go there tonight. I need to get out and since I'm not under arrest or anything..."

She left that comment kind of hanging and I could tell it was a verbal invite for me to join in the conversation.

"No. You are not under arrest. So, I can't stop you from going but I will be going with you."

She looked at my slacks with approval but there was a bit of a dorky smirk on her face when she looked at my mint green polo shirt.

"I brought another shirt in the gym bag."

"Oh good," she said, sighing with relief. ""I'll be ready in about fifteen minutes."

She dashed back upstairs. Firehouse Four is a decommissioned

Miami firehouse that has been converted into a restaurant bar. It is a beautiful Mediterranean-style building that has a palm tree-shrouded brick courtyard. There are two levels to the bar restaurant and a small stage for a notoriously good house band. It is in the Brickell Avenue area, and not too far away from Tobacco Road. I texted C.C. and let her know that the *"homeowner wanted to go to Firehouse Four, notify who you feel you need to or trust. If necessary."* I changed my shirt and slipped the quick release pancake tan holster onto my belt. The length of the Guayabera shirt hid my Glock.

When she came back downstairs, it was an incredible transformation. She was wearing sexy champagne-metallic colored lace-up heels. The height of the heels really accentuated her muscular tanned calves and thighs. She had on a short, matte rose gold sequin mini skirt, and a very tight square white top that barely contained her large breasts. Her hair cascaded down in layers of deep reddish brown. Her make-up was perfect; not too much and just enough to accentuate her beauty. She was heart-stoppingly gorgeous. It was not going to be easy to keep the bar flies off of her, and to keep her protected from drunks, lecherous Romeos, and least of all, Zeus. If I look like I'm in the friend zone, or her brother from the other side of town, there will be lots of men circling around. That would make protecting her even harder. I felt seriously compromised on this assignment.

"Well? What do you think?" she asked, pirouetting to display her astounding beauty to me.

"I think that without me saying it, you are a very attractive woman. You have a great sense of fashion and style."

"Thank you. A guayabera? I don't think of you as the type?"

"Actually I'm not, but you know the expression: When in Rome, do as the Romans do. Every male in Miami should own at least one guayabera. Ramon at *Casa de Guayaberas* helped select this one for me." I said.

She nodded once, smirking a little in a look of approval. I asked her if she had any Scotch tape. She said there was some in the kitchen in the drawer by the refrigerator. I went and got the scotch tape and a pencil out of the drawer. I noticed a drawer pull was off from the adjacent drawer.

"What happened to the drawer pull?"

"Detective Burns actually brushed against it with his holster this morning and it snapped off. I had to tell him that going forward I'd prefer a gym bag from him, too. Why do you need the tape?"

"It's just a little something I need to do before we leave."

I quickly went to all the ground floor French doors and put a two-inch piece of tape somewhere across the seams where they came together. If someone broke in while we were gone, I would quickly know just by looking at the covert places where I placed the tape. Contrary to popular belief, burglars and assassins are known to lock doors behind them in case an alarm trips. Responding police officers will check exterior doors and if they're locked the police will move on. With this method, I could tell in seconds if a door has been breached and Zeus is in the house waiting for us.

"Ready? Then let's go," I suggested.

We stepped outside into a beautiful purple-tangelo-colored sunset. After locking the front door I propped the pencil against its far corner. If the front door is opened the pencil would fall over, and once again I'd have a quick indication that Zeus might be inside.

I opened the car door for her and she sexily slid into my passenger seat. I closed the door and was a little momentarily dazed—because in the briefest of glimpses, I don't believe she was wearing any panties. The drive to Firehouse Four is a very short distance from where she lived. As we neared the front of the place, I could see lots of people milling about in front of the bar and inside of it. There was also a cadre of doormen and bouncers all dressed in identical black t-shirts and black tapered slacks. Each one was festooned with an earpiece discreetly tucked into their ear with a rattail coil wire running down the inside of the back of their black t-shirts.

The car valets were in black pants and white short sleeve shirts. Each valet seemed to have a small oval nametag—the nametag is a byproduct of an occupation fueled by the barest of personalization to assist in the necessity of a gratuity.

"I have a friend who says to me, 'being cheap is not a very endearing quality.' I'm not being cheap, but I need to avoid the valet. There are too many things in this car that cannot be replaced—most notably, you. So bear with me as I look for a space." I said cruising past the front door.

She seemed to understand. I went past Firehouse Four, not only looking for a parking space but also getting a little intelligence of the place before we went inside. The multilevel balconies and awnings were nice accents and the exterior lighting made for a very inviting place to be. I turned off of South Miami Avenue onto Southwest 10th Street. There was a loading zone in front of a storefront with brown butcher paper in the window, and a *Coming Soon to This Location* sign. Perfect. I pulled into the loading zone, confident no one would be accepting deliveries on a Saturday night to an empty storefront.

"Stay here," I told her.

I got out and looked around the street and up at the rooflines of the buildings. When I was comfortable, I went around the car and opened her door for her. Confirmation: no panties as she stepped out. We crossed the nearly empty street and went in through the front doors. The bouncers and doormen took one look at her and happily stepped aside. Places like this in Miami love having beautiful women present. Thee green tiled rooms towards the back looked like party rooms. There was a real tight quintet with a sax on stage playing a pitch perfect version of the Blow Monkey's *"Digging Your Scene."*

The entire bar had a real nice vibe to it. Everyone was having lively conversations and the drinks were flowing. The crowd was energized with fun and positivity. The burnished wood of the bar blended well with the brass accents, and the still-intact smooth firemen's poles from when it was an actual City of Miami firehouse bespoke of true individuality. Soft, yet prominent, lights illuminated the "Palm Court" where settees and comfortable couches were placed in the palm tree courtyard. We were fortunate to find a few open seats on an L-shaped couch. Suezie made a point to sit very close to me, her body pressing against me. She had no issue with her thigh resting against mine. A young cocktail waitress came by and laid down paper napkins on the lacquered table in front of us. Suezie asked for a Singapore Sling. I requested a ginger ale with a lemon slice in a tall glass with ice.

"Now how am I supposed to take advantage of you if you don't drink?" she said, smiling at me.

"Suezie, as appealing as that sounds my first objective is to keep you safe."

"I know. But it's been a while since I've actually been attracted to a man—and if you haven't noticed I am *very* attracted to you." she said raising her eyebrows as she softly bit her lower lip.

"You could have your choice of any guy in this place," I said.

She looked around the bar and took in the visual aspects of all the people, focusing a few times on a man here or there. She then looked back at me.

"Where's the challenge in that? Ever since you first saw me at the airport, I felt your intensity. You are a very intense person, Cade Taylor. Intensity means passion. I like a man with passion. I like a man with passion and discipline! You have discipline too, which I bet you can wield in the bedroom very nicely."

I just looked at her, wondering where she was going with this type of talk.

"Too forward for you? I mean disciplined men like you can forestall your own pleasure for your partner; *that* kind of discipline. What did you think I was talking about?" she asked.

The waitress brought our drinks, and Suezie put in an order for two personalized vegetarian pizzas and a charcuterie board "with no figs, but heavy on the gouda." We toasted to the wonderful Saturday night sunset that rode in with us. She took a healthy draw of her drink through the straw and she briefly closed her eyes, savoring the taste of the Singapore Sling. When she opened her eyes, they bore into mine.

"You're not getting out of this one. What did you think I was talking about?" she asked me again.

"I was assuming you wanted me to bring the bull whip and you could bring the Cool Whip."

She laughed out loud and let her left hand fall on my thigh as she seemed to sip continuously on her drink. Her fingers ran in a tight circle on my thigh. I looked up and whether they had a date with them or not, I could feel the envious eyes of nearly every man in the place. Within a few minutes, Suezie had consumed her drink and was busily ordering another one and sharing a whispered laugh with the waitress.

Her next drink came with the pizzas and the charcuterie board. I kept my eyes wandering between the front entrance and on any man who ventured close to us as we ate. I felt myself really enjoying the sexy vibrancy of her company. Early in my VIN career, one of my earliest dignitary protection assignments was standing in a hot hotel kitchen while Bolivian President Jaime Paz Zamora gave a speech in the ballroom. This detail with Suezie sure beat the Bolivian President by a country mile. Suezie was enjoying herself too, and we talked about many things. Mostly her travel experiences. She still found ways to remind me of her interest and tossed in a few sexual innuendos. By the time the waitress had cleared the pizza and charcuterie remnants away leaving the black cloth napkins behind. Suezie was on her third Singapore Sling. They seemed to have a directly proportional effect on her inhibitions, as she became even more bold with her sexual advances. At one point she placed my hand on her thigh, looked me in the eye and said, "Go ahead, I won't stop you." I quickly withdrew my hand and kindly reminded her that I was there to protect her.

"What better way to be close enough to protect me than to be inside of me?"

I realized that this was not going to work. I caught the attention of the waitress, slipped her my U.C. Mastercard and told her to tab us out. It was at this point that Suezie got up from the table and started to do a very seductive bump and grind on the fire pole. The band picked up on her gyrations quickly, and in mid-song, stopped what they were playing and quickly switched to an instrumental of TLC's *Red Light Special.*

This wasn't good. This wasn't good at all.

My protectee—not the "homeowner" anymore, but my protectee—now was putting herself *and* me in a very precarious situation. The whole place had their eyes glued to her dancing. She started mouthing the words to the song and gave me a come hither finger motion. A few patrons started singing loudly the lyrics and clapping. One asshole in the corner shook a beer bottle and, mimicking his thoughts, sprayed the corner of the palm court as he held the beer bottle near his crotch. I dashed up from my seat. I must've looked like a seriously jealous husband as I grabbed her and pulled her down from the fire pole. I had to be careful to not expose her as I did. She wrapped her arms around my neck and tried to wrap her legs around my waist. I turned my hips and ended up with one arm around her waist and the other holding her skirt from rising up. I eased her away from the pole, all to the consternation and dismay of the crowd. Especially the males in the crowd. There was a moment during this wild embrace when she whispered in my ear very clearly, "I knew I could get a rise out of you."

The band returned to their set and went into playing a spot on vocal and guitar riff of The Church's *Under the Milky Way.* She kept both her arms around my waist as we walked back to our seats thus causing me to drape my arm around her. She got lots of compliments from nearly everyone, whereas I got jeered for being such a spoil sport. We sat down and the waitress brought my credit card back to me. She had even drawn on the check a stick figure of a long-haired girl with boobs holding a pole. Wonderful. I spoke to Suezie with my head bowed as I signed the bill.

"My goal is to keep you alive. When this is over, I still need to go back to my undercover world and persona. I can't—actually, *we* can't—for your safety *or* mine, be the center of attention."

I looked up at her for her reaction. In doing so, I saw something behind her. My attention was immediately drawn from her to the front door of the place. I wasn't hearing her or anyone else or noticing anything else, only laser-locked on the entrance. She picked up on the change in my demeanor and looked behind her, asking me what I was looking at, but I was too intent to answer. She began to push with more urgency, asking me what I was looking at.

Standing at the front door, about ready to walk into the crowded bar, was Tovar.

Chapter Twenty-Seven

ILEANED IN VERY close to her. I tried to hold her gaze with my eyes, but I needed to keep my focus on Tovar. He was chatting with two of the bouncers, but was getting ready to cross the threshold of the front door.

"Listen to me. I don't have time to repeat myself. We are going to get up and I want you right behind me. You hear me? I want you right on my back. Right on me. Lift my shirt and grab onto to my belt and do not, for *any reason*, let go. You understand?" I commanded sternly.

"Cade, you're scaring me."

As she was talking, I leaned forward on the couch and slowly took one of the black cotton napkins from the table. I surreptitiously pulled my Glock from the holster under my shirt and draped the napkin over my hand holding the gun. I held the black-shrouded handgun against my black slacks and stood up with my back to the front door.

"Do as I said and do not let go. Up. Let's go!"

She stood up amid murmurs from the people near us, as they were probably hoping for another impromptu show from Suezie. I felt her hand slide up and under my shirt and grab my belt tightly. I could feel her up against my back. I started moving through the crowd, parting the thick crowd using my left hand. Some gently, some not so gently. I was prepared to use as much force as necessary to get anybody out of my way. My pace was as quick as the crowd could permit. Each step was punctuated with either an "excuse me," "pardon me," "I'm sorry," "coming through," or a more direct, "move." I wiggled past, angled around, shoved through, or displaced whatever bar patron was in my way. Suezie was holding on, and when I didn't feel her on my back I slowed, and over my shoulder admonished her to "keep up." I wanted her right up against me. We made our way to a side door that, if I had my bearings correctly, would put me right on Southwest 10th Street. Right where my car was. The door was monitored by a very tall and muscular Hispanic bouncer. His t-shirt was form-fitting over some massive muscles. His jet-black hair was gelled stylishly and he pursed his lips, betraying a slightly bored affect, most likely due to the continual tediousness of repeating to patrons that the door behind him was not an exit. He saw me coming at him with Suezie right behind me. As I got within ten feet of him, he was already shaking his head no.

I kept walking at him and now he was saying, "Wrong door buddy, front door is behind you."

"My wife is really sick, we need to leave."

"Front door. You can't go out this door."

I was now about three feet from him, and getting ready to close the gap even more.

"Please. She's really sick, we just need to go."

"Not here. Front door only."

Hi arms had been crossed across his large chest and now he had his hands on his hips. With his height advantage he was looking down on me. I put my Glock right up against his balls. The surprise and the comingled fear in his eyes will always be highly memorable to me.

"Unless you want to pee out of your ass the rest of your fucking life, open this fucking door or I'm going to put a hole in you so big I can drive a truck through your dick."

With his left arm he reached back and wordlessly pressed the push bar. The door opened out to the night air. I continued to press the Glock against him as I pivoted him out of the doorway, turning counterclockwise in doing so. Suezie slipped out the door, followed by me. I slammed the door behind us. The Z-28 was right across the street. I opened it with the remote. I opened the driver's door, pushed the seat forward, and shoved Suezie into the small backseat.

"Get down and stay down."

As I pulled away, three black t-shirt-clad bouncers, including the one whose balls were against my gun, came pouring out of the door. *Idiots*, I thought. Had I actually been a shooter, the Glock holds eighteen rounds. That would have been six rounds for each of them. Keeping my lights off to help conceal my license plate, I gunned the car as fast as I could away from Firehouse Four.

After I was about three blocks away, Suezie asked if she could sit upright. I told her it was okay.

"What the hell was that all about?" she quasi-yelled at me from the backseat.

"We don't know who Zeus is. But Detective Clay and I have a theory about a certain individual, and I saw him at the door, getting ready to come into the club. I'm not taking any chances. Too many innocent people in there."

"Wait! What? You have a suspect and you never told me? What the hell, man?"

"Its operational necessity."

"That's just cop bullshit for 'don't tell the woman anything.'"

"It's a theory. There's no proof. He's just a potential suspect." I answered back.

"It's cop bullshit and there's no getting around it."

We soon were pulling up to her house. I put the car in park. Using the rearview mirror, I spoke to her as she sat in the backseat.

"You got a choice. I can come inside, but if you're unhappy with my actions for the remainder of my shift, I'll stay outside once I know the house is secure. I'll talk to Miami about being replaced."

"I want you inside and I don't want you replaced," she meekly said.

We walked up to the front door as I scanned the yard for any threats or changes. The pencil was still in place against the corner of the front door. We went inside and I checked all the French doors; the doors were all locked, the tape swatches all intact. Suezie went into the kitchen. After I was done assessing the security of her house, I followed her.

"You really put your gun against that guy's nuts?" she asked me.

"Unfortunately. Yes."

"I've never seen anything like that before. It was so scary, yet so thrilling at the same time. I hate saying that because I know it's not right, but *damn,* that was just so wild," she said.

"Weapons are meant to be felt, not seen. Many people aren't scared to *die,* but they are scared of getting hurt. That's why everyone scrunches their face up when you threaten to finger-shoot a rubber band at them. It's easier to plant the thought of pain, or even disability in their head, more so than death."

"Speaking of weapons...if the house is locked down, can I ask you to just leave your gun in the gym bag? I can't take any more guns around me tonight. Not tonight. It's just been too much. I especially don't want another broken draw pull," she said.

She set a kettle of water on the stove and asked me if I wanted some tea with her. I said yes. I looked at the clock on the kitchen stove—Carmen Reyes was due to relieve me in less than an hour. If Tovar was still at Firehouse Four, I wasn't too concerned about him showing up here in the next forty minutes. I was concerned why he did show up at Firehouse Four. I was questioning in my head who C.C. might have spoken to.

I decided to give C.C. a quick text message and ask her if she spoke to anyone about where Suezie and I were going. I wasn't happy about keeping my gun in the gym bag, but to appease the "homeowner," I did it this time. I went into the living room and put my holstered gun in the gym bag. I also changed back into the mint green polo shirt and I put the neatly folded guayabera in the gym bag too. I didn't want Carmen Reyes showing up thinking that something unethical was going on between me and Suezie. I also made a note to tell Miami P.D tomorrow that I needed to be removed from this detail They could fill it with one of their own people. This constant dancing too close to the flame was eventually going to burn me. I carried the gym bag with me back into the kitchen, since that was where it seemed we would be. In a flirtatious way, she pretended to pout when she saw me.

"You changed your shirt? I liked you so much better in the guayabera."

"Let me see what this guy did to this drawer pull. It should be an easy fix," I said.

I looked at the drawer pull that Detective Burns had broken. Just as I figured, it was an easy fix.

"Do you have any tools?" I asked her.

"They're in the closet behind the stairs."

I left the kitchen and went to the closet under the stairs, but before I opened it I received a text back from C.C.

"No. I didn't say anything. Good news! The FBI shoe lab says the impressions are Nike ACG Boots. So now I have to track the sales of those shoes too. Sucks."

I opened the closet. It was full of big coats and lots of clothes. Near the back, a metal tool box was on the floor. I slid it out, got down on my knees and opened it, looking for a simple screwdriver. But something else really caught my eye.

On the top of the assorted tools was a screwdriver. The handle of the screwdriver was odd. It had a clear, elongated, Lucite hexagonal handle. It also had ribbed, fragmented ridges in the side of it for grip.

It was the same tool that C.C. had shown me at Ellinport's murder scene.

The same type of European tool that fit the Torq-Set screws that Reggie and Jabo had with them when they were murdered.

My mind reeled. I needed to process this. I also needed to be logical about it. Both Suezie and her deceased husband were Israeli nationals and having a Torq-Set tool like this was not completely out of the realm of logical possibilities. This was a serious leap of conjecture and I needed to view it as such.

I pulled a regular screwdriver from the box and I closed the toolbox. As I started to get up from my knees, I received a second text from C.C.

"The FBI is so messed up. They are now saying the Nike ACG boots are a woman's boot! This is ridiculous."

After that text, my mind was really spinning. I needed a contingency plan, because my instincts were starting to get very heightened. I didn't want to panic or cry wolf. I most definitely didn't need any lights and sirens showing up because I found a European screwdriver. I was letting my mind get away from me. I simply texted her back.

"Can you come by here? 2624 Taluga Drive."

I walked tenuously back to the kitchen. The faint whistle of the tea kettle was growing louder. Suezie was reaching for two mugs in the cupboard when I rounded the corner into the kitchen. I took the screwdriver and started working on the drawer pull, all the while my mind trying to grasp what my instincts were telling me.

No one had ever seen Zeus. He was a phantom in a gray hoodie. Could Zeus actually be a woman?

Could Zeus actually be Suezie?

The draw pull was an easy fix and I was done within two minutes. I straightened up and she was pouring organic honey into both steaming tea mugs. I noticed my gym bag was moved to the far side of the kitchen.

She was between me and the gym bag.

If she *was* Zeus, she probably removed the magazine from the weapon and took the round out of the chamber.

She looked at me briefly as she stirred the mugs. Her facial

345

expression was different than what I was used to from her. I don't know. I couldn't explain it. It was just very different.

I wondered where C.C. was coming from and if Carmen Reyes would be showing up early tonight, like she did last night.

"Tea is ready," Suezie said.

"I'm going to put this screwdriver back and then I'll have some. It looks good," I said.

Actually, I was going to make a play to get out the front door and wait outside for C.C. and Carmen.

"Don't be silly. That can wait. In fact, just put it in the drawer," Suezie said. She opened the drawer and held it open, waiting for me to drop it in.

The screwdriver was my only weapon—but to show reticence would also reveal my inner thoughts. I dropped it in the drawer. She quickly closed the drawer. I was standing in the narrow opening near the stainless steel refrigerator. She was in the center of the kitchen. My gym bag was behind her on the counter. All of a sudden, I had a starburst moment of a realization.

"You don't know what a semordnilap is? They're words that can also be read backwards, but the backwards spelling forms an entirely different word. Like swap would be paws, peels would be sleep, evil would be live. Get it?"

Suezie.

Zeus(-ie).

i.e. Zeus.

This was too much of a coincidence. She worked where Ellinport, Cooper, and LaMarr worked. She had the tool necessary to fit the screws. The FBI said the killer was wearing women's boots. No one had ever seen Zeus. Her name backwards spelled Zeus.

"I need to make a quick call about the scheduling after Monday. I'm going to step outside on the porch for a second," I said.

"What about your gun?" she asked.

She turned to hand me my gym bag. For the briefest moment I

felt incredible relief. As she neared the gym bag, she opened a kitchen drawer and pulled out a Walther P-88 and wheeled around quickly.

"You figured it out didn't you?' she yelled, pointing the gun at me.

She held the gun in a manner that was clear she knew how to use a firearm. She was in a modified weaver stance, holding the weapon at her eye level, pointing it right at my head.

I immediately put my hands up in a surrender position. I felt my knees go weak. My heart was leaping through my throat. I was staring down the gun barrel of an accomplished, and very capable assassin.

"I recognized your car tonight. I saw it from the train," Suezie said. "You were chasing me. I had to get off at the Coconut Grove station instead of my normal Viscaya station because of you. I had to walk back here *eight blocks* in the rain. I thought no one saw me— but you were chasing me. How did you know I was on the train?"

I cleared my throat and took a deep breath, wondering if it would be my last breath.

"The Miami officer you shot at knew you were on the train. He told me."

"I should have just plugged that fat ass cop, but I felt sympathy for him. Lesson learned there, huh? No more breaks for anyone."

That comment didn't bode well for me.

"Where did you get your training?" I asked her.

"Why are you talking to me? Trying to stall your own execution? Aharon wasn't a lobbyist, you dumbass. He was Mossad. He was my trainer. He was the best. He taught me everything. *Everything!* I learned Krav Maga from Aharon. I learned evasion techniques from Aharon. He drilled me and drilled me on shooting and weapons. Constantly on the range putting me through exercises. By the way, your precious Austrian Glock is in the gym bag. You can have it. I dissembled it and took the magazine. You want it?" she said mockingly.

"Just how do you think you're going to get away with murdering me? There's going to be a Miami cop here in thirty minutes. How are you going to explain that?"

"Oh my sweet, adorable, stupid as the day is long Cade. You tried to *rape* me, my lovely man. So I killed you. Shot you while you were trying to do the nasty with poor innocent me."

"You really think they're going to believe I tried to rape you?" I asked.

"After I kill you, I'll pull your pants down around your ankles. To tell you the truth, I hope that I don't regret what I missed out on. I'll put strands of my own hair across your palms and intertwined in your fingers. I'll scuff the back of these heels—which I actually really like, by the way—with the toe impressions of your shoes. I'll straddle your thighs for a few minutes and get a good dose of DNA on both of our legs. They'll think you came in here while I was making tea and attacked me from behind."

"That will never work and you know it. They will never believe you. They'll trace that P-88 you're holding right back to Ellinport and the others. You're done," I said.

"I'm done? *I'm done?*" she shrieked as she tightened her grip on the weapon, and now had her finger in the trigger guard ready to pull the trigger. "You are really so dumb. Let me spell it out for you. There will be boatloads of witnesses who will come forward and say they saw us at Firehouse Four. They'll say how jealous you were when you pulled me from the fire pole. You were enraged. Sexually charged and feeling left out. You were so angry you pulled a gun on me and made me leave with you. I was scared for my life. You threatened the bouncer with that very same gun. He will definitely be a good witness to your anger and your aggression. You threw me in the backseat and drove me back here. Those witnesses will give my story tremendous credibility. I'm going to shoot you right through your throat. That soft tissue is no match for a 9mm round. It'll go right in and right out again. While you're on the ground bleeding out, crying and panicking I'll quickly reassemble your Glock. You very well know that's only a twenty second chore. I'll shoot you again exactly in the same place, only this time you'll be on the ground and the round will bore right through the same hole, messing up any rifling evidence from the P-88. The round will lodge somewhere in my beautiful Dade County pine floor. That's the round they'll recover. The wound will be inconclusive, but the round retrieved will be from your Glock. I'll spend about ten minutes pressing your gun to the back of my neck, right side of course. I want a good front sight impression in my skin where you held it. In hindsight, I should've just shot you with your own gun from the start, but I don't know... Somewhere in the back of my mind I thought maybe, just maybe, we could've had a chance of being more than we were. I mean, I really liked you. What I said about intensity and passion? I meant that. But like I said, no more breaks going forward."

"So why Ellinport and the young men? Why kill them?" I asked her with my arms still raised.

"Ellinport was a such a douche. He kept setting cameras without telling me. It was just a matter of time he'd put one somewhere, see something that was going to be the end of me and my operation. As for those two absolute dimwits, I told them repeatedly—money or cocaine. Leave everything else alone. No watches, no cameras, no jewelry, nothing. No *anything* that a legitimate passenger would report missing. You know that idiot Jabo once took an urn, thinking it was jeweled vase? The fucking hoops I went through just to sneak that urn back on the tarmac so it could be found by a janitor were incredible. They were bringing heat. Both of them. They had to go. No one had tapped into that stream of cocaine and cash going back and forth from Miami to New York on those airplanes. It's practically a daily run. Ripping off the couriers is very lucrative, and they don't report their losses. It was idiot-proof—as long as you don't have idiots working for you.

"Both of those young men had European screws that only a European tool can turn. I saw that tool in your toolbox." I said.

She chuckled but kept her modified weaver stance and even seemed to lean closer to me with the gun. It was as if she was debating whether to shoot me through the teeth or through my open mouth.

I still had my arms raised. As we talked, I was slowly trying to get my elbows tucked in and lower my hands just a little, not just for comfort but to be more agile.

And I was praying for Carmen Reyes or C.C. to show up.

"Screws? They had the Torq-Set screws? Those two assholes were definitely going to be the death of me. Every time we hit a big score and couldn't put it in mailbags, they were told to stash the coke or money in the plane's beverage carts. There's a whole room full of those carts at the airport."

I immediately recalled the conversation I had with Katie Eighty in Tobacco Road.

"Well, those beverage carts are actually made in Europe and the latches and compartments on them are a bitch to try and figure out. Nothing more embarrassing than opening drawer after drawer to get some fat ass a Cheez-it bag and you can't find it. Plus, they seem to be really heavy sometimes and really light other times. You'll wreck your back if you try and push one, thinking its light."

"Cade enough is enough. I'm sorry. I'm not sorry about the others, but I did like you. I liked you a lot. I wish it could have been different. No more stalling. Goodbye, Cade."

Chapter Twenty-Eight

Don't blame me, babe
Don't' blame me, babe

~ Runaway Trains by Tom Petty

"**D**ID YOU SAY goodbye to Aharon? Is that what you said to Aharon before you pushed him off the cliff?" I asked in a last ditch effort to buy time.

"What? Aharon *fell*! How dare you even say his name, let alone accuse me of killing my husband?" she screamed at me.

"Detective Clay checked with the National Parks Police in California. When they recovered Aharon's body there were no binoculars with him. You said he asked you to go get a different pair than the ones he had. He had no binoculars. You killed him. Detective Clay and the California authorities know that," I bluffed her.

She was so angry at my bluffed assertion she was visibly turning red.

"No. No. That isn't true. You're lying. You fucking bastard. You lying piece of shit! I hope you burn in Hell—"

It was at that moment that I instinctively quickly dropped my right arm. I swiftly reached out and pulled the refrigerator door open. She was nearly as quick. She fired three rounds from the P-88. The door acted like a ballistic shield, which was exactly what I had hoped it would do, and it absorbed all three rounds.

I was already running from the kitchen through large splotches of ketchup, milk, and orange juice on the floor, streaming down from somewhere on the inside of the door shelves. Fluids splattered in every direction and also on me.

I ran as fast as I could upstairs. I'd never have gotten all the locks turned on the front door before she came around the corner and would kill me. Upstairs, as crazy as it seemed, was my best chance of survival. She must have been expecting me to go for the front door because I could hear her thin heels clacking, trying to catch up to me. I took those stairs two at a time and I reached the landing just as she neared the bottom of the stairs. On the landing I turned right, but not before blindly flinging books off the landing's bookshelf down the stairs at her as she charged up behind me.

"You motherfucker," was all I heard from her as I took the three-step rise in one big jump and went right into the first door on my left. It was the big mahogany door that led to the small vestibule. I slammed and locked it behind me. Even through the thick wood, I could hear her heels hurrying up the stairs.

I crossed through the vestibule and into the next room, looking for something to break one of the front-facing windows. As I reached for a floor lamp, I slipped on the Saltillo tile. My shoes were covered in ketchup and other liquids from the refrigerator. "Shit," I said, getting up as fast as I could, and remembering that I needed to lock the other side door; the entire vestibule, front room, and room with Aharon's stuff in it was just a semi-circle of three spaces connected by two doors from the staircase landing.

I ran to the other room filled haphazardly with box after box of Aharon's stuff. The first time I saw the room days ago I remembered it being nearly impassable. Getting past all the boxes, kayak paddles, Hawaiian slings and other things was difficult, especially in my panicked state. I did make it to the door and started to lock it, when she was already turning the knob to enter the room. She must've bypassed the first door I'd locked and she ran right to this door. I tried to push the door closed but she had it partially open, pushing the gun in her right hand through the opening.

She was very well-trained. Most people would push the gun into an opening and shoot but she turned her wrist where she thought I was and fired a round that whizzed right by my head. The round went through one of the boxes marked as "Aharon's things" and cracked a huge chunk of plaster off the wall.

My natural inclination was to move away from the threat. That gave her an even bigger opening in the partially opened door to shoot me. Shoving the door hard with my left hand, I reached for the wooden desk with the spindly legs. I pulled it hard between me and the partially open door while she was pushing hard and railing at me how she was going to really enjoy killing me.

She had a slightly bigger opening to work with, letting her once again forge her hand through and turn it to fire another shot at me. This one went right into the stucco between the vertical windows. She knew all my efforts were being employed to get the door closed. The two rounds were fired so fast that I couldn't get the door closed on her hand. Just as soon as she put her hand in to shoot me, she would withdraw it.

I needed to get as low to the ground as I could. She expected me to be upright near the door. I kept pushing on the desk, but now lowered myself to floor level, and I could see the shadow and the placement of her feet where the door just had a half-inch clearance from the floor. I could gauge when she was going to give a hard push, and I would prepare myself to push just as hard back. With my right foot I lodged myself between the back desk leg and the door.

We were at a momentary stalemate. She couldn't push it any further open and I couldn't close it any further. I wondered if I could hold her off until Carmen Reyes got here.

I also wondered if Carmen would have the wherewithal to break in through the French doors when no one answered the front door.

Suezie was shoving against the door. *Thump, thump.*

"You're fucking dead, Cade! You hear me? You fucking asshole!"

She really hit the door hard with her shoulder. I grunted, bearing down against the desk leg. To my utter dismay, the back leg of the desk snapped in half. The desk, now a three-legged albatross, wavered.

With Suezie's next shove, the desk fell on top of me.

Luckily my arms weren't trapped under it, but the desk had crumbled onto its side across my chest, pinning me to the floor.

The door betrayed me even more. She was now able to get a quarter of her body into the opening, and gaining more momentum with each push.

From my compromised position I was only able to use my left hand to reach up and grab her forearm. She tried to pull her arm back but I held on firmly. I needed to get my hand on the gun. If I could press the magazine release button, the magazine might fall onto my side of the door. That would leave only one round in the chamber.

I might be able to survive a single bullet wound.

Sweat was pouring off me. Adrenaline and cortisol were vying against each other in my system as she kept trying to break her arm free of my grasp. I was worried she might just switch the gun to her other hand, so I kept my eye on the opening. At one point she tried to do exactly that, but I drove the door closed a little more, almost trapping both her hands in the opening. With my right arm I began reaching for whatever I could and got my hand on a kayak paddle, which caused a whole bunch of stuff to fall against me. I pulled the paddle free from the avalanche of stuff and tried to swat at her hand with the paddle, but the long length of the paddle hindered the effectiveness of that strategy. I finally let the paddle go and now it, too, fell against my chest.

Fatigued, I groaned, trying to simultaneously hold her left hand, push the door from a prone position, and keep her outside of the room. She had the upper hand; the door opened more and more. It was inches, but those inches were adding up. It was only a matter of time until she got her shoulder through—that would be seriously detrimental for me.

It seemed like I was on the ground with the desk on me for an eternity. My breathing was becoming shallower. I was taking great gasping gulps of air as the desk pressed on my lungs and solar plexus. At first, I wasn't aware of the pain but the adrenaline and cortisol that had once been vying to fuel me was depleting, starkly bringing the ache into my consciousness.

I tried to reach the snapped-off leg of the desk, thinking I might be able to break her forearm or hand by hitting her with it. Each time I tried to reach the spindly, shattered leg it just rolled further away. I diverted my attention from her hand for the briefest of moments as I tried to use the paddle to roll the broken desk leg closer to me. It was at that moment that she gave a big heave against the door. To my complete disadvantage she had breached the opening enough to get most of her body through.

Her hair was matted to her forehead with sweat and her make-up had smeared from exertion. Her exhaustion showed in her heaving breaths, but she still had plenty of fight in her.

Now I was worried about her Krav Maga skills, and knew if she got her other hand in the opening, I could be the victim of a serious eye gouge or throat pull.

Her breaching of the door caused even more of the piled boxes and things in the room to shift and fall.

Teeth gritted, she was seething with anger at me. Expletives in every manner, shape, and form were spewing from her. Now partially inside the room, the desk was the only barrier to keep her from being directly on top of me. I saw the fingers of her left hand start to push on the door from her side of the threshold. She seemed to be getting more determined, and she was gaining momentum. My left arm was now fully extended and she was pulling her right arm back.

I was losing and severely disadvantaged. It wouldn't be long that I could hold her off.

She had the gun in her right hand. If she could open the door even two inches more, I could sense she'd switch the gun to her left hand and kill me as she laid across the desk in the opening.

In all the fray, a lot of Aharon's stuff had toppled over or spilled out of the boxes. I spied one of his Hawaiian slings, barely within the reach of my right hand. I put the Hawaiian sling across my chest. Suezie had now gotten low to give herself a better center of gravity. She wedged and pushed as I put my fingers into the surgical tubing of the Hawaiian sling and pulled it back as far as I could.

I made the decision to let go of her arm with my left hand to quickly grab the sling and hold it up.

Her right hand now free from my grasp, recoiled back from her pulling. Then she reset and was swinging her hand back to shoot me.

I released the tubing from the Hawaiian sling and the tri-prong spear shot out of the end of the sling and hit her right above her clavicle.

The spear went right through her throat.

Blood erupted from the wound like a geyser. Her eyes widened and involuntary tears poured out of her tear ducts. She made a gurgling sound. She tried to breathe but only a small gasp came out. Blood gushed everywhere. It ran out of the spear hole in her throat and blanketed her, and flowed onto me, covering me. Her mouth gaped open in pain. She wavered before her eyes closed, and she fell into the partial door opening, dead.

I went limp, drained, with her dead body hanging inches above me. My eyes struggling to stay open, I watched the blood flowing across the contoured angles of the desk and off the edge. Some places in drips and in others a continuous, slow flow. Under all the weight of her and the desk, panting, I tried to get my heart rate back to normal. I don't know how long I laid there with her lifeless body appearing to hover over me. I finally heard a lot of banging on the front door of the house, snapping me back. Carmen Reyes was outside, calling my name. I started calling for Carmen.

"Carmen, I'm upstairs. Upstairs. Upstairs. 3-15. Carmen, I'm here. I'm upstairs," I just kept yelling, my voice hoarse.

I heard the French doors being smashed in, and Carmen break inside, calling for me. I kept calling back to her, and then I heard her on the stairs. "Suezie's dead, I'm trapped inside," I called out.

Carmen's face peeked in the door around Suezie's dead body. I knew then it was over. It was over.

Zeus was dead.

Chapter Twenty- Nine

TWENTY-EIGHT MEDIA REQUESTS, twenty eight denials, and two weeks later, I was still on administrative leave at Coral Gables. Both C.C and I had spent nearly an entire afternoon with Godfrey and P.G Pinder. He thanked me for "jumping the curb." C.C had no idea what he meant by that and I just looked at her and told her I would explain it later.

I'd been mandated by Major Brunson to see a psychologist, a therapist, a hypnotist, and a bereavement counselor. The latter made absolutely no sense to me. I was getting tired of Ileana's telenovelas and the way that microwave butter popcorn smells when nine different detectives and administrative assistants make it daily. Gary and I had been talking. He told me one of his buddies had a house in Cocoa Beach that was half a block away from the water and a great surf shack.

"The guy's backpacking in Thailand until Thanksgiving. I got the keys. You ever surf before?"

"No, but I always wanted to." I answered.

"Dude, why don't you go up? Its less than four hours away. October swells are the best, bro. I'll come up on the weekend and give you some surfing pointers. There are shorties and long boards in the house. Check it out! The house is on a street called "Kelly

Slater's Way." How cool is that? A street named after Kelly Slater, my personal favorite pro surfer."

I sat in the VIN office and looked at Big G.

"I'll be right back."

I walked down the hallway to Major Brunson's office and asked Charlene to check the leave book. The next week was wide open. I put myself in the book .

"I'll fax you the leave papers," I said to her.

Back in the VIN office, I told Gary. He wrote the exact address down, opened his desk drawer and handed me the keys to the house.

"I'll come up Friday, bro. Leave the back bedroom for me. You can have the master bedroom. Get some organic greens, too. I need them for my morning smoothie."

"I'll see you Friday."

I got in the Z-28. After going home and packing a bag, I was ready. I called C.C. from the car. She answered right away.

"Have you ever been surfing?" I asked her.

"No."

"Can you get away?"

"You want me to go surfing with you?" she asked me.

"Yeah. I got a house in Cocoa Beach for the week. Gary's coming up Friday, but he shouldn't be a bother."

"When are you leaving?"

"Now," I answered.

She thought about it and I could sense her mulling it over in her head as the phone was momentarily silent.

"Come on, jump the curb on this one." I implored of her.

"Fuck it. Sciarotta is here, and so is everyone else. I'm just going to tell D.P I'm taking the time off," she said.

"Still no Tovar?"

"He's being moved to Traffic Homicide. That legal attaché really screwed him."

"Sounds to me like he screwed himself. I'm in the car, so what days do you think you can be there." I asked her

"Come get me," she said brightly.

"Now?"

"Right now. Come get me."

"I like the sound of that."

"Whatever I need, I'll buy, and whatever I don't need—like pajamas—I'll just go without."

"I like the sound of that even more."

The sun was shining, and there was no rain in the forecast. I had the keys to the house on Slater's Way in my hands, my bags were packed. C.C. would be with me for the week. I was getting pretty pumped as I headed out of Paradise Point on my way to get C.C. when my cellphone rang.

"You can't get out of it, C.C., I'm already on my way," I said with a grin when I picked it up.

"Cade! It's Santiago."

THE END

CPSIA information can be obtained
at www.ICGtesting.com
Printed in the USA
BVHW032147020621
608716BV00005B/41

9 781734 407549